Oilman

Oilman

Robert Stuart McLean

Order this book online at www.trafford.com
or email orders@trafford.com

Most Trafford titles are also available at major online book retailers.

Printed in the United States of America.

ISBN: 978-1-4269-7388-8 (sc)
ISBN: 978-1-4269-6970-6 (hc)

Library of Congress Control Number: 2011910820

Trafford rev. 06/24/2011

www.trafford.com

North America & International
toll-free: 1 888 232 4444 (USA & Canada)
phone: 250 383 6864 • fax: 812 355 4082

OILMAN PART 1

By Robert Stuart Mclean

Chapter 1

Billy Cochran sat on the wooden chair trying to balance on its back two legs. For just a fraction of a moment he was balanced and then the chair slowly began to tilt back. Billy arched his neck to touch the wall with his head and gingerly eased himself back into a perfect balance. When the chair began to tilt forward he raised and lowered his feet until he regained balance. Each time he achieved perfect balance he got the feeling he was in a state of weightlessness. With his eyes closed Billy rocked ever so gently ... back and forth ... as his mind wandered over the tumultuous last 10 days.

A slight smile flickered over his face as he thought back to the Friday afternoon during the last period of classes, when he looked over to his best friend Dave and said, "Let's get out of here and shoot some pool." And without a moment's hesitation both of them boldly got up, headed for the exit, then turned back and bowed deeply to their startled classmates. Billy opened the rear fire escape door and they made their exit, fleeing down the steel steps to freedom and the familiar environs of Dean's Pool Hall and Barbershop.

As soon as they were safely out of sight of the school they began musing about whether they would get caught or not. Billy reasoned that dizzy old Miss Horton would never miss them when she arrived at class. Dave cautioned that Sally Smith would surely snitch on them. Both knew that the punishment for truancy was a strapping from Jack Forester. The prospect of another strapping from old Forester quickly dampened the euphoria of the moment.

Jack Forester ruled the Nanton School with an iron hand and any offence was sure to result in a trip to Forester`s office with a high possibility of the strap. There was no question what was in store for them if they were ever found out skipping school. Both of them had been strapped by Forester since grade one and knew the pain they were in for. In grade eight alone Billy had been strapped eight times for various misdemeanours, including being sent to the office for copying someone else's homework. One encouraging thing was that this year, grade eleven, he had not been strapped 11 times, at least not yet.

As they walked downtown the discussion turned to the idea of quitting school for good. Billy said that he had already gone farther in school than any Cochrane he knew. Dave wasn't so sure. He felt his parents wouldn't let him quit. Besides what would they do?

"No problem," said Billy. " I hear there's all kinds of work on oil rigs around Leduc. Roughnecks they're called, and all you have to do is look up a tool push and ask for a job."

"That simple," mused a sceptical Dave, "so how do you know all this?"

"I've heard it around. As a matter of fact Skippy Thompson used to work years ago at Turner Valley and he told me."

"Skippy Thompson! He couldn't find his own ass with a flash light," Dave replied with a snort.

"Well, whatever. I've had about all I can take of school ... Forester ... Nanton ... my old man... everything! It's time to get a job and make some real money. Do you know what they're paying roughnecks?" Billy exclaimed in an authoritative voice.

"No, how much?" a hesitant Dave asked, realizing that he was giving credibility to Billy and Skippy Thompson. He didn't want his best friend Billy to quit school nor did he want to give any credibility to the stories of the quick riches to be made in the oil patch. "How much?" asked Dave again, in a much firmer voice.

After a short pause Bill gestured with open arms, "Tons."

As soon as they walked through the pool hall doors, every one of the old regulars looked at them and then at their watches. " School out early?" asked Dean as he began brushing hair from around the ears and neck of a customer. A crimson flush spread across both their faces as they realized how intimate a small town was and that everyone knew what was going on around them. "Time off for good behaviour," Billy brazenly quipped as he began searching the rack for his favourite cue.

Behind each of the four venerable old tables was a rack of cues and beneath each rack was a dirty bent spittoon. All beginning players followed an unwritten rule that required them to play on the back table. As your skill improved, you moved up a table. The first table was always left open for the regulars who mostly played "golf." Billy was seldom asked to be a partner in one of the golf games as they considered him too wild and because the game was played for money.

On Saturdays, all four tables were usually busy and Billy had a set routine. Each time he came in he would search for his favourite cue, and then go lean against the counter and listen to all the stories being told as Dean cut hair. Holding a cue gave the signal that he was available to play and it somehow legitimized his presence among the adults. Billy was always pleased when Pat Riley was present as he always had some outrageous story to tell.

Pat Riley's legs were so bowed that Billy was sure he would be four inches taller if he could only stand straight. As it was, he only stood 5'2". Pat always wore a huge cowboy hat and that, combined with his short stature, made him look a little ridiculous. Most of his stories were about riding broncos at the Calgary Stampede and other assorted adventures in which he managed to triumph. At the conclusion of each of his stories someone would invariably say, "You're bullshitting again Pat," and Pat would reply with an emphatic, "Are not!" or sometimes, "I aren't." Billy supposed that Pat's bowed legs could have come from riding horses and he had heard that Pat did actually ride in the Stampede.

Today, Pat showed up at the pool hall about the same time that Billy and Dave did. He walked over and plunked himself down on the barber chair all out of breath and seemingly very agitated. Billy wasn't surprised as Pat walked with difficulty swinging each of his bowed legs in a semi-arc with each step he took.

Old Sol asked, "What brings you to town on a Friday afternoon?"

Pat, catching his breath, told the assembled gathering that he had car troubles.

"What kind of car troubles?" Sol pressed.

Pat removed his huge hat, wiped his forehead with his shirtsleeve, and said, "I don't rightly know, but it doesn't have enough power to pump piss down a stairwell."

Billy let out a loud laugh, but reined it in as Pat gave him a withering look. Billy quickly realized that Pat wasn't trying to be funny. Sol continued his interrogation with Pat, knowing that Pat's reply was bound to be funny in one way or another.

"Pretty fancy new shirt you wearing today Pat. Getting married?"

Pat turned to Sol and took three quick breaths. Pat always took three quick breaths before he launched into one of his stories. "You know that pencil-necked haberdasher down the street. Well I went in to buy this shirt and he comes over to me rubbing his hands together and peers over his glasses and says, What would be your fancy? So I told him that I fancy fucking and pheasant hunting, but I'll settle for this shirt."

Everyone got a good chuckle out of the story but Billy didn't dare laugh again and he wondered if the story might even be true. Then Pat turned to Billy, and asked if he wanted to come and help with the Rocking T branding next Saturday morning. Billy had attended the Rocking T branding last year and was thrilled to be invited back. Billy knew that the Rocking T gave Pat a place to stay at the ranch and that he, in return, performed some menial chores for his room and board. Pat had worked for the Rocking T for nearly 50 years and most all of the big ranches rewarded their old hands in this way.

Billy enjoyed listening to Pat as he told story after story about the early days on the ranch, before the turn of the century when there would be huge round-ups in the spring to look for cattle that had drifted as far away as the Montana border. All the cattle had to be sorted out based on their brands, and the cows and newborn calves were herded back to the home ranch. Wolves, Indians, rustlers, and blizzards were all dealt with. And each time Pat told one of his stories the dangers grew larger and his heroics became bolder.

Ranches were settled along the Alberta foothills because the periodic warm chinook winds melted the snow cover, allowing the cattle to graze on the lush prairie-wool grass. Pat was always lamenting about the good old days before fences and about how putting up hay for winter feed had replaced the open range. Proud cowboys should never have to leave their mounts and now the modern cowboy had to pound staples and ride around on some type of haying contraption.

"Now you are expected to sit on a mower and look at two horses' asses, and ride around in a circle all day long. Then you have to go back a week later, when the hay is dried, and look at the same two horses' asses again all day long as you run a dump rake and bunch up the hay. Then you have to harness up those two horses to a hayrack and spend days building haystacks," Pat grumped. "If you ask me, ranches should be run like they were in the old days."

Everyone in the group, including Pat, knew the answer to this dilemma. They knew very well why it's no longer possible to run ranches as they once were. Just after the turn of the century there were two consecutive hard winters in a row in 1907/08, when the chinooks didn't come and the cattle couldn't get at the grass through the icy snow. Up to 80 percent of the cattle starved, leaving nearly every rancher on the verge of bankruptcy. All the ranchers could do was stand by and watch their herds die. Buffalo, with their massive heads, could bulldoze their way down to the feed, and horses could paw their way down, but cattle couldn't compete against the snow, and they starved

The annual branding of the 400-odd calves took only four hours. None of the other big ranches branded all their cattle at once.

Whether it was because they would have to travel to another part of the ranch or because the owner didn't want anyone to know how many head of cattle he owned, Billy didn't know. All everyone cared about was getting finished and getting at the cold beer and heaps of food that came at the conclusion of every branding. One of the reasons Billy was so excited to help out at the Rocking T was its reputation for excellent food and a plentiful stock of beer.

"I'm not sure Jack Forester will be very pleased with me for letting truants come here during school hours," Dean broke in, jolting Billy back from his thoughts about tomorrow's branding. Billy was not sure whether Dean was joking or not. Best bet was to continue on racking the balls and wait to see if Dean kicked them out. Billy liked Dean and was especially proud that Dean let him sit in the barber chair when no one needed a haircut. In any event there was no question now whether or not Forester would find out about their truancy … the whole town knew!

"Fuck Forester," Billy muttered to no one in particular. "I'm quitting school and getting a job roughnecking." Just as soon as he said this he wished he hadn't. Things were moving far too fast and he was painting himself into a corner. What had started as an impulse was taking on a whole new dimension.

The satisfying sound of a crisp clean break and the clattering of the ivory snooker balls went unnoticed, as Billy became absorbed in his thoughts again. Rather than the usual banter with Dave and all of the old regulars, Billy was uncharacteristically quiet. Invariably he would ask old Sol, who had to be at least 90, at what age one loses interest in sex and Sol always gave his pat answer, "You'll have to ask someone older than me." Billy always teased Sol with this question and the answer was always the same. But today he was in no mood for joking around.

Billy abruptly put his cue back in the rack and told Dave that he had to go wait for his school bus and its ride home. Walking down to the intersection and waiting to flag down the bus gave Billy some time to be alone and think things through.

Chapter 2

The hard-backed chair veered out of control and the front legs hit the floor with a loud bang startling Billy and causing Larry Wannop, the owner of Larry's Tire Shop, to look up from the Greyhound paperwork he was working on. Billy stood up, stretched ... and in his new Dayton steel-toed boots he felt he was at least six feet tall. "What time did you say the bus would be here again?"

Larry replied, "For the third time ... 10:30!" That meant he had another three-quarters-of-an-hour to kill.

In the back shop Bill Bondy started beating on a stubborn tractor tire with a sledgehammer, trying to break the tire seal. Billy walked back and watched as beads of sweat began running down Bill's face. But watching Bill work was not what had motivated Billy to come to the back shop.

He turned his attention to the 1948 Calendar Girl that was tacked up on the wall. Going straight to the pin-up girl would have been too obvious, so he had to linger over Bill's labours before he nonchalantly sauntered over to the calendar. This was no ordinary pin-up girl. She was beautiful with her blonde hair done up and sticking out from under her red cowboy hat. She was in a side profile kneeling position and wore a matching red halter top and red shorts. Her inviting blue eyes were enough, but there was more. The calendar was covered by a clear plastic cover and when you lifted the plastic up, the hat, the halter top, and the shorts came off and there she was, completely naked. Well not totally naked, there was a patch covering each nipple, and of course because she was in a kneeling position ... Billy's imagination would have to tell him what her crotch looked like. Still, Billy had never seen anything like it, and his throat became dry. His mind and heart began to race.

Realizing he was about to get a hard-on and wanting to let on he was only marginally interested, he let out a low whistle and turned to Bill exclaiming, "I sure wouldn't kick her out of my bed for eating crackers." Bill only grunted and didn't even look up from banging on the old tractor tire. Billy was relieved and quickly returned to his fascination with the sensational naked woman. He would lift the plastic cover up and down very slowly imagining he was taking her clothes off, piece by piece. The calendar was a hot topic of conversation. Judging by all the greasy smudge marks on the bottom of the plastic, he wasn't the only one interested.

Billy sauntered back to the office and stood in the open doorway watching the highway traffic. Don Lougheed drove by in his new Cadillac. Don farmed a lot of land and was said to be the richest man in Nanton. Don always volunteered to drive the hockey team when they went out of town and Billy always made sure he got to ride in Don's new Cadillac. Someday I'm going to own a new Cadillac, Billy promised himself.

Billy returned to his chair and began anew to bring it to a perfect balance on its two rear legs. As he leaned back and pushed off with his feet, he marvelled at his new work boots, which made him feel mature and certainly taller. The boots also gave off the satisfying smell of new leather and Neetsfoot Oil, which Billy had painstakingly rubbed in. As he teetered back and forth he fought for balance using his feet, and every time he had to raise his legs in the air he would gaze again with pride on his new boots.

Billy's eyes wandered from his boots to the battered duffel bag on the floor. He had just emptied out his hockey equipment, as he needed the bag for a suitcase. He wished he had done it earlier and aired it out for a while, maybe gotten rid of some of the musty smell. Now what few clothes he had would all smell mouldy. On the side of the bag was stencilled "Pvt. Ray Smith." Billy couldn't remember where he had got the duffel bag and he didn't know a Ray Smith. He wondered if Ray Smith was killed during the war. He hadn't bought the bag at the Army and Navy surplus store in Calgary, so how did it come into his possession? Billy let his mind drift back to the calendar girl.

In a few minutes Billy's thoughts turned to girls in general and he wondered if he was ever going to get laid. He felt he was reasonably good looking and yet he had not even felt a girl up let alone seen one naked, like the calendar girl. Around guys, on the school bus, at school, at the hockey rink, everywhere, he was full of confidence, but alone with a girl he just lost it. Even at the monthly teen dances he felt awkward asking a girl for a dance. He had rehearsed his routine over and over. If a girl refused to dance with him he would sarcastically say, "You thought I asked for a dance … what I said is you look fat in those pants." He never did use that line, but all the same he feared walking across the dance floor and being rejected and then having to retreat back to his knot of friends and face the ridicule. It was much safer instead to horseplay around and look totally disinterested in any of the girls. The couple of times he had been alone in a car with a girl, she casually fended off his advances and he'd just end up feeling incompetent and foolish. Although all the talk among his friends was about sex and who was doing "it," Billy's knowledge about sex was strictly limited to farm animals and their mating rituals.

The one exception was Rebecca Mitchell, a redhead who rode on the school bus. Rebecca was a buxom grade nine farm girl, a little on the tubby side, but she had great breasts. Billy could provoke her into a mock rage either by calling her "carrot top", by teasing the hell out of her, or by snatching something from her and pretending he was going to keep it. Any of these ploys would cause her to fly at him with flailing arms and fists. The melee would usually result in Billy finding a way to squeeze one of her voluminous breasts. One of his tricks was to stuff a balled up piece of paper down the front of her blouse. Rebecca would grab his hand and resist with all her strength, but at the same time he usually got to feel a bit of her cleavage. Except for one time. Her grip for some reason faltered and his hand and the ball of paper, or whatever he was using, plunged deep into her bra and he got a full feel of Rebecca's large breast. Not the nipple though. Just as it was with the calendar girl, the feel or glimpse of a girl's nipple still eluded him.

Billy often wondered if Rebecca meant to let him "get a feel" or if it was truly a slip. Each time it happened she would give a squeal of outrage and return to her seat in a dramatic huff. Usually she would say, "I'm telling on you!" and Billy would mock her reply in his best girlish voice, " I'm telling on you!" "I really am," Rebecca would retort, wagging her finger at him. And again, Billy would mimic her by saying; "I really am," while exaggerating a finger waggle. This exchange usually resulted in her stamping her feet in mock anger or exclaiming, "Brother!"

The other trick Billy liked to play on Rebecca was to provoke her into a tantrum, and when she started to flail away at him he would pin her down on her back. He would hold her arms and pretend he was going to spit in her face. To do this he would build up a big spit ball and let it slowly ooze out of his mouth and just before it dropped he would suck it back in. Each time the spitball started to slip from his mouth she would scream, "Quit it Billy!" This response only resulted in a bigger ball of spit and it would ooze out a little farther. Again Rebecca would yell out, "I'm warning you!" Again, another spitball would appear, larger and more ominous than before. Rebecca would squirm and turn her face as far as she could, but there was no escaping Billy's strength and grip. He would continue to torment her with his spit routine until her squeals and protestations started to be for real and Billy would let her go.

Then one day it happened … Billy didn't suck his ball of spit back fast enough and the whole slimy gob dropped on Rebecca's face. Billy quickly let her go from his grasp and began to apologize in earnest for his actions. For once, Rebecca was speechless and she furiously sat up and returned to her seat. Billy followed close behind repeating, "I'm sorry, I really am," over and over. Rebecca said nothing as she wiped up his spit with her handkerchief, but her face was as crimson as her hair. It was several weeks before he was able to goad her into attacking him again. Billy cursed his stupidity, not for his spit routine act, but for allowing the spitball to get away on him. Billy enjoyed pinning Rebecca down, as well as the sensation it gave him as she squirmed underneath him. Billy was quite sure Rebecca enjoyed it too, at least up until the revolting gob of spit dropped smack between her eyes. All of the young riders loved to watch Billy tease and torment Rebecca. They raucously egged him on with no clue of the sexual overtones involved.

Now when he said, "How's it going this morning, carrot top?" she would only reply, "Don't call me carrot top." Even when he responded, "Okay, I won't call you carrot top again … carrot top," she'd just ignore him, didn't even look at him. Not able to get a rise out of Rebecca, Billy would begin his prowl down the bus aisle looking for more victims to torment. Teasing the younger school kids was one way to break the monotony of the nearly hour-long bus ride each morning. The afternoon ride home was not as tedious because he was first off, unlike the morning ride where he was first on.

The twins, who lived a couple of miles from him, were always good targets and Billy regularly grabbed one of their lunch pails. He would make a dramatic gesture in opening it up and then exclaim, "Look what we have here! Chocolate cake. My favourite." And when he said "favourite," he dragged out every syllable, stretching it out to keep the suspense even longer. With that he would hold the lunch pail in front of his face so the twins couldn't see, and reaching in with his right hand, he'd pretend to eat the cake. Of course this produced a howl of protests from the twins. Satisfied that he had created the right amount of commotion he would give the lunch box back, and proceed on down the aisle roughing a head of hair here and landing a friendly punch there until he found someone he wanted to sit down and talk to. If someone was sitting in a seat near this person he would merely say, "You're sitting in my seat," and the kid would dutifully get up and give the seat to him.

Johnny Horton was a good target. When Billy spied the top of the royal blue velvet Seagram liquor bag sticking out of his coat pocket he'd snatched the bag, knowing full well it contained Johnny's marbles. He'd expound, "Whoa! Who did you cheat to win these?"

"I never cheated," protested Johnny.

"Yes you did," said Billy, "I saw you cheating yesterday. You were hunching!"

"I wasn't!" protested Johnny. Billy would purposely ignore him as he carefully examined the contents of the marble bag.

Playing marbles and flying kites was a sure sign in Alberta that spring had arrived. Usually a marble contest consisted of drawing a circle in the dirt and each contestant would put an agreed on number of marbles into it and then crouch behind a line also agreed on by the players. Then each in turn would roll his shooter, which was usually an extra large marble or a steel ball bearing called a "steely," trying to knock the marbles out of the circle. Each time a player knocked a marble out he got to keep it. You could tell the good players by the size of their marble bag. The losers shed many a tear. Hunching over the line when throwing the shooter was considered cheating. Billy hadn't ever watched Johnny play marbles, but by claiming the younger boy was cheating he knew would get a rise out of him.

As Billy examined Johnny's marbles his attention focused on a brilliant "cat eye" He exclaimed, "Who did you cheat this one out of," knowing very well that Johnny would never risk losing such a beauty by putting it at risk in a game of 'keepsies'. "If Forester ever finds out that you are playing keepsies he will take all your marbles away," admonished Billy.

At that point Billy announced, "I think I'll keep this," placing the precious cat eye in his right hand and putting it into his pocket. Johnny let out a predictable scream and frantically tried to get his hand into Billy's pocket to retrieve it. The struggle continued until tears began to well up in the younger boy's eyes as his desperation grew. Billy, seeing that Johnny was about to cry, opened up his right hand and there was the marble that he had palmed all along. "Here's your precious marble crybaby," he said as he got up and returned to his seat, leaving Johnny sniffling. Another boring day ahead thought Billy when he looked up at the stark brick two-storey Nanton School as the bus rolled slowly to a stop.

Not that Billy was a bully. He'd earned his authoritative status, firstly by being the oldest on the bus, and secondly from the incident three years ago when old Joe the bus driver got stuck going up the Coulee Hill after a spring snow left the road nearly impassable.

Billy realized that Joe didn't have enough speed to make it up the hill. The old bus powered out and became stuck three-quarters of the way to the top. He watched, as Joe seemed to freeze at the prospect of backing down and taking another run at it.

Billy didn't even know Joe's last name. To everyone he was just Joe the bus driver. Joe was a small man and in Billy's opinion he sure didn't know much about driving. Joe sat ramrod straight behind the wheel and held it with a death grip. When he drove ahead he always revved the engine too fast and released the clutch too quickly, resulting in a sudden lurch that threw the students back into their seats. Anytime he had to gear down he could never get the engine speed right as he double clutched, resulting in a noisy gear grind. Joe seldom acknowledged any of his passengers and when he did it was in a high Cockney accent that was hard to understand anyway. Joe always dressed in a tweed jacket and tie, which made him look out of place in a farming community like Nanton. Someone said Joe was a World War I vet but Billy couldn't get an answer from Joe on this, or anything else for that matter.

Billy impulsively stood up and went up to Joe and said, "Here, let me do it." Perhaps it was Billy's authoritative manner because he didn't ask or suggest, he just said, "Let me do it" and old Joe obediently got up and turned the bus over to him. Billy was confident he could do it as he'd been driving farm equipment and vehicles since he was old enough to see over the steering wheel.

Billy knew the trick was to keep in the ruts while backing up or he might slip over the steep bank and the bus would surely be upended. Billy had never driven anything quite like the school bus, but no matter, he put the gearshift into reverse and gingerly backed the bus down the hill. Carefully, he avoided spinning the wheels which might cause the bus to jump out of the main rut and he would lose control. If the bus got out of the ruts it could easily spin sideways, and in the mud and snow Billy knew it would be unlikely he'd have any room to manoeuvre. Trying to go back and forth at this stage was impossible, with a real probability of going off the road into a steep ditch. A couple of times Billy had to goose it to keep the bus going because if the back wheels jumped out of the rut, Billy would have to stop right there and go to the nearest farmer to get him to pull the bus up the hill with his tractor. His only alternative was to steer the bus back into the ruts himself. Miraculously, the bus seemed to find its own way back into the ruts and Billy continued his descent down the hill.

Once he reached the bottom of the hill Billy continued backing up, expertly looking over his shoulder out the back window and then back to the rear-view mirror. He backed up all the way past the bottom of the coulee and part way back up the other side, far enough until he was certain he could get up enough speed going forward that he could make it to the top. Billy didn't give old Joe a chance to take back the wheel. He reckoned that he would have to leave the transmission in second to have enough power and speed to climb the hill. Billy slammed the gearshift into first, shouting "Hold on!" and then floored the gas pedal. Shifting into second, the bus sped toward the hill with the engine at full rev. Snow and mud flew everywhere as the bus bounced along, throwing all the kids around in their seats. The old bus shook and rattled and the engine sounded as if it was going to blow up at any second. No one had ever seen Billy in such a state of concentration before.

The engine scream began to dull as the old bus made its ascent up the hill with Billy steering wildly to try to keep the wheels in the old ruts. Old Joe and the rest of the passengers never made a sound. A couple of times it looked like they were going to get stuck again, but the back wheels found a bit of footing, and with Billy urging the bus on under his breath, swearing at it and pleading with it at the same time, they suddenly lurched forward and then inched over the top of the hill. A round of cheers went up as Billy triumphantly pulled the bus over and gave it back to old Joe

Joe never said a word then or since to Billy and Billy never spoke of it to old Joe. But everyone at school talked about it, making Billy out to be some kind of folk hero. Everyone in town was talking about the event as well. Billy's father's only comment was; "I hear you're driving the school bus now." Billy didn't know if that was a compliment from his father or what. He never could figure out what his father was thinking. He even heard old Joe was going to be fired over the whole incident. Nothing ever came of it though. Billy, himself, was nonplussed and considered the whole thing no big deal. At any rate, he reasoned it sure beat everyone getting out of the bus and shovelling snow to clear a path. Besides, all the farm kids he knew could drive at the age of 14. It was something he felt he could do and he instinctively knew that old Joe couldn't. But from that day on Billy was king of the bus. No one, including old Joe, told him when or where to sit.

Billy stopped trying to balance the wooden chair and began rocking it instead, alternatively pushing off the floor with his feet and off the wall with his head. His mind was still racing over the events of the last week and his decision to quit school and leave home.

For the first time he began to have misgivings about the whole plan. "What if there are no jobs on an oil rig?" he thought to himself. "What if I get a job and can't hack it?" At this thought Billy looked down at his strong forearms and muscled chest. He was certain he was stronger than most grown men he knew. Still, he thought back to last fall when he helped stook 200 acres of wheat along with two grizzled men who made their living with a nomadic thrashing gang. After the first day Billy was in a complete state of exhaustion and would have quit if it weren't his father's farm they were working on. The two stookers, neither of who were as big as Billy was, never took a break and never seemed to tire. Surely, stooking wheat bundles was a lot easier than working on an oil rig. Methodically, like a pair of robots, each man stooped to pick up bundles of wheat and then stood them on end to create a stook. Hour after hour in the hot fall sun the men worked on, leaving Billy praying for rain or even for school to start — anything to get out of stooking.

After the events of this morning, Billy was certain he could never go back to school in Nanton. Besides, after all his big talk of quitting and leaving, he couldn't face the ridicule of returning home with his tail between his legs. No. There was no turning back. Suddenly, he let the chair come to the floor with a crash and stood up.

This time his hand tapped his back pocket to feel if his wallet was still there. The loss of his entire life savings ($40 less the $8.35 for the bus ticket) was a potential disaster, and he worried about it. Billy's father had always been good about giving him a calf or a pig, and when they went to market Billy had promptly banked his earnings. No telling how long this money would have to last him.

Just as he was getting ready for a good long stretch, the pug-nosed Greyhound bus rolled to a stop. The driver waited for a minute to let the dust clear and then bounded out the bus door and into the tire shop. The moment Billy had imagined and fantasized about was here. So this is it, he thought to himself. Billy jammed his hands into his pockets, trying to look relaxed and confident, as though this were just another bus trip for him. Inwardly his heart was racing. He was doing it. He was leaving home. He was quitting school.

The driver ignored him as he and Larry went over some paper work, and then suddenly turned to Billy and said, "Ready to go, kid?" Bristling at being called "kid," Billy just nodded and nonchalantly slung his duffel bag over his shoulder saying, "After you, old man."

As he followed the driver out the door, Larry called after him saying, "Good luck Billy." Billy took some comfort in this as Larry had hardly spoken to him all morning. Billy looked back and flashed Larry a smile and a thumbs up and disappeared into the Greyhound bus.

Chapter 3

The bus was only about one-third full and the passengers were nondescript looking. Choosing an empty seat, Billy stowed his duffel bag in the compartment above, sat down, and folded his arms. His hands were still throbbing from the morning strapping. The odyssey was about to begin. The Greyhound bus, with its fabric seat, sure beat the old school bus. And best of all, there wasn't the nauseating smell of rotting orange peelings and apple cores or the crusts of someone's half-eaten sandwich. Old Joe wasn't that good at sweeping out his bus, despite Billy's constant ragging.

As the bus gathered speed, Billy's gaze was riveted on the passing countryside he knew so well. The foothills and distant shimmering mountains were a comforting sight to him. A sense of well-being surged over him, and a feeling of confidence in his decision set in as the bus wound its way through the countryside, stopping at every town as it headed towards Calgary. Sometimes a passenger got out or someone got on. Each town was familiar to Billy, as he had competed against its hockey or ball team since he was old enough to play. And each town held some memory for Billy.

As the bus ground to a halt in Okotoks, Billy sat bolt upright as he relived the fight in last winter's hockey game where he decked Okotoks' tough guy. The resulting brawl cleared both benches and the game itself was suspended. Wouldn't it be something if someone from that team got on the bus, thought Billy, as his imagination began to race. He was sure there'd be a bounty on his head if he were ever sighted alone in Okotoks. However, when the bus driver returned to his seat the only person following him was some old lady who could hardly make it up the steps.

A slight glow of satisfaction arose in Billy as he fondly recalled the brawl, and then he considered that he might be finished with hockey as well as school. No matter, he thought, it was onwards and upwards. He rubbed his hands together and was surprised to feel the lingering sting of Forester's strapping still had not left.

Billy's mind now flipped back to that morning's events at school. The buzz all Easter holidays had been that Billy and Dave were going to get the strap on Tuesday morning when they returned to school. Billy knew it too. There were only two things he could do. Go to school and get the strap or take the bus to Leduc. Billy had weighed these two options over and over, and he came to the conclusion that he didn't want to be remembered for being a chicken and leaving his friend Dave to face the music by himself, especially when it was his idea to skip that last class in the first place. He would never be able to hold his head up in Nanton again if he did that.

The task of telling his parents he was quitting school was much easier than he anticipated. His father said very little and did nothing to encourage him or discourage him. His mother tried to talk him out of it, pointing out that there was only a little over two months left in the school year and it would be a shame to quit now. Billy countered that grade ten was further than any other Cochrane had ever gone in school. Besides, he wasn't sure he was going to pass anyway. Getting up every morning at 5:30 had meant going to bed at 9:30, leaving little time for homework. Chores began as soon as he got home from school and changed his clothes. Trying to read at night with only the weak glow of the coal oil lamp was no easy task either. Besides, being ragged by his teachers for never having his homework done was a pain in the ass.

Billy was adamant that he was quitting school and going to look for work on an oil rig. His mother soon gave in and the matter was settled. No more milking cows, feeding pigs, cleaning the barn, separating the milk, riding the school bus, feeling too big for the school desk. No more! Billy realized then that the reason neither of his parents could offer him much advice was that they didn't know what to tell him. Billy's father, as usual, had little to say, and his mother did all the talking. They both realized that Billy was headstrong and independent. Billy's mother just kept saying, "Are you sure this is what you want to do?" Then she cautioned him. She had heard that oil rigs were very dangerous and that the people who work worked on them were unsavoury types.

Billy pretended to listen, but his mind was made up. Besides, what did his parents know about oil rigs? His father grew up on the farm, and then took it over from his father who had homesteaded it in 1904. As far as Billy knew, the only time his parents had ever left the farm was once when they took a short vacation to visit relatives in North Dakota where his grandfather had come from. Other than that, their whole life was working the farm.

When Tuesday morning came, his mind was firmly made up. He was going to school. He'd take his whipping and then immediately leave the school, catch the bus to Leduc and then — freedom!

First on the bus as always in the morning, Billy had sauntered to the back and flopped his duffel bag on the seat beside him. The next to get on were the twins. As soon as the bus door opened, they shouted in unison, "You're going to get it from Forester, Billy!"

The next on was Rebecca, and instead of flouncing down in her usual seat she came straight to Billy and sat beside him. With a painful look, she said, "I hear you're quitting school this morning." When Billy only nodded, instead of coming out with a smart-ass remark, her eyes welled up with tears. "Please don't quit," she softly implored as she touched his hand. At that moment, Billy saw something in Rebecca that he hadn't noticed before. Instead of the carrot top he loved to torment, the redhead beside him seemed, somehow, to have grown up.

The last to get on the bus was Nathan, a grade oner, who huffed his way to the back where Billy was sitting. With great round eyes, he lisped through his missing front teeth ... "You're going to get the strap from Forester when you get to school Billy."

"Thanks for the warning, pal," Billy deadpanned.

During the entire trip to school, Billy was uncharacteristically silent. With each new warning from his school mates, each believing he or she was the only one to warn Billy of his upcoming fate, he gave off only a bemused smile. Everyone on the bus, including old Joe, sensed an impending loss they couldn't explain.

Billy sat resigned in his desk as the nine o'clock bell rang. And just as the usual classroom commotion settled down, the huge figure of Forester filled the doorway. Without any acknowledgement to Miss Horton, he pointed his finger at Billy and Dave and said, "Cochrane, Nelson, come into my office."

Forester always left his office door open when he gave somebody the strap because the sound could be heard throughout the whole school. This time was no different. Forester chose Dave first. Billy watched the routine he knew so well. Only this time he was not filled with fear, only anger. When Forester dismissed Dave after giving him three whacks on each hand, he turned his attention to Billy. "So … he spat out in his high voice, which seemed out of place coming from such a large man, "I imagine you're the ringleader in this whole incident. Hold out your right hand!" Forester demanded. He seemed to pirouette on his tiptoes as he put the full weight of his body behind the strap. "Left," he grunted as he repeated the process. Billy knew what the next act was.

Forester would lecture for a minute, letting the sting take hold, then start again. After the second strap Billy's hands really began to hurt, but he refused to wince and he glared directly back at Forester. After the third strap, Billy's hands were on fire. He was relieved the punishment was over.

As he waited to be dismissed, Billy's heart shot into his mouth when Forester barked out, "Other hand!" Billy had never been strapped four times on each hand, and he had never heard of anyone else getting four on each hand either. Billy looked Forester right in the eye with a deadly rage on his face. And Forester realized that, for the first time, he himself might be in danger.

Billy stared for a long time contemplating his next move and then calmly held out his right hand again. The pain was excruciating but Billy never removed his stare from Forester's face as the sound of the strap reverberated through the school.

Forester quickly stepped away and muttered, " I hope you have learned your lesson." Billy stared at Forester with a measured look of contempt. Both realized, in a split second, that four times on each hand crossed the line from punishment to personal vendetta. "Forester," Billy said in as even a voice as his rage and pain could muster, "You can shove this school up your fat ass!" With that he spun around in his new Dayton boots and defiantly marched back to his classroom. He went straight to the cloakroom, slung his duffel bag over his shoulder, and paused on his way out long enough to tell Miss Horton that his school books were in his desk and that he was never coming back to the Nanton School.

Passing the Chinese cemetery indicated that the City of Calgary was soon to come in to view as Billy continued carefully to massage his red swollen hands. The bus finally reached the depot and he collected his bag and got off. Having to wait an hour to transfer to the Edmonton bus, Billy wandered aimlessly around the bus terminal to kill time, keeping a close check on his wallet. Never had he seen so many weird-looking people and he was sure every one of them was out to rob him. Eventually, he decided his best course of action was to just sit on his wallet and put the duffel bag on his lap.

The bus trip north eventually got underway with no unusual incidents. But now, instead of familiar countryside, the view out the bus window began to look foreign. The Rocky Mountains started to fade out of sight and the landscape began to roll, with trees visible in every direction. Some of the towns he had heard of, some he hadn't. In any event, the old Greyhound bus pulled in to each of them and made its obligatory stop. Each stopover started with a cloud of dust entering the bus as the driver opened the door. People got on, people got off. Billy lost interest in the comings and goings. The bus trip was beginning to feel like riding the school bus. He began to feel queasy from his stomach to his esophagus. He closed his eyes, pressed his head against the window.

"Red Deer," announced the driver. "There will be a 10-minute stop if anyone wants to stretch their legs." Billy was only too glad to oblige — anything to break the monotony and the sick feeling. Soon the bus lurched forward again, continuing its winding laborious and nauseating journey. Billy went back into his closed-eye routine, trying to block out the boredom. His mind returned to Nanton where by this time of day he would be home from school and starting chores. Rather than being comforted by the thought of not having to do chores, he felt a strange pang of uneasiness. Misgivings about his brash decision to quit school and leave home were building up. Already he was starting to miss the farm routine with all the dogs, cats, and even the milk cows. Revisiting the bravado scene of the morning was beginning to make him feel foolish. Gone forever would be the teasing of his neighbours on the school bus.

"Ponoka!" barked the driver. Billy never even opened his eyes, preferring to recall pleasant thoughts that shut out the never-ending bus trip. Still, Billy was aware of the commotion around him. Someone had sat down beside him and the seats had filled up in front as well. He never acknowledged his new travelling companion, and it was only the acrid smell of smoke that made him open his eyes. Sitting in front of him, kneeling on their seats and facing backwards were two small Indian kids wearing buckskin jackets. Both were staring intently at Billy with their piercing dark eyes. One had a runny nose that dramatically heightened his nausea. This time he was pretty sure he was about to get sick.

He closed his eyes and desperately fought back the nausea. He was sure he was going to lose the chocolate bar and coke he'd had in Red Deer. Forcing back his urge to vomit, Billy became aware of the unmistakable sound of suckling. His mind cleared as he realized that the woman beside him was nursing a baby. The woman began burping the baby by patting its back while making cooing noises. Billy sat upright and, ignoring the two pair of dark eyes that were still staring at him, slowly turned his head towards the nursing mother. He moved his head just far enough to get a furtive glance out of the corner of his eye at the woman next to him. Then, suddenly, there it was, a fully exposed naked breast — nipple and all. A first.

The Native lady placed her baby back on her breast and continued nursing. Billy wondered if she was aware that he was watching, or if she even cared. With his nausea now gone, Billy started to think about what his first move should be when he reached Leduc. He thought the most obvious place to start looking for a job would be to hang around the hotel.

The bus started to brake and Billy opened his eyes. Painted in large bold letters on the side of the grain elevator was LEDUC. Billy sat upright in his seat at the same time the driver announced, "Leduc." The bus hadn't even come to a stop when Billy pushed his way past the Indian lady and her baby. He was already standing in the stairwell of the bus when it finally came to rest.

Chapter 4

The hotel wasn't hard to find. With only one main street of business, it was the only large building in town. The fact that Leduc appeared to be about the same size as Nanton comforted him as he made his way down the main street.

Strolling through the hotel entrance, Billy walked to the front desk where a small man was engrossed with some kind of book work. When Billy cleared his throat, the clerk peered up and looked quizzically at him over the top of the glasses, which were perched on the tip of his nose. "Can I help you?" he said, in a clearly irritated voice.

"I was wondering if any of the oil rig bosses might be in the bar?"

"Oil rig bosses?" The way the clerk repeated his request indicated he had absolutely no idea what Billy was talking about.

"Yeah, you know, the guy who does the hiring and stuff like that."

The clerk gave Billy a long disdainful look and then turned his attention back to his book work. As he picked up his fountain pen he muttered, "There's always some tool pushers in the bar. The way he pronounced "tool pushers" embarrassed Billy. He realized he had shown his ignorance.

"Look," Billy persisted, "I'm looking for a job and I sure would appreciate it if you would tell one of the tool pushers I'm here so I could talk to him."

Again there was a long silence as the clerk continued his column of figures. Finally, he sighed and put his pen down. "I'm pretty sure Al Schultz is in there. I'll tell him you're here."

As the night clerk disappeared into the bar, Billy took a chair in the small foyer. When the little man returned, he went back to his task, paying no attention at all to Billy.

"Thanks," Billy offered, but the clerk never looked up at him or even acknowledged the thank you.

Panic grew as Billy realized he'd never asked for a job before and that he had no experience or training to qualify him for whatever it was that he was applying for. His first decision was to lie about his age. Nineteen would sound a lot better than 17 would. Then he'd lie and tell this Schultz guy that he'd worked on a water well drilling rig. Last year his dad had a new well drilled on the farm, and Billy had watched the two men drill the well with their old cable tool rig. It was a pretty big stretch from watching a well being drilled for water to having drilling experience, but he remembered a few terms and thought he might be able to pull it off. His mind raced through other work-related experiences but as he cross-examined himself he realized that it would take only a few questions to expose his deception. The longer he sat preparing himself for Al Shultz the more his hopes began to sink. With World War II over just three years ago, there were still lots of veterans coming out of the service and they were sure to get first shot at any work.

Ten hours ago he had boarded the 10 o'clock bus in Nanton and he was tired and hungry. The main door to the bar continued to open and close as people came and went. Every time the door opened Billy could hear the rumble of voices, loud laughter, that would fade away as the door slowly closed. Each time the door opened, he'd sit up ramrod in his chair at the expectation of Al Schultz. But each time the person was just another patron on his way somewhere.

Finally, after about an hour, he approached the night clerk and asked if Al Schultz was still in there. All he got was a grunt in response. Billy dejectedly returned to his chair to resume his wait, not daring to go into the restaurant to get something to eat. Soon he began to lose interest in who came and went from the bar and began to doze off. Later, he was only vaguely aware that a very large man had come out of the bar, stopped at the front desk, and said something to the little man. But instead of heading to the exit door he walked towards Billy.

Suddenly every hair on Billy's neck seemed to stand on end as he realized this must be Al Schultz. Billy rocketed out of his chair to stand attention to meet the man he had been waiting two hours for.

Billy had never come up against a man of Al Schultz's stature before. He was wearing khaki pants with one pant cuff jammed into the top of a very worn leather boot. The leather toe of the boot was worn away, exposing the steel. Both boots were unlaced and they had the unmistakable look of being as tough as the man who wore them. Schultz's khaki shirt was also partially open, showing a mass of chest hair. Each hair looked like it could be used as a bedspring. The three-day old growth on his face was equally overwhelming. Each whisker looked to Billy as large as a pencil lead and just as black. Billy stood as tall as he could, but even in his new boots, he felt dwarfed in Al Schulz's presence. He became acutely aware that he could only manage to grow a little peach fuzz on his cheeks and there wasn't even a hint of hair growth on his chest.

Billy was too intimidated to talk and stood frozen in one spot, tongue-tied. Al Schultz said nothing and continued to stare right through Billy with his coal black eyes. Finally, Al Schultz grunted, "You a farm kid?"

From just those three words, Billy recognized the American accent. He wasn't sure how he should answer this question, as he didn't know if being a farm kid was a good thing or a bad thing. After a short pause, Billy said, "Yes, sir."

Al Schultz said nothing in reply and after what seemed an eternity, he removed the match stick from his mouth and while examining the chewed end said, "Be here at 11 o'clock." Billy was speechless and Al Schultz returned to his beer drinking.

In contrast to the rest of his day, the next two hours flew by. Questions began to overwhelm him. Where do I stay? What do I wear to work? How do I make a lunch? But each question he turned over in his mind became trivial as the realization sank in that he had triumphed. He was about to become a roughneck. Billy could hardly contain himself. He was consumed with happiness, yet there was not one person in all of Leduc that he could share his joy with.

Eleven o'clock was the closing hour for all hotels across Alberta, so he knew Al Schultz could not keep him waiting long. Billy watched as the stream of bar patrons went past him, all in various stages of intoxication. From the far end of the foyer the Ladies and Escorts entrance doors also swung open as a mix of men and women made their way past Billy. At last, Al Schultz, whose size stood him apart from all others, emerged. As he passed by Billy, he nodded his head in a gesture to follow, and Billy stepped smartly in behind him with his duffel bag over his shoulder.

Schultz opened the door to his brand new 1948 Chevy half-ton. On the side of the door Billy could make out the lettering TEX CAN DRILLING. Schultz said nothing and Billy offered nothing in return. Occasionally Schultz would let out a large beer belch that stunk up the cab of the truck. But Billy, just thrilled to be where he was, paid no attention. On the western horizon, Billy could faintly see the lights of various oil rigs. At least he thought they were oil rig lights.

One light kept getting closer, and as the gravel road they were on gave way to a rutted trail snaking through the bush, Billy realized that this must be it. He was about to begin working in the oil patch.

As soon as Billy stepped out of the truck, he was overwhelmed by the size of the rig and the deafening noise it made. Standing 125 feet tall the rig was the largest piece of equipment Billy had ever seen. Following Schultz up the steel steps to a small metal office, Billy felt his knees go weak. He was completely intimidated by the noise and vibration that crushed his senses and he fought the urge to flee.

Once in the steel enclosure with the door closed, his panic began to subside. Schultz went straight to the geolobox and studied data being printed out, which, Billy learned, indicated the depth that was drilled by the previous shift. As he looked over the printout, a squat man pressed close trying to make a case that the last shift drilled for too long and should have changed the bit two hours ago. He argued that it wasn't fair because he would now have to do all the work of tripping in and out to change the bit.Billy learned he was the driller.

Schultz paid no attention to his driller's complaints. But just as he was about to leave, he casually said, "I brought you a new weevil." Then in his heavy Texan drawl, he spoke to Billy for the first time since their meeting in the bar. "Kid, when I see you moving around this lease I want to see daylight under both feet at all times, and your shirttail better be sticking straight out. This here is Nick Ramchuck, your boss when I'm not in sight," and then he turned to the driller and said, "When I was his age men were made of iron and the rigs were made of wood, and now it's the other way around." Then, pleased with his little joke, he let out a loud guffaw.

Ramchuck repeated the joke in a high singsong Ukrainian accent and laughed hysterically. Billy thought the laugh was strained and sensed he was fawning on Schultz. Ramchuk followed Schultz to the door and shouted out after him,"We make lots of hole tonight. You see, you see."

Schultz paused briefly and said to Ramchuck, "Give this weevil a hard hat, I'll dock it off his paycheque."

Ramchuck reached into the locker and pulled out a steel hat and plopped it on Billy's head. The hard hat was comical looking. It was bright silver in colour with a wide brim and a high crown, but Billy felt 10 feet tall with it on. This must be the official acceptance in the oil fraternity he thought.

Ramchuk closed the door and looked at Billy, showing absolutely no hint of the humour of the last exchange. Ramchuk then turned his attention to a logbook and began printing up Billy's personal information. As he asked each question, Billy stifled an urge to laugh. He had never known a Ukrainian, nor had he heard such an accent before. While Ramchuck laboriously took down Billy's information, Billy had a good chance to study him. The man didn't have a neck, making his round head look like a bowling ball sitting on top of his shoulders. Each time he asked Billy a question, he'd peer up at him with his small round expressionless eyes. Billy noticed his teeth. They were about half the size of an average man's teeth and they were a brownish yellow. Maybe he ground his teeth or something. Maybe he was born that way. Were they brown because of the water or from chewing snoose? What Billy noticed most was that the man was barely literate. Billy had to repeat the spelling of Cochrane over and over, each time more slowly, as Ramchuck struggled to print the letters.

At this point, the door burst open startling both Billy and Ramchuck. All five men from the afternoon shift filed into the "doghouse" at once. There was a great deal of laughing and bantering as they picked up their lunch buckets and prepared to end the day. The driller looked at the geolobox and said to no one in particular, "Three hundred feet, not a bad day." Perhaps he meant his remarks for Ramchuck, thought Billy. He wondered if Ramchuck was as plodding at drilling as he was at printing. In the mist of all the light-hearted banter, the night shift came in the outside door, packing the small doghouse. One of the afternoon guys hollered out, "Hey Shoe, you leave any beer for us?" They all laughed, knowing that if there were any beer anywhere, Shoe would have drank it. Billy immediately started feeling comfortable in the mist of all the ribbing and horseplay.

As the afternoon shift disappeared out the door, Ramchuck said, "Get ready, we trip now." Shoe spat out, "Those assholes stiffed us again." Ramchuk said nothing and pointed from Billy to Shoe saying, "You go with him now. Him tell you."

Billy followed Shoe dutifully out of the door to the main floor of the drilling rig. He was once again overwhelmed by the noise of the three huge diesel engines and all of the rest of the unfamiliar noises from the rig's moving parts.

Shoe stopped, and while scratching his head as if deep in thought, he turned and said, "What's your name, weevil?"

"Billy Cochrane."

"Well I hope those aren't your Sunday goin-to-meet'n clothes, cause if they are, they sure are going to get dirty! Get yourself a pair of coveralls cause you won't be ridin' in my car covered with mud and grease. It looks like it's about time to break in those fancy new boots too."

He paused, and then continued, "Well boyo, it goes like this. Those three noisy sons of bitches over there power the draw works here, indicating both with a sweeping hand motion. The draw works is the control centre that powers that spool of cable that feeds the blocks. That lifts the pipe in and out of the ground. It also powers the turntable there that turns the drill stem. On the bottom of the drill stem is a rotary bit that digs the hole. You still with me?" Billy nodded but he had very little idea what Shoe was talking about. "Also," continued Shoe, "those three little puppies run the mud pumps that pump mud up that pipe and through that Kelly hose and then down the drill pipe. That's the dog house," he said, pointing at the steel building they had just been in. "And way up there's where my office is, and that's called the monkey board. This big ugly looking wrench hanging from this here cable is called a 'tong', and that my friend is where your office is, and on your desk is a sign-Dummy Corner.

"Down there," pointed Shoe as he led Billy over to the railing, "is the change house where you leave your dirty coveralls at the end of the shift, if you ever get around to buying a pair." While Shoe was pointing over the railing he let loose with a large stream of brown spit. "This here is where the driller stands and runs the show. See these two levers?" Shoe continued. Billy nodded as Shoe pointed at the brake handle and another lever that stuck out from the control panel. "This is lever A and this is lever B. Don't ever pull on this lever B because it will activate the blowout prevention and a hydraulic ram will slam shut and crush the pipe. The whole fucking shebang will fall down the hole and you'll be looking for a new job."

"Why do you pump mud down the hole?" Billy asked, shouting in order to be heard. "Well you see, boyo," continued Shoe, "the mud is pumped down the inside of the drill pipe and it comes up around the outside of the pipe carrying all the rock cuttings from the drill bit. The mud she go around and around, the table she go around and around, and you and me go around and around making sure everything she go around and around. One other thing, if anything goes wrong, run like hell or look for something big to hide behind!"

"What do you mean by something going wrong. How do I know if something is going wrong?" Billy pressed, trying again to be heard over the noise.

Shoe just shrugged and said, "You'll know when you know. Here's an extra pair of gloves I'll lend you. If you don't wear gloves you'll get your hands cut all to rat shit." Just as Shoe said that, the engine noise subsided, causing Billy to look around. Ramchuk had taken up his position at the controls of the draw works.

"Let's go, weevil, it's time to go to work." The other roughneck was smiling when he said this and Billy took no offence to the order. Billy introduced himself to the two other floor hands with a hearty "Hi, my name's Billy Cochrane." One introduced himself as Len and the other as Bruce. Billy assumed that they were two local farmers trying to supplement their meagre farm income with work on an oil rig. Len showed him how to work the tong, which would be Billy's main job.

The engines gave out a mighty roar as Ramchuck stepped on the foot pedal. Billy thought the whole derrick was going to collapse on top of him as the entire string of drill stem slowly lifted off bottom. With the three Waukesha engines screaming in protest, Billy was transfixed as the pipe moved skyward.

Just as the first joint between the square Kelly pipe and the round drill stem appeared, Ramchuck took his foot off the gas and slammed on the handbrake. This signalled the three floor men to drop the cone-shaped slip around the drill pipe, preventing it from sliding back down the hole. Len demonstrated how Billy was to lock his tong on the top of the pipe joint, while he in turn locked his tong on the bottom side. Ramchuck, the driller, then engaged what Show told him was the cathead, by pulling the spinning chain that was fastened to the end of the tong. With a groan and a pop, the joint was broken. Len and Billy removed their tongs and Ramchuck gunned the rotary table in reverse, spinning the two pieces of pipe apart. When the two pipes were completely separated, Ramchuck's next move was to raise the Kelly and all three of the floor hands wrestled the 40-foot-long piece of pipe, the swivel at the top of it, and the mud hose that was attached to the swivel. The whole assembly was guided down a specially dug hole so that it would be out of the way while the rest of the drill stem was removed. With the Kelly freed, all that was left was the block and the elevator attached to it.

Ramchuck lowered the elevator carefully and Billy watched intently as Len locked the elevator around the top of the drill stem that was sticking up on top of the drill table.

From out of nowhere Shoe appeared and stepped up onto the elevators. With a cocky smile he saluted the three floor men. Shoe wore his hard hat at a jaunty angle and this gesture reminded Billy of someone out of a pirate movie. Ramchuck gunned the motors and again the whole rig squealed in protest as the pipe slowly ascended skyward. Billy stood in amazement as he watched Shoe and the pipe go higher and higher. Finally, 90 feet in the air, Billy watched Shoe nimbly jump off the elevators on to the monkey board. Billy couldn't believe Shoe's bravery, or maybe stupidity. Any slip and Shoe would have fallen to a certain death.

The appearance of the joint on the third drill pipe was the signal for Billy and the rest of the crew to set the slips and break the pipe. By this time Shoe had put on a safety harness and wrapped a piece of rope around the top of the pipe. He looked down as the three men steered the now unfastened pipe across the rig floor onto a portable pipe stand. Shoe released the elevators and as they coasted back down the derrick, he used the leverage of the rope to pull the pipe towards him, and then placed it in position on the monkey board.

As Billy set the tongs and pushed the pipe around, he began to feel more confident. The engine noise and all of the other loud sounds of metal banging against metal and the reverberating noise in the pipe became less terrifying. Billy took satisfaction in knowing that he could keep up physically.

Over and over the process was repeated. Ninety feet of pipe was broken off and stacked on the rig floor. No time or motion was wasted, and very little was said.

When the second-to last stand of pipe was broken off, a spray of mud erupted, soaking all three of the floor hands. Billy was covered in mud from head to toe. He was too startled to say anything, but Len and Bruce were cursing furiously. Billy looked over at Ramchuk for some reaction, but there was no hint of expression on his broad face.

Finally, the last piece of pipe was hoisted from the hole and there, attached to the bottom, was the drill bit. Billy stared intently at the bit, as he was curious to see what it looked like. So this is what made old Howard Hughes a millionaire, thought Billy, as he rubbed his finger around the teeth of the three cones of the drill bit. He could see at a glance how the bit worked. The three interlocking cones chewed the rock it passed through to shreds under the weight of the turning drill stem.

While Billy was marvelling at the drill bit, Ramchuck sent the elevators up one last time to retrieve Shoe. Upon reaching the rig floor, Shoe stepped off the elevators, and looking at the muddy state of the three floor hands, called out, "Having fun, lads?"

The cold spring morning air pressed against Billy's mud-soaked clothes and his teeth began to chatter. Shoe turned to him and in a loud voice told Billy to go down to the end of the catwalk and bring back the pipe stretcher. While the rest of the crew disappeared into the doghouse to eat their lunch, Billy began dutifully searching for the pipe stretcher. But he could find nothing lying around that looked like it might be a pipe stretcher.

Billy dejectedly returned to the doghouse to report that he had failed to find the pipe stretcher and admit that he didn't know what a pipe stretcher looked like. "What's the matter, kid?" Shoe asked in a surprised voice.

"Can't find it ..." Billy began to explain.

"Maybe the last shift moved it, did any of you guys see the pipe stretcher tonight?"

Both Len and Bruce shook their heads and Billy thought he detected a slight grin on Len's face as he took another chomp on his sandwich. "Forget it for now. Where's your lunch?"

Billy weakly said, "I'm not hungry." Shoe recognized the fib and thrust out a half of his sandwich. Billy weakly protested, but took the sandwich saying, "If you insist." Billy was ravished and he was grateful to Shoe for the gesture.

Shoe then turned his attention to Ramchuck who was quietly sitting in the corner eating his lunch. Shoe said to him, "So what are you going to do with all the money you're making now that you're a driller? Going to buy a boar for your pig farm? All those sows would probably miss you!"

Billy's back stiffened and he looked over at Ramchuck for some kind of reaction. Ramchuck let on as if he hadn't heard Shoe's insult. He merely stood and said, "We go to work now." Billy guessed that Shoe was bitter that Ramchuck had been set up as a driller instead of him.

Running the drill pipe and new bit back into the hole wasn't much different than pulling it out. The one thing that intrigued Billy was the job of the motorman. Len would wrap the spinning chain six times on the bottom joint of pipe. Then up in the derrick Shoe dropped the pipe in the elevator and as it was hoisted off the floor, the three floor men steered it into position as it was lowered onto the previous pipe joint. Len gave a deft flick of his wrist and the spinning chain climbed up the stand of pipe. Ramchuck then activated the cathead, spinning the whole 90-foot section of new pipe securely together. The tongs did the final tightening. The whole routine was repeated over and over until the entire pipe was back in the hole. The final step was reattaching the square-piped Kelly. As soon as the square pipe was lowered into the square hole on the turntable, the rig was ready to drill.

The sun was now shining, and Billy noted with satisfaction that his clothes were drying out and there were only two more hours left to work.

Shoe took Billy over to the change shack, pointing out a locker he could use. "I suppose you need a ride to town too. Well I'll give you one this time, but that's why we have a change shack. You change from your really dirty clothes into your normal dirty clothes so you don't get my car all mucked up."

Just as they were about to drive away, Billy shouted, "Stop! I forgot my duffel bag." Running up the steps to the doghouse, he marvelled how the rig didn't sound as loud as it had at first and he took little notice of the shaking beneath his feet. What seemed like mass confusion eight hours earlier wasn't nearly as intimidating as it had been at first.

As soon as he got back in to the car, Shoe asked, "Got a place to stay?" When Billy shook his head, Shoe let out a low whistle. "This might be a problem," he said. There are a lot of rigs working here and I doubt like hell if you'll find a place. We'll try Ma Williams. She runs a boarding house across the tracks."

Ma Williams greeted them warmly, and said, "I've got one-half of a bed you can share, take it or leave it!" Billy looked up at Shoe and when he nodded, Billy said, "I'll take it."

"I'll pick you up here at 11 tonight," said Shoe, and then he tugged on Billy's arm and whispered, "Can you spot me $10 until payday?" Billy was grateful for all the things Shoe was doing for him, so he quickly fished out a ten-dollar bill from his wallet.

Sharing a bed with a complete stranger was something Billy had never contemplated. Nor, to his chagrin, was sharing a very small room with three strangers. Ma Williams cheerfully pointed out that he might get lucky. Maybe his new bedmate would be working an opposite shift from him. "Besides," she continued, "the bed will always be warm in the winter." One thing that Billy was particularly grateful for was that the house had electricity. This was a big improvement from his farmhouse. The little wash basin at the end of the stove was totally inadequate to wash all the mud off, but it would have to do. After eating Ma Williams' hearty breakfast of pancakes, ham, and eggs, Billy quickly fell into a coma-like sleep.

Chapter 5

Billy woke with a start and decided to explore the town and buy a pair of coveralls. Leduc was just like every other small town he had been in. A couple of grocery stores, a pool hall, other assorted businesses and just as he would have guessed, a Chinese café. Stopping in the café Billy noticed two booths were filled with high school kids. He perched himself up on the stool at the counter, ordered a coke and lazily drank it while he tried to eavesdrop on the conversations. Billy was immediately attracted to one very pretty young lady. He stretched and spun from side to side on his stool keeping time to the jukebox. Every so often he got up and walked to the door and looked out as if he was expecting someone. He made sure she noticed him, while pretending to take no notice of her. He returned to his stool nonchalantly and then tapped his toes in time to the music, knowing that his work boots would have to be noticed.

Eventually, as he had hoped, the dream girl got up to go to the bathroom and walked right past him. Billy rehearsed a few lines to say on her return. In a couple of minutes she emerged and, just as she reached the spot where Billy was sitting, he spun his stool around and said to her, "I'm new in town, just hired on with Tex Can Drilling." But before he could get the next line out of his mouth, which was going to be, " What's there to do in this town?" she brusquely said, "I know. I can smell you."

A strange feeling came over Billy. Just yesterday he could have been with a group of friends much like those in the two booths. Now he felt they had nothing in common. He made his exit by walking as tall as he could, He wasn't going to let on the girl's sarcasm had hurt him.

He eventually eased off on his pace and went into the General Store to buy a pair of coveralls, a lunch bucket, and two pairs of cotton gloves. Then Billy made his way back to Ma Williams' for supper.

At the boarding house Billy met his roommates and his bedmate. They were all young guys like him and Billy didn't see any problems. His bedmate asked him flippantly if he had "cooties."

Billy replied, "Do I have what?"

"Cooties. You know, crabs, lice, bed bugs, stuff like that."

Billy threw a mock punch and they all trooped into the kitchen for supper. After supper, Billy's new friends introduced him to the fine art of playing poker, which helped to kill time until Shoe came to pick him up.

The rest of the week fell into a routine. His coveralls were no longer new but encased in grease, diesel fuel, and grime. His new Dayton boots had turned black. Every night Shoe arrived, he was at least half-pissed. Ramchuk, or Hunky as Shoe called him, slyly asked Billy, "How much money did Shoe bum from you?"

Billy's face turned red as he realized that Shoe must be well known for borrowing money and probably just as well known for not paying it back. "Ten dollars," he said defensively. "Ah, you lose it," said Ramchuck dismissively, in his funny Ukrainian accent.

First off on this shift Shoe told Billy to climb to the top of the derrick with a five-gallon pail of water and fill the water table. One hundred and twenty five feet straight up, one rung at a time, Billy finally reached the top. Once he got there, there was nothing resembling a water table, nor was there any part of the crown that would even hold water. Billy quickly realized he had been had again. But instead of being upset he took the opportunity to gaze out into the night sky. He felt as though he could reach up and touch the stars. Off on the horizon he counted 15 other oil rigs with their lit-up derricks. Billy took his sweet time climbing down the derrick as he reasoned no one could give him shit after pulling such a prank on him. On his way down he stopped to examine the monkey board where Shoe, his derrick man, worked. I could work derrick, thought Billy. I'm not scared of heights.

When he had finished climbing down, he was met by a gale of laughter. Even Ramchuck seemed to be enjoying the joke. Billy just said, "You assholes." He knew it was all part of a weevil's initiation.

Each afternoon he stopped in at Fats Café, hoping to see the breathtaking girl. She looked just like the calendar girl in Larry's tire shop back in Nanton, he thought. His persistence paid off. One afternoon, returning from the bathroom, she poked him lightly in the ribs on her way by. Billy responded with a loud grunt, thrilled that some form of communication had taken place.

Friday, Len informed Ramchuck he was quitting because he needed to devote more time to his farm. The next person in line for Len's motorman job was Bruce. When informed of this, Bruce merely shrugged his shoulders and said, "Give the job to Billy." Later, Billy was taken aback when Ramchuck mentioned that Schultz had said Billy was to be the new motorman. Panic set in. He didn't know how to loop the spinning chain and he knew absolutely nothing about the Waukesha motors. He turned to Shoe and said, "What should I do?"

"Fuck all to it boyo, you'll learn."

Billy was incredulous that after only four days on the job, he was promoted two positions, and a ten-cent-an-hour raise to boot. One dollar an hour. Billy couldn't wait to tell his pals in Nanton about his good fortune.

On Sundays the midnight shift short changed to the daylight or morning shift. This meant there was only an eight hour break between shifts. After a brief sleep, Billy was raring to go. At the rig a new hand was there to take up the dumb corner position. Looking at the new man and realizing that he was about the same age as he was, Billy asked, "What's your name, weevil?" The new guy replied, "Johnny Laboucan," and as Billy shook his hand he thought that Johnny was probably just another tough farm kid like him.

Getting the knack of spinning the chain from one joint up to the next piece of pipe wasn't as easy as it looked. His first several attempts resulted in only four of the six wraps finding their way up to the top joint. This meant that Billy would have to push the last two coils up with his left hand and he was afraid that Ramchuck would engage the cathead and crush his hand. However, by the end of the trip in, he got the hang of it. As the crew began the general clean up after changing the bit, Billy said in an overly loud voice, "We're going to need the pipe stretcher. Johnny, you run down to the tool box and bring it here." Billy pointed in the direction of the toolbox and Johnny promptly left to hunt down the pipe stretcher.

The only thing Billy had to know about the motors was periodically to check the oil.

"Have a look at this, boyo," Shoe said, pointing at Al Schultz's small trailer, which was parked at the end of the lease. Emerging from the trailer was Schultz's gorgeous wife. Even from 100 hundred yards they could see her large breasts.

Billy gave out a low whistle.

"Don't get any ideas Billy, Schultz would kill any man he caught sniffing around her."

"What's a good looking babe doing with a brute like Schultz?" Billy wondered out loud.

"I hear she's got a real itch too," continued Shoe. "But he's probably too pissed all the time to scratch it. Anyway, don't get any bright ideas because if anyone is going to get into her pants, it's going to be me."

Billy gave a low whistle and exclaimed, "I sure wouldn't kick her out of my bed for eating crackers!" While they continued their gaze, the motors changed pitch, signalling another single of pipe was about to be added to the drill stem.

Billy particularly enjoyed this part of his job as he got to run the cathead that lifted the length of pipe off the catwalk, while the other two men had to wrestle it into position. Bruce didn't seem to mind that he was still doing the grunt work. This puzzled Billy because, with this promotion, the only additional thing he had to do was wrap the rope around the cathead and guide the pipe up to the floor. Billy thought that Bruce must be one of those people who didn't want any responsibility and was happy just taking a cheque home to his wife and kids.

The rig was slowly becoming a part of him. Every sound gradually became clear, no longer just a jumble of noise. And every time Schultz came around, Billy made himself scarce, as he didn't want any confrontations. He did find it funny though to watch Ramchuck grovel at Schultz's feet. Ramchuck was intimidated by Shoe too, probably because he realized that Shoe knew more that he did, having worked in the patch longer. Johnny was a hard worker and Billy felt a bond growing between them. He sensed that Johnny was not all that smart, but his face was always beaming and he was quick to laugh at any joke or funny situation. He liked Shoe too, but he didn't like the idea that Shoe had taken advantage of him and was going to stiff him out of the ten dollars.

Billy enjoyed the responsibility of taking shale samples over to the geologist's trailer. The cuttings from the drill bit were pumped up around the drill pipe and caught in a shale shaker as the drilling mud was circulated back into the mud tanks. Billy's job was to shovel the cuttings into the sump and then wash up a small sample for the geologist. Extreme care had to be taken to mark each sample with the depth drilled. On occasion, when he had a little time, free from adding singles or the other multitude of tasks that needed to be done, he would try to engage the geologist, Dave, in conversation.

The geologist was very young and Billy could relate to him. Billy would ask Dave what he was looking for and hope that Dave would take time out to explain in layman's terms what his job was. Billy sensed that Dave was probably a little bored and enjoyed conversation. Billy was impressed with the microscope and the other tools of the geology trade, which were laid out on the table in the small trailer.

"Have you ever heard of the Great Barrier Reef in Australia?" asked the geologist one day. Billy nodded, trying to think back to which grade the topic was studied. "Well, some 350 million years ago the land we are on now was a warm shallow ocean. A large reef grew here just like it's doing now in Australia. Living in the holes of the reef was a multitude of sea life that was well fed by the nutritious warm water. Then the earth began to change, sometimes gradually and other times violently, so that the reef is now some 5,000 to 6,000 feet beneath us."

"Wow!" exclaimed Billy.

"We call that reef the Devonian Reef, and what you're doing is trying to dig a hole down to find it."

"How did you pick this spot?" Billy pressed.

"Well, we had seismic tests done and from the results it looked like we might be over a porous formation that, hopefully, contains oil. We think that when the ancient sea life died it was trapped in the holes in the reef. Over a long period of time, it turned into oil."

"Tell me what you see in all the bags of shale I'm bringing here."

"Well," continued the Dave, showing impatience with Bill's elementary questions, "we have samples from around the world to compare them to, and if nothing else, I lick them to see if they taste like oil." He said this with a straight face and Billy wasn't sure if this wasn't just another prank being played on him, so he excused himself saying he had better get back to work.

Billy was fascinated with every aspect of the oil rig, but no one took the time to explain things to him. He wouldn't dare ask Schultz, Ramchuck wouldn't answer his questions, and Shoe just gave him smart-ass answers. Most of the time he was simply shown how to do something, and just told to do it. No one ever explained why it was being done. Most of the time he had to figure out for himself. He wished he looked older than 17, rather than younger, so he could go into the beer parlour after work where he was sure there would be people he could sit and listen to and learn from. But maybe he would just turn into a drunk like Shoe and Schultz.

When he got back on the rig floor, Ramchuck agitatedly asked, "Where you be gone?"

Billy knew he had nothing to fear from Ramchuck, so he merely shrugged and said, "Shovelling shale, tidying up the tool box, taking a sample over to the geologist," reasoning that this should cover for his absence. He knew Ramchuck could not leave his job of constantly releasing the brake to make sure there was a steady weight on the drill bit. He had no time to go looking for Billy.

Besides, every night last week when they were not tripping, Shoe had curled up under the tarp on the cement bags and gone to sleep. Any time Ramchuck asked him where he had been, Shoe used the same runaround, knowing it was unlikely that Ramchuck would come looking for him. But Shoe had warned Billy that if anyone was looking for him, he'd better come and wake him up. And if he didn't, Billy would get his ass kicked. This night when Ramchuck asked him where he'd been, Shoe replied, "Mixing mud."

"Mr. Shultz ... he say, you go change oil in wife car." Ramchuck blurted out in his sing-song Ukrainian accent. Billy stared at him for a second trying to get the exact meaning of what Ramchuck said. Ramchuck continued on, "You know how to change oil?"

"Of course I do, I'm a motorman ain't I," Billy replied, finally realizing what he was being asked to do.

Billy glanced over towards Schultz's trailer just in time to see the dust of Schultz's half-ton as he left for town. Without further comment, Billy went down to the tool shack under the doghouse and rummaged around for some wrenches, a funnel, and a five-gallon pail of oil. When he had gathered them up, he lugged them all over to Schultz's 1946 Chevrolet car.

Billy lay on his back and squirmed under the engine and oil pan. It took no time at all to unscrew the oil plug and let all the oil spill out on the ground beside him. With the plug secured firmly back in place, Billy placed his hands on the running board and slid out from under the car. As his head emerged from under the car, he looked up, but instead of seeing daylight, he was looking right up the skirt of Schultz's wife as her two legs straddled his shoulders. She neatly stepped away and as Billy sat up she laughingly asked, "Need any help?"

Billy was completely speechless and after what seemed like an eternity, he mumbled something about starting the car up and letting it run for a few minutes before topping it up with oil and checking the dipstick.

"That ought to do it." Billy smiled at her, packed up his things and retreated back to the rig. On the way back his heart was beating out of control. What did he actually see as she stood over him and looked up her dress? He remembered seeing a lot of her legs, but how high up did he see? Did he in fact see her panties? Maybe she wasn't wearing panties. Did he see her pussy? As his mind raced he began to imagine he had got a glimpse of it. But on cross-examining himself, he couldn't even remember the colour of her dress, or for that matter he couldn't even bring up a clear picture of her face. Probably because he had been too embarrassed to look at her face, he thought to himself. Why did she do that? Was she just joking around? Did she mistake him for someone else? Was she just lonely? Was she horny? What did the whole episode mean? Questions and answers kept Billy's head spinning for the rest of the afternoon.

Should he tell Johnny and Shoe about the juicy details of his adventure? Better not, he reasoned to himself. If word ever got out and Schultz heard about it he would be fired, and more than likely he would have every bone in his body broken. The rest of the shift was a blur. He hadn't even asked her name, he thought to himself. What if he had started up a conversation and just acted amused as if this kind of thing happened all the time?

When Ramchuck worriedly asked him, "You oil change okay?" Billy just shrugged and said, "No problem." He smiled to himself and thought that if Ramchuck knew what had just happened, he would probably have a heart attack.

On the way to town after the shift, Shoe asked Billy and Johnny (who was now also paying Shoe for his ride) if they were going to stop in the hotel and have a beer with him. Both thought this was a good idea, but they were pretty sure they wouldn't get served. Shoe pressed on saying that the beer parlour would be so busy on a Friday afternoon that the bartender would never even notice them.

"I will if you will," Johnny beamed and Billy, rising to the challenge, replied, "Alright, let's do it ... all they can do is kick us out!"

"Just follow me and let me do the talking," Shoe warned.

As they entered the bar Billy's heart raced with anticipation. There must have been 200 hundred men in there and by the looks of them any one of them would fight at the drop of a hat. They squeezed around a small table and Shoe signalled the bartender by making a circular motion with his hand. As they waited for their beer, Billy thought the bar was nearly as loud as the oil rig.

Billy spotted Schultz talking animatedly with a half-dozen other men and a chill went down his spine as his afternoon adventure came back to him. He turned back to his two companions and in a matter of fact voice stated that a cool beer was going to taste pretty good. Billy could tell that Johnny could hardly contain his excitement and that he wanted to appear that this wasn't all that big of deal to him. The bartender neatly wiped their table off with the towel he had tucked in his apron and set two glasses each in front of them. Both Billy and Johnny looked down at the table trying to hide their faces, as was their game plan on the way from the rig. And the bartender said, " You boys old enough to be in here?" Billy's heart dropped as he muttered, "Yup."

"Got any identification?" Billy looked to Shoe for guidance and Shoe said, "For fuck sakes, Pete ... give the guys a break ... They've been busting their asses all day."

"Sorry boys," and with that said, he picked up their beers and put them back on his tray.

Billy felt that whole room was watching and laughing at him as they slunk out. Johnny later said, as they were playing pool, that not one person even noticed them leaving. This made Billy feel a little less humiliated.

Shoe walked into the pool hall a short time later and laughingly said, "Don't worry about it, Sunday's short change and payday as well and I'm going to take both of you on a real adventure."

Billy looked over at Johnny and snorted, " What kind of adventure can happen in eight hours."

You'll see," promised Shoe.

Chapter 6

Billy stared in awe at his first paycheque one hundred and eight dollars for 12 days work. Shoe looked up from his cheque and looked over at Billy and said, "Well boyo, you got the world by the ass on a downhill pull." Billy said nothing and carefully folded his paycheque and put it in his wallet. The morning shift was uneventful, the drilling was going slowly and they didn't even need to trip. This gave Billy spare time to visit with the geologist and putter around the lease. He was hoping that Schultz's wife might notice him and walk over or at least show herself so Billy could get a close-up look. He even thought about suggesting to Ramchuck that maybe he should do Schultz a favour and wash his car. He reasoned that Ramchuck would go along with this as it would be a good way for him to suck up to Schultz, but then he dropped the idea as being too risky.

Down at the change shack Shoe made both Johnny and Billy rewash their hands and every other piece of skin that was exposed to the day's dirt and grime. When they stood for inspection for the third time, Shoe announced, "Alright, let's boogie." All three piled into Shoe's old Ford. They weren't even off the lease when Shoe reached under the seat and pulled out a bottle of whisky. Bouncing down the rutted trail, Shoe took the cap off the bottle, held it up, and gave a salute, "Here's to that dirty, greasy, noisy, smelly, ugly piece of pig iron. But," he winked, "the paycheques ain't dirty."

Billy was sure he had never been happier in his life as he forced a little swallow of the burning whisky down his throat, then passed the bottle on to Johnny and said, "Bottoms up pal."

"Where are we off to?" Johnny inquired from the back seat.

"Edmonton, lads, we're off to see the big city," Shoe boomed.

"In that case, let's stop and get some mix for this fire water," Billy pleaded.

"Are you guy's roughnecks or pansies?" Shoe asked scornfully. "Pass that bottle back up front. We'll stop at the hotel and get my paycheque cashed at the front desk. I'll lend you guys some money if you need some, but if you're going to drink my whiskey, you're going to drink it straight!

Shoe pulled his car up to the hotel and bounded out with his usual cat-like agility. Upon returning to the car Shoe handed Billy a ten-dollar bill. Billy tried to look surprised as if he had forgotten about the loan.

"What's this for?" he asked.

"It's the $10 I owe you," replied Shoe.

"Oh, yeah," Billy said, and stuffed the bill in his wallet. He was pleased that Shoe had paid back the loan without him having to ask for it. His stock in Shoe was rising.

Billy had never been to Edmonton before and was looking forward to the trip and the adventure, whatever it might be. A warm feeling began to spread across his body as the liquor took hold.

Turning towards Shoe with his left arm draped over the seat, he said, "Shoe, how did you ever get a name like that?"

Shoe thought for a second, and then said, "Well you see, it's like this, I was bagging this guy's wife one night and he comes home early. I grabbed my clothes and jumped out the window, but I didn't have time to get my shoes. Then, while I was walking down the street some friends picked me up and wondered why I wasn't wearing any shoes. Everyone started calling me Shoeless, and then after awhile it just became Shoe." Billy laughed at the story and thought it might even be true, but then again it might be all bullshit.

Hank Snow started singing "Moving On" on the car radio and all three of them sang along. When the song ended, Shoe carried on with his own lyrics …

The old tom cat was feeling fine
when we brushed his ass with turpentine.

He's moving on, he'll soon be gone,
He passed the gate like an eighty eight,
He's moving on.

All three howled with laughter, giddy with happiness and whiskey.

"Shoe," piped up Johnny from the back seat, "I heard a story that you once took a length of spinning chain into the bar and started swinging it around. You had people hiding under tables and running for their lives. Then, when the cop came and asked you, 'What the hell do you think you're doing?' you told him that you were keeping the Indians away. When he looked around and said there were no Indians here, you said, 'Doing a good job, ain't I' Is that story true?"

Shoe rubbed his chin and said, "Maybe it is, maybe it isn't, I know I spent the night in the can for doing something."

Soon they were passing through the outskirts of Edmonton. Billy noted with interest the new and used cars for sale in various car lots. A brand new Dodge was parked high up on a ramp with a huge sticker price written beneath it ... "$2800!" A little further on, a used car lot was advertising, "Best selection of used vehicles in Edmonton!" Billy wondered what he could get for $400. He should have that much in the bank in another three months.

Shoe eased his old Ford down the steep bank of the North Saskatchewan River, crossed over the Low Level Bridge, then geared down for the equally steep climb on the other side. Passing by the majestic Macdonald Hotel, he made a right turn at Jasper Avenue and continued on a few blocks. Then he pulled into a side street and stopped in front of a dilapidated old apartment building.

"What the hell is this?" demanded Billy as he sat upright in his seat and surveyed the seedy neighbourhood they were in.

"This," announced Shoe triumphantly, "is where we are going to get laid. Just wait here a second and I'll check things out." Shoe bounded from the car and disappeared inside the building. In a moment he was back and grabbing the remains of the whiskey bottle, saying, " Follow me!"

Billy looked back at Johnny and said, "I don't know about this." Then, shaking his head, he slowly stepped out of the car. He had barely stood up when he was almost bowled over by Johnny, who was acting like a rambunctious dog that couldn't wait to get out. Johnny quickly fell into step beside Shoe as Billy slammed the door shut and somewhat reluctantly followed.

What paint there had been on the old building was almost weathered away and the wooden steps were rotted to the point that Billy had to watch his step. He followed his two pals down the grimy corridor and into the back suite. There, sprawled on a sagging sofa, was the object of Shoe's adventure.

"Boys. I want you to meet Gerty," said Shoe as he briskly rubbed his two hands together.

"Afternoon boys," Gerty replied. This very fat lady made no effort to stand, but continued, with a dismissive wave of her hand, "Find yourselves a place to sit."

Shoe quickly offered Gerty a drink of whisky and she drawled, " Don't mind if I do."

"Billy, pour this lady a drink," Shoe ordered, as he plunked himself down beside her. Billy raised his eyebrows and began looking around the room for some sign of a glass. Besides the sofa Gerty and Shoe were sitting on, there was little else for furniture. In one corner of the room there was a cupboard, a small table, and two wooden chairs, which had about as much paint on them as was on the outside of the building. Next to the cupboard was a washstand. On it rested a chipped enamel basin and a water pail. Beside the washstand was a slop bucket that was half full and in need of being emptied.

Billy opened the cupboard where there was a pitiful collection of dishes, assorted cups and glasses, and a few other kitchen knick-knacks. An old stove stood along the other wall. Next to the sofa was a door that looked like it might lead to a bedroom. He picked out what he thought was the cleanest of the dirty glasses and poured a shot of whiskey. "Water?" He asked, looking over at the dissipated-looking Gerty.

"A little darlin'... if you would," she replied in a surprisingly girlish voice.

As Billy politely handed her the drink he had a chance to look her over more closely. The dress or housecoat she was wearing was loose fitting, but he could see it hid a very ample body. Her black hair was unwashed and badly in need of attention. Jowls were beginning to form on her cheeks and Billy guessed that the rest of her body was just as mushy.

Billy didn't linger over her very long as her cigarette was smouldering in an already overfilled ashtray beside her, and the spiral of dead smoke was about to make him gag. He retreated to the other wooden chair beside Johnny who was sitting backwards in his chair and his face was beaming more than usual. Shoe and Gerty were engaged in some idle banter and Johnny was taking it all in.

Gerty didn't seem self-conscious at all and after a few minutes she turned to Billy and Johnny, "So you boys have come to town for a little entertainment. Well, which one of you is first?" she said, as she slowly turned her head and looked at each one of them for a brief moment.

"I guess you would be talking about me," said Shoe, and then he stood and gallantly bowed, holding out his hand. He and Gerty disappeared into the bedroom, leaving Billy and Johnny alone. "Wow!" Johnny exclaimed, "Can you believe this?"

Billy said, "Here, have a pull on this," and he reached for the whiskey. "We're going to need all the fortification we can get."

In no time at all Shoe emerged through the door with a triumphant look on his face. "Who's next?" he asked, as he looked first at one and then the other. Billy looked at Johnny and said, "You go."

Shoe took about three big swigs from the bottle of whiskey and then let out a forced loud belch. "Motorman, people are like those Waukesha engines, they got to get their oil changed on a regular basis."

"You're fucking A right," replied Billy, "and its about time too." He hoped his brazen reply sounded more convincing than he felt. He was about to continue with some more tough talk when the bedroom door swung open and Johnny resurfaced. He stood in the doorway pretending that he was propping himself up and then he did a wobbly-knee walk towards them imploring them … "Help me … help me."

"You couldn't have been in there four minutes," Billy exclaimed. Johnny's only reply, in a very weak voice, was "Whiskey … whiskey." Shoe was bent over laughing. Then he straightened up and pointed Billy to the door, unable to speak because he was laughing so hard.

Billy closed the bedroom door firmly behind him and gazed over at the naked Gerty, who was still lying on the bed. She was smoking a cigarette and sipping on the whiskey Billy had poured her. Yep, she was fat all right. Her huge breasts hung to each side of her body and nearly touched the dirty gray sheet she was lying on. A mass of pubic hair began at her navel and spread downward from there. Billy looked at the size of her legs and wondered how anyone could fit between them.

"Before we get down to business darlin' I want to see your five dollars." Billy continued to stare at the mound of pasty white flesh as his mind raced for a way out of his predicament. How could he save face, and yet not piss-off the fat lady? If he was to say that he had no money, he knew she would bring this up with Shoe, and then Shoe would wonder what was up. If he said he had some kind of injury or disease, she would demand to know what the hell he was doing here in the first place.

Finally, he said, "Look, I don't want to go through with this right now. I'll give you the money if you promise not to tell my two friends … okay?" Gerty took a long drag on her cigarette and fixed Billy with a lingering stare. He stood there while she took her time finishing her smoke. He didn't say a word but thought she might be giving him enough time to save face, more likely save her own face. Finally, she rolled onto her side and swung her legs over the edge of the bed. Billy fished five dollars out of his wallet. As Gerty stood with her hand out to take the money the flab of her belly sagged down so far that it covered her pubic hair. "This is a new one on me," was all she said.

Billy couldn't wait to get out of the room with its putrid smell of unwashed flesh, soiled linen, and dirty clothes. He opened the door while forcing a smile on his face.

"Get over here boyo," Shoe ordered. Billy replied, "What's up?" And then Shoe said, "Alright everybody, cocks out." All three of them stood exposed in a tight little circle and Shoe splashed whiskey on each of their cocks. Billy wasn't sure if this was to prevent disease or if it was some kind of an oil patch rite.

As they left the apartment Shoe called out to Gerty, who had yet to come out of her bedroom, " So long sweetheart, see you soon." Billy thought maybe so, but it won't be with me. Johnny chirped up, "Let's get out of here before this dump falls on our heads."

Everyone was back in the car, when Billy asked, " What now?" Shoe looked at his watch and replied, "I think we've got time for some Chinese food before we get back for the midnight shift, and I know just the place."

"I hope it's cleaner than the last place you took us to," Billy sarcastically replied, rolling down the window to get some fresh air.

Billy took over the wheel on the drive back to Leduc. Shoe was right about knowing the Chinese restaurant, for as soon as they were seated, the waiter brought over a large teapot filled with whiskey. Billy could see that both Johnny and Shoe were pretty drunk. He would be too, except that he had often put the bottle to his lips without drinking any when it was passed to him. Billy had only driven a few miles out of Edmonton when Johnny blurted out, "Stop the car. I'm going to puke." Billy watched in amusement as his friend brought up all his Chinese food.

As Johnny got back in the car, Billy said to his ashen-white friend, "You just puked up two bucks worth of Chinese food." Johnny's only response was a loud groan. Billy looked into the rear-view mirror to see what Shoe was doing, but he was either passed out or asleep. Twice more on the way back to the rig, Billy had to stop to let Johnny out to throw up.

Chapter 7

Billy was relieved when they finally pulled up in front of the change house. The cars from the afternoon shift were still there, meaning they weren't late for work. "Alright boys, rise and shine, it's time to go to work." Billy had to shake each of them hard to get them awake. Shoe stood beside the car and, looking up at the rig, said, "The Kelly's high and so am I. You know where to find me." Billy turned to Johnny and warned, "You had better straighten up partner or you'll get your ass run off." The thought crossed Billy's mind that he was one to talk. He wasn't in much better shape than they were.

Ramchuck never even looked up as Billy and Johnny filed past him in the doghouse. Bruce was already tidying up on the rig floor and Billy briefly told him that they had gone to Edmonton and got pissed, and asked if he would cover for them as much as he could. "I'm going to park Johnny somewhere and I'll come back and give you a hand," he promised. Luckily everything went smoothly for the rest of the night and every time they were needed to add a single, Billy and Bruce did all the work. When Ramchuck demanded to know where Johnny was, Billy said the last he saw of him, he was mixing mud with Shoe. The answer was plausible as Shoe's responsibility as derrick man was to keep up the consistency of the mud's thickness. This took some skill, as a proper viscosity had to be maintained and Shoe knew what he was doing. And Shoe had the authority to order

Johnny to haul and break the bags of mud into the mud tank, while Shoe stirred the mixture.

The best thing about working the night shift, Billy thought to himself, was being able to hang out at Fat's Café in the late afternoon. Billy made sure he didn't oversleep, which was never a problem as the boarding house was really noisy during the day. The problem was getting enough sleep. Each afternoon when he got up he took great care combing his hair and brushing his teeth. He lathered the soap on his hands and face hoping it would cut the smell of diesel fuel that seemed to have sunk into every pore of his body. Every afternoon he walked to the café hoping to get a chance to talk to the most gorgeous girl in all Leduc. Usually, she was there after school with her friends and he constantly schemed up ways to draw her into a conversation. He told Johnny about her and sometimes his friend would show up so that Billy didn't have to look so obvious sitting by himself.

By now Billy knew that most of the townsfolk didn't care much for the oil people who took over their town. The girl had probably been warned to stay away from the oil field outsiders, who were constantly coming and going. He was aware that he and his fellow workers were referred to as "rig pigs." He'd have given up on this girl long ago except that, when he quickly turned his head in the pretense of looking out the window, she was invariably looking at him. When he made eye contact, she looked away. But she was taking notice of him. If only he knew her name.

The gulf between the Nanton school kids and Billy was now complete. He wasn't the least bit interested in their school lives. In fact he rarely even thought about his old school chums. Nanton seemed such a long time ago.

Another thing he enjoyed about the night shift was playing cards at Ma Williams's house while he was waiting for Shoe to pick him up. Poker was the game of choice among the boarders, with Ma often joining in on the action. One of his three roommates was from Nova Scotia and he loved to play his guitar. Billy had never heard of most of the songs he played, except for the Hank Snow ones. They all had the same beat and his down-home roommate played each one with the same unbridled enthusiasm. With a little beer and very little coaxing, the easterner could also be persuaded to do a little step dance.

The day shifts were the busiest. If any of the top brass were to come to the rig, it would be during the day, and Ramchuck was very conscientious about everyone being busy. If there were no other tasks to do, he would order the floor hands to wash everything in sight. It was during these shifts that the geologist was in his trailer and Billy always went to him with questions that no one knew the answers to or that they would not bother explaining to him. It was during one of these stolen moments, when he took the sample bag over, that he asked, "What do you see in those rocks today?" As usual, the geologist didn't dismiss him but replied studiously, "It looks like we're about to enter the Viking Gas Zone." Billy quickly looked over his shoulder to see if he was being watched, as he pressed closer to the geologist. The young scientist continued, "We know it's here, but that's not what we're looking for, we're looking for oil, and if we're lucky we should hit the oil reef about another thousand feet down. In the meantime, this gas zone is going to cause us problems.

"How's that?" Billy asked.

"Well," continued Dave, "gas will escape from this zone and come to the surface with returning drill mud or, it might even force its way up the inside of the drill pipe, depending on the pressure, and cause all kinds of problems, such as catching fire."

Billy looked incredulous. He had trouble believing that the geologist could tell all this just by looking at the little sample of shale cuttings, and he blurted out, "So what are we going to do?"

"What we are going to do, my lad, is drill through the zone, which should be about 100 feet thick, and then seal it off by running a casing down the hole and then pump cement down through the drill pipe and force it up around the casing. When the cement has set, we'll have sealed off the gas zone. "Simple huh!"

Billy nodded, but continued his questioning. "But why, I mean who, doesn't want the gas?"

"'Who' is Imperial Oil, or perhaps I should say Standard Oil. And 'why' is that they've already found lots of natural gas. They want oil. You probably thought Tex Can Drilling was going to own the oil." Billy's face reddened a little as he could see that the young scientist could read his thoughts. The geologist took no notice of Billy's naïveté and continued with his discourse. "The government owns all the mineral rights beneath the ground. Imperial Oil negotiates a deal with the government for a share of the gas or oil revenues and then hires a drilling contractor, such as Tex Can, to drill the well for them. Imperial has a few rigs of their own, but not near enough to keep up with this oil play."

"Sometimes, you'll find a farmer who owns the mineral rights, if they bought the land from CPR before, I believe, 1912. The Canadian Pacific Railroad had never thought about any subsurface wealth before that time, and as soon as they realized their mistake and figured out that some little guy might make some money, they changed the rules. The railroad company reserved all the surface rights. But whoever thought about oil one mile beneath the surface of the ground when they built the railway? There are many farmers who homesteaded in Alberta and they bought additional land from the CPR before 1912. And these guys still own the mineral rights. This means that if any oil or gas is found on their land, they'll get 13 percent of the royalties. If they also own the mineral rights, then the oil companies have to deal with them directly before drilling."

"If you remember your history classes, the CPR was given 20 miles on each side of the railroad, by John A MacDonald, as an inducement to build it. Back in 1885 this land was all wilderness and American settlers were drifting north. MacDonald knew that possession was nine-tenths of the law and that it would only be a matter of time before the Americans would claim the land. Just imagine the mineral rights that the CPR originally held!"

"I wonder how many people hold the mineral rights around here now?" Billy mused.

"I'm sure all the oil companies are wondering the same thing," the young man replied as he pushed his glasses high up on his forehead and peered into his microscope. This was his signal that the conversation was ending. As Billy was turning to leave, Dave made one more comment as he adjusted the focus on his microscope, "I'm sure that, at this minute, there are land men at the Land Titles office poring over land registration documents. But to get back to your original question," the geologist suddenly continued, "we should be finished drilling through the gas zone by tomorrow morning and you're going to have to run casing. And you had better get back to work before Schultz catches you, or you'll never see tomorrow."

The next morning, Billy was proudly explaining his new-found knowledge to Shoe and Johnny on the way to the rig. Shoe demanded to know how he knew all this and Johnny just listened in bewilderment. Billy airily replied that Schultz had called him over and had asked him what was the best way to proceed. Shoe hadn't even finished cursing him out when they pulled on to the lease and there, parked beside the rig, was a cement truck. Another truck was unloading casing onto the pipe rack.

"Alright men," Billy ordered, "lets get changed and run that casing."

For the first time since Billy had been there, Schultz was on the rig floor giving orders. Ramchuck was running around the floor with the rest of them as they got set to run the casing. Schultz was at the controls screaming out orders and abuse. For a moment or two Billy panicked, because he didn't know what to do, but when he looked over at Ramchuck he realized that the Ukrainian was more panic-stricken than the rest of them.

The casing, because of its fine threads, had to be handled gently and a whole different set of equipment had to be used to accommodate its large diameter. Each 30-foot length was screwed together with care before Schultz gently lowered it down the well. Running 4,000 feet of casing was going to make for a very long day, Billy thought to himself, especially with Schultz screaming and swearing just 10 feet away from him. Unlike a regular drill stem that could be screwed together with a spinning chain, each section had to be tightened with hand tongs, and that required a lot of work.

Schultz lowered the casing very gently down the hole with a deft touch that only experience could bring. Every order that Schultz gave, Ramchuck repeated in his heavy Ukrainian accent as he hurried around getting in everyone's way.

There was a considerable crowd gathered in the doghouse, including the geologist, an engineer, and the cementing crew. Billy felt a sense of importance, being in the middle of it all. When the last joint of casing had been lowered into the hole the cement truck swung into action. A hose was connected from the cement truck to the casing. And with a mighty roar from its own specially mounted engine, it began to pump cement down the hole and then back up the outside of the casing, creating a cement wall between the casing and the wall of the hole. Billy, Johnny, Bruce, and even Shoe and Ramchuck were put to work carrying cement bags to the mixer hopper. For eight long hours everyone bust their tails, without so much as 10 minutes off to eat their lunches.

Tired as he was, Billy took great satisfaction in the day's work. Schultz was soaked in his own sweat and Billy winked at Shoe, saying, "It looks like Schultz might be down a few quarts of beer." The Imperial Oil engineer and the geologist spent the whole day going over their calculations about how much cement was needed and keeping an eye on the quality of the cement itself.

Billy was relieved when the four o'clock crew pulled up on the lease, signalling the end of their day. Billy was about to go to the change house when the afternoon driller came over to him and said, "Want to work another shift? My motorman is sick." Billy felt his shoulders sag, but he couldn't very well say no. Shoe slapped him on his back and said, "Have fun boyo, at least you still have your lunch."

Surprisingly, the next eight hours weren't that tough. They put on a new smaller bit to fit down the newly-run casing, ran the drill pipe down the hole, and then drilled out the cement plug, which had been put in place to keep the cement from oozing back up the casing. The thing that Billy found most interesting was working with a new crew, and especially a new driller. The derrick man climbed the ladder to the monkey board, unlike Shoe who dangerously rode the elevators up. The driller took time out to talk to him, asking questions about how the morning had gone when they ran the casing. Billy hoped that he had impressed everyone with his ability in using the spinning chain. One never knew where or when he might be asking the driller for a job.

Even more important, the extra work meant he could bank extra money for a car. Three more paydays and he was going to get serious about looking for one. What if the girl from Fat's Café were to go out with him? What would he do without a car? Back home he had always had a car to drive, well at least since he'd turned 13. That was one good thing about my old man, he mused, he always let me have the car to go to ball or hockey practises. There was never a problem having the car for a Friday night either.

Once Billy had got a good night's sleep and was back on his regular nightshift he repeated Len's warning to Johnny about the dangers involved in steadying the pipe as it was being lifted from the floor when they were tripping back into the hole. He told Johnny that Len had said to always keep the pipe crooked into his arm and to keep his feet wide apart and out of the way, in case there was a snag. Billy had never seen it, but apparently there was always a chance that Shoe might not get the elevators locked. And if they came open, 90 feet of pipe would drop onto your foot.

Late in the Friday shift, Ramchuck grew careless. Perhaps it was the monotony of the same routine, over and over. The floor hands dropped the slips in the turntable, released the elevators, and Ramchuck floored the accelerator skyward. From experience he knew when to let off the accelerator and let the blocks coast slowly by Shoe who'd be cradling the top of the stand of drill pipe in his arms. When the elevators came into reach Shoe would push against the column of drill pipe with all his might, and then in a fluid motion he'd reached out and grab the elevator horns and snap them together, locking the pipe into the elevators.

But his time Ramchuck misjudged the speed, and the blocks were going past Shoe far too fast for him to react in time. Billy, as always, watched Shoe as Shoe dropped the pipe into the elevators. He immediately sensed a problem as he saw Shoe frantically wave his arms. Before Billy or Ramchuck could react, the stand of pipe was jerked violently off the ground with Johnny desperately trying to hold on. The pipe was almost eye level when it dropped between Johnny's feet. Billy had a sickening sensation as he looked down expecting to see Johnny with a missing foot.

Johnny was ashen white and was only able to mutter, "That was close." Looking up, Billy saw that the top of the pipe had fallen to the other side of the derrick. Shoe had already taken off his safety harness and was climbing around the side of the derrick with a rope in his hand. He put one wrap of rope around the pipe and then climbed back onto the monkey board and put his safety harness back on. Billy could not believe the strength Shoe had as he pulled the pipe back towards him. Shoe dropped the pipe into the now stationary blocks and Ramchuck gently picked the length of pipe up and the three floor men stabbed it into place.

This was the last of the drill stems to be lowered and no sooner had Ramchuck lifted the drill stem up, enough to take the weight off the slips so that they could be pulled, than Shoe came sliding down the 90 feet of pipe, landing as light as a feather. And in one bound he was in Ramchuck's face. Shoe grabbed the much bigger Ramchuck by the neck and screamed at him. "You dumb fucking bohunk! If you ever do that again I'll break every fucking bone in your body!"

Everyone was speechless as they watched Shoe stomp away toward the mud tanks. Billy looked over at Ramchuck for some reaction. The Ukrainian, with a blank stare, merely pointed to the Kelly indicating that it was business as usual. There was no doubt in Billy's mind that Shoe could give Ramchuck a beating. Shoe was much lighter but he was well muscled in his arms, shoulders, and back. Billy was sure Shoe could be cat-like quick and he hoped that he would never have to tangle with him.

Later, while cleaning up, Billy and Johnny examined the circular indentation in the floor planking. Billy gave a low whistle and said, "I guess Len knew what he was talking about. We just about had to call you stumpy."

On the way to town after work, Billy said to Shoe, "That was quite a little performance you put on today."

"Which was that, retrieving the pipe, sliding down the pipe, or nearly beating Ramchuck's brains out?"

"All of them," Billy quipped. "Tell me, weren't you scared up there when you had to take your harness off and climb over to get that pipe?"

"Nah," said Shoe, "when I started out working derrick, I used to drop at least four stands a trip, but that was my fault, not some bohunk driller's."

"It seems to me that you don't much care for Mr. Ramchuck," Billy replied, in way of an understatement. This comment caused Johnny to let out a loud guffaw from the back seat.

Billy continued his questions. "Aren't you ever scared that the rope that ties your safety harness to the rig might break? I stand down on the ground and watch you lean out over the floor and pull strand after strand back with all your weight only supported by a piece of rope. If it broke you'd do a three-gainer dive and you might land on me and kill me in the process."

"There are all kinds of ways to die, boyo, and that sounds about as good a way as any."

"How would you get off the derrick if it were to catch fire?" Johnny chimed in.

"Didn't you boys see that safety line that runs from the monkey board to the ground?" asked Shoe in mock amazement as he turned to look at both of them. "I've got my own personal escape buggy to hang onto, then I'd ride the brake to the ground. Come on up the next time you get a chance and I'll let you try it out."

"Have you ever fallen off the monkey board and been saved by your harness?" Billy pressed on.

"Hell yes!" Shoe exclaimed. "One night I was drunk and fell off three times. Each time I was upside down looking at all the boys on the floor."

"What did you do then?" Johnny asked.

"I just climbed up my rope to the monkey board and went back to work."

"What did your driller have to say about that?" Billy joined in.

"Oh yeah, well, when I got down he ran my ass off," Shoe continued as if it were no big deal.

As usual Billy couldn't make his mind up whether Shoe was bullshitting or not. But it didn't matter one way or another, thought Billy, it made for a good story.

The car pulled up to Ma William's house. What really mattered now was that Ma would have one of her great meals prepared.

Chapter 8

April and May passed quickly by and with that last paycheque in the bank, Billy had now saved the $400 he thought he needed to buy a decent car. Shoe and Johnny were as excited as Billy was at the prospect. Each constantly offered advice and began to bug him about when he was going to make this purchase. Shoe suggested that he drive them to Edmonton where there'd be a better selection. "There's also a hotel there that'll serve even you two baby faces," he added.

"Alright," Billy said, finally relenting to their constant badgering, "Lets go this Saturday and have a look." Riding in Shoe's Ford coup was becoming something of a routine, always with Shoe and Billy in the front and Johnny in the back. Shoe, as usual, was telling them about how he got laid last week. Johnny was strumming his imaginary guitar, keeping beat with whatever country song was playing on the radio, and Billy was just plain happy, drinking in the camaraderie and the passing countryside.

They stopped at four different car lots and nothing caught Billy's eye. They gave each car the salesmen showed them a thorough going over, grilling the salesmen with every question they could think of — often all at once. Then they'd look under the hood, under the car, and in the trunk. They started and stopped over and over, and after each car they looked at they would withdraw from the salesman and compare notes.

Finally, at the fifth car lot, Billy declared, "That's the one!" He had chosen a 1941 Ford coupe. The very same car that Shoe had, only this one was black in colour and Shoe's was gray. Billy counted out $390, the best price he could haggle the salesman down to, and placed the bills on the salesman's desk. The salesman wrote up the Bill of Sale and told Billy that this was all he would need if he were to be stopped by the police. "But," he cautioned, "you need to buy licence plates as soon as possible."

Billy triumphantly approached his two buddies and said, "Now where's that bar you were talking about?"

This time Shoe was right. The bartender didn't ask their ages or even seem to care about how old they were. Shoe raised his glass and said, "To your first car purchase and to your first time in a bar." Billy and Johnny joined him and raised their glasses with a hearty, "Here. Here."

"Now it's your turn to buy a car," Billy said as he turned to Johnny. Johnny looked a little sheepish for a second and replied, "I've got nearly enough money but I don't have a driver's licence yet." Both Shoe and Billy seemed amused and a little stunned at this revelation. Neither one said anything though, fearing they might embarrass Johnny.

Billy changed the conversation and asked Shoe how he knew about this hotel. Shoe replied that he had been coming in here since he was 16. Billy thought for a moment and then asked, "How old are you now Shoe?" Shoe became coy and asked in return, "How old do you think I am?"

Billy took a large gulp of beer and said, "Oh, I don't know. Somewhere around … 24? … 25? Somewhere around there." Shoe fixed them both with a grin and his shoulders shook with a silent chuckle.

It was now his turn to take a long drink, and he let the drama build before he answered. Finally, he said, "I'm 20." Both Billy and Johnny were thunderstruck with this revelation. Billy wondered if this were true. Shoe looked and acted far older than 20. From all the stories he told and the stories told about him, it seemed almost impossible for Shoe to be only 20.

Shoe read their minds and said, "Is there something wrong here?"

Billy came out of his state of shock, and quickly mumbled, "No, no, it's just, you know, I thought you were older."

"Hell, you're not old enough to be in here either!" Johnny had just figured out the implication of Shoes' confession.

They all ordered another beer and the topic of conversation quickly returned to the many girls that Shoe had screwed in Edmonton. Billy sarcastically remarked, "Yeah, I've seen some of those women."

Johnny, looking at his watch, said, "I think we've got time for some of that Chinese food before we have to go to work."

Billy replied, "Good idea, but you're going to ride home with Shoe. I'm not having you puke in my new car."

Billy followed Shoe out of Edmonton, but as soon as they were out of the city limits he floored the gas and shot by them. Shoe rose to the challenge and they were soon both doing 80 miles an hour. Shoe wasn't able to pass Billy, however, and Billy gave the dash a pat as he pulled up to the rig saying, "Good work girl, I think you and I are going to be great friends."

Billy stopped as he went through the doghouse and gave the geolobox a quick once over. Ramchuck was labouring on some kind of a report and Billy looked over his shoulder and asked him what he was doing. He didn't expect an answer so he wasn't surprised that Ramchuck's response was only a grunt. Billy continued to watch Ramchuck as he struggled with the English language. He thought about volunteering his service, but then thought better of it, as it might embarrass the man. He wondered why Shoe hated Ramchuck so much. Perhaps he felt he should have been set up as the driller instead of Ramchuck. Billy knew the reason for that though. He and everyone else knew that Shoe was too much of a loose cannon to be given that kind of responsibility. Billy thought to himself that there was really nothing to like or dislike about the man. He decided that, until Ramchuck did him a disservice, he would reserve all judgement about him. It was obvious that the man was insecure and that must be the reason why he didn't stand up to Shoe.

A few days later, Shoe asked Billy and Johnny as he was dropping them off, "You guys want to come with me to the dance this Saturday after work?"

"Sure" they said in unison.

"Where is it?" asked Billy.

"Out at the Meadow Bank Hall. And another thing," snarled Shoe, "give me a couple of bucks for the booze, you cheap bastards."

Billy and Johnny headed for Fat's Café and Shoe, as usual, headed for the bar. "How are we going to keep our clothes clean enough to go to a dance? And the dance will probably be over by the time we get there anyway," moaned Johnny.

"Well, we'll just have to spiff ourselves up the best we can." Billy replied.

"Oh sure, and do you think your little hot pants over there will dance with a 'rig pig'?" Johnny said sarcastically, as he gave a nod towards the corner booth where Billy's dream girl and her friends were sitting.

Billy thought about this for a second and then just shrugged, "We'll see." Then he suddenly stood up and said, "I'm heading home for supper. Want to go for a drive later?" Johnny nodded, and Billy strode out of the café without trying to make eye contact or conversation with the hot little brunette.

Walking down the main street of Leduc, Billy waved and said hello to several of the people he passed. He didn't know many names, but the faces were becoming familiar. The pool hall was a different story, as he now knew most of the regulars by name.

The Saturday afternoon shift dragged on and on with Billy anxious for it to end. His excitement built all day in anticipation of the dance. When midnight finally came, Shoe, Billy, and Johnny had already changed and cleaned up the best they could. The next shift had barely pulled up to the rig when they all jumped into Shoe's car and were down the dirt trail in a cloud of dust.

Once again Shoe made a big production of hauling the whiskey bottle out from under the front seat. He unscrewed the cap and said, "Here's hoping you get to meet Step-and-a-half."

"Step-and-a-half?" Billy repeated, giving Shoe a puzzled look.

"Yeah. She's an old Indian gal who likes little white boys like you two."

Johnny reached up over the back seat for the bottle and said, "Why do you call her Step-and-a-half?"

Shoe was pleased that Johnny had taken the hook and retorted with a laugh, "Because she has a gimpy leg and she limps."

Johnny thought about this and tried to visualize the woman. He took a drink and passed the bottle to Billy, "Drink up, we've got a lot of catching up to do."

Billy let the whiskey slowly burn down his throat, turned the bottle back to Shoe, and said, "I'll hold the gun to your head and you drink. By the way, do you know where the hell we're going?"

Before Shoe could answer they came over a hill and there, in a clearing, was the hall. Cars and trucks were parked all over the place.

Shoe nosed his car into the ditch and each of them had one more gulp of whiskey before heading in. It had taken exactly 14 minutes for the three of them to kill the. As Billy entered the hall, the sudden blast of heat from all the sweated up dancers swept over him. A sudden wave of nausea overcame him as the whiskey kicked in. Billy struggled to clear his head and then looked over the room.

The familiar strain of a schottische was being played as the room swirled with dancers. There was every combination of groups of three that Billy could imagine. There were two women and a man, three women, three ten-year-old girls, two men and a woman, and even three men, who were obviously well into their cups. The dancers would take three quick steps and then, in unison, all hop on one leg. Then in time to the one-two-three-hop steps they'd pass over, under, around and just about every configuration one could imagine. Round and round they went while Billy's head and stomach also went round and round.

As Billy fought to regain his composure he began to take stock of his surroundings. He couldn't see Schultz in the thick knot of people over in the corner, but he could hear the rumble of his voice. The crowd appeared to be an even mix of farmers, town people, and oil patch workers. All the farmers were identifiable by their red necks and sunburned forearms. Shoe and Johnny disappeared into the crowd and Billy lost sight of them.

The band was trying to bring the Schottische to a close. The lady on the piano banged the keys in a triumphant conclusion and crossed her arms. The tenor saxophone player ignored her and continued on. The banjo player, taking his cue from the saxophone, continued on with his beat. Looking frantically around, the lady on the piano started playing again. Finally, after two false tries they brought the number to an end.

As the floor cleared, Billy's stomach settled down. The band struck up a waltz and as he returned his gaze to the crowd, his heart gave a jump. Sitting across the hall was the girl from Fats' Café — and more than that — she was staring right at him. Billy nodded his head towards the dance floor and she nodded hers in consent.

He hadn't taken three steps towards her when a body came sprawling right in front of him. Billy looked up to see Schultz in the middle of a full-scale brawl. Within seconds, everyone was throwing punches and wrestling on the floor. Trapped, Billy looked helplessly in his dance partner's direction, but the band had quit playing.

Just then Billy realized that somebody was tugging at his arm. Looking down, he was surprised to see Schultz's wife. "Come on, she shrieked, you're getting me out of here!"

Billy looked around in shock as she dragged him out the door, and numbly said, "Where are we going?"

"You're driving me home ... away from that asshole!" Billy was nervous and reluctant, as Schultz's wife dragged him toward her car. Billy's sense of survival tempted him to break free and run, but then again, this was the boss's wife. She handed Billy the keys, and his shoulders sagged with resignation and he got behind the wheel as he was ordered, "Just take me as far as town. I think I can make it the rest of the way from there," she murmured.

On the way into town, a new sensation began to take hold as Billy thought about the oil changing incident. He noticed that, instead of being upset about the whole dance fiasco, Schultz's wife sat calmly, taking off her lipstick with some tissue paper.

"We have never formally met. My name's Billy Cochrane."

"Pleased to meet you Billy, my name is Judy," and with that she proffered her hand for a handshake. The handshake was not your normal grasp and pump affair, rather it was her just squeezing his hand.

"You're not from Texas, I gather," Billy said, trying to make conversation.

"No, I'm just a silly Alberta girl who married that asshole Texan," said Judy. And then she said in a very seductive voice, "Sweetie ... would you pull down that road there? She pointed to a trail that looked as if went nowhere. "I can't wait until I get home. I have to take a pee." Billy was a little taken aback by her bluntness, but he did as she asked, realizing only then that Judy was more than a little drunk.

He left the car idling and then reached across Judy to open the door for her. She softly caressed his arm and thanked him for his thoughtfulness. Then, instead of disappearing out of sight, Judy started undoing her jeans directly behind the taillight. Billy sat transfixed as he watched her out of the rear-view mirror. Between the taillight and the full moon, there was nothing left to Billy's imagination. Judy seemed to struggle with her zipper for a few moments, and then came back and got back in the car.

She leaned back against her door and said in a little girl voice, "Honey, this darn zipper is caught in my panties and I can't get it undone. Would you be a real doll and help me?"

Billy's mouth went dry. His heart was racing, as he looked down at the half-undone zipper attached to her white panties. Judy thrust her hips in the air as if to help him. Billy slowly ran his finger around the snagged zipper and in the process felt the outline of her pussy.

Right about then, Billy decided that if Schultz himself was coming down the road, he wasn't going to stop. Slowly he worked the zipper up and down while Judy gave him mild admonishments, telling him to keep his mind on his work.

Suddenly, the zipper came free and Billy pulled Judy's jeans down to her knees. She gave a little gasp, and then teasingly said,

"What are you going to do now?" Billy thought that was a pretty good question as his body was shaking out of control. Even his teeth were rattling.

Luckily, instinct took over and saved the day.

Chapter 9

Someone was calling his name and shaking him, but all the commotion fit into the dream he was having. Finally his eyes opened and Johnny stood over him, calling out for him to wake up.

"What's up?" Billy said as he looked up in bewilderment, and then it dawned on him that they had to be at work at eight o'clock. "What time is it?" he asked as he hurriedly reached for his clothes. Panic set in because it was his turn to drive and he thought he had overslept.

"It's six o'clock," replied Johnny. Billy gave Johnny a long incredulous stare and with a loud groan fell back into bed. "For fuck's sake Johnny, I've only had two-and-a half-hours sleep."

"Billy … Billy … it's Shoe."

Billy once again opened his eyes and tried to focus on Johnny. "What about Shoe?" He was now wide awake.

"He's in jail," Johnny announced.

"What's he in jail for?" asked Billy. As he looked up he noticed that Johnny had a black eye.

"At the dance last night … remember … when we all went outside?

Billy looked at Johnny and said, "Yeah."

"Well didn't you see Shoe hit that policeman?"

"No, I must have left just before that. I got a ride into town." Billy hoped that Johnny wouldn't ask any questions.

Johnny continued, excitedly, "This cop came up behind Shoe and grabbed him, and Shoe thought it was some farmer and he spun around and punched the cop. They got him in jail right now."

Billy let out a low whistle and mumbled, "Cops don't take it too kindly when they get bopped. Well, what exactly am I supposed to do about it Johnny?"

"You have to get him out of jail. You have to get him to work on time or Schultz will fire him for sure. You have to do something, Billy!"

Billy's shoulders sagged as he looked down for his socks. He had no idea what he could or should do. But for Johnny's sake he had to try.

"Okay, okay, let's go find the jail and we'll break him out."

Johnny's eyes opened wide at the prospect of breaking Shoe out of jail. "Do you really mean it?" he squealed. Billy grabbed his lunch pail from Ma William's kitchen and with Johnny in tow headed for his car.

"So where is this jail?" Billy asked"

"It's in the fire hall."

Billy looked at Johnny with raised eyebrows and headed his car to the fire hall. Their knock on the door was answered by Sparky, the same little man that worked at the hotel.

"We've come to see Shoe," demanded Billy in the firmest voice he could raise. He thought Sparky would automatically deny his request, but to his surprise Sparky nodded his head and beckoned for them to follow.

Shoe was sound asleep and his snoring echoed around the fire hall. The jail was little more than a dog cage, and Billy figured that if anyone really wanted to, they really could break out. It took considerable banging on the cell bars and shouting before Shoe woke up. He was confused to see his pals there and wondered why they were making all that noise.

Billy asked him what they could do and Shoe said, "Nothing." The way he said "nothing" sounded like he wondered why they would ask such a stupid question.

Shoe said the police would be around at nine o'clock and then he'd be set free. "The pricks are too cheap to feed a person. This is not my first rodeo you know."

"What should we tell Ramchuck and Schultz?" Billy asked.

"Tell them I'll be late for work. Schultz was in as many scraps as I was. He's lucky he's not in here with me."

Billy looked at Shoe and then at Johnny and said with a laugh, "It looks like the two of you better do a whole lot more ducking and a lot less talking at the next dance. Somebody beat on you like a red-headed stepson."

"Let's go, amigo," Billy said, grabbing Johnny around the neck, "We got work to do. Shoe ... go back to bed. You look tired."

All the way to the rig Johnny babbled on about the big brawl, how he got sucker punched, and what Billy thought they were going to do with Shoe. Billy's mind was on his own problems. What if Shultz's wife told him about last night? Pulling up to the rig Billy began to brace himself for a possible confrontation with Schultz. He made up his mind that if Schultz came at him, he would stand and fight. Schultz's truck was pulled up to the rig, and this meant that he was on the floor. Billy smiled to himself. That Judy was worth a whipping, even getting run off.

Looking up at the rig a new concern came over Billy. The derrick was full of pipes. Who would go up in the derrick to run it all back into the hole? Billy thought to himself that Ramchuck must have worked derrick before he became a driller. Maybe he was going to work it, with Schultz taking over the brake. Maybe that was why Schultz was here this early in the morning. Maybe it had nothing to do with his wife.

As soon as they entered the doghouse Billy could see that Schultz was still drunk from the night before. The skin was gone from Schultz's right knuckles and he had an angry red knot on his forehead. Schultz gave Billy an uneven look and said, "Kid, you're going up the stick," and then he left without another word.

Billy's heart raced with panic. He had watched from the floor at least a thousand times as Shoe dropped the stand of pipe into the outstretched horns of the elevator. Billy looked searchingly into Ramchuck's face and expected to be given some instructions or advice. But Ramchuck just headed for the door saying, "We go work now."

Billy looked at Bruce and Johnny and said, "Here goes nothing, watch your toes." Billy climbed hand-over-hand up the derrick for 90 feet. Upon reaching the monkey board, Billy walked carefully over and scrutinized the safety harness. Putting the harness around his shoulders, he walked to the edge of the platform and looked down at his friends who were getting the floor ready to trip in. The monkey board was about as high as a 10-storey building. Billy checked to see that the rope was securely attached to the harness and to the derrick. Then he walked over to inspect the safety buggy that Johnny had been quizzing Shoe about. Billy could see how the contraption worked, and shuddered to himself, hoping he'd never have to use it.

He then walked back to the edge of the platform and leaned out, with only the harness keeping him from pitching face first to the floor below. Next, he turned his attention to the racks of pipe that the previous derrick man had stacked and tied in place. The tops of the pipe were about eye level and his job was to pull each stand of pipe out of the rack, walk it over and drop it into the waiting elevators. Now, he thought, can I do it?

Billy heard Ramchuck gun the engines and he watched as the blocks and elevators came hurtling up towards him. Billy pulled the pipe, from the fingers it was resting in, towards him and was surprised that it wasn't heavier. Ramchuck had stopped the elevators at the right height and Billy carefully manoeuvred the drill stem toward the open elevators. He pushed the stand of pipe with his chest, and with his hands free he was able to close the elevators around the drill stem. Ramchuck lifted the elevators up, and Billy was reassured when they caught around the collar of the pipe. At that point, he looked down with satisfaction as he watched Johnny and Bruce doing his old job.

By the time the elevators had come back up to him, Billy was waiting with the next stand of pipe. By the fifth stand, Ramchuck didn't stop the elevators, and as they slowly coasted by, Billy dropped the pipe into them and slammed them shut, all in one motion. As the morning went on, Billy became less and less aware of his safety harness and of the dizzying height he was working at.

As the last stand of pipe disappeared down the hole, Billy undid the harness and climbed down the ladder to the floor. He was sure that if any derrick jobs came up in the future he'd be ready, willing, and able to do the job. As his boots touched down on the floor he turned, and there was Shoe standing right in front of him laughing. "So," Shoe announced, "I sleep in a bit and you take my job!" Every time Shoe laughed, his missing front tooth was noticeable.

The thing Billy enjoyed most about working the dayshift was being able to cruise around Leduc in his car in the evening. After supper with the gang at Ma Williams, he usually drove over and picked up Johnny at his chicken coop. Johnny's residence was an 8-by-12-foot shed behind the main house and Billy was sure that it used to be a chicken coop. I guess there is more money to be made in renting out available space to people in the oil patch than selling eggs, he thought. The line he heard was that if you give someone in Leduc an inch … they will rent it.

Billy and Johnny usually drove up and down Main Street with the windows down and the radio blaring tunes. "Buttons and Bows," "I'm Looking Over a Four Leaf Clover," "Peg O' My Heart," and "Shoo Fly Pie and Apple Pan Dowdy" were their favourites on the Edmonton radio station. Shoe and Schultz's vehicles were always parked in front of the hotel. Most times there were an assortment of people milling around on main street. Billy would pull his car up to the curb whenever he saw two or three teenage girls hanging around. Billy and Johnny both leaned out their windows and called out to the girls. Most of the time the girls came over and leaned against the car, but sometimes they got in and cruised the never-ending circuit with Billy and Johnny.

Billy had learned the girl's name through various conversations, without making it look that he was particularly interested. But he was soon silently repeating over and over, "Candace is her name. Candace. Candace."

Where could she be? He had not laid eyes on her since school got out for the summer. Every time he talked to any of the local girls, he would work the question in of Candace's whereabouts, but no one seemed to know where she was. Someone thought that she had gone to visit relatives in Banff and someone else had heard that she was in Edmonton.

Johnny was interested in one girl in particular, and became really agitated with Billy when he said she had an ass on her like a Peace River breaking-plow. Billy teased Johnny relentlessly about this girl. And every time he sighted a fat woman, young or old, Billy exclaimed, "There's another one for you, Johnny!"

Johnny indignantly replied, "I don't see you with anyone. The chick from Fat's won't even talk to you."

Realizing that he was getting under Johnny's skin, Billy pressed his attacks even more. Every time they saw Johnny's girl, Billy would start singing the new hit song, "Baby Face." But instead of singing the line "You got the cutest little baby face," he would sing, "You got the ugliest little baby face."

"Fuck you, Cochrane," was Johnny's only defence.

A new movie came to town each week and the two of them usually went to see it. Going to a movie, playing pool, and driving around took up up most of Billy's free time. Getting Shoe to get beer for them was never a problem either. Cruising Main Street, drinking beer, and smoking cigarettes - life doesn't get much better than this.

One night, Billy pressed Johnny about getting his own car. "You're making good money, why don't you get your driver's licence and buy a car?"

Johnny became strangely quiet for a while and then slowly began to tell Johnny why. "I send most of my money home to my mother," Johnny began. "See … I come from a large family, six sisters and three brothers. My two older sisters left home and got married. I still have six younger brothers and sisters at home and my old man wasn't around much. He comes home only long enough to knock the old lady up again. When he does come home, he doesn't have any money. I grew up pretty poor Billy. We all lived in a one-roomed cabin about 15 miles outside of Grande Prairie and there wasn't much of anything to go around . . . especially food and clothes."

"Where did you all sleep?" asked Billy incredulously.

"Oh, we had bunk beds nailed against one wall and we would sleep three to a bunk."

Billy thought about this for a second, and then asked, "What did you eat?"

"Not much," replied Johnny. "I'd been shooting wild game since I was eight. My old man, when he used to be home more, taught me how to hunt and trap. The first time I ever ate beef was when I came to Leduc. We had a garden and a root cellar to store the potatoes and other vegetables in the winter. A bag of flour, and that's about it."

"How far did you have to go to get to school?" Billy asked.

It was Johnny's turn to become silent. Then, he reluctantly answered, "You see, that's the other problem Billy. I never went to school. The nearest school was in Grande Prairie, and there was no way for me to get there. The only time I went to school was when I was 10. We were all taken to Grande Prairie and placed in different people's homes. I had to go to school and they put me in grade two. I was really embarrassed because I was the biggest kid in class and I didn't know nothing. I did learn the alphabet and how to do a little arithmetic. Then summer came and we went back and rebuilt the cabin."

After another period of silence, Johnny continued, "I'm surprised my old man stuck around long enough to do that. I feel really bad for my mother. She's about worn out raising all of us kids. I used to make a little money trapping muskrat and beaver during the winter, and I promised her that as soon as I was old enough to get a job, I'd send money home to her. And that's the reason I haven't got my driver's licence. How could I ever write the exam? I'd never pass it." While Billy was trying to figure out an answer to this question, Johnny grabbed him by the elbow and said, "You won't tell anyone about this, will you?"

Billy replied, "No, of course not," but his mind was racing with all the implications of the story Johnny had just told him. He was thinking about 11 or 12 people living in a one-room cabin, miles away from nowhere, and all of them illiterate. He had a million questions he wanted to ask his friend, but he could tell from Johnny's plea to not tell anyone that it was a very sensitive issue.

"But what did you do all day?" Billy asked as his curiosity again overtook him.

"Like I said, I hunted and trapped most of the time, at least ever since I can remember, Johnny replied. Then he sat upright in his seat, turned to Billy, and said, "Have you ever shot a deer?"

"Of course I have … several as a matter of fact."

Johnny slumped back into his seat again and said, matter-of-factly, "I shot my first deer when I was nine."

"Bullshit!" Billy shot back.

"I did!" Johnny exclaimed and he shot upright in his seat again. I was out looking for a rabbit to shoot with my 22, and was lying on my back on a beaver dam enjoying the spring sun when I heard rustling in the bush. I never made a sound or a move. All of a sudden, a two-point whitetail stepped out of the willows about 20 yards from me. It looked around and then stood up on its back legs and began nibbling the tops of the pussy willows. I slowly lifted my gun up and shot him right behind his ear. The deer dropped dead. Never even heard or smelled me.

Billy knew that Johnny was telling the truth. He was much too naive to make up such a story. "What did you do then?" Billy pressed.

"Well, I ran about a mile back home and told my mom. Me, my Mom, and all my brothers and sisters came and we drug it home. Boy, were they ever proud of me. My mother cut the deer up and we all had deer for supper. Beats the hell out of rabbit. Sometimes during the winter days we would play 'I Spy With My Little Eye' and other games like that. The only problem is that I'd always get confused when words started with E, B, C, or D. They all sound alike to me. But my younger sister would always guess what the object was. She was six when our cabin burned down."

Billy blurted, "Your cabin burned down!"

"Yeah, when I was about 10, the roof caught fire from the chimney and the whole thing went up in flames. We saved a few things. Then some people came and moved us all into Grande Prairie for the rest of the winter. That was the only time I ever went to school," Johnny repeated, then went on with his story. Billy, for the first time, listened with complete attention.

"I hated it! All of us were put into grade two together. Me and my two older sisters were nearly as big as the teacher. The people I stayed with were nice and all that, but I couldn't wait for my old man to rebuild the cabin. My younger sister, the one that always won the 'I Spy' game, stayed in Grande Prairie for two years and continued on in school. When she came back to live with us she tried to teach us to read, but I never had much time for it."

"So you actually moved back to the bush."

"Yep, my old man built the very same cabin on the very same spot. He even used the same stove that burned the thing down in the first place. It looked the same after the fire as it did before."

Billy interrupted him suddenly, exclaiming, "Hey! Here comes Step-and-a-half!"

"Who?"

"Step-and-a-half. Now this is the one for you, Johnny."

As the Indian lady limped past, Billy let out a low wolf whistle. To his surprise and embarrassment she stopped and came over to his open car window. She leaned against the door and looked at the two occupants with a big smile, which showed that her two front teeth were missing.

"What fine handsome boys two," she said between clenched teeth. "You got some beer for Suzy?" Only when she said Suzy it sounded like she said "sushi." The familiar smell of smoked buckskin drifted into the car.

"I'm sorry Suzy, I haven't got any beer." Billy looked over at Johnny and said, "You got any beer Johnny?" hoping to draw Johnny into the conversation. Johnny merely shook his head.

Suzy pressed ahead and said, "Why don't you boys give Suzy money to buy some beer. Be nice boys." All of her speech came in a slow clenched mouth cadence, interspersed with happy chuckles.

Billy fished into his pocket and held out a quarter and a nickel in his open palm. "Alright, alright, here's 30 cents. That should be enough to buy three beers."

Chapter 10

Billy watched as Suzy limped toward the hotel. Then he turned to Johnny and said, laughing, "What's the matter, you not into squaw humping?"

"That's not very funny Billy."

"Why not? I hear she has fucked nearly every roughneck in Leduc."

Johnny was silent. He lit another cigarette.

"Shoo Fly Pie Apple Pan Dowdy" started to play on the radio and Billy reached over and turned the tune up and slapped the steering wheel in beat with the song, forgetting the whole conversation.

The street was full of people who had come to town to shop and visit. All of the husbands were in the beer parlour and the wives walked up and down the street gossiping and killing time. Billy noted that the wives of the oil patch workers never mingled with the wives of the locals. The three cafes in town were overflowing with customers and Billy knew it was no use trying to get a seat. Besides, he thought, he would rather sit in the car and watch people.

The song ended and Johnny spoke. "You know something Billy … my mother is three-quarters Cree and my father is part Cree. That makes me about … "

And while Johnny paused trying to figure out the math, Billy said, "A half-breed." It was Billy's turn to become introspective, and he thought about the encounter with Suzy. He was trying to figure out if he had said anything that offended his friend. Not knowing what he should do or say, he blurted out, "You sure don't look Indian!"

This off-the-wall comment seemed to lighten up the moment and Johnny returned to his cheerful naive self.

"You should see my younger brother, we call him Geronimo."

"Here comes your lard-ass friend again, Johnny."

The girl spotted Johnny and immediately came to his window. Her friend stood on the street with her arms folded and looked on with disapproval. Billy began to hum "Baby Face" and Johnny reached over and punched him in the arm.

Billy turned his attention to the scrawny girl who was standing with her arms folded and asked her how old she was. She rocked back and forth, all the while glaring at her friend. After a short deliberate silence she turned her focus to Billy and replied, "16." Billy scoffed and said that if she was 16, he was 50. Caught in her little lie, she flustered and blurted out that her mother said never to talk to roughnecks, that they were all animals.

"Is that a fact?" Billy sarcastically replied. He then turned to Johnny, who was still talking to his new friend and said, "Are you an animal?" Then Billy began yipping like a coyote. Johnny caught on what was going on and he joined in barking like a coyote.

When they finished with their coyote act, Billy turned sober and asked the young girl if her parents owned the hardware store down the street. When she nodded yes, Billy sarcastically pointed out that the girl's mother was quite happy doing business with roughnecks.

Billy then spotted Shoe making his way down the street. Billy liked watching the way Shoe walked. He had a kind of rolling gait that made him look like a cat ready to pounce on its prey. Billy, when alone, often tried to imitate Shoe's walk. And he and Johnny both tucked their package of cigarettes in the sleeve of their T-shirts, just as Shoe did. About the only thing Billy didn't copy from Shoe was his haircut. Shoe wore his blond hair in a close-cropped brush cut. Billy thought about getting a brush cut but stayed with combing his hair straight back. What to do with his hair was always a problem. He would part it first on the left and then on the right. Most of the time he'd tried to copy the style of the actor in the latest movie he saw. Johnny on the other hand never seemed to comb his mop of hair at all and was constantly pushing it out of his eyes with his hand.

Shoe strode up to Billy's window and the two girls took their cue and ambled off down the street. "What are you two weevils up to? Shoe asked," at the same time reaching through the window and cuffing Billy's hair with an open hand. Before Billy could come up with a witty reply, Shoe held out his hand and demanded that Billy spot him 10 bucks until next payday.

Billy began grumbling that he was tired of having to lend Shoe $10 every two weeks.

"Shut your cake hole … I pay you back every time don't I!"

Billy continued with his lecture, " Your room, the restaurant, the beer parlour, and cheap whores, suck up every dime you make."

Shoe shot back, "You seem to enjoy using my bathtub. I'm not going to bath every Saturday in some little square tub with cold water that has been used three times before me, or live in a chicken coop, or wait to take a shit in some outdoor two-hole shithouse that already has two people in it. No siree bub, not this boy! Now give me 10 bucks or I'll drag you out of your fucking car and beat it out of you." Shoe was the most imaginative swearer Billy had ever heard. He turned most two-syllable words into three by inserting "fuck."

"Okay, okay, here's 10 bucks. Don't do anything with it that I wouldn't do. Do me a favour though, can you pick up a dozen beers for tomorrow? We'll drink them on Ma William's porch and listen to the Nova Scotian sing and play his guitar."

As Shoe ambled back to the hotel Billy yelled out, "Hey Shoe, Step-and-a-half was just looking for you. She said that she'd be waiting for you in the Ladies' and Escorts' section." Shoe didn't look back but acknowledged the remark by giving them the finger. Johnny piped up that he sure wouldn't like to have to fight Shoe. "Me neither," replied Billy.

After a long silence, Billy spoke up. "We got another hour to kill before the bar closes and the fights break out. We'll watch them for 15 minutes and then go to work. I heard that the tool push at Brinkerhoff asks everyone if they're good fighters before he hires them. They say he only hires scrappers."

Billy wanted to hear more about Johnny's life, so he asked where Johnny's two older sisters were now.

Johnny pushed his hair back and told him that his oldest sister left with an American serviceman who was stationed in Grande Prairie while the Alaska Highway was being built. One day this guy in a uniform drove up and knocked on the door and his sister opened it up and introduced him to their mum. Then the two of them drove off to get married. "I never saw her again. I think they went to the United States somewhere. My next sister left home and we think she's in Edmonton or somewhere like that. We haven't heard from either of them since they left."

Billy replied, "That reminds me that I got to phone home. I haven't talked to my parents since I came here."

Both fell silent again, each with their thoughts about home. Johnny suddenly sat up straight again and started his sentence with the usual breathless, "Guess what Billy… one time a grizzly came up to our cabin one night and was trying to get in. We were all terrified and the girls began to cry. The grizzly boar was standing on his back legs and banging on the walls with his front paws. Then he came to the door and began banging on it. Just before the door caved in my mother took the 30/30 off the wall and fired through the closed door at the bear. We thought the shot scared the bear away cause we didn't hear any more from him. We were all scared to go back to sleep so my mother sat the rest of the night in a chair with the gun across her lap. In the morning we all stood behind her as she slowly opened the door to peek outside. And there was the bear, stone dead. The bullet went right through his heart. And do you know what? My mother skinned the bear and nailed its hide to the wall over my bunk. Me and my two little brothers slept under it ever since. I bet the skin is still there. And so's the hole in the door."

Both of them fell silent again as they reflected on the tale Johnny had just told. Billy finally broke the silence and said quietly, "You must have had it pretty tough growing up."

"I never thought so," said Johnny. "Shoe thinks we have it tough now."

"Yeah I know he does," Billy replied. "I like living at Ma Williams' place, except for trying to sleep during the day in the heat. There's always sticky flies crawling over you and she makes more noise than an oil rig, banging her pots and pans all the time. I never heard more racket than she makes. She's the one that's got it tough in my opinion though. I don't know if there is, or ever was a Mr. Williams, or how she came to own that big old house."

Ma Williams was a large lady who, as far as Billy knew, owned only two dresses. Other than the colour difference, both were identical and both were ill fitting and hung over her large frame. Billy marvelled at the loose skin and fat that drooped down whenever she stuck her arm out. A dirty apron, which Billy suspected had never been washed, completed her wardrobe. Billy felt sorry for her having to stand over the cookstove in the heat of the day preparing meals and lunches for six borders. Her round face was usually beet red from the heat. Billy did what he could for her by dumping the slop pail out behind the house and he made sure there was always kindling wood split up and in the coal pail. He also checked the shaker box and dumped it when it was full. The other chore Billy volunteered to do was to pump water and make sure the reservoir was topped up. Ma Williams returned these favours by making sure that Billy's lunch bucket got the leftover pork chops, sausages, or steak.

Breakfast began at 6:30 a.m. and ended at 8:30, depending on the schedules of the men's shifts. Usually, everyone was present at 6:00 p.m. for supper. The kitchen table impressed Billy. It was round with two tiers. The bottom tier sat up to eight people and the top tier held all the food and could be spun around. Billy had never seen such a table and thought it most ingenious.

Ma Williams didn't seem to mind her lot in life and was always in a good humour, taking the ribbing and handing it out in equal measures. And, in spite of her large girth, she always had lots of energy.

Billy thought he was pretty good at teasing people but he was an amateur compared to Bill McDonald, the Nova Scotian. McDonald was forever pulling pranks on everyone and constantly teasing Ma. He had a thick Cape Breton accent that amused Billy. Words like "sure" came out "shore," and with his huge jug ears and lantern jaw, he kept everyone in stitches. But what Billy liked best about McDonald was his ability to play a guitar and sing. Sunday afternoons was party time and everyone gathered on the veranda, drank beer, and listened to him play his guitar. All of the songs were about places and happenings in Nova Scotia. During the more lively ditties, McDonald enthusiastically stomped his foot up and down in beat with his music. Sometimes he'd jump up in the middle of a song and do a jig, much to everyone's delight.

McDonald drove a crude-oil tanker and the only time Billy saw Ma Williams put her foot down regarding something he did was when she made him park his truck down the road because it stank so bad.

Shoe showed up on Sunday with the beer while everyone was lounging on the veranda listening to McDonald play and sing. It was during one of McDonald's ballads about home that Billy remembered that he still hadn't phoned home. He went over to Ma Williams, who was enjoying the show along with the boarders, and asked her if he could make a long-distance call. The two of them agreed that he would get the charges and pay her for the call later.

The phone was a little different from the one he was used to back in Nanton. His home phone had a button on the side that you could press and ring each person on the party line, if you knew their ring. Everyone on the line knew everyone else's ring and when anyone on the line was making a call, it would tie up everyone's phone on that party line. May Scott and her daughter both had houses on the same farmsite, about 50 yards apart, but they were forever phoning each other and tying up the line. If people needed to use the phone they would simply pick up the receiver and tell the two women that they needed the phone, knowing full well that both women would rubber in and listen.

Billy rang the operator and asked for Nanton and for the long-distance charges. After a short pause, the familiar voice of Betty, Nanton's operator, came on the other end. "What number please?"

"Betty, give me three eight ring two please."

"Billy Cochrane! Where are you?"

Billy was a little taken aback to have Betty recognize his voice so quickly. Then he realized that what everyone in Nanton said was true — Betty knew everything that was going on. His father once phoned and asked Betty if she knew where the person he was trying to reach might be and she told him where that person could be found and then proceeded to connect the phone call. Betty tried to be discreet and feign ignorance of any juicy gossip, but everyone knew otherwise. Billy could visualize her sitting behind the bank of cables, which she deftly connected and disconnected, all the while keeping up a running dialogue with each new caller. Her hair was pulled back in a tight bun and she wore glasses with thin wire rims. Both her glasses and her hair seemed to be held in place by the ubiquitous speaker headset.

"I'm roughnecking up in Leduc," he announced with a cavalier air of nonchalance.

"Well, I declare! Everyone here thinks you fell off the face of the earth. Let me see if the Scott girls are on the line, and if they are I'll ask them to hang up. I'll tell them there's an important incoming long distance call waiting."

Billy could see his mother and father in his mind. It was Sunday afternoon and his father would be sitting in his over-stuffed chair listening to the radio, with his mother sitting in her chair knitting. His parents were not overly religious, but Sundays were always spent going to church in the morning and relaxing for the rest of the day. There were a couple of unchallenged rules in the Cochrane house. The first rule was that no one was allowed to sit in Dad's chair and the second was that no one was allowed to make noise of any kind when the news or the grain and livestock market report came on.

Many an anxious moment had been spent in front of the radio during the war years, listening to CBC's Lorne Green, with his deep baritone voice announcing the news. Other times it was Mathew Halton doing the broadcasting. Nanton, like most every small community in Canada, had many of its young men and women serving in the armed forces. Billy knew of at least 20 young people who went overseas during the war, and the whole community knew where each one was stationed. When Lorne Green began the news by announcing a city or area in Europe where heavy allied and enemy casualties were reported, everyone immediately became fearful if it was an area where a friend or neighbour was serving. Every grown-up person in Nanton would collectively hold their breath for a couple of weeks, dreading the arrival of a telegram announcing someone's death or that the person was "missing in action."

Following the news, the familiar strains of Alford's Colonel Bogey March came on, signalling the daily update of the grain and livestock prices. And again, everyone had to remain silent as Billy's dad noted each of the daily price changes.

Billy's mother answered the phone, and in a faltering and credulous tone of voice said, "Billy, is that you?"

After a brief scolding about being so tardy in letting his parents know how he was doing, Billy brought his mother up to date on his job, his car, his friends, and where he was living. Then he answered all her questions. During this initial small talk, Billy could hear the telltale sounds of the line clicking as each party line person began listening in.

Billy then asked his mother if there was anything new happening in Nanton. She informed him that two days after he left, his father had sold all the milk cows and pigs. She said it was time for Dad to slow down a bit and only do only grain farming, along with raising a few beef cattle. Billy asked if she had sold her chickens too, and she exclaimed, "Heavens no, I have to have something to do!" She said the red-headed neighbour girl,she couldn't remember her name, asked about him every time she saw her. "She even phoned to see if I had a phone number for you. Gracious me, I can't think of anything else to tell you. But as soon as we hang up I'll think of lots of things."

Billy wrapped up the conversation by asking his mother to say hi to his dad. He knew talking to his father would be strained, not because there was any tension between them, but because his father didn't like talking on a phone. Besides, his mother always did the talking, and Billy knew that his father would have put down whatever he was reading, turned down the radio, and be listening raptly to the conversation anyway.

Billy returned to the Sunday afternoon festivities and opened a beer. Shoe inquired, sarcastically, "Did your mommy miss you?"

Billy didn't respond. He reflected a minute and then began telling everyone a story about Pat Ryan.

"This old hillbilly got drunk one Saturday night, and when he went home around midnight, he rang his own phone number. He rang it over and over. Each time, he listened for the pop on the line that indicates that someone is listening in. He knew that all his neighbours would be dying of curiosity about who would be phoning Pat Ryan at that hour of the night. Finally, when he was satisfied that he had a sufficient audience he announced, 'All you girls can go back to bed now. It's just old Pat Ryan up having a piss.'"

Everyone had a good laugh at the story and McDonald picked up his guitar and strummed a crescendo. McDonald then took a swig of his beer and asked Billy, "What part of the country did you say you came from?"

Billy couldn't resist the opening and came out with another Pat Ryan story. Billy tried to put on the breathless look that Pat Ryan had when he launched one of his yarns. Billy opened his eyes wide, took three short breaths and stuck out his hand in a dramatic fashion. "I came riding out of the mountains on a grizzly bear, barbed wire for a saddle. With a rattlesnake in one hand and a bobcat in the other, I whipped that bear up to the Waldorf Hotel, dismounted, and strode inside. I told the bartender to get me a quart of sulphuric acid. I drank it down in one gulp. The whole bar grew deathly silent, staring at me. Finally, one old-timer spoke up and stammered, 'Where did you come from stranger?' I slowly turned to him and said … I come from Nanton. The tough guys chased me out."

Chapter 11

Billy hated the midnight shift. After drinking beer all afternoon and enjoying a good roast beef supper, all he wanted to do was go to bed, not go to work at midnight. His mood was further fouled when he entered the doghouse and looked at the drilling record. He knew immediately that the previous crew had again delayed changing the bits, leaving it to Billy's crew. "Looks like we been fucked again," he said to no one in particular. Then he went out onto the floor and began preparing for the night's work. They had to pull nearly a mile of pipe out of the ground, put on a new bit, and run it all back down the hole again. The crew was running the pipe when a heart-stopping crisis arose.

Billy's job was to tail each string of pipe as it was being lifted off the floor and muscle it into the waiting joint of the previous 90 feet of pipe that was held in place by the slips. Johnny and Bruce operated the tongs to screw the pipe together. Ramchuck was supposed to lift the entire pipe up enough so that the men could pull the slips up and then let the pipe fall freely down the hole. At the exact moment Ramchuck pushed down on the handbrake bringing the pipe to a stop about three feet above the floor, the crew would slide the conical shaped slips in around the pipe to keep everything from falling down the hole. This procedure was repeated over and over until the entire pipe was connected.

Everything was going smoothly until the pipe hit a bridge in the hole where it had caved in. The pipe came to a sudden stop and the freewheeling blocks came crashing down on top of it. The noise was deafening and Billy had no idea what was happening. He'd followed Shoe's advice from the first day he started, and he immediately dived behind the leg of the derrick. By the time Ramchuck realized what was happening and slammed the brake handle down, the drill cable was spinning off the drum and out of the draw works onto the floor. Billy could see Bruce's face peering out behind the opposite derrick leg. Ramchuck's eyes were big as saucers and Johnny was transfixed as the cable snaked around the floor.

The weight of the blocks crashing down on the top of the pipe drove everything through the bridge in the hole and the pipe began to free fall again. The slack in the drilling cable snapped tight as the pipe came to a jarring halt. The cable sounded like a whip cracking when it became taut again. The cable spooled all around where Johnny was standing and, miraculously, he wasn't touched by any of it. When the cable snapped taunt it could have easily taken an arm or a leg off. The whole derrick shuddered and bounced when the pipe came to a stop. Billy was sure the whole thing was going to come down on top of them. For a moment all was still, except for the din of the motors.

Ramchuck tried to lock the brake down with the piece of chain that was used for that purpose, but his hands were shaking so badly he couldn't fit the chain into the slot on the brake. After a few moments, when he was sure everything was safe, Billy ventured over to the draw works to see if there was any damage. Some of the cable was snarled around the drum, just like a fishing reel, but other than that there didn't appear to be any structural damage. Ramchuck gingerly lowered the rest of the pipe down the hole and the snarled cable played out without any incident.

Everything settled back to normal very quickly after the incident. Shoe told Billy, "You know where to find me," and disappeared down to the mud tanks. Billy knew that Shoe was going to crawl under the tarp that covered the bags of mud. The mud bags were still warm from the day's sun and they made an ideal place to sleep. Shoe trusted Billy to wake him if need be, and not to tell anyone of his whereabouts. Johnny was spraying down the floor with the water hose and Ramchuck had just taken up his position with one hand on the brake and his eyes riveted on the weight gage.

The weight gage was attached around the dead end of the drilling cable and the gage measured the stress on the cable, giving a rough indication of the weight. Schultz had obviously told Ramchuck the weight range he wanted on the bit for optimum drilling performance. The full weight of a mile of pipe on the bit would ruin the bit or even twist it off. As the bit chewed through the mantle of the earth, the weight indicator would show less weight on the bit, and this was Ramchuck's signal to lift the brake handle and let out another foot of cable. Each time he released and reset the brake the brake drum would emit a loud squeal which could be heard a mile away. This sequence soon became a comforting sound to Billy, a signal that all was well.

Billy went into the doghouse to grab a quick bite of his lunch and found Bruce already there sipping on a coffee and munching a sandwich. Billy sat down and said, as he opened his lunch bucket, "That was a close call. It sure didn't take you long to take cover."

"I guess that was my combat training," Bruce responded.

"You in the war?" Bruce merely nodded his head.

"What branch?" Billy was suddenly taking an interest in Bruce, who said little and never seemed to come to town, or to associate with the rest of the oil patch fraternity.

"Army, Loyal Edmonton Regiment, or as we were more commonly called, 'The Loyal Eddies`."

"Really! Were you in Europe?"

"Yep." Bruce seemed reluctant to talk, but Billy pressed on.

"Where in Europe?"

"Italy." Bruce was studying the egg salad sandwich his wife had made as if there was something wrong with it.

Billy's curiosity was peaking and he again pressed his attack. "Where in Italy?" Bruce chewed thoughtfully on his sandwich and before he could answer, Billy answered his own question. "I bet you were in Rome drinking wine and chasing Italian girls."

"Ortona."

It was Billy's turn to become silent as the words of Lorne Green and Mathew Halton came back to him … "In Ortona today heavy fighting continued door-to-door and street-to-street. Heavy Canadian casualties were taken …"

Billy respectfully stopped his questioning, now realizing why Bruce was so jumpy when there was unanticipated loud noise. It was just this afternoon that he was laughing as he told the story about Bruce throwing himself on the rig floor when he accidentally dropped a drill bit that had made a loud bang. "I heard it was pretty rough going there."

Again Bruce only replied with a nod.

Billy kept pressing, trying to get a story out of Bruce. "What was it like, did you kill any Germans?"

Bruce gave the stock answer that all veterans seem to give, "Not that I know of."

Finally, Bruce opened up a little bit and volunteered that the noise was about three times louder than the oil rig and that he went days on end with very little sleep and little to eat. Most of the time he spent crawling on his belly through blown-up buildings trying not to get shot.

Billy's curiosity and imagination raced, and he blurted out, "Did you see lots of dead people?"

Bruce was studying the black fingerprints on the white bread of his sandwich, and before he could or would respond, the heavy metal latch to the doghouse clanged open and Shoe and Johnny stomped in. This broke the spell and the conversation ended.

Billy leaned back and enjoyed the rest of his coffee, and not just for the taste. Only on the graveyard shift could all four of them take a lunch break together. If Schultz was around, a person dared not sit down and eat, and on many a shift Billy went home with his lunch untouched.

Billy shifted topics and asked Bruce where he lived. It had just occurred to him that he knew nothing about Bruce after two months of working side by side. Bruce told Billy that he'd purchased a quarter-section of land about 10 miles south, with a veteran's loan. After a brief pause Bruce, in his quiet modest way, asked if any of them wanted to make a little extra money and help him put his hay up in the barn loft.

Billy asked if the hay was raked and bunched and if it was dry. Bruce said it was all ready to go. Billy looked at Johnny and Shoe and asked, "What do you think girls, up for some hay pitching?" He looked at Shoe and when Shoe shrugged his shoulders in agreement Billy turned and told Bruce that they would follow him home after work. Billy didn't even look at Johnny for agreement. He knew that Johnny would want to be included.

Bruce looked at the three of them with an incredulous look and simply said, "Great!" Then Bruce turned to Johnny and told him he'd been very lucky earlier that night and that he could have easily lost his life. Bruce told them about an incident that had happened a short while ago, he wasn't quite sure where. He explained that the same thing had happened on another rig, only the cable wrapped around a guy and when the bridge broke free the cable snapped back. The unfortunate man was pinned against the drum and the draw works. "I guess it broke nearly every bone in the guy's body, but it didn't kill him outright. I hear it took quite a while to get the cable free, and all the while he was talking to co-workers as they tried to free him. Then, as soon as the pressure was off him, he died."

Billy felt his stomach turn and he lost his appetite for the sandwich he was eating. "I think I'll go squeak the brake and give Ramchuck a chance to get a cup of coffee." He had gained Ramchuck's trust enough to take over the driller's job for short periods.

Following Bruce back to his farm that morning after work, they passed Schultz's wife, who was out for a walk. She turned and gave them a big wave and looked Billy right in the eye as he drove by.

Shoe turned to watch her as she faded out of view, "That's one hot dame and she wants me!"

"How do you know that, Shoe?" Johnny asked from the back seat. Shoe was just starting to warm up and he shot back, "Did you see the way she just waved and stared at me as we drove by? She wants me all right, and I'm going to give it to her. I'm going to take her up to my room, grab her by the hair and throw her on my bed, and then I'm going to reach up under her dress and grab her panties by the crotch and tear them apart. Shoe's lip was starting to curl up as continued his narrative. Johnny, by this time, was leaning over the front seat and his eyes were beginning to glass over. Then I'm going to grab each of her ankles and pin them back behind her ears …"

"Yeah! And then what?" Johnny's breathing was becoming laboured.

Shoe stretched his legs out and started rubbing himself. "Then I'm going to ram my cock into her and give her a fucking like she's never had before. And she'll beg for more, squealing like a stuck pig."

Billy couldn't contain himself any longer and asked Shoe what he thought Schultz would be doing while all this was happening.

"Fuck Schultz, I doubt that drunken asshole could even get it up."

Billy pondered this statement. Shoe might be right on that point. "Maybe she was waving to all of us," Billy said.

"Naw, I'm telling you, she wants *me*." Shoe seemed to slump as the drama of his story unwound.

Johnny sat back in his seat embarrassed by his eagerness to listen to the story.

Next to Schultz's trailer was the farmsite that belonged to the owner of the land the drilling rig was on. Peter Kostura had inherited it from his father, who was one of the original Ukrainian immigrants.

The oil rig was only 300 yards behind Kostura's house and there was a never-ending stream of trucks and cars coming and going at all times of the day. Peter Kostura had done little to improve the homestead and it looked to Billy like nothing had changed since it was first settled. Billy thought the chicken coop back home was better than Kostura's house. It had been built with poplar logs and they were all twisted and rotting. The barn behind the house was no bigger than a shed and it looked like it was about to come crashing down. Every vehicle that came onto the lease had to pass through Kostura's yard to get to the oil rig.

Invariably, there were chickens or pigs on the road, which scattered in all directions when a car passed by. Usually there were two or three scrawny kids watching from the edge of the road. Billy couldn't tell if they were boys or girls as they were all dressed the same, and equally dirty. Also, he could never figure out how many there were, because they seemed to come in different ages and sizes each time he came through.

The one feature that was out of place was the new 1947 Chevrolet car that was parked in front of the house when Kostura was home. It looked out of place, the only piece of machinery on the property capable of running. Billy slowed as he passed the house, fearful of running over something or someone.

Any time Shoe was driving, however, he sped up and tried to run over a chicken or two. He'd leave a cloud of dust that settled over the house and drifted in through the one open window. A mangy dog, which was always on the alert, usually bounded out to bark and snap at every vehicle that passed down Kostura's lane. Each time they entered or left, Shoe would swerve to try and run over the dog as it raced along barking at his front tire. But the dog had always leapt out of the way, until this one time.

One day when Shoe was driving, he said, "Watch this … " and he sped into the yard. "I'll teach this son of a bitch to not chase cars." The dog predictably bounded towards the car and Shoe quickly opened his door and, with a loud thump, sent the unfortunate dog tumbling end over end. All three of them had looked back and laughed as the dog rolled down the road. From then on the dog glowered at everything that went by — but he never chased cars again.

Johnny shook his head and said, "Those people must be really poor." He wondered how they ever lived through the thirties.

"Well they ain't poor any more," Shoe shot back from the passenger seat. "Some time ago, I heard that some fast-talking oil man from Calgary had paid old man Kostura $100,000 for the mineral rights on his land. Turns out it was Frank McMillan. Where do you think the money came from to buy that fancy new car? The stupid son of a bitch should have held out for three times that amount."

Johnny piped up again, "With all that money you'd thinking Kostura might spend some of it on his family and his farm instead of buying a new car.

And Shoe replied, "A bohunk would never think like that. I bet the drunken asshole didn't even put the money in the bank. Those bohunks never trust banks you know. He'll have the money buried somewhere out in the trees, probably beside his still. I say we come back here and rob him."

Billy shot Shoe a sideways glance to see if he was joking or not. He wouldn't put it past Shoe to pull off a stunt like that.

Billy quickly changed the topic, asking Shoe to explain how mineral rights worked. Johnny listened with interest, as he wanted to know as well. Shoe was aware that both looked up to him for his worldly knowledge, so he turned sideways in his seat to address the two of them. "When the government started giving the land away, they kept the surface mineral rights, so that they could keep any gold or coal that might be found. But who was to know back then, 50 years ago, that oil would be found a mile beneath the ground. Anyone who filed for a homestead before the turn of the century also got all the mineral rights below the surface.

Usually an oil company comes in and makes a deal with the farmers to lease these rights from them. And then, if they ever drill on the land, they give the farmer 12 percent of the oil that comes out of the ground. So, if an oil company does strike oil they get 88 percent of the revenues. But from what I hear, Kostura never had a contract or an agreement with any major oil company. Well, of course, Frank McMillan smelled this out somehow and came courting.

Everyone in Leduc knows the story of how Frank McMillan, a slick oil stock promoter from Calgary, got rich. He knew about the first two oil strikes that came in and deduced that the Leduc oil field was going to be huge. He'd sent a land man to Edmonton to look at all the land titles in order to find out who held the mineral rights to each piece of land. The large oil companies pretty well had all the farmers tied up, but for some reason Peter Kostura's quarter-section had been overlooked. McMillan sprang into action and drove out to make the deal with Kostura.

Rumour has it that McMillan brought a suitcase with $100,000 in it, along with a case of rye whiskey. He probably got Kostura drunk, which he probably was already, and told that dumb Ukrainian that there was a 99 percent chance that no oil would ever be found and that, most likely, he'd never see a dime.Then he probably made the generous offer of $100,000 for the mineral rights. Probably told Kostura that he would take all the risk himself.

The story goes that McMillan opened up the suitcase, dumped all the money on Kostura's table or dirt floor or wherever. The poor son of a bitch didn't know that much money existed, let alone seen it all piled up like that on the floor of his kitchen. I heard he signed McMillan's offer right there on the spot."

"So McMillan's pretty confident that we're going to strike oil?" Johnny asked.

"From what I hear, McMillan's no fool. And if we do strike oil, he'll be a multi-millionaire."

They continued on their way to Bruce's farm and Billy asked if Shoe or Johnny had ever seen Kostura driving his new car around Leduc? Before anyone could answer, Billy, in a lame imitation of Kostura, squared his shoulders back into the drivers seat and sat ramrod straight, putting both of his hands firmly on the steering wheel and pasting a solemn and self-important look on his face. He looked straight ahead, and nowhere else. This brought a laugh from both Johnny and Shoe. Everyone in Leduc joked about Kostura's sudden wealth and his pomposity over it.

"I wonder why he doesn't buy his kids some clothes and fix the place up?" mused Johnny.

Shoe sarcastically responded that Kostura was too busy getting drunk each day and beating up on his wife and kids.

Billy wondered if there weren't a grain of truth to Shoes' comment, because their rare glimpses of Kostura's wife revealed a distraught-looking woman no better dressed than her kids were.

Billy changed the topic and announced that the geologist had told him that Schultz had come up from Beaumont Texas with the rig, and that he had heard that Schultz was on the run from the law for killing a man.

Johnny leaned forward again over the front seat and exclaimed, "*Killing* a man!"

"Yeah, Billy continued, "Dave said that he'd heard three stories. One was that Schultz hit a guy over the head with a beer bottle. Another was that he shot the guy, and another that he kicked the guy in the head and killed him. He told me the Spindle Top Oil Field was a real rough place and that he believed it was quite possible that Schultz had killed someone, and then fled to Alberta to escape the heat. Dave also said that Schultz was raised in the oil patch and really knows what he's doing."

Shoe was thinking, just taking the story in. He finally commented that he believed the story because he knew of an incident last winter when Schultz had broken a guy's leg in a bar fight by jumping on it when the guy was down.

"So, you still want to fuck his wife?" Johnny piped up from the rear.

"Damn right! He don't scare me none."

All three of them fell into silence for a couple of minutes. Then Johnny suddenly leaned forward again and dug a crumpled piece of paper out of his pocket. He passed it to Shoe and asked him to read it for him. Shoe turned and said, "Why don't you read it yourself?"

Johnny mumbled something about not having his glasses with him. Billy cursed himself for not telling Johnny that the piece of paper was an invitation to Ramchuck's daughter's wedding. He was quite sure that Ramchuck would not be inviting Shoe, and this was not the way he wanted Shoe to find out. Ramchuck had unobtrusively handed out the invitations that morning.

Shoe took the handwritten invitation and smoothed it out. "It says, Johnny Laboucan"

Billy glanced over and noted the writing was in calligraphy, the same as his, and the page was decorated with neat scrolling along the corners and along the border.

Shoe opened the invitation. The writing was calligraphy and the invitation was decorated with neat scrolling on the corners and around the border. He read the contents silently first. The invitation read —

Mary and Nicolas Ramchuck
Are pleased to invite you to the wedding of their daughter
Elizabeth
to
Metro
Son of Marion and Steve Stefanyshyn
Saturday, July 31, 3 p.m.
Saint John the Baptist Ukrainian Orthodox Church
Reception, Dinner and Dance will follow at the farm of
Mary and Nicholas Ramchuk
RSVP

Shoe read it again and Johnny, sensing that it might be important, nudged Shoe, "Well what does it say?"

"It says," Shoe began in a deliberate and formal voice, "Johnny Laboucan, you are invited to our bohunk wedding on July 31." He paused for a dramatic effect, and then continued using his best Ukrainian accent … "Please bring fat pig for present. If there are no fat Ukrainian *babas* to dance with, you may dance with pig. Eat *pyrohy* and drink *horilka* until you puke. Rest in peace — or whatever RSVP stands for in Ukrainian."

Billy gripped the wheel tighter, staring straight ahead, and said, "I believe RSVP is French and it means that they want you to let them know whether you are coming or not."

Shoe was obviously irritated and tossed the invitation back at Johnny saying, "You figure it out, you're the Frenchman."

Johnny sat back and tried to decipher what Shoe had just read to him. By now he'd guessed that Shoe was spoofing and that it was simply a wedding invitation. "You get one Billy?"

Billy just nodded and was hoping that would be the end of the conversation. If it wasn't, he knew that Shoe would begin pouring more invective on Ramchuck.

After another short silence, Johnny piped up again, "Did you get one Shoe?"

Just as Billy had thought, Shoe launched into another rant, spouting that he wouldn't be caught dead at Ramchuck's wedding or eating some bohunk slop. The rant continued as Billy followed along behind Bruce.

Chapter 12

Shortly after Shoe's rant, Bruce turned into his acreage in front of them. Bruce introduced the three of them to his wife and two children, a boy of seven and his younger sister, who Billy guessed to be about six. Both of the children were shy and disappeared into the next room as soon as the introductions were made. Bruce's wife, Linda, was soon fast at work making them breakfast. In no time flat, bacon and eggs were served.

While they were eating, Billy noticed two heads peeking around the corner. Just as they were about to finish, Bruce's son made a furtive entrance back into the kitchen and was edging over to his father when Billy reached out and scooped the boy up onto his lap, demanding to know what he thought he was up to. Billy guessed just about every stunt a child could pull and at the end of every question the boy would answer an emphatic "No!" Soon the boy began to giggle, clearly enjoying the attention. Pretty soon the girl edged closer, shyly sidling up to Billy as well.

Billy suddenly stood up and asked the two children, "Are you two ready to stack some hay?" That was the signal for everyone to get to work. Bruce led them to the barn explaining how he thought they should proceed. He had two hayracks but only one old tractor and a team of horses. He thought that they should let each person take a turn driving the tractor while the other three forked the hay. Billy listened, asked about the team of horses in the corral, then suggested, "How about Johnny and I take one rack with the team and you and Shoe pull the other rack with the tractor?" Bruce looked at him closely, "You know how to handle a team?"

"Show me the harnesses," was Billy's instant response.

The only question Billy had to ask Bruce while they were harnessing the two old horses, fat ones at that, was which one pulled on the right. By now both of Bruce's kid's had lost all their inhibitions and were intent on helping with the harnessing. They were talking non-stop and arguing with each other about which piece of harness went where, both darting under and around the mammoth old beasts. Neither of them showed any fear and they obviously knew that both horses were as docile as the nondescript old dog that had materialized out of nowhere to join in the commotion.

"Alright city boy, let's see what you can do!" Billy yelled over to Shoe as they all headed out to the hayfield. A sense of exhilaration overcame him as he listened to the two old horses snort and felt the bouncing of the steel-rimmed wagon wheels under his feet. Johnny said very little but watched with interest as Billy took over and gave directions. Both children rode with Billy and Johnny and clung close to Billy as the hayrack bounced over gopher holes and rocks.

Shoe and Bruce zoomed by them on the tractor and were soon stopped next to a pile of hay. They had already loaded the first bunch by the time Billy and the team caught up with them. Billy stopped the team beside the first pile of hay he came to and both he and Johnny jumped down with pitchforks in their hands. Billy showed Johnny how to load the rack so that the load would'nt fall off on the way to the barn.

When each bunch of hay was forked onto the rack, Billy would jump back on and steer the team to the next pile of hay. At each pile, the yellow mongrel dog would wait expectantly for the last bit of hay to be forked onto the rack. This procedure usually exposed a mouse or two and the old dog would pounce like a cat on his unsuspecting prey.

Every time Billy grabbed the reins, Todd, the oldest child, pleaded with Billy to let him drive the team. Each time Billy gently said, "Not yet," clucked his tongue and gave the reins a jerk. And the two old horses grudgingly pulled the load over to the next hay pile.

The work soon became as rhythmic as tripping pipe at the rig. Billy loved the aroma of fresh cut hay and he frequently asked Johnny, "Don't you just love the smell of fresh cut hay!"

Johnny just shrugged and said, "I guess so."

Each load was forked from the hayrack to the barn loft. One man forked it up into the loft and the other pushed the hay back and piled it up in the back of the hayloft. All four men had their shirts off, and their muscular torsos glistened with sweat.

Bruce's wife came out to the field at lunchtime with a large picnic basket loaded with everything imaginable to eat. Everyone sat under the shade of one of the racks and ate off an old sheet that was spread on the ground. The two old horses snorted, pawed the ground, and shook their harnesses, providing background music for the lunch.

By four o'clock in the afternoon, the 10-acre field was almost cleared and everyone was tired. The two children, who had moved from riding on the rack to riding on the two horses, were also tired and getting a little bored. Billy and Johnny were just pulling away from the barn when Billy pulled the team to a halt by Bruce's rack.

"I'll make you a little wager," he said. "I figure there's about two loads each left to clean up this field. I bet you that Johnny and I can bring in our two loads faster than you can. But, because you can travel faster on the tractor, you have to spot us the time it takes you to unload the load you have on."

Shoe and Bruce had a short conference, turned to Billy, and said "How much you willing to bet?"

"The loser has to buy the winners a case of beer, right Johnny?" Billy said, as he realized that Johnny might want to have a say in the bet. Johnny smiled and nodded.

"You're on," both Shoe and Bruce echoed.

"Hang on kids," Billy shouted up to the two children, "I'm going to see if these two old plugs have got a high gear."

Billy took the ends of the reigns and slapped the backsides of the old horses, but he could only get them into a slow trot. Both the boy and the girl had their legs wrapped around the horse's necks and were holding on to the top of the hames for dear life. The ride invigorated everyone and they were soon filling the rack with a new load of hay.

Billy and Johnny worked furiously loading and unloading, but due to the now long distance to the barn, they could tell the tractor was gaining on them. The old horses seemed to be caught up in the excitement as well, but were too tired and out of shape to move very fast.

Billy and Johnny finished their last load and headed to the barn. They knew it was going to be a close race when they looked back to see Shoe and Bruce finishing the last of their load. Billy was now hollering at the horses and both of the kids were screaming as well, each spurring on his or her horse. Perched on top of his load, Billy could see the tractor rapidly gaining ground. A mere 200 yards from the barn, Shoe and Bruce, who were both riding on the tractor, began to gain on them.

Bruce was waving with a silly smile on his face and Shoe was holding up an imaginary beer bottle and having a drink. But just as their hayrack went by Billy's, the front wheel hit a badger hole. Their load of hay swayed to one side and then back again, and then the back wheel ran over the same hole and slowly — the load of hay began to slide off the rack.

Bruce brought the tractor to a sudden stop and Billy and his crew plodded past them. Both kids held their arms up in triumph, cheering wildly. Johnny cupped his hand under his armpit and made farting noises, and Billy thumbed his nose. The dog joined in on the commotion and began to bark. It seemed to Billy that the old team even had a slight prance to their step as they finished the last short pull to the barn.

All of them used the horse trough to splash the dust and grime off their sweaty bodies. As Johnny stuck his head in the water, Shoe reached down and grabbed both of Johnny's legs — dumping him head first into the trough. Johnny just sat in the trough yelling, " You asshole, Shoe, I'm going to get you for this." The idea of Johnny getting even with Shoe was even funnier than the dunking. Then, while Billy was laughing, Shoe made a sudden lunge for him, grabbed him in a bear lock, and began wrestling Billy towards the stock trough. The suddenness of the move had caught Billy off guard and he fought vigorously to regain his balance.

Billy arched his back, spread his legs, and finally braked Shoe's assault. Just as they were right front of the stock trough Billy slowly began to get the upper hand. Then, all of a sudden, Billy was holding Shoe in a bear lock. Billy lifted Shoe off the ground and plunged both himself and Shoe into the water tank. All three of them howled and splashed water over one another. Bruce could only shake his head saying, "You guys are crazy!"

Although nothing was ever said between Shoe and Billy both knew, from that time on, that Billy was the stronger of the two.

Bruce, in his quiet way, began to thank his crewmates for their hard work and apologized that he wasn't prepared for them that day and that he'd get money from the bank and pay them the next day. Billy shrugged his shoulders and said that as far as he and his partner sitting in the horse trough were concerned, the only thing they had coming was the case of beer that they'd bet.

On the way back to town Shoe suddenly turned and said, "I'll tell you what. This is the first day of the Edmonton Exhibition. Let's get a little shut-eye after work tomorrow and you two meet me at the hotel about three o'clock. We'll go take in some of the action. Laboucan, give me a couple of bucks for the beer."

After they dropped Shoe off, Johnny climbed into the front seat with Billy. A moment or two after they drove off, Johnny said, "Shoe sure doesn't like Ramchuck very much, does he? Are you going to the wedding?"

"Hell yeah. I hear a Ukrainian wedding is the most fun a person can have with his clothes on. But the first thing you and I have got to do is go down to Brody's store and buy us a suit. We'll go together on a wedding present."

The following morning after their nightshift, Bruce pulled his truck up beside Billy's car, announced that he had something for them, and produced three cases of beer. Billy, Johnny, and Shoe were in high spirits on the way in to Edmonton. Shoe opened each beer with a loud pop as he expertly used another beer to pry each top off.

Standing at the entrance of the Edmonton Exhibition grounds, Johnny looked up at the wording over the entrance gate and asked what it said.

"It says bring your fucking glasses," Shoe replied sarcastically

Billy cut in and said, "It says ... 'Through these gates walk the finest people on earth, our customers,' Royal American Shows."

Johnny blurted out, "But how did they know we were coming?"

No sooner had they entered the grounds than Johnny spied a cotton candy vendor and asked his two friends to hold on. It was something he had never seen before and he wanted to try some. Johnny got one and spent the next 20 minutes looking at it and wondering where to start.

The first booth they passed proclaimed the strangest marriage in the world - the fattest woman on earth weighing over 800 pounds and the smallest man on earth. The canvas on the front of the tent had a garish painting of a very fat woman holding hands with a midget.

Johnny was beside him with excitement, "Let's go in!"

Inside the tent was an enormous bored-looking woman reclining on a sofa. The midget was reading a newspaper. "We better get out of here before you two get turned on," Billy quipped. "I don't want you two walking down the midway with hard-ons."

"That was a rip off," said Shoe as he linked arms with the two of them and proclaimed, "The three musketeers! Now what?"

They passed booth after booth, each covered with paintings extolling the wonders that beckoned inside. They stopped at each booth and looked at the paintings. A barker was inevitably in front calling them over: two-headed animals, snakes, and people who could do fantastic stunts. They were all there. Johnny was so overwhelmed by all the sights and sounds that he'd delayed tackling his candyfloss.

They stopped at a booth that featured a mouse race. You placed a wager on a certain colour of mouse hole. When all the bets were down, the operator poured out a half-dozen live mice from a box. They would take a second to get oriented, and then scramble down the table, which was made to look like a racetrack, and disappear down holes at the end of it. All three watched this race over and over, trying to figure out if one particular colour won more often than the others.

After tiring of the game, they continued their meander around the midway. Shoe brought everyone to a stop when he spied the entrance to the toilets, "Wait here, I've got to get rid of some of that beer." As he left he pushed the cone with the cotton candy into Johnny's face, just as he was opening his mouth to take a great big bite.

While waiting for Shoe to come back and for Johnny to recover, Billy eased over to two good-looking girls who were standing nearby. "Having fun, ladies?" Billy said, trying to strike up a conversation.

Johnny joined in and stuck out the lopsided remains of his pink cotton candy. "Want some?"

Both the girls tittered and one reached out and pulled off a little tuft off the cotton candy. Before Billy could think of another line, the girls' two boyfriends made their exit from the toilets and stepped into the middle of the group. One snarled, "Get your own girls!" Johnny mimicked him, echoing, "Get your own girls!" The two began calling Johnny and Billy names and made like they wanted to fight. Billy beckoned them towards him, and said in a deadly voice, "Come on."

Just then Shoe came back and the two boyfriends, realizing they were outnumbered, grabbed the girls and quickly moved away, all the while muttering threats. Shoe asked what that was all about and then both he and Billy started laughing. Johnny was totally oblivious to the fact that his face, eyebrows, and hair were still covered with sticky candyfloss.

"I guess when they realized that they were up against the incredible living candy man, they headed for the hills, quipped Billy. "Maybe we should set up a booth and call it the world's only living candy man, half-candy and half-man."

Johnny, as always, was good-natured about the ribbing, and vowed to get even with them. His chance came soon as the next booth they passed was a shooting gallery.

The booth was lined with prizes and the object was to knock over a moving line of ducks. The top prize was awarded if you could knock over 10 out of 10 ducks. There were lesser prizes for hitting stationary targets or hitting some of the ducks while they were moving. Shoe ordered everyone to stand back because they were at risk of getting shot. Billy joined in by asking the crowd that was milling around to place their bets, as Deadeye Dick was about to give a lesson in marksmanship.

But it was Johnny who paid his money and picked up the gun. He was starting to take aim from a standing stance, when the attendant told him he might have better luck if he were to use the counter to steady his aim. Johnny merely said, "Stand back," and with 10 rapid-fire shots he knocked over the 10 moving ducks. Everyone, including the attendant, broke into applause. Billy noted that for the first time, Shoe gave Johnny a look of respect. Johnny took his time and selected a large stuffed black and white panda bear as his prize.

Moving on, their attention was caught by a man who was selling knives, knives that could cut through anything and still remain sharp. The three of them were more impressed by the oratory and the convincing sales pitch than they were by the knife.

Next they spotted the towering Ferris Wheel in the distance and they moved on. They were slowly making their way in that direction when a barker called them over to the Crown and Anchor wheel. He spun the wheel and called the boys over to make a bet. Billy was explaining the game to Johnny as the wheel spun, making a staccato-sounding noise as the stopper bounced off the slots. Shoe had already placed 25 cents on spades. Johnny watched, mesmerized as the wheel slowed and the clicking became more distinct. He could see the three spades slot slowly coming up, but was sure the wheel would stop before it could get to them. The wheel appeared to stop one spot away from Shoe's spades, teetered, and then advanced the one more click, giving Shoe three spades and a 75 cent win. Johnny let out a whoop and jumped straight up into the air. He was already digging into his pocket for change when Billy suggested that Johnny play anchors and he would play crowns.

Each time the wheel spun Johnny would stare, transfixed, as the blur of colours slowed into focus. Then, as the wheel became slower and slower, he sank lower and lower behind the counter as one of his anchor slots came closer to payday. Whenever he won, he would pump his fist in the air and leap from his crouch straight into the air. When he lost, he would groan and fall to his knees on the ground. Shoe observed Johnny's antics with a look of disgust and announced, to no one in particular, "The kid doesn't get out much."

Billy was concentrating on the spinning wheel and didn't notice at first the presence of a person shoving in between Shoe and himself. Billy turned and the big newcomer snarled, "Shove aside, pal." Billy then felt the presence of several other guys pushing in close. It was then he recognized the two guys that had the girlfriends he had been talking to. Before he could say anything or even react, Shoe spun around, and with one motion threw a left hook right on the point of the big guy's chin. The sound of Shoe's punch was not unlike the sound of a home run hit in a baseball game. The big stranger dropped to the ground and Shoe followed through with a vicious kick to his face with his cowboy boot.

Billy turned to face the rest of the gang and counted four more, five of them in all. He balled his fists and stood side by side with Shoe, ready to do battle. The other four immediately backed off when they saw their leader unconscious on the ground.

Billy took a quick step forward and said, "Which one of you punks is next?" The remaining four cowered back even further and Billy knew the battle was over, but he couldn't resist the temptation to take another step towards the one guy he recognized. He drew his fist back for a punch. The guy turned and fled, leaving the remaining three holding up their hands and pleading that they didn't want to fight, didn't want any trouble.

Let's get out of here," said Shoe, deliberately stepping on the unconscious combatant's chest as he left in a show of contempt. Billy turned to Johnny who was still fixated on the game and was oblivious to what had just happened. Johnny turned and, with a look of bewilderment on his face, picked up his large Panda Bear and obediently followed.

All three were almost giddy as Billy recounted the fight. He was bouncing up and down, shadow boxing and flattering Shoe's performance. Suddenly he stopped, as he caught sight of a fortune-teller's booth ahead. "Let's get our fortunes read. Maybe we 're destined to become rich and famous."

The three of them approached the old woman, who had dark deep-set eyes., obviously the fortune-teller. She wore a strange looking gown and a kerchief covered her hair. Trinkets dangled from the kerchief, adding to her mysterious aura. Her booth consisted of an awning, which was attached to a small trailer. Most likely where she lives, thought Billy. The trailer was decorated with all kinds of astrological symbols.

"How much do you charge to read a fortune?" Billy asked.

"Fifty cents," she replied, motioning him to sit down on a chair beside her table.

"How much for all three of us?" Billy countered, pressing their bargaining position.

"One dollar and fifty cents," she deadpanned, her face showing no emotion at all.

"Alright, alright," Billy said as he laid his 50 cents on the table and sat down.

The old lady took Billy's hands and slowly turned them over and back again, intently studying them. She ran her fingers over his palms, tracing invisible lines on them.

Both Shoe and Johnny pressed close, watching and listening intently.

Finally, she began, "You will live a long time and become very rich. You will marry and raise three children. One of your children will bring you much sorrow," she intoned in a strange accent.

Johnny couldn't contain himself any longer and blurted out, "How can you tell that?"

The old fortune-teller looked up at Johnny with her soulful dark eyes and, after a moment's hesitation, explained some of the mystery of her art. "Do you see how the tip of his little finger extends above the crease on the top knuckle of the ring finger?" Both Shoe and Johnny pushed closer to look. Johnny nodded that he saw.

"This means that he will work for himself and be his own boss. See how all his fingers fit close together, this means he will be able to hold on to money and other important things in life." She traced her finger along a crease in his palm and said that this was the lifeline, and that Billy would have a long life.

Shoe plunked himself on the chair saying, "I'm next." He turned both palms up and Billy and Johnny immediately pounced, pointing out that Shoe had stubby little fingers and that gaps showed between them. Shoe shot back, "Shut up, you weevils. If I wanted any shit out of you two, I would kick it out of you."

The fortune-teller, momentarily distracted by the exchange, returned to examining Shoe's palms. She suddenly straightened up, looked very alarmed, and said, "I can go no farther!"

"Why not?" Shoe demanded.

"You will soon have very bad luck. You have not long to live. Here." She pushed his money back to him and disappeared into her trailer.

All three walked away *very* subdued. Billy broke the silence with a forced laugh and said, "You really don't believe in that fortune-telling bullshit, do you? Fuck it, let's take a ride on the bumper cars."

The mood seemed to lighten as they raced to get to their cars. Billy managed to steer his car into the side of Johnny's car with a resounding jar, and then the whole fleet became snarled in a gridlock and no one could move for some time. The buzzer sounded all too soon, signalling the end of their ride. Shoe bounded out of his car and gave it a kick, yelling at the operators that he had been ripped off. He followed that with, "Let's get out of this fucking place!"

Johnny pleaded that he wanted to go on just one more ride.

"Alright, you two go on that one, as he pointed at a ride that spun in vertical circles and tumbled end over end as it spun. I'll hold your fucking bear."

Johnny gritted his teeth as the ride began. He was aware of people screaming all around him and that his stomach was beginning to erupt. All of a sudden the cotton candy and beer spewed out his mouth and down the front of him. Mercifully, the ride came to a halt and Johnny literally staggered out when the door opened. Billy also felt queasy by the time the ride stopped, but when he saw Johnny covered in puke, he to began to gag.

Shoe showed no sympathy and told Johnny that if he didn't get cleaned up, he would have to walk back to Leduc.

As soon as they drove out of the city limits, Shoe opened the three remaining beers. Each drank quietly, reflecting on the day. Shoe broke the silence by muttering, "Fucking gypsy. What does she know anything anyhow?"

Billy changed the subject by saying that the Edmonton Exhibition was a poor-assed show compared to the Calgary Stampede. He boasted that the Stampede had a rodeo, an Indian village, and more rides. It was bigger and better in every way. The only thing the Edmonton Exhibition had was a flower show and an award for the best dill pickles. "The Calgary Stampede, now there's a real show," Billy boasted, giving the impression he had been there many times.

"Take me to the rig, Jeeves, it's time to go to work," was Shoe's only response.

Billy was always amazed that there was never a completely dark period during the night shift. He had never stayed awake all night before coming to work in Leduc and always assumed that the night hours would be inky black. But there was always a slight northern glow that gave way to daybreak around 4:00 am.

Billy spied Bruce eating his lunch as usual, around four in the morning, and sat down beside him hoping to press Bruce for more war stories. Bruce noticed that Billy didn't have a lunch and politely offered him a sandwich. Billy thanked him but said he had eaten a greasy exhibition hamburger just before work. He related some of the day's events, and then quickly shifted the conversation back to the war. "So what made you decide to join up, being that you were married and all?"

"Well," Bruce replied slowly, feeling obligated to answer Billy's questions in light of the day's work Billy had donated, "there wasn't any work to be found during the depression. Besides, I felt it was the right thing to do."

"Tell me more about Ortona," Billy pressed.

Again Bruce looked slightly pained, but he continued between mouthfuls of coffee and sandwich. Again, he proffered a sandwich and this time Billy gave in to his hunger and took one.

"We advanced on Ortona on December 10th and fought the Germans for eight days straight. Ortona is a small very old city with narrow winding streets lined with four-storey houses. The Germans blew up houses in various areas to block the streets and our tanks, so we had to fight from house to house to advance. You couldn't show your head on the street or a German sniper would blow it off.

"What we ended up doing was blowing a hole in the upper floor of a house with a beehive demolition charge. We'd take cover on the bottom floor, and as soon as the hole was blasted we'd charge up the stairs and through the hole before the Germans regained their senses and cleared them out."

"By clearing them out, you mean killing them," Billy interjected.

"Yeah," Bruce nodded, muttering it softly.

"Did your unit have many casualties?" asked Billy.

Bruce's eyes began to well up with tears. After a long pause, as the memory of the events receded a little, he slowly regained his composure and said, "I lost a lot of friends there."

Then, without prompting, he continued. "The worst was one time on Christmas Day. My best friend said he was going to take a chance and go back to the base and get a Christmas dinner and a beer. He was killed by a sniper as he ran out onto the street."

Billy thought about the story while both of them chewed their sandwiches in silence. Finally, Billy broke the stillness and asked Bruce if he had ever been wounded.

Bruce winced at the question and then answered with a steady voice, "Not in the way you might think."

Billy raised his eyebrows in a questioning manner, and Bruce continued, "I suffered 'battle fatigue' or, as it is more commonly called, 'shell shock'. "

Billy didn't dare ask any more questions. He knew that many veterans were loath to talk about shell shock because they worried they might be accused of malingering. He responded by saying, "Sorry to hear that," but he quickly figured out that was why Bruce had a facial tic — and why he is so jumpy around sudden noises or movements.

Chapter 13

Saturday was shift change and Billy and his crew were about to start the day shift. Billy liked the day shift, because he was now responsible for checking the oil on the three Waukesha engines. The first thing he'd do each shift was check the oil levels and then measure out the amount of oil he'd need from a 50-gallon drum. After topping up the oil he would check the radiator water level and then grab the grease gun and methodically grease all the nipples. He now knew the location of each grease nipple that kept the myriad of moving parts on the oil rig lubricated. The terrifying noise of the engines, the mud pumps, and the constant crashing of steel on steel, which he had encountered on his first day, were now music to his ears.

It was the unusual sounds that alerted his attention now. They'd often signal a bearing that needed to be replaced or something that needed to be tightened. Billy learned to carry out his duties at a measured pace, fast enough to keep Schultz off his back, but not so fast that he would have to pick up a bucket and scrub brush and join Bruce and Johnny scrubbing down the draw works. He'd rather be tripping pipe than do mindless scrubbing. He had also learned the art of grabbing a wrench off the tool board and hurring out of sight, giving the impression of tending to some urgent matter. Although it was strictly forbidden, he'd regularly join Shoe for a smoke behind the mud tank.

Everything was ticking along, like the start of any other day shift, when Shoe came striding past in a very agitated state. He went straight to the doghouse and looked at the geolobox. Then he went over to the pump pressure gage and looked at the reading. And then he marched up to Ramchuck and started screaming at him. Billy dropped his grease gun and crowded in closer so he could hear what was going on.

Shoe's face was contorted in rage as he gestured at the mud pump gage and the geolobox, "You dumb son of a bitch! We have only been here half-an-hour and you've drilled 30 feet. The last crew only drilled 100 feet in their whole shift!" Do you ever look at the mud pressure gage or are you so fucking stupid that you only look at the weight gage! We're losing circulation! Look at the mud pressure. It hardly registers!"

Shoe's face was only inches away from Ramchuck's and the way the veins in his neck were sticking out Billy thought he might hit Ramchuck. Billy said nothing. He wasn't sure what Shoe was talking about, but he pressed between them before Shoe could do anything drastic.

Ramchuck was obviously shaken and rattled. His face was red and he seemed paralyzed as to what to do next. Billy sensed that Shoe was right and that Ramchuck knew it. Usually Ramchuck was stoic, but his eyes were now round and he seemed to roll them heavenward, looking for some answer to his predicament. Finally, he chained the brake down, turned to Billy and said, "You get Schultz and the geologist."

Billy headed towards Schultz's trailer immediately, replaying in his mind the sequence of events that had just occurred. When he thought about it, the sound of the squeaking brake, which indicated that Ramchuck was lowering the pipe to keep pressure on the rotating bit, was faster than it had been for the last few days. But what did that mean? What did Shoe mean by loss of circulation? Where did it go?

As he tried to make sense of what had just happened, he knocked on Schultz's trailer door. He had barely knocked when the door opened and Schultz's wife stood there in a terry towel bathrobe. She leaned against the door frame and took a long drag from the cigarette she was smoking. As she exhaled the smoke, she asked, "What do you want?" It was the way she said it that took Billy aback. The way she emphasized the "you" giving the question a suggestive meaning.

Schultz, obviously still in bed and hung over, bellowed out from the back of the trailer, "Who's there?"

Billy said, "Tell Al that Ramchuck wants to see him, we've got some kind of problem."

Schultz again bellowed out, "Who's there?"

Normally the sound of Schultz's voice would send a wave of fear through Billy's whole body, but this time he calmly and boldly untied the belt from Schultz's wife's bathrobe and ran the back of his right hand around each of her breasts and then slowly down her stomach until he reached her soft pubic hair. Only then did she flinch, not away from him as he would have expected, but her hips came invitingly forward. Billy never took his eyes off her expression and slowly backed away, giving her time to tie her robe, in case someone from the rig was watching. Schultz again hollered out and Billy thought he had better not press his luck any further.

As Billy turned to go fetch the geologist his heart was pounding at the audacity of the act he had just committed. His mind raced with a plan that would allow him to sneak over to the trailer while Schultz was in town drinking. There was no way to hide his car unless he was prepared to crawl on his belly like a coyote for two miles. He was still mulling over a plan when he reached the geologist's trailer.

Billy stuck his head in the open door and Dave gave him a hearty, "How you doing, Billy?" Billy hurriedly explained the situation the best he could. Dave didn't say anything, just made an "Hmm" noise and pulled at his chin. Then, after a few moments, he stood up from the microscope and the table that was covered with cuttings and muttered, "I was afraid this might happen."

Billy peppered Dave with questions and the geologist explained that they had just gone through a very porous formation. All the drilling mud had leaked into the formation instead of returning up the outside of the drill stem and back into the mud tank. Dave said it might be a simple matter if the mud sealed the leaks on its own or, in the worst case scenario, they might never be able to seal the hole off — and the well would have to be abandoned.

Ramchuck had gathered his composure by the time Billy and Dave arrived at the doghouse. Schultz came clattering up the steel steps to the doghouse, tucking in his shirt as he came. Ramchuck explained the situation and without hesitation, Schultz stepped out the door leading to the rig floor. He turned the pump switches on and gunned the engines. Watching the pressure gage intently, he quickly backed off the throttle and turned the pumps off.

Schultz stepped back into the doghouse and pointed at Shoe. "Get these weevils down to the mud tank and mix all the mud we have left just as thick as the pumps can pump it. I'm fixin' to go to town and get more mud. When I get back, if y'all ain't done you can all stick your heads between your knees and kiss your asses good bye." Dave asked Schultz what was going to occur if the mud didn't seal off the formation.

Shultz turned to the geologist with a withering glare, and in his heavy Texas drawl replied, "If the dog ain't stop to shit, he'll shit a-runnin'."

Billy guessed that was Schultz's way of saying that he was in charge around here and the only one in charge.

Shoe explained to Billy the different strategies he'd heard about that would stem the loss of circulation, including pumping sawdust and even chicken feathers down the hole. But he was still ranting, "That ignorant asshole Ramchuck! He could have burned the mud pumps out!"

A few minutes later Schultz came by and told Shoe to keep mixing mud and pumping it down the hole while he went in to town to order another load in.

The truck with the load of bagged mud pulled up about 3:30 that afternoon and everyone set about unloading it. The next crew arrived for their shift and both crews were gathered around the truck. Each bag weighed about 70 pounds and the men had worked up a sweat unloading the truck and piling the bags by the mud tank. Shoe suddenly stopped what he was doing and said to Johnny, "I bet you 50 cents that you can't carry two bags over your head the 10 yards to the pile over there."

Johnny looked suspiciously at Shoe, and then realized that the two crews had stopped and were all looking at him. Johnny thought about the weight and, figuring that the two bags wouldn't weigh any more than 120 pounds together, decided that they wouldn't pose that big a problem for him. Johnny then asked Shoe if he had to lift the bags in place over his head or whether someone would stack the bags on his upraised hands. Shoe assured him that the driver would stack the bags for him. Johnny felt this was an easy bet to win but he was still wary. He looked around at the rest of the men for some telltale giveaway.

Johnny then looked up to the rig floor. Both Schultz and Ramchuck were watching. This was the final inducement, and he said to Shoe, "You're on!"

Johnny stood with his back to the truck and his hands above his head. The driver set one bag on his up-stretched palms and then carefully placed the second bag on top of the first. Johnny wobbled a bit at first and then he began a slow deliberate walk to the tank with his load perched well above his head. Johnny had covered about half the distance when Shoe stealthily stole up behind him and slit the bottom bag with his pocketknife. The fine powdery mud contents cascaded down on Johnny like an avalanche. He stood there frozen momentarily, not realizing what had happened. The mud clung to Johnny's sweat-soaked shirtless torso. It was in his hair and eyes and for a moment he couldn't breathe. When he finally clued in, the spectators were beside themselves with laughter. Even Schultz could be heard stomping his foot and guffawing.

"You asshole Shoe! I'm going to get you for this!" Johnny raged. Then, stuck for some kind of a closure, he demanded, "Where's my 50 cents? You owe me 50 cents!"

Shoe was still laughing when he announced that Johnny owed him the 50 cents because he hadn't finished the contest.

Billy turned the water hose on Johnny and tried to console him by saying that he hadn't seen that one coming either. Then he chuckled and said, "You must admit, it was pretty funny."

As Billy dropped Shoe off at the hotel he said, "So it's Saturday night in Leduc. Let me guess ... you're going to drink beer tonight."

Shoe replied as he got out of the car, "Maybe," and then he reached back through the open window and ruffled Johnny's hair, "And I suppose you're going to try and lay that fat-assed redhead." That was Shoe's way of saying to Johnny, "No hard feelings?"

"I'll tell you what we should do tonight," Billy said as they drove away, "First thing after supper, we go over to Brody's and buy us a suit for Ramchuck's wedding and then we'll take in the nine o'clock movie." Johnny began to question why he had to wear a suit to the wedding. Billy pointed out that they would always need a suit for special occasions like a wedding or perhaps a funeral, or even their own wedding or funeral.

Johnny moaned, "Oh, alright, I'll buy one with you."

Billy drove up in front of Johnny's chicken coop only to find Johnny standing by the road waiting for him. As Johnny climbed in the car Billy could smell the fresh scent of soap on him and his raven black hair was slicked back with Brylcream. "Whoa, look at you! Who is the lucky girl tonight?" Billy beamed.

Johnny flashed a huge smile, enjoying the compliment.

Billy then showed Johnny a copy of the driver's test manual he'd picked up and explained to him that he could take the test orally, and that he would read the manual to him and help him with the questions. "It's time you got your own goddamned car and quit bumming rides from Shoe and me." Johnny pointed out that he always chipped in for the gas. Billy kept right on pushing, "Just think how proud your mother is going to be when you drive up in your very own car. And you'll be able to take all your brothers and sisters for a ride."

As they were getting ready to enter Brody's clothing store, Billy grabbed Johnny by the arm and told him to let him do all the talking. "When we're buying two suits at once, I'll be able to beat Brody up on the purchase price."

The store was quite busy and the two of them meandered around looking at various clothing items. Finally, Mr. Brody himself approached them and politely asked if he could be of any assistance. Brody was very well dressed in contrast to Billy and Johnny's usual attire of khaki pants and tee shirts. Billy felt his negotiating skills ebbing, and his confidence. "We're both looking to buy a new suit and we're looking for a real good deal." Billy tried to make a strong emphasis on the "real good deal" part but his voice trailed off when he said it.

Brody pointed out in a soothing voice that he had some excellent suits to choose from and that they were on sale, as well. "Gentlemen, if you will step over to the suit rack with me, I am sure we have just the right suits for both of you."

They tried on several suit jackets and looked in the full-length mirror at the results. Brody circled around them pulling at the sleeves and shoulders, all the while making approving noises as he worked. His head bobbed up and down and he constantly took a step back to admire his handiwork.

Billy had never experienced anything like this before and he found the experience both intimidating and exhilarating. And if he was going through this kind of an emotional roller coaster, he could only imagine what Johnny was thinking. Looking in the mirror, Billy had a whole new image of himself, one he had never envisioned before. He sensed that he looked much more mature.

Johnny settled on a brown suit and Billy opted for a dark blue one. Billy thanked Brody and was about to leave when Brody said, "Hold on a minute, we're not finished yet. We've got to measure you for the pant alterations." Brody then took the tape that was draped around his neck and measured each of their waist sizes and then, to their embarrassment, he reached up each one's crotch to measure the inseam distance. Billy took a nervous glance around the store to see if anyone was watching. Then he thanked Brody again and was about to leave when Brody put his hand on Billy's shoulder and asked if they needed new white shirts to go with their dazzling new suits.

Billy was about to make up a story about having lots of dress shirts, but the realization that he needed a dress shirt suddenly dawned on him. Before he could say anything, Brody deftly steered the two of them over to a table covered with packages of shirts. Brody soothingly informed them that those two smart new suits wouldn't look right without crisp new shirts. Billy looked at Johnny, shrugged his shoulders, and said lamely, "I guess so."

Brody then announced, " I'll set these aside for you for when you come in to pick up your suits. They'll be ready this Wednesday." Billy started to thank him for the third time, but Brody put his hand up and said, "Oh, another thing, could I interest you in a new tie. I'm sure both of you have lots of ties, but I'd like to show you some of the latest designs."

Billy, again realizing he was trapped, gamely said, "I suppose we've got time to look at ties."

Getting into the car, Johnny blurted out, "Jesus Christ, Cochrane! I thought you were going to negotiate a *deal* on a suit. We came away with a whole new wardrobe!"

Billy airily waved his hand and said, "Relax, we got a good deal, the suits were on sale." But inwardly, he was telling himself that he sure hadn't planned on spending $45! He also hadn't planned on being so easily manipulated by a salesman and he was feeling a little sheepish.

"We've got a little time to kill before the nine o'clock show. Let's cruise around for a bit." Billy had driven no more than half-way down the block when Johnny suddenly asked him to pull over. Billy angle-parked at the first opening and asked, "What's up?"

Johnny was rolling his window down when Billy spotted the tubby redhead and a group of her friends heading their way down the street. Immediately, Billy began humming "Baby Face," but Johnny disregarded him and leaned half-way out the window, trying to look nonchalant.

The redhead spotted Johnny immediately and began to squeal as she hurried over to the car to say hello to him. The rest of the group continued on down the street except for her friend, who was as skinny as the redhead was fat. Johnny confidently asked her if she wanted to come along for a little spin.

Billy quit humming and looked over at his friend in disbelief. The redhead quickly said yes and asked if her friend could come along too. Billy's mouth nearly dropped open when Johnny said, "Sure!" Billy didn't know what to say or do. He was astounded that Johnny would invite two 14-year-old girls into his car without asking him first. Johnny opened the door to let them in, and Billy pulled the passenger seat down and ordered, "Get in the back." There was no way he was going to be seen driving around downtown with a scrawny 14 -year-old sitting beside him.

Billy had no sooner backed his car out onto the street and was about to drive forward, when he looked in the rear-view mirror to see Johnny and the redhead all over each other and kissing passionately. This sudden turn of events shocked Billy. He never dreamed Johnny had any idea about how to approach girls or to make out with them. How had he figured all this out when he'd grown up in a cabin in the middle of nowhere? As Billy drove, he kept one eye on the street and the other on the rear-view mirror. The other thing that amazed him was the attitude of the skinny girl. She was completely unconcerned about the heavy petting that was going on beside her as she smiled and waved at people she knew as they drove down the street.

After a while, Billy regained his ability to speak, "It's time you two love birds came up for air, we've got a movie to go to and I'm sure it's past your bedtime."

"What's the name of the movie?" challenged the redhead, obviously peeved that her night was ending so soon.

Billy regretted saying that they were going to a movie, but having said it he wasn't going to relent and be seen taking two juveniles, as in jailbait, to a movie.

"So,what's the name of the movie?" the redhead petulantly asked again, stepping up her attack.

Billy gripped the steering wheel hard and leaned forward so that his body seemed to be wedged flat against the windshield. "It's called `Angel and the Bad Man`, starring John Wayne. And no, you are not coming."

When they were alone again, Billy said, between clenched teeth, "Listen, Laboucan, don't ever pull that stunt again on me again. And if you ever do invite another two girls into my car — make sure mine is worthwhile!" Inwardly, Billy thought the whole incident was quite humorous. Also, he began to see Johnny in a whole new light. Johnny said nothing, and after a short pause, Billy said, "Where'd you learn all those moves anyway? You were all over that girl like a hobo on a hot dog!"

Billy was lounging against the wall waiting for the seven o'clock crowd to exit. He was absent-mindedly picking away at a bag of buttered popcorn, paying little attention to the stream of people passing in front of him when suddenly —Candace was in front of him — materializing like some mirage on an Arabian desert. Billy's breathing tightened as he came to attention. He was speechless at first, but then mumbled, "Was the movie any good?"

A good-looking companion whose clothing suggested that he was probably a university student accompanied her. He was obviously somewhat older than Candace. She replied in an even voice, "Not bad for a western," and then continued, "I'd like to introduce you to Brad." Brad, her date, was looking past all of them with feigned disinterest.

Billy stuck out his hand and this seemed to catch Candace's date's attention. He looked at Billy's proffered hand and then at the bag of popcorn Billy had been eating. He placed his hand on Candace's shoulder and calmly announced, "We best be going." Billy bristled inwardly at the snub.

Johnny, oblivious to the drama that had just unfolded, blurted out, "Billy! Isn't that the girl that hangs out at Fats after school?"

Billy ignored the question, seething inside. He was thinking that if that creep had shaken his hand, he'd have squeezed it so hard he would have broken every bone in it. Maybe he should have decked him, right then and there in the theatre. His mind continued to race. If the asshole was worried about a little butter, how would he react if he were grabbed around his throat by hands that were coated with it?

Billy was preoccupied with thoughts of revenge as he and Johnny took their seats. When his rage finally began to subside he started to think about Candace. She was breathtakingly gorgeous, and she seemed more mature than when he had last seen her. Also, it was she who had stopped to say hello. That must mean something, he reasoned. And that geek who was with her clearly felt threatened. The more he thought about it the better he felt about the encounter.

The packed theatre grew silent as the curtains opened, giving the movie a stage-like presence. As always, a news bulletin on some world event preceded the main feature. A motion picture camera rotated until it focused on the audience and, to the accompaniment of a crescendo of music, an announcer with a baritone voice explained the unfolding newsworthy events. A Bugs Bunny cartoon followed the news.

During the movie, Billy looked over at Johnny and, just as he'd thought, Johnny was watching with spellbound intensity. No matter what movie they went to, Johnny was totally engrossed, sitting on the edge of his seat with his hands on his knees. He always looked as if he was about to stand up and cheer. In fact, he once did during a Saturday matinee. All the kids in the front row were cheering the arrival of the Seventh Calvary and Johnny stood up and cheered too. Billy ragged him about that one for a long time.

After the movie, Billy suggested that they head down to Fats, have something to eat, and watch the circus unfold, as all the drunks coming out of the bar usually headed to Fats.

"Fats" was a misnomer if there ever was one, Billy thought. Fats, who owned the café, was a cadaverous-looking old Chinese. The skin on his face stretched taut over his cheekbones and his eyes disappeared into their sockets. There wan't an extra ounce of flesh on his whole body. He had one misshapen front tooth, which was much larger than the other front tooth. However, it wasn't often that anyone got to see his teeth because one, he seldom smiled and two, he always had a cigarette dangling from his mouth, which he only removed when it went out. Billy always watched in fascination as to where and on what the never-ending ash would fall. Billy once saw the ash fall into a plate of food that Fats was serving and he continued on as if nothing had happened. Billy wondered if the white apron Fats always wore was ever washed. Ma Williams's apron looked sparkling clean compared to Fat's. To top off his wardrobe, Fats wore a chef's hat that only accentuated his scrawniness. The hat stood up like a stovepipe and was nearly as dirty as his apron. Sticking out the back, from under the grimy chef's hat, was a surprisingly neat braid of hair. The other amusing and distinguishing feature about Fats was that he never lifted his feet when he walked. Neither foot ever left the ground, and his slippers made a gritting sound on the muddy wood floor as he shuffled by.

Every time Fats came up to Billy to take his order, Billy asked what kind of pie he had and Fats always gave him the same answer, "Apple pie and laisin pie."

Billy would then mimic him, asking what kind of pie was "laisin" pie. Fats never smiled or acknowledged Billy's joke. He'd just stand by impassively until Billy ordered something.

Fats had recently brought his wife and two grown-up sons from China, and they were all busy helping him run his café. People in Leduc chuckled at the "wife and sons" story because, as far as anyone could recall, Fats had not been back to China for at least 25 years. Neither his wife nor sons spoke English. Billy thought that they must be working there under some form of slave labour.

As long as there was a customer to be served, Fats stayed open. The first breakfast crowd arrived at six o'clock, and on Friday and Saturday nights the last drunks might not leave until two or three in the morning. Somehow, between cooking Chinese food, cleaning dishes, and all the other chores that go along with running a restaurant, 40 to 50 bag lunches had to be made up each day for the various oil crews.

Billy quietly ate away at his hamburger absentmindedly watching Fats go about his work. He turned to Johnny and noted that Fats, his wife, and his two sons or whatever they were, might be the hardest working people in the whole oil patch. Suddenly, an old jingle that he and his friends used to chant to taunt the old Chinese café owner in Nanton popped into his head.

Chinky Chinky Chinaman
Sitting on a rail
Along came a choo choo train
And cut off his tail.

Usually, two or three of the Nanton boys would stick their heads through the café door and chant the ditty in unison, then run off. This generally got a reaction from old Feng, and he'd make a quick motion towards the door as if to give chase. Those who did the goading were the back-up for the brave two or three who stuck their heads inside the cafe. They would all flee in terror down the street, with one of them yelling that Feng was in pursuit with a meat cleaver. It was only after a terror-stricken three or four block run that they'd notice that Feng wasn't chasing them. Everyone would be babbling at once about his close call with Feng and the cleaver. They'd all compete to determine who the bravest of them was that day, and then debate how far the hero had ventured into the café before beginning the jingle.

The next order of business back in Nanton, one that was sure to get the adrenaline flowing, was playing Knock out Ginger or raiding gardens. Knocking on someone's door required careful planning. The target had to be old enough not to be able to catch them, yet young enough to pose a threat. Billy ruefully remembered the time they miscalculated and he, being the youngest and the slowest, was run down and got his ass kicked.

If it was winter and snowy or icy, they would have a game of street hockey going, and if a car came down the street, they would all slowly step aside and let the car through. Then, as soon as it passed, they would grab hold of the rear bumper and get towed. The object of the game was to see who could hold on the longest as the car picked up speed. Billy remembered the time an elderly gentleman, who drove an old Model A Ford, drove by. So many kids were clinging to the bumper and each other, that they stalled the car. This pursuit always carried the risk that the driver might be rather athletic. It was possible these types would see you, stop the vehicle, and suddenly plunge out of the car chasing you. He had seen more than one ass-kicking meted out when playing this game.

If they couldn't get a rise out of Feng with the jingle, then taunting him with the Chinese phrase "hoo mucka hi" was sure to bring some kind of response. Although he had never had the slightest idea what "hoo mucka hi" meant, Billy now realized out that the "choo choo train cutting off his tail" must be referring to the pigtail that a lot of the older Chinese wore. Until this moment, the jingle had never made any sense to him, because Chinese people didn't have tails.

People usually started trickling into Fat's café shortly after "last call" was announced in the bars. They'd quickly down the last of their beers and head over to the café. Billy and Johnny sat at the horseshoe-shaped counter and watched as the wooden booths on each side of the room began to fill up. If Schultz and any of the other tool pushes that he drank with came in, anyone in a booth would automatically stand up and offer his booth to the tool pushes.

Shoe came in and for a change he wasn't too drunk. "What are you bums up to?" he asked as he plunked himself down on a stool beside them. "How was the show?"

Billy told him that the show was very good. John Wayne got the woman, the bad guy turned good, the good guy turned bad, and everyone lived happily ever after, pretty much like all the westerns. Billy was in the middle of his summary when the afternoon shift from their rig came into the café, just off work. Shoe called the derrick man over and asked how they made out stemming the loss of circulation. Billy listened intently as the derrick man told Shoe that they had mixed the whole load of mud as heavy as they could and had finally regained circulation about nine o'clock that night.

One of the other crew members was leaning against a booth telling four very drunken roughnecks about the stunt Shoe had pulled on Johnny. They were all having a good laugh and pointing at Johnny. Soon the whole restaurant was laughing and pointing at Johnny. Johnny didn't know what to do, so he just looked down into his Coke glass.

From one of the other booths a roughneck stood up and hollered over, "Hey chief, been doing any mud dances lately?" The roughneck put both of his hands over his head as if he were holding something aloft, and stomped in a little circle in a poor imitation of a powwow dance. He then started a war-whoop, fluttering an open hand over his mouth as he continued his dance, and raising his knees in an exaggerated fashion. He then yelled over to Johnny again, "Hey chief, aren't you going to join in?"

Shoe slid off his stool, and in that deadly menacing gait that Billy recognized so well, moved in on the troublemaking roughneck. Billy couldn't hear exactly what Shoe said, but it was something like "I'll dance with you asshole." The restaurant grew silent as everyone sensed what was about to happen next.

The roughneck stopped his dance. His face took on a belligerent look and he immediately went into a fighter's stance. Shoe anticipated the roughneck's roundhouse right, and as he was ducking he drove his right fist square into the guy's solar plexus. It was a few seconds before the blow took effect, and then the roughneck's eyes grew wide with terror and pain. He and everyone else knew he was badly hurt. Just before he collapsed to the ground he lunged at Shoe, dragging him down with him.

The next moments were a blur. Another roughneck jumped on Shoe and in a flash Billy was on the floor punching and trying to drag the man off him. The fight didn't last long. Old Fats was screaming and hollering as he circled the melee of bodies on the floor — "No fight! No fight!" Order was soon restored and everyone returned to his seat. Shoe continued to glare at his adversary, who was by this time crumpled up in his booth in obvious pain.

Billy, catching his breath, laughingly said, "That was interesting."

Johnny never moved from his stool during the entire fracas, but when Shoe and Billy returned to their seats, he said, "You didn't have to do that for my sake, Shoe. I get called names all the time."

Shoe snorted derisively and said, "I didn't do anything for your sake, all that yodelling and kyeyiing was getting on my nerves. I was just shutting the asshole up."

Billy had never seen Fats move that fast or show so much emotion. Everyone knew that he would never call the police because it was a well-known fact that Fats bootlegged whiskey out the back door of his restaurant. Billy heard that he'd been arrested once and that he wanted no part of the police. Also, if Fats trusted you, you could order his special tea, a teapot filled with whiskey.

In no time at all, everything was back to normal with the usual constant din of laughter, clanging plates, and the ever-present cloud of cigarette smoke. Billy sipped his Coke and marvelled at Fats. He wondered if Fats, his wife, and his two sons ever slept. They must have to clean the kitchen up sometime. But a glimpse into the kitchen through the two swinging doors cast more than a little doubt on this statement.

Most of the faces from the other rigs were becoming familiar. Everyone bragged about how much hole they had made that day or told some outrageous story about a prank that was played on a new hand. Billy was quite at ease with this banter and could now talk oil patch lingo with the best of them.

Billy's thoughts drifted back to the movie and his encounter with Candace. He resolved to phone her up and invite her to a movie. But first he had to find out her last name and then her phone number. The more he thought about it and the more he experimented with some opening lines of conversation, the more he began to lose confidence. He thought of all the reasons why she would say no. She was probably going steady with that university guy. Her parents probably wouldn't let her go out with a stranger from the oil patch anyway. And why did he think that she would even want to go out with him? Hadn't she already said once that he stunk?

He was about to dismiss the whole idea and then he thought about her making the initiative to say hello at the movie. His mood brightened and he started counting off the positives he had going for him. He was reasonably good looking, owned a car, had some money to spend, and was just as good as any university creep. Yes, by God, he would make the phone call! He almost banged his fist on the counter but Shoe interrupted his thoughts by suggesting that they go out to the regular Saturday night dance and see if there were any leftovers.

Chapter 14

Johnny stood up and said it sounded like a good plan to him. Billy got up as well, reminding Shoe that the last time they were at that dance he'd ended up spending the night in the slammer. Shoe smirked, paid the bill for the three of them, and they were off to the dance. It was only a little after 12 o'clock and the country community hall was packed. The three of them stood at the back and surveyed all the people, trying to spot any girls that might be single.

All the familiar dances were being played. When a polka began, Billy thought the floor was going to collapse with everyone up dancing. Shoe wasted no time in asking some farm girl to dance and Billy noted that he had the same cat -like grace on the dance floor that he had with his normal walk. Billy was thoroughly enjoying himself watching all the couples twirl around and around as they danced past him. The same orchestra was playing as the last time and they were in especially fine form when playing the polka. The heavy-set lady at the piano was banging the keys so hard that Billy thought the piano would break. The saxophone player, bass fiddle player, and banjo player were all having as much fun as the dancers.

Two of the dancers intrigued Billy. The man was very thin, almost skeletal-like. His shoulders protruded through his snap button western shirt. His face and hands were brown and wrinkled, weathered from working outside, Billy guessed. The top of his head, the area covered by his hat, was pure white. The man's partner, obviously his wife, also looked like she had spent her life working hard. Still, she had retained her good looks and was constantly smiling. She exchanged pleasantries with the other dancers as she whizzed past them. They were dancing a fox trot, but it was their footwork that intrigued Billy. They seemed to dance in double time compared to everyone else. Their steps were quick and jerky, like two spiders locked in a deadly combat. Despite the awkward-looking footwork, they danced in perfect time to the music. The man stared straight ahead as if in total concentration, seemingly not enjoying himself. But Billy noticed as the night went on, the couple never missed a dance.

Billy was tapping his toe in time to the music when he spotted two overweight farm girls sitting on the bench along the wall. He elbowed Johnny and shouted to him above the din pointing them out. Johnny didn't know for a second whether Billy was making fun of him or if he was suggesting that they both go over and ask the girls for a dance. Johnny cupped his hand in Billy's ear and was beginning to tell him that he didn't know how to dance when Candace and her date from the movie passed in front of them. Billy went rigid when he saw them. He didn't hear a word of whatever Johnny was trying to tell him.

When the dance ended, it was easy to tell the locals from the oil patch crowd as they returned to their separate sides of the hall. Billy watched as Candace and her date disappeared into the crowd at the far end of the hall. Shoe never released his hold on the girl he was dancing with and continued to walk in a giant circle around the dance floor awaiting the next dance. Billy could tell by the look on the girl's face that Shoe was making progress.

The saxophone player directed everyone to get a partner because the next dance would be a waltz. For a change the entire band started out on the right note and beat. Billy craned his neck, watching and waiting for Candace and her date to emerge on the dance floor, but they never did. Shoe had his partner in a close embrace and Billy could see that she was enjoying it. Billy stewed for a few moments and then on a sudden act of impulse, he muttered, "Fuck it" I'm going to ask her to dance."

The walk down to the other end of the hall was the longest and most lonely he had ever taken. His jaw was set and he told himself he didn't care if she did reject his request to dance with him. He decided he might as well find out then and there if she was interested in him or not. Billy shouldered his way through the small throng of people who weren't dancing and strode right up to where she was sitting.

Candace was immersed in conversation with a small group of friends and her date was standing idly by, listening. She looked up, suddenly aware that someone was standing in front of her. Billy miraculously became confident and self-assured. With a gallant bow he asked her if she would honour him with a dance. Candace, startled by this sudden turn of events, looked first at her date and then at her friends, and finally at Billy's outstretched hand. Her face reddened and she made no comment as she stood up and took Billy's hand. Billy caught the glare of her date as he led her onto the dance floor.

The four-piece orchestra was doing a pretty good job of Glen Miller's "Moon Light Serenade" and Billy easily began the three-quarter time waltz steps. However, his impulsive decision to ask her to dance had left him completely unprepared for conversation. Realizing this, he finally he blurted out, "This is my favourite Glen Miller song." Candace murmured some kind of reply and they continued to dance in silence. After three or four bars Billy tightened his grip on her waist and spun her in a tight turn. During these turns Billy could feel her body close to his and smell the gentle fragrance of her hair. By this time he had reached the end of the hall where Johnny was standing.

He was obviously bursting with pride as Johnny closed his thumb and forefinger into a circle and thrust them out as a show of approval.

Billy sensed that Candace was beginning to relax and he was thankful he'd taken his Saturday night bath. They danced past Shoe, still grinding against his dance partner.

All too soon the dance came to an end and the two of them began the slow promenade back to her seat. Just as they reached her group of friends, the band struck up another waltz. Billy stopped and lightly grabbed her arm and asked if she would care to dance again. To his surprise, she said "Sure," and they did an about turn back onto the dance floor. This waltz was much faster and Candace seemed to be enjoying the fast-paced turns and the little dips and missteps that Billy threw at her. Billy still couldn't think of anything intelligent to say, so he merely gazed spellbound at her face and hair. After a few turns she made eye contact, smiled beautifully, and then quickly looked away again.

When the dance ended, Billy knew he would be pressing his luck to ask for a third dance, so he took the longest route he could to return her to her place. Then, in the middle of the dance floor, he suddenly stopped and asked her if she would go to a movie with him sometime. He thought saying " sometime" might make it a little harder for her to say no. After a short pause she said she would have to think about it. Then she said this week was definitely out as she was going out of town with her parents.

This gave Billy the chance to announce that he was going to a wedding this coming weekend, so it was out for him too. This, he thought, should make him look a little less eager. He hoped she would ask him whose wedding it was but she seemed lost in her own thoughts.

Billy thanked her for the dance and as she was about to push through the throng of bodies, he took a couple of quick steps and then grabbed her elbow saying, "Wait, I don't know your last name."

"Crawford, Candace Crawford. And your name is Billy Cochrane." She flashed him a big smile and disappeared back into her crowd of friends.

Billy's heart was pounding and his head was spinning as he walked back towards Johnny who greeted him like a lost dog and seemed more excited than Billy was. "You sure are a good dancer!" "I wish I knew how to dance like you."

"Fuck all to it," Billy responded. "I'm sure there has to be some gal around here that'll show you how. I was lucky, I had an older sister who showed me." Billy scanned the hall to see if there were any likely prospects he could set his friend up with. "If Step-and-a-half were here, she could teach you the step-and-a-half and then you could figure out the other half-step and then you would know the two step." Billy laughed exuberantly at his own joke as he slapped Johnny on the back.

Everyone had left the dance floor but Shoe, who was standing in the middle of the floor in a tight embrace with his dance partner.

At the end of the evening, the banjo player bellowed out for everyone to get a partner for the "Home Waltz." After a couple of bars the whole band was on key and in rhythm and the familiar strains of the waltz washed over the crowd. There was a mad dash as everybody hooked up with his or her partners or potential partners for the night.

For a fleeting moment, Billy's wishful thinking had him believing that Candace might come over and ask him to dance. He waited in brief anticipation for her to appear out of the melee of bodies, then realizing it wasn't going to happen he came back to reality. His heart sank as he saw her walk out on the floor with her date.

Shoe shuffled by and Billy could see that his right hand was firmly fixed on his partner's behind.

Candace and her partner glided by, but they seemed too engrossed with the dance or their conversation to notice him. Billy watched with resignation as they twirled out of sight.

An older couple danced by and Billy elbowed Johnny in the ribs and pointed them out. "That," he said, "is how to dance." The couple were obviously married and had danced together for years. The gentleman's back was ramrod straight and his wife anticipated his every move as they gracefully dipped and turned to the music.

Billy and Johnny watched in silence as the dance came to a close. The band finished the waltz and played a few bars of "God Save The King." Everyone stood at attention and faced the flag that hung at the end of the hall. The banjo player bid everyone a good night and announced that all the proceeds of the next Saturday's dance would be going to the Goodwin family, whose house had recently burned down.

Shoe must have done something right because his dance partner accompanied the rest of them to Billy's car. Billy thrust the car keys at Johnny and announced, "Here, you drive home." Johnny protested that he had never driven at night before, but Billy dismissed him by saying that was why the car had lights.

Johnny edged the car out onto the main road back to Leduc and Billy started telling him about the upcoming week, when he began to notice the pressure of the back of his seat being crunched from behind. Billy ignored the commotion going on in the back of the car and continued his conversation with Johnny. "The first thing we do tomorrow is study the driver's manual. I'll read out the instructions and then I'll ask you questions. All the answers are multiple-choice. The driving examiner will read out each possible answer and you'll tell him which one of them is right. Understand?"

Before Johnny could agree another violent push came from the back seat. Billy looked back and exclaimed, "Settle down back there!" Then he began to laugh as he realized that Shoe was lodged between the floor and the back seat with his new-found love on top of him. "Jesus Christ! Everyone gets to make out in my back seat but me," Billy exclaimed, raising both of his hands up in a gesture of futility. The wrestling and pushing became much more noticeable as Shoe and the girl struggled to get up from their entanglement.

"As I was saying," Billy continued, "I'll pick you up tomorrow at around three and we'll start studying. Then we have to figure out what to buy for a wedding present for Ramchuck's daughter, because the wedding is this week." He was just getting immersed in his thoughts again, when Shoe's new pal reached around Johnny from the back seat and covered his eyes with her hands.

Johnny, in a panic, let go of the steering wheel and pried her hands from his eyes, causing the car to swerve towards the ditch. Billy quickly grabbed the steering wheel and forced the car back to the centre of the road. "You dizzy bitch," he exclaimed, "Do you want to get us all killed or do you just want to walk back to town!"

Shoe shot back, "Watch your mouth!" and his date rocked back into her seat with a gale of giggles.

Billy's anger surged. His car was of prime importance to him. "Fuck you Shoe! Do you want to settle this right here and now? Stop the car Johnny!" Billy hollered.

Johnny was near paralyzed by the sudden turn of events and he slowly braked the car to a stop. Just before the car stopped, Shoe reached up from the back seat and gave Billy a slight shove on the head and said, "Hey settle down, we're just having a little fun back here."

The tense standoff was broken and Johnny continued his drive back to Leduc. The car became silent. Billy slumped back into his seat and Shoe continued his wrestling match with the girl in the back. Billy couldn't believe that he had just challenged Shoe to a fight. As his anger subsided, his thoughts drifted back to Candace and he started making plans about how he was going to approach her for a date.

He'd have to phone her, he decided. He'd simply have to screw up the courage to phone her. But when? She said she wasn't available this upcoming weekend. Next week though, he'd be working days so he'd be free any night to take her to a movie. When would be the right time to give her a call? If he asked too far in advance it might give her a reason to say no. Two days in advance, he decided, would be about right. If she were to say no, he would have a chance to suggest another day. But what if she flat out said no? He could apologize and tell her that was the only time he was free. Then he could airily dismiss her snub with a "perhaps another time."

Then another problem popped into his head. Where was he going to go to make the call? If he were to try to call her from Ma Williams' house, there always was someone around who would overhear his conversation. If Ma or the Nova Scotian ever got wind that he was lining up a date, he'ld never live down the ragging.

But more important, what was he going to say when she answered the phone? Billy began to rehearse some opening lines. They sounded sexy and might grab her attention. If only he could sound like Cary Grant. Eventually, he settled on, "Hi Candace, this is Billy Cochrane calling. There's a great movie playing this Wednesday, and I wonder if I could take you to it." Then he began to rehearse those two opening lines, experimenting with all the different places he could moderate his voice to make himself sound more confident and sexy.

Billy was suddenly jolted into consciousness when Johnny announced, "Welcome to Leduc, ladies and gentlemen. On your right is beautiful shack town." On the outskirts of town was an assortment of one-room houses built on skids, home to many of the married oil workers. Most of the shacks were no more than 12' by 14' and many had only tarpaper for a finish. There was no other accommodation and the families had to make the best of it. Billy felt sorry for the wives and children who had to put up with no power or no water. And on top of the primitive conditions, the town women ostracized them.

Johnny stopped in front of the hotel and waited patiently beside the car with the door open while Shoe and his gal rummaged around the back seat for various articles of clothing.

Billy was watching Shoe and his new friend disappear into the hotel when Johnny got back behind the wheel and began to babble excitedly. " Boy that was close, Billy. You and Shoe nearly got into a fight! But you know something Billy, I think you would have taken him!"

Billy shook his head and laughed, "If Shoe had got out of the car I would still be lying out in that ditch."

Johnny stopped the car in front of his home, and as Billy slid across the front seat to take the wheel, he said, "See you Monday at three." Billy hesitated - his conscience told him he should ask his friend to come over to Ma Williams' place and join in on the usual Sunday afternoon party, but he was a little tired of Johnny's company. Besides, Sunday was his day to hang out with all Ma's boarders.

Then he wondered if he should invite Candace over. He wrestled with this thought all the way home. Would she be offended by the rough and tumble crowd that drank beer, swore, and sang all Sunday afternoon? Or maybe she'd fit right in and join in with the singing. Maybe he should just call her and invite her for a Sunday drive. Billy shut the car off and went to bed, too tired to think anymore.

On Monday afternoon, as promised, Billy picked Johnny up and began tutoring him for the driver's exam. Billy read the instructions and then threw out questions for Johnny to answer. To kill time for the rest of the afternoon they drove to Fat's for a coke. Sitting in the booth Billy posed the question, "So what kind of car are you going to buy?"

Johnny became evasive and meekly replied, "Oh … I dunno."

"Well, you must have something in mind?"

After a long pause, Johnny finally volunteered, "You know something Billy, I've never passed a test in my life and I don't think I can pass this test, so there's really no point of even thinking of owning a car."

"Don't be silly, of course you're going to pass the test. And next week after Ramchuck's wedding we're going to start looking for a car."

"You really think so, Billy?" Johnny replied.

Billy could see his spirits picking up. "And that reminds me, let's take a walk down the street and see if we can find something for a wedding present."

Rummaging around in the Variety Store they weighed the merits of this against that. They ruled out an electrical appliance, as there was a strong likelihood the new couple would live where there was no power. Finally, they asked the lady at the counter what she thought would make a good wedding present. She asked a few questions about the newlyweds and both had to admit that they'd never even seen the bride or groom before, let alone know anything about them. "Hmm," the lady replied, "I think a nice set of sheets and pillow cases would be greatly appreciated."

"Done!" Billy exclaimed and Johnny nodded his head in approval. Both were relieved to have the decision made for them.

"Would you like these wrapped?"

Again, both quickly answered yes.

"Would you like a card to sign to go with the present?"

Billy started to feel a little stupid, just like when they were in Brody's buying their suits. "Of course," Billy replied emphatically as if that was going to be his very next request.

While the saleslady was wrapping their present, Billy suggested that they might as well sign the card right now. At the bottom of the card Billy just signed his name, as he couldn't think of anything else to write. He handed the pen over to Johnny and stood back as Johnny printed his name. Billy watched Johnny print in big laborious letters. By the time he had printed the L A B in Laboucan, he realized that he was going to run out of room, so he started making each additional letter smaller and trailed them off down the card so it would all fit in.

Johnny finished and was seriously examining his work. Billy could hardly restrain himself from laughing, thinking that if Shoe ever saw that card he'd fall down laughing. "We'll just store this in the trunk of my car until Saturday and remember that your exam is this Wednesday at 2:00 p.m. I'll drive you home after, I've got to get back for supper."

When Billy pulled up to pick Johnny up for his test on Wednesday, Johnny was standing on the street waiting for him. He had no sooner got into the car than he began bombarding Billy with questions about driving. Billy let Johnny drive while he leafed through the manual trying to find the answers.

Billy suggested that Johnny practise one more parallel park before they went into the provincial building. Billy wished Johnny good luck, and left him his keys, saying, "See you when it's over." Then he strolled out of the building. He figured the whole exam and driver's test should take around an hour so he headed to the pool hall to kill time.

Heading back, he spotted Johnny sitting in the car, and muttered to himself that this didn't look good.

Johnny hadn't see Billy coming until he was almost to the car, and when he did see him he leapt out of the car and jumped straight up into the air yelling over and over, "I passed, I passed!"

Billy didn't know whether he should hug Johnny, slap him on the back, or what, so he just stuck out his hand and said, "Congratulations sport."

"You know what, Johnny," Billy tried to copy Johnny's speech mannerisms, "This calls for a celebration."

"Like what." Johnny asked.

"Like we're going to go over to the bar, march in like we own the joint and order a beer."

"All right! Let's do it!" was Johnny's enthusiastic response.

Billy led the way into the bar from the back door and quickly spotted three of their crew members from the morning shift sitting at a table. Confidently striding over to the table he pulled up a chair and sat down. Johnny followed suit and dragged a chair from a nearby table and plunked himself down as if he was right at home. The other crew shared a couple glasses of their beer, and as the waiter walked by Billy took a healthy gulp from his glass, looked the server in the eye, and said, "You had better bring another round for the table." The waiter nodded and continued with his rounds.

The conversation quickly turned to what the morning crew did on their shift. The derrick man figured they must be close to pay dirt because all the big shots from Calgary were there. Frank McMillan was there with his fancy new Packard car and his big cowboy hat. And the place was swarming with engineers and geologists.

Don, the driller, figured they'd probably core the rest of the hole until total depth had been reached. Everyone agreed that

Billy and Johnny were lucky to be working the graveyard shift and wouldn't have to put up with all the people getting in the way. As the conversation continued about who was an asshole, which company was the best to work for, and other rig-related topics, Billy excused himself.

He headed for the restroom, but instead made an exit into the lobby and went over to the pay phone. He thumbed through the phone book until he came to Crawford. There was only one Crawford in the Leduc pages and he dialled the operator and gave her the number. His actions were so quick and impulsive that he forgot the lines he had rehearsed a few nights before. Listening to the telephone ring at the other end he was suddenly startled when Candace's voice came on with a distinctive "Hello". The "Hi Candace, this is Billy Cochrane" routine that he had hoped would sound like Cary Grant came out with a rush of words in a high pitched voice. He caught himself, took a deep breath and continued, "You said that you would be tied up this weekend, but you didn't mention Friday." He continued on gaining more confidence, "I was hoping you might go to the movie with me on Friday night."

There was a long pause as he waited for Candace to respond. Panic set in and he regretted his sudden impetuous act. The thought of rejection ate at his stomach.

Suddenly Candace spoke and said, "I don't know … I'll ask my mother."

Billy could hear a mumbled conversation in the background and his spirits began to soar. Clearly she had not rejected him out of hand.

Candace quickly came back on the line and said yes, but that it would have to be the early show, as she had to be home by 11 o'clock. She went on to say that they weren't leaving for the weekend after all.

Billy, now full of confidence said, "If you tell me where you live, I'll pick you up at 6:30 and have you home by 11:00. I have to be at work by midnight myself."

Billy was numb as he walked back to his table. Several newcomers had joined in while he was away and an older man was debating the merits of drilling with cable tools, as he had done in Turner Valley, compared to all the new fangdangled rotary rigs that were now in use. Billy absently listened as the old-timer recounted stories of 40 below zero, no steam, and all kinds of other hardships he had encountered. Another guy said that was nothing and he began a long-winded story about being stuck on a rig in Saskatchewan in a howling blizzard for three days before being relieved.

Normally, Billy would have enjoyed all the stories and bullshit, but his thoughts were on his upcoming date. That is, until one of the other crew spoke up and said, looking at Johnny, "I didn't think they allowed Indians in the beer parlour." Johnny took the shot with good nature and responded that he was French.

The topic returned to rig experiences. There was a feeling of closeness in the group that set them apart from the farmers and town people who were drinking at other tables.

Billy finished his beer and announced, to no one in particular, that if he wanted a warm supper he had better get going. He stood up and said, "You coming?" as he looked at Johnny. Johnny got up and they both headed for the door.

Once in the car, Billy again congratulated Johnny on passing the exam. Then he said, "Banning Indians from the beer parlour … how about banning a17-year-old Indian from the beer parlour!" Both of them laughed at the day's good fortune. Johnny had passed the test and they had been admitted the local bar without being challenged.

Chapter 15

Billy woke with a start Friday afternoon and looked at the ticking alarm clock. He couldn't understand his panicky feeling, because it was only 4 p.m. What was it that he had to do? What did he miss, he wondered, as he slowly regained his senses? Finally, he realized the cause of his anxiety. This was Friday and tonight was his date with Candace. He looked at the clock again to reassure himself. He had lots of time. He could wash his car and still go down to the hotel for a bath.

Billy fell back on the bed again and thought about how the evening might unfold. This was the first time he'd ever slept straight through during the day without being wakened by Ma banging pots and pans around.

Billy washed his car inside and out and polished the outside for good measure. Then he headed over to Shoe's room at the hotel for a bath. Shoe answered the knock on his door with a raspy, "Come in."

Billy went straight to the window and gave a tug on the roller blind. The blind shot up so quickly that he almost lost his grip. He locked the blind about three quarters up the window and let the room flood with daylight. By this time Shoe had swung his legs over the bed and was sitting there in his underwear.

"What time is it?" Shoe sleepily asked, and while he was asking the question he was lighting a cigarette.

"Around five."

Shoe's next question was, "What's up?" Then he reached down beside his bed and pulled a beer out of a box. He pointed at the box and offered Billy a beer.

"Don't mind if I do."

Shoe took a big swallow and let out a loud belch. "Good old Calgary Brewing and Malting, a good friend to wake up to."

Billy answered Shoe's last question with a request to use his bath.

"Use my bath! This is only Friday. You usually bath on Saturdays. You must have a big date or something."

Billy didn't evade the question and grunted, "Yup."

He took a drink of his warm beer and waited for the insults and ridicule that Shoe was bound to throw at him, but Shoe was strangely silent and softly said, "Good for you." Billy had braced himself for the onslaught and looked up to see Shoe scratching his chin. The remark was so out of character for Shoe that Billy was taken aback.

"Ever have a serious girl friend?" Billy ventured, sensing vulnerability in Shoe he had never seen before.

"Naw, not really. Find'm, feel'm, fuck'm, and leave'm. You know me."

This was more like the Shoe Billy knew, he thought as he finished his beer. When he stood up to go have his bath, Shoe made a statement that stopped Billy in his tracks. "Did you know that I spent a couple of stretches in the Bowden Juvenile Detention Centre a few years back?"

Billy quickly sat back down and wondrously asked, "For what?"

"Oh, just a bunch of kid stuff. Stealing cars. Break and entry. Shit like that. It wasn't like we were stealing the cars. We always left them where they could be found. It was more like we were just borrowing them for a night or two."

"Wow! I never knew that! Was it pretty tough in there?"

"Not much more worse than some of the foster homes I grew up in," Shoe said quietly.

Billy sat back and began to look at Shoe in a whole new light. Who was this guy, he wondered?

Shoe continued, "Don't need no women in my life telling me what I should or shouldn't do. I'm just going to go down life's highway, doing what I want to do and when I want to do it."

"Ever know your parents?" Billy hesitatingly asked, as he never knew when Shoe might erupt. Somehow he sensed that Shoe was in a different mood today.

"I doubt that I ever had a dad, but I think I remember my mother. She probably was just some kid who got knocked up and finally realized that she couldn't look after her and me too. I don't hold it against her."

"Do you think it might be possible to look her up and find her?'

Shoe just shrugged and said, "Why? I never needed her or anyone else before and I sure as hell don't need her or anyone else now."

Billy wanted to pursue the conversation, but he was running out of time.

"If you don't mind, I gotta get going, and if you don't mind I'll use your bath."

Mindful of Candace's comment that she'd known he was a roughneck because of his smell, he was determined to scrub out as much oil, grease, and grime from his pores as he could. While the bath was running Billy stuck his head out the door and asked Shoe if he could use his razor.

Shoe said, "Go ahead, you're not going to dull the blade with that peach fuzz."

Looking in the mirror Billy noted that the peach fuzz on his cheeks and upper lip were giving signs of becoming real facial hair. Standing back from the mirror he also noticed that his face looked older and his shoulders were more filled out. I must have gained 10 pounds in the last three months, he thought.

While he scraped the lather off his face he continued to talk with Shoe. "You mentioned 'we' stole cars?"

"Yeah, I always hung out with older kids."

"What happened to your friends?" Billy asked.

"Dunno. I heard one of them joined the army and got killed in Holland. Probably got knifed in some Dutch whorehouse."

Hard as he tried, Billy couldn't scrub the black from under his fingernails and his hands still looked dirty. He simply could not remove the stubborn grime that was ground into the calluses on his hands either. Billy exited from the bathroom with his hair slicked back and thanked Shoe for the use of his tub as he always did.

Shoe, still sitting on the side of the bed with a cigarette sticking out of the side of his mouth, asked who the girl was.

Billy shrugged him off with an off-handed comment, "Oh just some local bimbo I met." Billy shuddered to think what Shoe might do or say if he were ever to see him and Candace together.

Billy quickly drove home, wondering what he should wear. He had three choices. His usual wardrobe of khaki pants and white T-shirt, his new suit, or his suit pants with his button-up shirt. Wearing a suit to a movie was a bit much, he thought, so he opted for the suit pants and his white shirt. Ma Williams always washed and ironed his clothes because of the chores he volunteered to do for her.

Billy didn't even stop to trade insults with the assorted gathering of boarders as he hurried to his car. He could hear Ma's high-pitched laugh as everyone tried to venture an opinion about what he might be up to.

Billy found Candace's house with ease. It was a large stone house with a big yard on a corner lot. It might be the biggest house in Leduc, he thought as he walked cautiously to the front door. Candace answered his knock and opened the door. She was dressed in a summer skirt, with a white sweater buttoned around her neck. The sweater was draped over her shoulders, leaving her arms free.

Billy began to feel more at ease, as he was pretty sure he was dressed appropriately.

"Billy, I want to introduce you to my mother and father." Candace's mother had emerged from the kitchen, where she'd been doing dishes and lightly said, "How do you do?" Candace's father stood up from a gigantic armchair and put down the paper he was reading. And before Billy could respond to Mrs. Crawford's greeting, he stuck out his hand and introduced himself as Jack Crawford.

Billy shook his hand firmly and, without a moment's hesitation, looked him straight in the eye.

"Where do you hale from, Mr. Cochrane?" asked Mr. Crawford.

Billy replied, "Nanton, a little town just south of Calgary."

"Ah, I know the town well. When I was a youngster and just starting out in the banking business, I was posted to the Royal Bank in High River. I don't recollect hearing of the Cochrane name in Nanton. Are you perhaps related to the original Cochrane family that started the ranching empire just west of Calgary?

"I wish I was sir," said Billy, sensing that he was under intense scrutiny.

"So! You came to Leduc hoping to find fame and fortune in the oil business?" He hooked one thumb under his suspender and with the other hand placed his pipe back in his mouth.

"Something like that," was all that Billy could come up with while saying to himself, "So Candace's dad is a bank manager." In his experience, the most powerful men in the small towns were the banker, the hotel owner, and the car and truck dealer.

Candace, sensing Billy's growing uneasiness, tugged at his arm, which was a subtle hint that if they didn't get going they would be late for the movie. Candace hurriedly gave her mother and father a hug and led Billy out of the house. Mr. and Mrs. Crawford stood in the doorway, arm in arm, watching Billy and Candace get into Billy's car. Billy had never seen that kind of affection shown before. He couldn't remember ever hugging his mother or father nor had he ever seen his parents hug.

Candace stood back while Billy purchased their tickets and then came close when he beckoned her over to the concession stand. They each settled on a bag of popcorn and a coke. Candace leaned into Billy as some other people pushed their way up to the concession and he caught the delicate scent of her hair. It was all he could do to restrain himself from putting his arms around her and kissing her right then and there in the lobby of the theatre.

The movie was a comedy, which Billy didn't see much humour in. But when Candace laughed, he chuckled along with her. Rather than concentrate on the movie, Billy agonized on how bold he should get. Should he reach over and hold her hand? Should he put his arm around the back of the seat and caress her shoulder? Should he put his hand on her knee? In the end, he did nothing and pretended he was totally engrossed with the movie.

Back in the car Billy asked her if she wanted to do anything, it was only nine-thirty. As soon as he had posed the question he knew that he'd made a mistake and given her an easy way to say she should be getting home. He cursed himself for not just driving down to Fat's and saying, "Let's go in for a coffee or something?" Sure enough she said that she'd better get home. Billy mentioned that she had been out with her boyfriend much later than this last Saturday night.

Candace gave a short laugh, and said, "He's not my boyfriend silly. He's my neighbour." Billy didn't press the issue but felt relieved when she had said that. Maybe she didn't consider the guy her boyfriend, but Billy knew he hadn't imagined the guy's hostility when they were introduced at the dance.

They pulled up in front of Candace's house. Billy felt pretty good. All in all the evening was a success, and he was sure that he had made a favourable impression on her. They chatted for a short time about the movie and some other mundane topics, and then she suddenly opened her door and said, "I better run now." Billy was taken aback by this quick turn of events as he had hoped to turn the conversation onto a more personal level.

"Wait!" he implored, as he opened his own door, "I'll walk you to the door." As Candace was about to enter the house Billy put his arm around her waist and pulled her aside. Instinctively, she put her arms around his shoulders and they embraced in a passionate kiss. She broke free and murmured, "I got to go," but then she quickly turned back to him and gave him one more little peck on the lips.

Billy felt light-headed and giddy as he walked back to his car. He was certain that the way the evening had gone and the fact that she kissed him must mean she liked him. Billy felt like walking down Main Street and shouting to anyone who would listen, "I kissed Candace Crawford!" He felt his chest was going to burst. The short drive back to Ma Williams to pick up his lunch for the night shift and change his clothes was a blur. Billy could barely contain himself as he waited for Shoe and Johnny to pick him up. He sat on the veranda clenching and relaxing his fists as he recounted every minute of the evening with Candace. Billy stood up, walked around in a circle, and then he sat down again trying to compose himself.

Shoe finally drove up and Billy had no more than got into the car when Shoe started his interrogation. "So how did it go, stud?"

Billy tried to ignore the question, but Shoe persisted, and each question became more personal. Billy responded to each taunt with either okay, not bad, or all right, and was relieved when they drove through Kostura's yard and onto the lease.

The night flew by and by 7 a.m. the rig floor began to fill up with engineers and other assorted production people. Billy was not able to listen in on any of the conversations, but he could tell something important was happening. Long round pieces of core samples were carefully laid out on the floor and all the experts were on their hands and knees carefully making notes and examining the evidence.

Finally, he got the opportunity to tug on Dave's arm and ask him what was going on. The geologist took the time to tell him that they had struck oil, and bent down to point out evidence of this in the core samples. The solid black tubes of rock were riddled with holes and Dave told him that they were full of oil. Dave then picked up a piece of the sample and pointed out various imprints of the ancient sea life that were fossilized in the rock.

Billy was fascinated with the whole conversation and wanted to ask a million more questions when the geologist suddenly stood up and said, "I've got to get back to work." Quickly Billy asked what would happen next and Dave said, "We'll swab out the well today and see if we can get some production, but maybe we'll drill a little deeper. We'll see."

Billy, Shoe, and Johnny talked non-stop on the way back to town from work. They were excited to be part of something that was going to be big news. When Shoe stopped to let Johnny out, Billy told him that he'd better get to sleep quick, as they had to be at the church by 2:30 p.m. — and that they were not likely to get any sleep for the next 24 hours.

The alarm woke Billy up from a dead sleep and he sprang into action. Laying his new suit out on the bed, he dressed carefully and at the last minute realized he didn't know how to do a tie knot. He sheepishly went out into the kitchen and asked Ma Williams if she knew how to tie a knot in a tie.

Ma was in the midst of baking and she burst into laughter. "Of course I do," she replied and began to wipe off the flour that covered her. Her voluminous body shook with mirth as she painstakingly showed Billy how to tie a Windsor knot. When she finished she took a step back and gurgled in approval. She then stepped closer to Billy and while she patted the lapels on his suit jacket she said, "You look so good … I could just eat you!" Billy took this as a compliment and dashed out of the house.

Chapter 16

Johnny was waiting for him in front of his chicken coop and Billy gave him a wolf whistle through the window when he stopped. "Man, he said, you look like a million dollars in that get-up. If you can't get laid tonight, you never will."

The church was easy to find, but Billy had never seen a church that looked like this one. It was set off from the road in a little clearing of trees. In front of it was a giant wooden cross, but the cross had an extra bar that was on an angle to the cross bar. There was an onion-shaped dome on the little church. The yard was full of cars and trucks and there were even a couple of teams of horses hitched up to a hitching rail.

Both boys nervously entered the church not knowing what to do or what to expect. An usher led them to a seat. The summer heat was oppressive and Billy looked around the room and saw the icons and Ukrainian embroidery that adorned the little church. A hush settled over the congregation. The priest walked to the back of the church and returned escorting the bridal party. He was as forbidding a man as Billy had ever seen. He was covered from head to toe in a full-length gold and white robe. His head was covered with a strange cap and he had a long flowing white beard. Out from under the cap and beard stared the most piercing blue eyes Billy had ever seen. The man was even more intimidating than Schultz.

The imposing religious figure began singing in Ukrainian and everyone stood up. While he continued his monologue, the congregation sat down. This went on for some 20 minutes, with Billy and Johnny always one moment behind as people stood up and sat down. Not one word of English was spoken. The whole thing was becoming tedious in the hot and crowded little church. Billy closed his eyes and tried to picture himself somewhere else.

All at once there was a new commotion and when Billy opened his eyes a young women and a man were standing in front of the priest holding two ribbons aloft that supported a crown. Nick Ramchuck, his wife and the groom's parents were also standing near the priest.

Billy was amused at the sight of Ramchuck in a suit. Ramchuck had obviously had someone from his family cut his hair with only a pair of scissors. A rooster tail stuck up at the back, and where he parted his hair another rooster tail stood up on the short side of the part. Billy had never seen Ramchuck before without his hard hat on. Ramchuck could not button his collar up around his massive neck and his necktie hung down the front of his shirt untied.

Billy looked at Ramchuck's wife, a pleasant-looking woman who was as tall as her husband and a little on the hefty side. She wore a richly embroidered dress, not unlike the dresses of the two bridesmaids, who were obviously her daughters.

The priest beckoned the bride and groom to come forward and as they paraded three times around the altar under the ribbon arch, the bridesmaid took the crown and placed it on the bride's head. The priest had bound the bride and groom's hands together with a strip of embroidered cloth and bade them to drink from a chalice that he held forward. The rest of the ceremony dragged on another hour before it came to an end.

Billy gulped in the fresh air when they got outside. He looked at Johnny and said, "What did you think of all that?" To his surprise Johnny said he enjoyed it. "All I can say that if I marry a Ukrainian, remind me to hold the ceremony in a Protestant church."

It was a short drive from the church to Ramchuck's farm. Ramchuck greeted them with an enthusiasm and warmth that neither had ever seen in him before. He offered two glasses filled with home brew and said, "Welcome, drink, drink," in his usual singsong Ukrainian–English. By now Billy knew what to expect and braced himself for the burning drink. Ramchuck laughed as both of them screwed up their faces, then he slapped both of them on the back.

Billy could barely whisper, "What do we do with this?" as he held out their present.

Ramchuck was still laughing, which revealed his little nubs of teeth, and pointed towards the house saying, "You take."

Heading in the general direction Ramchuck had indicated, Billy noticed a large platform and a firepit with two pigs on a spit being barbecued. As they stopped to watch, a young girl slipped up from behind and stepped between the two of them. Grabbing each of their arms, she said, "You must be Billy. And you must be Johnny."

Billy, recovering from his start, replied, "Actually I'm Billy and this is Johnny, and you are? "He let his raised eyebrows finish the question for him.

"I'm Mary," she cheerfully replied. "I am Nick's youngest daughter."

"Of course, of course, you were one of the bridesmaids."

"How did you know who we are?" Johnny joined in.

"I'm the one who sent you the invitations, silly."

Billy was now taken aback and asked, "Are you the one who printed the invitations?" Before she could reply he continued, "Where did you learn to print like that?"

"Where do you think? In school of course," she cheekily replied. "I bet both of you would like a beer after sitting in that hot church."

"Sure would," Johnny quickly answered.

Mary led them to two wash tubs filled with ice water and beer.

Billy took a beer and offered the present in return, saying, "Do you know what to do with this?" Mary took the gift from him and stayed to talk. The tenseness of the afternoon soon melted away in the presence of Mary's bubbly personality.

"Where is everyone?" Johnny asked.

"Oh, they all had to go home and do chores, they'll be here soon, Mary said. Let me show you around, dinner won't be ready for a while yet."

The first stop on the tour was a small building that was falling apart and had been for some time. The roof was gone and a poplar tree was growing up from the centre of the old structure. "This was the original homestead house that my *gido*, that's Ukrainian for grandfather, built when he and my *baba*, my grandmother, emigrated from the Ukraine in 1898," explained Mary. The old twisted poplar logs could clearly be seen. Most of the original caulking had fallen out, exposing just how the building had been built. Looking in through the single window, they could see the remains of an old earthen stove and chimney. It must have taken up a quarter of the floor space in the house.

"What did they do for a roof?" Johnny asked.

"They made rafters out of poplar logs and then used sod to build the roof. Dirt for a roof and dirt for a floor."

"Sure must have been cold in the winter," Johnny speculated.

"Yes it was, my baba tells me stories about how it was in the early days."

"Can you speak Ukrainian?" Billy interrupted.

"I can understand it better than I speak it. I have to, Baba doesn't speak any English." Without prompting Mary continued with her narration. "My gido was a great man, a man of vision. Anytime there was a dispute in the community, the people would come to Gido. When two Canadians have a dispute, they go to a lawyer. When two Ukrainians have a dispute they go to the priest, but there was no priest in the early days, so they came to my gido. Nothing went on in the early days without him being involved.

When Gido heard about the Canadian government giving away 160 acres of land just for the taking, he convinced three other young couples from his village in Bukovina, which is now part of the Ukraine, to come with him to the new land. Baba says that the most land Gido could ever hope to have after working a lifetime in the Ukraine might be seven acres and they had to pay taxes on everything.

The brochure that the Canadian government sent promised that there would be no taxes in Canada. In the Ukraine Gido and Baba would have always remained peasants. But Canada offered them a chance for equality and to become rich. Baba told me they were all very young and very scared. They sold everything they owned, and they stitched all their money into their clothes. The three couples brought all the tools they thought they would need and headed for Canada. None of them had even left their village before. And now they were sailing across an ocean."

Mary sensed that the two boys were genuinely interested in her story and continued on. "Baba said that the worst part of the trip was the train ride from Montreal to Edmonton. They sat on wooden seats that made down into bunks at night and the trip seemed to last forever. Mostly they survived on sunflower seeds and a little soup they made on the cookstove that was in the back of each of the railway cars. When they finally reached Edmonton, they didn't know a word of English and didn't know what to do. The agent at the settlers' office showed them in sign language where to look for land and how to register their homesteads.

It was only March so it was very cold. They carried all their belongings, even a plough, on their backs and walked the 20 miles from Edmonton to here. Gido stopped when he found some red willow bushes growing. He said it was a good sign because red willows only grow on good land. They dug down into the frozen earth and saw how rich and black the soil was, then said a prayer and set out the next morning to stake their claim for a homestead."

"How did they do that?" Johnny inquired.

"It was quite easy, actually," Mary replied. "All the land had been previously surveyed and they just had to find the survey stakes that indicated which quarter- section, township, range, and so on that you were on. All they had to do was look for the quarter-section that they felt was the best one. Then they built a house."

It was Billy's turn to interrupt and he gave a low whistle and shook his head. "It must have been pretty tough going for the first few years."

"It was. Baba said she cried every day because she was so homesick. Baba was sure they would all die, be eaten by bears or wolves, or be killed by savages, or at the very least starve to death. She told me she begged Gido to return to the Ukraine, but he wouldn't hear of it. But the point-of-no-return really came when the newborn baby of one of the other couples died suddenly, and they had to bury the baby without a proper service. You see, none of the group could ever leave one of their own behind in a strange land, so from then on they were committed to stay and they had to make the best of it.

"Little by little things began to brighten for them. Spring came and the vegetable seeds Baba had brought with her began to sprout. Gido had cleared and broken about three acres and the wheat seeds he had planted were also growing."

"Are your grandfather and grandmother, I mean your gido and baba, still alive?" Billy asked.

"Baba is still alive and you will get to see her later, but Gido died before I was born. He was pulling stumps with a team of horses and one of them kicked him in the stomach. He rested for a few hours and then went back to work, but that night he became very ill. He died the next day."

"Gido was a good man," she added in a subdued voice. "He was responsible for the church being built, for classes being held in the church, and for everything you see around here." Mary then brought the conversation to a sudden close by saying she had to help with dinner. "Go help yourself to another beer," she shot over her shoulder as she left.

Billy and Johnny continued the tour on their own, noting how neat and orderly the farm equipment was lined up. They talked about the size of the barn and the house. After a while they stopped to watch the men lift the two hogs off the spit and onto a table to cool. They decided it was a good idea to sit in the shade of a big tree and watch the guests, who were just now starting to arrive.

As each person arrived the boys came up with a string of wisecracks. They watched as Ramchuck greeted everyone in turn and poured each one a shot of *horilka*. No one refused his hospitality.

"Here comes one for you," Billy quipped as a young fat girl waddled up the lane. Johnny responded with a punch to Billy's ribs.

"How do you suppose Ramchuck can make it to work tonight if he has a drink with everyone who comes in?" Billy wondered out loud.

"Look at this," said Johnny, his voice raised a notch. "It's the priest! Let's see if he takes a drink." The priest was now dressed in a full length black cassock and he had his wife by his side. Ramchuck, for the first time, was very subdued with his greeting. The boys couldn't hear the conversation but the priest took the shot of horilka that Ramchuck offered and downed it with ease.

"It doesn't look like that's the first drink he's ever had," offered Billy.

Bruce and his wife made their entrance. As they passed by the tree where Billy was lying on his side, with his head propped up with his elbow, Billy called out in a falsetto voice, "Oh yoo-hoo! Bruce!" Johnny took up the chant and Bruce turned and walked over to the boys, "What are you two scoundrels up to?"

"We're watching Lord Ramchuck greet his subjects, said Billy. I swear some of them would have kissed his hand." Bruce's two children spotted Billy and Johnny and rushed over squealing out their names. Both of them straddled Billy as he lay there and he gave out a loud grunt. Bruce's wife lightly scolded the children and made them get off Billy.

Billy sat up exclaiming, "My, what a beautiful young lady we have here!" Are you going to save me a dance this evening?" At this compliment Bruce's young daughter flashed a huge smile, which revealed that a front tooth had gone missing since Billy had last seen her.

"What have we got here? Did your brother knock your tooth out?"

"No, I pulled it out myself," she said, turning serious.

"How did you do that?" Billy asked in an incredulous voice.

"I tied a piece of thread around it and gave it a big pull," she responded and her face broke out in a grimace as she demonstrated how she did it.

The four adults talked for a bit and Bruce asked if they had gone to the church service. Billy said yes and that he thought Bruce should have come and partaken in the sacrament. "It was a grand way to spend a hot summer afternoon," he added sarcastically. "I didn't understand a word that was said but I think the priest must have blessed everything he could think of."

Johnny announced, "It looks like we're going to have a very drunken driller tonight if Ramchuck plans to down that stuff drink-for-drink with every one of his guests. I reckon he's already downed a bottle of hooch so far and the night has just begun."

Bruce countered that Ramchuck was a good Ukrainian and it would take a lot more than that to put him down. He also pointed out that they might get lucky and only have to circulate and rotate for the whole shift.

"Why do you say that?" Johnny asked.

Maybe they'll wait until morning before they continue with their testing."

Next to come through the gate were Kostura and his wife. Kostura walked in a slow measured gait with his shoulders thrust back. He had the same self-important look that he had when he drove his new car through town. His wife walked slightly behind him and looked like a deer caught in a car's headlights. Her hair was held in place by a series of hairpins. Neither of the boys had ever got a good look at her before. She was wearing a newly-bought dress, but it looked like Kostura had picked it out and purchased it for her, because it was very plain and also ill- fitting. Both Billy and Johnny were sizing up this unusual couple when Mary again came bouncing up from behind the boys.

"Here you two are, I've been looking all over for you," she said as she handed them two fresh beers.

"We were just looking at old man Kostura and his wife." Johnny replied.

"Oh them ..." was her response. "Daddy probably would never have invited them if it were not for all their money. They are Galicians, you know. Daddy says you can never trust a Galician. They lie, cheat, and are horse thieves. Daddy says that not all Galicians are horse thieves but he is sure that all horse thieves are Galicians."

Billy chuckled at her joke, but he could see by the look on Johnny's face that the quip had gone right over his head.

"I doubt that Kostura needs to steal a horse when he drives a new Chevy car," Billy chided.

"I came to get you for dinner. Come on, it's time to eat. Hurry now so you can find somewhere to sit while the food is still warm."

Billy quickly jumped up, "You don't have to ask twice."

But before he could take a step, Johnny grabbed his pant leg and excitedly said, "Look! Look! Get a load of this!"

Billy turned his attention back to the lane. And there was Schultz, his wife, and Frank McMillan going through the greeting ritual. All three had obviously been drinking all afternoon, as Schultz's wife was giddy and hanging all over McMillan. Billy could see her cleavage hanging out of her skimpy dress from where he was standing. This should make for a very interesting evening, Billy thought to himself.

Ramchuck showed little of the solicitousness he usually displayed around the rig when Schultz showed up. On his own turf he was obviously the lord of the manor.

"Who are they?" Mary inquired, and both Billy and Johnny filled her in on the way to the dinner line-up.

"Have you ever seen this much food before?" Billy exclaimed. Johnny just shook his head in amazement.

"What's this, " Johnny asked as he pointed at a huge bowl of what looked like dumplings.

"Those are called *pyrogies* and this is *holubtsi cabbage rolls,* and these buns are called *pyrizhky*," and then saucily went on , "and these are called carrots and these are potatoes and these are peas."

"Why are the potatoes all covered with grass?" Johnny asked with his face screwed up in a show of distaste.

"That's not grass silly, that's dill weed."

Billy filled his plate until it was overflowing and then he piled a large chunk of the roasted pig on top of it all. Never had he tasted food so good. He was well into his meal when he looked up to see Frank McMillan walking around passing out a bottle of whiskey to each table. McMillan stopped and chatted at every table and usually slapped one or two of the men at each table on the back. Billy watched McMillan work the crowd like a politician and guessed that he must have distributed at least two cases of whisky.

All the guests of honour were sitting up on the platform that Ramchuck had built for the wedding. Before the head table began to eat, the best man stepped forward bearing the traditional greeting of bread and salt. As soon as everyone had finished eating, the best man, who also acted as the master of ceremonies, stood up and began the introductions. He made a weak attempt at speaking Ukrainian and everyone starting laughing. Not sure whether they were laughing at him or with him, he switched to English. Ramchuck had a big smile.

Suddenly, with a flourish, the best man dismissed the head table and announced it was time to party. From out of the crowd came a man with an accordion, another with a violin, and another with a strange looking many-stringed instrument that he played across his knees. Billy had never seen an instrument like that before. They stepped up on the platform and began preparations to play. The violinist announced, "Ladies and gentlemen, the first dance of the evening will be, The Butterfly."

In a flash Mary leaped in front of Billy and Johnny saying, "Come on you two. Let's dance!" Billy groaned that he was too full to dance, but Mary would have none of it and dragged them both up on the dance floor. The music began with a furious pace and each took his turn spinning Mary around by locking arms with her and then releasing her to the other, who would in turn lock arms with her and then spin her around. When it was Johnny's turn to spin Mary, Billy shuffled his feet and clapped his hands in time to the music. Billy was out to give Mary a hard time. Every time Johnny released her to him, he would turn her in a circle as hard and fast as he could go. He was sure she'd beg for mercy and plead with them to slow down. But when the dance ended Mary was clapping and laughing, and it was Billy and Johnny who were begging to go sit down.

The music continued, with most of the tunes being polka and fox trot. Women danced with women, small kids danced with anyone or alone, and the floor was always full. Someone from the crowd had joined in with the small band and was playing a pair of spoons to the beat of the music. The band had just broken into an infrequent waltz when Billy felt a tug at his arm.

"Billy, you promised to dance with me," implored Bruce's missing-one-tooth daughter.

"Why it would be my pleasure," Billy responded with a gallant bow. "Do you know how to waltz?" Billy inquired as he led his small friend up on to the dance floor. She shook her head and Billy assured her that it was all right and told her to stand on his feet and hold on tight. As soon as Billy was confident she was't going to slip off, he made longer strides and exaggerated turns. When the dance ended his young friend raced off the floor and ran to her mother in delirious excitement.

Billy was surprised to see quiet shy Bruce lead his wife onto the dance floor. Although he seemed pained by the experience, he did a passable job on the polka. While they were dancing, their two kids had a great time crawling all over Billy and Johnny. Billy was distracted by his efforts to tease the two, when Johnny furtively shook him. Billy stopped playing with the kids and followed Johnny's gaze out onto the dance floor. Frank McMillan was dancing with Schultz's wife. She was wearing his big white Stetson and it seemed as though she was too drunk to dance, or maybe she just couldn't dance thought Billy. McMillan knew what he was doing on the dance floor and cut an impressive image with his expensive suit. Every time he made a tight turn with his heels kicking up, she would lean back, and Billy was sure Schultz's wife's breasts were going to pop out of her low-cut dress. Billy glanced around and saw that nearly every male in attendance was watching her too. Schultz seemed not to be paying any attention at all. At least that was the impression he gave. Billy was relieved at that, because he didn't want to see Schultz in some kind of a brawl at his driller's wedding dance.

Mary popped up again, out of nowhere, and tugged at Johnny's arm, dragging him up on to the dance floor. Johnny protested that he didn't know how to polka, but to no avail. Billy exclaimed that there was no such thing as a man who was half-Indian and half-French who couldn't polka. Billy watched with interest as Mary began the familiar one-one-two, polka step, with Johnny stumbling along looking at his feet. Then Mary stopped and explained the step to him. Johnny was trying hard and starting to get the hang of it, at least as long as he stood in one spot. But as soon as he launched out and tried to get some forward momentum going, his feet got all tangled up and they would have to stop and start all over again.

Ramchuck and his wife were up dancing and breezed by his stationary daughter and Johnny. Billy was astounded at this new phenomenon of Nick dancing. So used to seeing his driller standing motionless at the brake handle, hour after hour, he was flabbergasted to see him, not only dancing, but also dancing well. Nick danced the polka in short quick steps, which was in variance with all the other dancers on the floor who were dancing in big wide turns, but he was impressive nevertheless. His wife was still wearing her clean-up apron over her mother-of-the-bride dress and it was obvious that they had spent a lot of time perfecting their steps. Nick stood ramrod straight when he danced. The only body parts that moved were his short legs. It was quite a sight.

The music stopped and Mary delivered Johnny back toward where Bruce, his wife and kids, and Billy were sitting on the grass. The violin player said they were taking a short break and invited everyone to go over to the table set up as a bar to have a drink on the Ramchucks.

Mary told them that she had to go see how her baba was doing and it was then that Billy noticed the old lady sitting motionless on a chair by the fire. Someone had kept the fire on which they had roasted the pigs, burning. Some of the men were now throwing green leaves onto it, making a smudge to help keep the mosquitoes away. The old lady seemed impervious to both the heat and the smoke from the fire. Billy wandered over to the bar to get a drink so he could get a closer look at the old baba.

She had a shawl over her head and thick woollen stockings covered her legs. The only skin that Billy could see was her wrinkled wizened face and hands. As Mary knelt down beside her, Billy could see that the old woman's dark eyes still glowed and that she was taking everything in. In the background were the remains of the original log house that her husband had built many years before. Billy was awed at the thought of all the hardships the old gal must have gone through. Thousands of miles from home in a different land with strange customs and not being able speak the language. With only an axe and shovel they had built their home and cleared the land. Not knowing if the three acres that they had cleared in their first year would bear fruit, the fear of starvation must have always been on their minds. What a relief it must have been, Billy thought, when her first garden had flourished. That same year her husband had harvested 20 sacks of wheat with only a scythe and hand flail. Their roots had taken hold and Baba had gone on to give birth to two sons and two daughters in the little log house. What must she be thinking now? Billy wondered, as she expressionlessly watched over all that was going on before her.

Billy walked back to his group, stopping here and there to exchange greetings with total strangers. Trying to make conversation, Billy noted that the crops looked really good when he and Johnny had been driving around that afternoon. This comment produced an outpouring of lamentations from everyone present. One of the farmers said that the muskrats were building their houses larger than usual, which meant it was going to be an early and severe winter. He was sure all the crops would be snowed in before they were thrashed. Everyone murmured in agreement. One man thought that there would be an early frost. His pigs were acting up, a sure sign of an early frost. Another farmer noted that it wouldn't matter anyway.

There would be a grasshopper plague that would eat all the crops before they had a chance to freeze. All of the farmers nodded and chewed reflectively on the tender ends of the grass blades in their mouths.

Finally, the oldest in the group made the solemn pronouncement that, even if they were lucky enough to harvest their crops, the Anglik that ran the Grain Exchange would cheat them out of their money.

Billy felt a complete sense of well being. He was happy mixing with strangers who made him feel welcome. He especially enjoyed talking about agriculture, which was the main topic of conversation in this group. The only thing he thought to himself that could possibly have made him happier would to be to have Candace by his side

Sitting back down with his fellow roughnecks, Billy noticed the priest get up. He'd been sitting in a comfortable chair. A steady stream of people had stopped to chat with him, and as the evening wore on and it was obvious that they held him in high esteem. The priest took three unsteady side steps as he stood up, righted himself and regained his bearing and dignity. Johnny laughed out loud and said, to no one in particular, "Did you see that?" "Let's see if he's going to get another drink or join everyone pissing on the back side of the old house."

Billy pointed out to Johnny and Bruce that Schultz and McMillan seemed in a hurry to leave. Bruce responded that if he had as much money tied up in the well as McMillan, he would be anxious to see how the tests went too. "Do you have mineral rights on your farm?" Billy asked Bruce.

Bruce shook his head and replied, "No such luck."

"I guess that's why McMillan never came over and dropped off a bottle of whiskey for us."

"Does Ramchuck have mineral rights?" asked Johnny, joining in on the conversation. Johnny was beginning to slur his words a bit and he kept squinting his eyes, trying to stay focused.

Billy mimicked Johnny by repeating his last question and then he punctuated the whole scene with a hiccup. "Better have another drink partner," he added.

Bruce ignored Billy and answered Johnny's question by saying, "I would imagine so, unless somewhere along the line the rights were sold off to someone. But knowing Ramchuck, I doubt that would happen."

Bruce touched his wife's arm and tenderly said, "We better gather up the kids and shove off. It's getting late."

Johnny unsteadily got up on his feet and began punching his fists out in front of him, repeating, "Good people ... good people ... I love you guys." His new white shirt had a little of everything on it. His combed back pompadour now hung in his eyes and, as usual, he kept pushing it back with his hand.

Billy looked askew at Johnny and said to Bruce, "I think our Indian friend is getting a little maudlin." Bruce clasped Johnny's shoulder and announced that he would see them both at the rig in a couple of hours. He dug into his wallet, pulled out a five-dollar bill, and asked Billy to drop it into the hat when it was passed around. Billy took the money and gave Bruce a questioning look. Bruce explained that passing the hat was a Ukrainian custom and usually everyone present made generous donations to help the newlyweds make a start in life.

Billy thought about taking Johnny home when the music started again and everyone flocked back onto the dance floor. The first tune must have been an old familiar Ukrainian folk song as the dancers one by one stopped dancing and began to sing in Ukrainian. Soon everyone in the crowd was singing along. The song had a haunting melody and many who were singing had good voices. The mix between the male bases and the soprano voices of the women created a very moving experience. The song ended and was followed by another fast polka. The background of laughter and talking got louder and louder as the alcohol took hold.

A few minutes later, between two dances, Billy noticed that everyone on the dance floor had made a big circle and were all clapping their hands and calling out to someone in the crowd. After much persuasion, a middle-aged man stepped up onto the dance floor and gave a deep bow. The band obviously knew what to do as they immediately broke into a fast tempo. The man crossed his arms and danced in a quick circle from a squat position in front of all the clapping spectators, and then he began Cossack dancing in the centre of the circle. First he kicked his right leg out and then his left. On his third attempt he fell over backwards and lay on his back, and the crowd howled with laughter. The music started again and everyone resumed dancing, simply dodging around the fallen Cossack dancer, who seemed content to lie there on the floor.

The bride was occasionally coaxed out onto the dance floor, but she seemed far less comfortable dancing than her younger sister Mary. Her veil stayed on her head all night long. Billy thought that in 10 years, with a couple of kids, she would look just like her father.

One by one, some of the older people began gathering up their folding tables and chairs and making preparations to leave. The MC brought the music to a halt. He got everyone's attention by having the accordion player play a loud crescendo. "May I have everyone's attention please?" he loudly called out. "Let's have the newlyweds come up here."

The crowd all cheered and clapped as the newlyweds stepped up onto the platform. "Don't they make a fine looking couple?" he bellowed out, as he stood between them and put his arms around their shoulders. "Lets also give a big hand to the Ramchucks for their fine hospitality." The MC, now well on his way to becoming drunk himself, was much more at ease than he was during his after-dinner introductions. "Time has come for the *propee*, I'm going to ask for some of my friends to pass the hat rather than have you come up to the newlyweds. I hope you all feel generous tonight.

Billy and Johnny, taking their lead from Bruce, put five dollars in the hat as it came by. As the older couples left, younger ones came in to join the dancing.

Mary came towards Billy and Johnny and asked if they were enjoying themselves. While she was talking, they noticed an older man crawling on his hands and knees around and under a table. The three of them rushed over to give assistance and Mary called to the man, "Metro, can we help you?"

The man straightened up onto his knees and proclaimed that he had lost his hat. Mary was a little startled at this statement and said, "Metro, your hat is on your head."

The old fellow exclaimed, "Thank God, I thought that I had lost it."

Several dances and a few drinks later, Billy took Johnny by the arm and said it was time to get going if they were to be on time for the graveyard shift.

Chapter 17

"I'm Looking Over A Four Leaf Clover" was playing on the radio and Billy and Johnny joined in singing at the top of their lungs on the short ride back to the rig. Both of them changed straight from their suits into their coveralls and made their way up the steps to the doghouse.

Entering the doghouse, Billy was surprised to see the geologist and the engineer, as well as McMillan, Schultz, and Ramchuck in deep conversation. The engineer was explaining to McMillan that the day's tests showed that there wasn't enough oil to warrant bringing the well into production and that — since they had drilled through the production zone and into bedrock — he should abandon the well. Billy held his breath hoping that the group would ignore him and allow him to stay and listen.

McMillan rubbed his chin in deep thought. He finally spoke up and asked the geologist what he thought.

"I'm sorry, Frank," Dave replied, but I have to agree with him, it would be pointless to drill any further. This is still an unproven field, and it looks like we just drilled on the very edge of it."

McMillan went back to stroking his chin. Billy could only imagine what he was thinking, for one thing the money that he'd lost. Or did he have some other plan?

After a long silence, Schultz spoke up. "Ah'm not sayin` this to make more money for Tex Can Drilling, but ah know there's oil down there. Ah can feel it in my bones. Ah say we drill another hundred feet. If'n we'd hit salt water, then we'd be fucked like Hogan's goat, but I think the main formation is still down there a little deeper."

McMillan looked first at the engineer and then at the geologist with a piercing glare, trying to read their reaction to Schultz's bold statement. The engineer hesitated, and then shrugged and said, "It's your nickel."

McMillan ruefully replied, "The point is … I'm out of nickels. I've drained my company, mortgaged my house, and borrowed everything I could to drill this well. Men, I'm a ruined man!" After another long silence, McMillan straightened his shoulders and pronounced, "Alright … another hundred feet. Get to work."

Everyone filed out of the doghouse. Schultz, McMillan, and the engineer down the steps and Ramchuck and the crew out the other door onto the rig floor. Just as Billy was leaving, Dave pulled him aside and said, "I want a sample brought to me every 10 feet. If I'm asleep … wake me. Do you hear me?"

Schultz returned with a new 80-pound bit cradled in his arms, and instructed Ramchuck to use it. "It's the toughest bit made in all of Texas, and that means it's the toughest som-a-bitch made in the whole world."

Shoe took his usual ride to the monkey board on the elevators. By the time the pipe had been run into the hole, everyone was dead sober, a little hung over but sober.

It was five in the morning before the first 10 feet were drilled. Billy dutifully took a sample of the cuttings, washed it clean, and took it over to the trailer. Billy lightly knocked on the door and Dave opened it immediately. Billy handed him the sample bag and turned to leave. The geologist asked why the hurry. "I'm awake now, you may as well come in and have a cup of coffee." Billy glanced at the rig and guessed it would be awhile before they would have to add another single.

"Sure, I'd like that."

Dave asked how the wedding went and explained that he couldn't get away while they were testing. Billy quickly recounted the highlights and told Dave that he had seen Ramchuck in an entirely new light. Billy then asked how they could tell there wasn't enough oil to be profitable.

The geologist told him that they had swabbed the well and they could tell by the amount of oil that they brought to the surface that it wouldn't be worthwhile to case it and bring it into production.

Billy asked, "What do think of McMillan's statement that he'll go broke?"

Dave laughed and sat back with his coffee cup steaming in his hand. "Wouldn't be the first time. Actually Frank McMillan is quite a story. From the rumours I've heard around the oil patch, he was raised in Trail, British Columbia, and got a job in the smelters right out of high school. Somehow he ended up in Calgary. The story goes that he was drinking in a bar and struck up a conversation with an old Indian. For a few dollars, and probably several drinks, the Indian said he knew where the lost Lemon Mine was located. The old man told him that his grandfather knew the Indians that supposedly beat up and robbed the old miner, whose name was Lemon. He said his grandfather swore him to secrecy. He was never to tell anyone about the location because it would disturb his ancestors' spirits. I think the old Indian probably sold his story at least once a week to any stranger he met."

"Anyway, Frank rushed out and bought a saddle pony and a pack horse and went into the foothills southwest of Calgary looking for the two mountains the old Indian had mentioned. Apparently, if they were lined up just right, their peaks would form a perfect W. Legend has it that you then had to ride towards the W until you ran into a stream. When you reached the stream, you had to go upstream until you reached a waterfall, and there you would find Lemon's abandoned mine and the remains of the sluice box by the waterfall."

Billy, mesmerized by the story, blurted out, "What happened to Lemon?"

"You see, that's the beauty of the story. When Lemon was beaten and robbed by the Indians he was left for dead. The Indians took everything except the bags of useless yellow stones. Lemon eventually came around and made it back to civilization, but he'd lost his mind in the meantime and couldn't remember where his mine was. He spent the rest of his life insane. And everyone has been searching for the mine ever since."

"Do you believe the story?" Billy gasped.

"Of course not. I'm a geologist and there are no gold-bearing formations in that part of Alberta. Anyway, the time spent in the wilderness focused Frank and he decided to become a stockbroker and concentrate on mining ventures. Around this time oil was discovered in Turner Valley and Frank changed his focus to oil. Being a gambler and an entrepreneur, he formed his own public company and began buying up mineral rights to various properties. The very first well, I'm told, turned out to be dry and that's the first time he went broke. I'm sure there are others that I don't know about though. He quickly bounced back, formed a new company, promoted his stock, and this time he found a modest amount of oil."

"The thing about Frank McMillan is that he always bounces back and there is no promoter like him. I'm sure Frank was the one who pioneered the business of spying on other companies to get useful information. He haunted the beer parlours in the Turner Valley area, bought drinks for all the oil hands, and pumped them for information. And he'd sit out in his car with a pair of binoculars and observe everything that was going on while a well was being drilled"

"I'm sure this'll be a big blow to his ego, going broke in Leduc, but he'll bounce back and find a new batch of suckers for his next venture. He might not be riding his palomino horse with his fancy saddle, waiving his big white Stetson in the Calgary Stampede Parade next year, but I'll bet he'll be in the parade the year after."

There was a moment of silence and Billy was afraid that if he said anything, the spell might be broken.

After a sip of coffee, Dave gave a little snort and said, "Frank is a gambler alright. Another story I heard was that he was in a marathon poker game in Calgary's Chinatown. When he finally went home to his acreage in south Calgary, he had to tell his wife that he'd lost the house and all of their purebred palominos." The geologist then turned his attention to his microscope and examined the last batch of cutting Billy had brought him.

After a short pause Billy inquired, "See anything interesting?"

"Just more bedrock ... should look the same from here to China."

Billy looked out the trailer door towards the rig and announced that he best get going. He then told Dave that Ramchuck had brought some extra food from the dinner and had invited Dave over if he wanted something to eat. The geologist enthusiastically replied, "I'm wide awake now and I missed supper, so I'll join you."

In the change shack at the end of the shift, Ramchuck told Billy and Johnny to come for breakfast at his farm. Billy declined, saying that it was a short shift and they all had to be back to work at four that afternoon, besides he was a little tired. Ramchuck insisted, telling Billy that he had spent all Friday eating and drinking with his new in-laws — and he wasn't tired. Then he insulted them both for being pussycats.

Billy looked at Johnny, then shrugged and answered for both of them, "Why not?"

When they arrived back at Ramchuck's, it looked like the party had never stopped. People were milling around everywhere. Most were in some state of inebriation. The band had disappeared but breakfast was in full swing. Ramchuck poured them a drink and insisted they down it on the spot. Johnny reasoned that if they had just got off the day shift, a drink would be in order. So … nine o'clock in the morning, just after a night shift, should be no different.

Mary came bouncing over, still full of energy, and led them all to the firepit where a huge griddle now straddled the lingering fire. Everyone filled their plates with fried eggs, pyrogies, kubassa, toast, then picked up a beer to wash it all down. Billy and Johnny gravitated to the same spot they'd eaten the night before. Johnny blissfully stated, "I don't know what I'm eating. But it sure tastes good."

"What do you think, partner, should we go home and try to get a couple-hours-sleep?" Billy yawned. Both had just got up and were headed towards Billy's car when Mary caught up with them.

"Where do you think you two are going?"

Billy merely shrugged his shoulders. And Mary grabbed each by the arm and turned them around, saying it would be impolite not to stay for the present opening.

The bride and groom were now on the dance platform and a steady stream of wedding gifts were being delivered to them. Johnny brought over a couple of whiskeys and said it looked like they were'nt going to get any sleep after all. Billy wasn't interested in all the oohing and aahing and soon got into a debate with several of the farmers about the merits of Angus versus Hereford cattle. Four drinks and two hours later all the wrapping paper and presents were removed from the dance platform. Out of nowhere the band appeared and the dancing began anew. Billy noted that it was still only 11 a.m.

Johnny came back from dancing and proudly announced, "Guess what Billy! I think I've learned how to polka!" Drinking, laughing, and merriment continued and time flew by in the hot August afternoon sun. Plates of food were again put out and everyone grabbed a piece of something as they walked by the food table. Billy grabbed Johnny in a headlock and said, "Guess what Johnny! You're pissed again and it's time to go to work." Johnny protested that they had half-an-hour to spare, but Billy, still holding Johnny in a headlock, pulled him back to the car.

On the ride back to the rig, Johnny began his "good people ... good people" routine, taking little punches with his fists as he talked.

Billy was surprised to see that Shoe's car was already at the rig when they arrived. Shoe usually arrived with only minutes to spare. As they entered the shack, Shoe was changing into his work clothes and was in a foul mood. He was cursing out Ramchuck as usual, saying that this was the last time he was going to work under that dumb Ukrainian. "The dumb son-of-a-bitch can fuck up an anvil," he muttered as he kicked his locker door shut.

Johnny piped up and said, "You're just jealous because you weren't invited to the wedding."

Shoe whirled around and threatened Johnny with closed fists. "You got something to say to me?"

Billy sprang between them and with a flash of anger held out his hands, palms up, motioning with his fingers for Shoe to come on. "You want to go? Let's go!"

Shoe eyed Billy with his icy blue eyes for a moment, and then he suddenly smiled and said, "Relax … " as he reached out and rumpled Billy's hair.

Billy sat down and began examining his work boots. "Three months ago, these boots were nice and brown and had that new smell of leather. Now look at them, they're black, scuffed, and they stink of fuel oil." The tenseness of the last few moments quickly evaporated.

Bruce offered up a rare comment, "Too much booze and too little sleep."

Chapter 18

As soon as Billy had changed into his coveralls, he headed over to Dave's trailer to find out what had happened during the last eight hours. The geologist was gone and two sample bags with the drilling depths clearly marked on them were sitting on the doorstep. This puzzled Billy as Dave had told him to wake him in the middle of the night every time he brought a sample. Billy then went up to the doghouse and waited for the shift to change. He looked at the geolobox and noted with amazement that there had been 20 feet of hole dug in the last hour. According to his calculations, at the speed they were drilling when he left at eight that morning, it should have taken until eight that evening to reach this depth. Billy sat quietly in the doghouse waiting for Ramchuck to arrive. The other driller was very agitated, as he had already completed his book work. But he didn't say anything to Billy and Billy didn't say anything to him.

Eventually, Ramchuck clomped up the stairs to the doghouse and the other driller explained that McMillan had taken Schultz, his wife, the geologist, and the engineer to town for an appreciation dinner and during their absence he had punched through the bedrock and drilled 40 feet in the past hour. He explained he didn't know what should be done.He was told to only drill to 5,028 feet, and he was now there.

Ramchuck agreed with him. It was his understanding that they were only to drill a hundred feet more to a total depth of 5,028 feet and then they would abandon and cement in the well. Both men felt that the best option was to trip out because, at the very least, the bit had to be changed. They decided that the bosses would be back soon and if they wanted to change the plan, there would be little harm done. At the very least, Ramchuck could run the pipe back into the well.

Billy took that as a signal to prepare for tripping out, and he began his routine inspection of the tong lines. He looked at the tong dies to check if they were worn out and at the spinning chain to see if it was still in good shape. Any malfunction could cause serious injury or even death if there was a breakdown. Bruce, Billy, and Johnny had just broken off the Kelly and clamped the elevators around the first stem of pipe when Shoe showed up, 15 minutes late. He jumped up on the elevators as usual, ignoring personal safety measures in order to avoid climbing the 90 feet to the monkey board.

Ramchuck put the drive into low gear and the engines bellowed to life as he stepped on the throttle. This time Billy noticed a subtle difference. Usually, the whole derrick would groan and it seemed that every bolt and rivet would pop as the 17-ton pipe was lifted into the air. Billy had always felt that the crown would fall in on top of them under that weight.

This time the three Waukesha engines were not putting up as much of a protest as usual. Shoe and the pipe lifted up with ease. Shoe nimbly jumped off the elevators to the monkey board and tied his safety belt around his waist. Billy and Bruce put their shoulders to the bottom of the freed stand of pipe and steered it into position. Ramchuck carefully lowered the 90 feet of pipe onto the rig floor, Shoe released the handles on the elevators, and with his rope looped around the top of the pipe, pulled it in. This routine had become so familiar to Billy that he could do it with his eyes closed.

The second stand of pipe came up even easier than the first one. The third stand of pipe hardly made the motors work. The third joint of the fourth stand of pipe appeared and this was always the signal for the driller to brake the draw-works, let the floor men set the slips, and ease the pipe down onto the slips' vice grip.

This time the third joint continued on skywards. Ramchuck threw his whole weight on the brake handle thinking that the drum was still engaged. The drill stem began to fly out of the hole.

Bruce slapped Billy on the shoulder and yelled, "Run!" just as the drill stem crashed into the crown of the derrick. Bruce headed down the 45-degree pipe ramp at a full run and Billy, on pure instinct, followed right behind him. At the end of the pipe ramp Billy stumbled as his body was going faster than his feet. On all fours he looked back. Ramchuck was still leaning on the big handbrake. Johnny was frozen behind his tongs, his eyes imploring Billy to help. Quickly looking up, Billy could see Shoe dangling from his safety belt, face down, with his body bent in half. The four tons of blocks were falling to the floor as if in slow motion.

Bruce screamed his name and Billy scrambled to his feet and dashed to safety along the pipe ramp. Bruce and Johnny regrouped at the edge of the lease in front of Kostura's farmsite and watched as one mile of five-and-one-half-inch drill pipe soared skyward. The drill stem shot into the air 200 to 300 feet — and then collapsed and snapped under its own weight. Both Billy and Bruce watched in awe and horror as the shattered drill pipe fell on top of the rig and obliterated everything around it. Billy's, Bruce's, and Shoe's cars were crushed under the falling pipe.

The carnage quickly ended and the area around the rig looked like a giant pick-up-sticks game. A sudden gush of oil shot up through the crippled rig like a monstrous fountain. Billy watched for signs of life from his pals. First he looked up to the monkey board and then at the safety line that ran down from it to the stake in the ground. "Come on Shoe! You can do it!" he called to no-one. Billy assumed that Shoe had been stunned by whatever it was that knocked him off the monkey board, but he was sure Shoe would quickly recover and with his typical cat-like quickness, haul himself back onto the monkey board, jump onto the escape buggy, and slide to safety.

He turned his attention to the rig floor and prayed that Johnny and Ramchuck would appear out of the fountain of oil and walk to safety. Surely they would have ducked under the legs of the rig and survived the falling blocks. Billy didn't notice the car screeching to a halt just behind him with McMillan and the group excitedly exiting it.

Schultz ran towards the rig, stopped and began to walk back. Then he turned and started towards the rig again, obviously in a state of confusion. Finally, the reality of it all struck home and he began to bellow, "Get back! Get back! It's going to catch fire!"

McMillan, meanwhile, threw his Stetson in the air and with his arms outstretched and head tilted back, let out a loud — "Yahoo! I'm rich! I'm rich!"

Schultz came running up to Bruce and Billy and asked where the rest of the crew were. Billy couldn't answer. He just stared at the rig, and then started yelling at Bruce.

When Billy finally returned to his senses, he looked at Bruce and saw that his friend's face was strangely contorted. Bruce was catatonic. At first Billy thought Bruce was smiling, then he noticed that Bruce's body was shaking violently. He was obviously in bad shape. His right eye was closed and his mouth was screwed up in the corner, giving the appearance of a lopsided grin.

"They're still in there," Billy said evenly.

Schultz's wife overheard the comment and started shrieking, "There are people over there! Somebody help them!" She paced back and forth crying and imploring everyone to save the trapped men.

Billy was thinking, "Would someone shut this woman up!"

Schultz came back over to Billy and demanded to know why Ramchuck didn't pull the blowout-preventer lever when the blowout started. Billy looked at him with an incredulous stare. Schultz turned away to look at the rig again and then suddenly turned back and demanded to know why Billy hadn't thought to pull the lever. "You had time to run here. You had time to pull the lever!" he shouted accusingly.

"That's enough!" the geologist angrily interjected. If it's anybody's fault, it's ours for not being here."

Suddenly Schultz cupped his hand to his ear and said, "Listen. The motors are still running." Turning back to Billy again he asked, "Do you think you could go back and pull the BOP lever? Maybe we can get this thing under control yet."

Dave spoke up again and said to Schultz "I wouldn't advise it. There's a good chance that there's some hydrogen sulphide gas and three whiffs of that, and instead of saying kill you, he snapped his middle finger and thumb.. Besides, as you said, it could catch fire at any minute." Then he added for good measure — "Why don't you go yourself?"

Schultz's shoulders sagged and a look of helplessness overcame him. He turned again to Billy, his eyes beseeching help to save his beloved drilling rig. Billy, for the first time, saw him for what he was — a bully and a coward. Billy looked at Bruce, and then looked back at the crowd that was beginning to gather. Kostura, his wife, and their gaggle of bare-footed, wide-eyed kids were looking on. Cars were coming from everywhere.

Billy looked at Schultz again, and then stoically said — "I'll go.

As he started toward the rig, Schultz grabbed him by the arm and asked if he knew how to shut the motors down. Then Schultz said something that Billy never dreamed he would hear. Schultz said, "Thank you."

Billy walked in deliberate steps towards the maelstrom. The noise grew more deafening as he approached the rig. The oil that had been compressed over eons of time was gushing to the surface through an eight-inch hole. Shale from a mile below the ground sounded like machine gun bullets as it bounced off the rig structure. The violence and the noise were absolutely horrific.

For no apparent reason, Billy thought back to when he and his friends used to play a game of chicken by riding their bikes to a dry gulch that ran under the railway track outside of Nanton. They would stand in the gulch with the train tracks only three feet above their heads and wait for the four o'clock train to pass over them. They could hear the rails begin to pop while the train was still out of sight. The tension built when they heard the sound of the oncoming steam locomotive. As the sound grew, so did the terror of knowing the train was going to pass only three feet over their heads. The monstrous steam locomotive ground at the steel rails, its huge iron wheels creating a deafening sound as it came closer and closer. One by one all the kids began to panic and run away. The first time they played the game, Billy fled in terror with the rest of them when the train was still a hundred yards away. The second time, he made an oath to himself that he wouldn't run. It was only noise and noise couldn't kill you, he reasoned. The next time they played chicken, Billy stood firm while one by one the rest fled screaming. After the train passed over him, Billy nonchalantly walked out from under the small trestle. From that time on he commanded respect.

The flashback of that long-ago event steeled his nerves as he approached the curtain of oil that surrounded the rig. He knew that everyone was watching as he entered the curtain. The oil poured down over him. The stairs to the rig floor were, amazingly, still intact and Billy negotiated his way up the slippery incline to climb around the piles of twisted pipe and cable. Once on the rig floor, he could see better because the spewing fountain of oil had created an umbrella. The blocks had fallen on the draw works and nothing was recognizable. Where the BOP lever was supposed to be, there was nothing. He could see Ramchuck's body lying lifeless under a pile of cable and rubble.

Johnny was sitting under the derrick leg and he seemed uninjured. His head was tilted back and it looked like he was sleeping. Billy was sure that Johnny's eyes would pop open and he would exclaim, "Guess what Billy!" Billy knelt down and shook Johnny and his body tipped over onto the steel floor. It was then that Billy noticed Johnny's hard hat lying beside him. It had a large crease in it. Billy tried to look up to the monkey board but the oil burned his eyes and he couldn't see through the spray.

Billy left Johnny and climbed over and under the debris to the three faithful engines, which were still running. He turned off the main fuel line and one by one they went silent. But shutting those engines down hardly made any difference to the noise level.

Billy went back to his best friend's lifeless body and tossed him over his shoulder, fireman style. He began the slow retreat back into the assembled crowd. No one said anything as he gently deposited Johnny's body on the ground. To no one in particular, he resolutely announced, "I'm going back for Ramchuck."

Billy followed the same route back, at the same pace, only this time he stopped at the tool shed and picked up a pry bar. On the rig floor he methodically began to pry off the cable and pipe that pinned Nick's body. Out of the corner of his eye he noticed something that looked out of place from the rest of the rubble.

As Billy moved closer he realized that it was Shoe. His body lay crumpled on top of some twisted metal and his lifeless form resembled a large rag doll that someone had thrown out with the garbage. His safety harness was still intact, as was the rope that secured him to the monkey board. The force of the oil and the shale coming out of the hole must have cut the rope in mid-air.

Billy grabbed Shoe by his arms and dragged him to the top of the stairs. He then grabbed the piece of rope from Shoe's safety belt and let the lifeless body slide down the oil-slicked stairs. At the bottom of the stairs, Billy hoisted Shoe over his shoulders and walked through the curtain of stinking eye-burning oil towards the assembled crowd.

Billy dropped Shoe's body alongside Johnny. Stopping to catch his breath and rapidly blinking to clear his eyes, he surveyed the gathering crowd, hoping someone would help him extract Ramchuck's body.

Schultz ignored his gaze. He seemed occupied in consoling his wife, who was sobbing uncontrollably in his arms. Frank McMillan was now deathly quiet as the tragedy of the situation registered. The geologist and the engineer avoided his imploring gaze and looked at the ground. Kostura and his family were rooted to the same spot they were when Billy had brought Johnny's body out. Kostura's wife lifted her apron up and pressed it against her face as she shrunk from the unfolding spectacle.

Billy's shoulders slumped with the realization that he would have to go back alone to get Ramchuck. Again, he disappeared into the curtain of oil towards the rig. The oil on the ground was now almost ankle deep. Billy picked up the pry bar and began removing the debris from around Ramchuck's body. With a reserve of strength he didn't know he had, he cleared everything away. Then lifting Ramchuck onto his shoulders he summoned the remainder of his ebbing strength. He wasn't sure his legs would hold out under Ramchuck's weight. Billy staggered and stumbled as he carried Nick over the fallen pipe. As he slowly emerged from the fountain of spewing oil, Dave rushed forward to meet him and helped him carry the dead man the last hundred yards.

Covered in oil, exhausted, and in a state of shock, Billy sat down, put his head in his hands and cried. Johnny was dead. Shoe was dead. Nick was dead. Grief and exhaustion overwhelmed him. His shoulders shook as he sobbed.

Frank McMillan leaned down and whispered into his ear, "I'm not going to forget what you did today."

Someone was gently shaking his arm, and as he slowly looked up, Candace came into focus. She fell on her knees, in tears, beside him, "I heard in town and I knew this was your shift …" her voice trailed off and she buried her face in his oil-soaked clothing.

OILMAN PART 2

By ROBERT STUART MCLEAN

Chapter 1

Billy Cochrane dreamed he was drowning, and he could hear his mother calling him. He struggled desperately trying to reach the surface of the suffocating water. Just as he was out of breath he awoke to Ma Williams gently calling him. Billy bolted upright, panic running through him – maybe he'd overslept and missed his shift at the oil rig.

As his head cleared and he slowly came to full wakefulness, he began reliving the events of the previous day in his mind. He hadn't overslept; there simply was no rig to go to work on. His friends Johnny, Shoe and Ramchuck were all dead. He and his friend Bruce had been the only survivors. His mind took him back slowly and painfully though the memory of going back to retrieve the three bodies that lay under the debris after the rig blew in. As he shook off the sleep from his mind, he ran through all the events leading up to the blowout, trying to think what he and everyone else could possibly have done differently to have averted the explosive disaster.

The images came back of the past three days, the Ukrainian wedding, two days without sleep, all the drinking, then the drill stem blowing straight up out of the hole, breaking under its own weight and falling back down on the rig.

Gradually, he became aware of muted voices coming from Ma William's kitchen.

Billy pulled on his clothing and made his way to the kitchen. Sitting there with Ma was Frank McMillan and another man Billy didn't recognize. He'd had never seen Ma so distraught. Usually, he was so always cheerfully loud and boisterous and often whistled when she was cooking. Billy had always been amused by that; he'd never heard a woman whistle before.

"Hi, Billy," said Frank. "This is my friend.... You sure were lucky getting out of that rig blowout the way you did."

"I guess that's because Bruce yelled at me to run," said Billy dryly. "He just shouted at me to get the hell out of there, and we were both able to scramble to safety."

"Do you know who Shoe and Johnny Laboucan's next of kin were?" said Frank.

"Shoe talked to me about it this one time. He never knew either his mother or father, because he was raised in a series of foster homes," he said, scratching his head.

Ma handed him a cup of coffee.

"I don't even know what Shoe's real name was," he said. "I do know he grew up in Edmonton though."

Johnny, one the other hand, had a mother and a sometimes father in Grande Prairie, Billy said. He'd told him the cabin they lived in was 15 miles or so from town, and Johnny sent money home to his mother by mailing to General Delivery Grande Prairie.

"Well, would you mind picking up Johnny's belongings and mailing them to his Mom?" asked Frank.

Billy nodded. Frank pulled an envelope from his suit jacket and handed it to Billy.

"That's for all your troubles," he said.

Frank and the other man stood up to leave.

"I'll arrange for the funerals to be held in Leduc as soon as possible," he said.

Billy nodded again, realizing there probably was no alternative to the location.

For the next three days he went around in a fog. He gathered up Johnny's scant few belongings and the little money he found, and mailed them to Johnny's mother, explaining in a letter how Johnny had died. Then he went to visit Bruce in hospital where he'd been taken after he lapsed back into the shell shock he'd been plunged into in the war.

"I'm okay, Billy," he said. "I'm feeling better and should be able to make it to the funerals."

During their conversation, Billy asked Bruce if he thought he might return to the rigs. Bruce's answer surprised him.

"I'll probably make it for a few more years," he said a little wryly. "That quarter section just doesn't pay the bills," he continued.

With time on his hands away from the hospital and the rig, Billy tried to think out his future, but he couldn't focus and his thoughts kept on going back to his dead friends. And several times his mind wandered to Candace and her sitting by his side after the blowout.

Maybe I'll go and see her, he thought, but then he knew she'd already be or in the process of going to the U of A.

The funerals took place at the funeral home with just a small group of rig-workers in attendance. Billy looked around and noted Frank McMillan, Schultz the Tool Push, Schultz's wife, who was weeping copious floods of unstoppable tears, and Dave the geologist. The rest were mostly roughnecks Billy knew or at least recognized but wasn't interested in.

He noticed though that during the sermon the pastor talked as if he'd known both the men intimately. Billy doubted either one of them had ever attended a church, or that they'd even ever known a church minister at all. And when the pastor suggested the two young lads had gone to a happier place, Billy silently scoffed to himself, reflecting that Shoe would likely have been happier down at the beer-parlor, drinking beer, smoking cigarettes and joining in the BS-ing. During the whole service, Billy hung his head and played with his hands. Several times he stared into his huge palms and thought of the words from the old Gypsy palm-reader they'd seen at the Edmonton Exposition.

"You're going to live a long time, and become very rich," she told him reassuringly. "And you'll marry and raise three children, one of whom is going to be quite a problem."

But when she read Shoe's palm, she suddenly stopped short and said she couldn't continue. When the three of them pressed her asking was her problem, she blurted out that he, Shoe, didn't have long to live. Billy, silently in thought during the service, wondered now if there wasn't something in what the old Gypsy knew, given Shoe's sudden death not too long afterwards. The three of them had just stopped at the fortune tellers both on a lark, thinking only it would be worth a laugh.

The minister droned on and on, and Billy thought to himself that McMillan must have paid him well to keep going on for so long.

At the internment afterwards, Billy became slowly aware he'd become something of a celebrity, as many of the rig-hands came up to shake his hand and congratulate him on having the courage to go into a fountain of oil to retrieve his three dead friends single-handedly At any moment, the blowout could have erupted in flames, they kept on saying.

Billy walked over to Dave the geologist, whom he'd always liked and admired, and smilingly shook his hand.

"It sure was generous of McMillan to give me that big check," he said.

"I don't think it probably had anything to do with generosity," Dave said a little ruefully. "It's probably more to keep you on side in case there's ever a lawsuit."

Billy looked at Dave incredulously.

"How could that be when the whole blowout was nothing but an accident?" he said.

"Don't you think there might be something amiss when three people die, working on a job site?" Dave said.

"Are you suggesting McMillan's trying to buying me off?" Billy replied.

Dave opened his eyes wide and tilted his head.

"Frank McMillan doesn't do anything without an ulterior motive," he said.

"Well I hope he gave Bruce $1,000 too," he said. "He can use it."

The next day, Billy attended the funeral for Nick Ramchuck the driller. It was held in the same little Catholic Orthodox church Billy had gone to just a week before, to attend Ramchuck's daughter's wedding. What a difference a week makes, he mused somberly; one week ago there was a real hoot and a holler of a celebration - and now this. The same priest that performed the wedding now officiated the funeral.

In contrast to Shoe's and Johnny's, Nick's funeral had to be held outdoors to accommodate the large crowd. Nick had not only been closely connected to his Ukrainian community, he was very well known in the Leduc farming and business community. The hour-long funeral for Shoe and Johnny was nothing compared to the way Nick's farewell dragged on, lasting almost two hours. But even though much of the service was conducted in Ukrainian, Billy somehow felt the time pass quickly. The presence of the all male-Ukrainian choir, singing hymns in rich baritone voices, and all the colorful pageantry served as a welcome diversion and the time seemed to just fly by.

Driving away after the funeral lunch and after expressing his condolences to the family he'd just met less than a week ago, Billy found himself able to focus better on what he was going to do with his life. Right now, all he wanted to do was get away from Leduc and go home to see his parents.

Chapter 2

Nanton hadn't changed noticeably in the four months Billy had been away, but it felt like a strange place to him. Even though his parents were happy to see him and his mother's cooking was as good as ever, Billy felt a vague sense of unease and edginess. His old sense of humor and ability to take a teasing - and to give as good as he got - seemed to have faded and he kept finding himself slipping into an indefinable but undeniable feeling of melancholy. Even his old bed and the room he had spent so many years in seemed slightly strange and almost unfamiliar to him now.

To keep himself busy, Billy quickly found work helping neighbors with the harvest. All through September and into October he hauled grain, drove a combine, swathed, and generally helped out with every task given to him in bringing in the fall crop. And being busy helped distract him so that he wasn't constantly thinking of the deaths of his friends. The occasional early-morning duck hunt turned out to be his only recreation though.

Sitting in the barber chair at Dean's pool hall and barber shop one day, Billy saw he had now become a member of the pool hall establishment. He was too young - especially where everyone knew him - to go into the beer parlor for a drink, so Billy continued to content himself with hanging around the pool hall during what little leisure time he had away from the harvest.

Some weeks later he was sitting idly by and joining in laconically with the nearby conversation, when Pat Riley came in. Billy always derived great delight from listening to Pat's tall tales of never-ending adventures. So he was among Pat's avid audience for some tall yarn Pat started spinning about some cattle rustlers he'd caught 40 years before.

When he'd finished, Pat suddenly turned to him and asked if he'd like to work for the Rocking T on their annual cattle drive from the West 20 to the home ranch. Everyone knew the West 20 was named after the 20 square miles of lease land the Rocking T used for summer-pasturing their cattle. And for good measure Pat gave a kind of harrumph and said the pay was $5 a day, plus all the grub you could eat.

"I guess you're going to be the one doing all the cooking, eh, Pat," said Sol, one of the other guys sitting around listening to his yarn. "So pretty much everyone's going to have to be real lucky not to come down with food poisoning."

Everyone had a good laugh at that, but Pat didn't seem to see the humor. All of about five foot two in his stocking feet, Pat always tended to take himself and his outrageous stories pretty seriously.

To take the sting out of the moment, Billy said it sounded good to him.

"You got a horse for me?" he said.

"I imagine the Rocking T has a few extra horses around," Pat replied in mock indignation at the question even being asked. "Be at the Rocking T at five sharp Monday morning - and bring a good sleeping bag."

Billy arrived at the ranch promptly at 5 a.m., which turned out to be just in time for breakfast. Alice Newton, the sole owner of the Rocking T, was busy helping cook the food. Once again Billy thought how out of place this refined-looking woman appeared to be with all the cowhands around her. They were sure a hard-bitten looking crowd if ever he'd seen one.

There were just eight riders going on the drive, including Billy. Pat showed Billy his horse and quickly took his sleeping bag and tossed it into the back of a two-ton truck. Pat had rigged a large tarpaulin over the top of the truck's grain box, and he proudly pronounced the truck his chuck wagon.

He started shouting orders, but everyone already knew Alice had previously given instructions on how the drive would work, so they all knew what they were meant to be doing and they quickly went about their business without too much fussing from Pat. It was still dark when the group set out on the 30-mile ride to the West 20. Alice waved goodbye as they rode off, and Pat announced he'd catch up with them with lunch by noon, which was still a good six hours away.

It took them until fairly early in the afternoon before they reached the West 20, meeting with a man named John, who worked for the Rocking T and lived in a small cabin on the West 20 year-round. A man of few words, he seemed to enjoy his solitary lifestyle watching over the cows in the summer. Billy guessed he probably spent most of his winters fixing fences knocked down by cattle in summer and the snow in winter.

John led them down a rough trail for ten more miles and stopped by what he called a small "crick". Soon enough Pat came bumping down the trail in his chuck wagon, and came out barreling out of the truck hollering orders on where and how to tether the horses, to set up camp and help him unload. Billy didn't really care what Pat was yelling about – and nor did the others for that matter. Like them, he was only too happy to get down from his horse. Almost instantly, Pat fell to cooking supper and served up one of the best meals of steak and beans Billy said he'd had ever eaten. That brought a few smiles and the group sat around the fire that evening telling tales of "cow-punching" and herding. Pat launched into a long yarn about how one winter he'd been driving some cattle over the divide when a fierce blizzard blew up. The cattle wouldn't turn their faces into the wind, so to get them over the hill, he simply backed them over. Billy couldn't see in the dark if Pat had kept a straight face when he told the story, but one of the older hands asked Pat how he managed to dream up all his bullshit.

"It ain't bullshit," Pat responded in a tone of injured dignity

At that, the conversation changed and everyone took a turn telling where they were born. When it came to Pat, he proudly announced that his was born in Mannyberries in the North West Territories. Alberta wasn't even a province then.

"I heard tell there are rattlers around Mannyberries," said one of the younger hands.

This was all the opening Pat needed to launch into yet another yarn, this time about all the rattle snakes around there.

"When I was a kid, I'd have to pry rattlesnakes off the milk cows' bellies after they'd leaped up and got their fangs stuck in the cattle's hide," he assayed with a straight face.

"There you go again, Ryan, always bullshitting," said the older man.

"Are not," was all Pat said with his usual measure of offended dignity.

"Hey, Cochrane," said one of the older hands, quickly changing the topic again, "I hear you've got quite a story to tell yourself, working on an oil rig in Leduc."

The word had probably got round that this was one topic Billy always clammed up on when people would ask him, so nobody in the group knew much about the details of the blowout.

"Not really," said Billy quietly, hoping the subject would go away.

"Come on, Billy" one of the youngest cowboys persisted, "tell us about it."

Billy realized no-one was going to say anything else unless he broke the silence, so after a long pause to draw breath and gather up his courage, he started to tell them. He began by telling them about the rig crew of five men, the driller who ran all the controls, and the derrick man who had to stand on a platform 90 feet above the rig floor and had to stack all the pipes into fingers. And he told them about the grunt laborers, of which he had been one, who did all the heavy lifting. Then he went on to tell them that for two days prior to the blowout, they had all been at the driller's daughter's wedding.

"If you've ever been at a Ukrainian wedding, you know that you don't sleep for two days," he said, a little abashed at the memory. "Anyhow, we'd all gone straight from the wedding to work at eight in the morning. We figured we'd have to drill another 20 or 30 feet to go to total depth, and the well would then have to cemented in. That's because we all reckoned it was going to be a dry hole. So when we got there, everyone from the other crew was standing around, as they had already finished drilling to the TD.

"All the big brass had gone to town to eat breakfast and no-one really knew just what should be done. The other driller said he'd punched through the last 40 feet like they were going through Swiss cheese. So both the drillers thought our guy should trip out of the hole, because if nothing else, the drill-bit needed changing."

Billy explained how, when they pulled up the pipe, it would be broken off every 90 feet and stacked up against the derrick. They had broken off about the first four stands of pipe and were working on the fifth, and the routine was for the driller to lift the pipe so the slips would be set in such a way that the next joint would be about four feet above the drilling table.

But when his driller pushed on the brake handle so that the crew could set the slips, the pipe didn't stop, it just kept flying out of the hole all on its own, under the pressure of the oil.

"I just looked up as the pipe soared right through the crown of the derrick," said Billy. "I couldn't believe my eyes and what I was seeing, and I didn't really know what it meant. I was just standing there staring up at all this pipe flying up in the air. And then my co-worker yelled at me to run for my life."

Now he had started, the words just kept flowing.

"There is a pipe ramp that runs at about a 45-degree angle up to the rig floor, and I must have been doing about a hundred miles an hour by the time I hit the bottom – so I just went sprawling right on my face.

"All I could do was scramble to my feet and run like a bat out of hell. The drill pipe was snapping in two and falling all around like metal pick-up-sticks. Oil was gushing out all over the place. I guess, if it hadn't been for my friend and his World War Two reflexes, I wouldn't be here talking to you. I think he saved my life.

"I still don't know why the driller froze over the brake and never engaged the blowout-preventer. And I don't know why my pal Johnny didn't run as well. Poor old Shoe, the derrick man, never stood a chance."

Billy would have been content to leave the story at that, but everyone kept on at him and said they'd heard he'd gone back to the rig after all the pipe was blown out, and had single-handedly brought out the three bodies.

Billy was quiet for a while at that, before he finally admitted it was true.

"Weren't you scared?" the young kid asked.

"Yea, I was." Billy said quietly. "Looking back I think I was just about scared out of my wits, but I reckon I must have been in some kind of robotic state to go back and climb up on to the rig floor in that fountain of oil. If I really think about it now, that whole thing could easily have burst into flames at any time. All it would have needed was a spark."

"So why didn't your friend who escaped with you help you?" asked the older cowhand.

Billy took his time again in answering.

"That's the funny thing," he said slowly, staring down at the ground in puzzlement. "When we finally stopped running, I looked over at Bruce and he was just kind of standing there with the side of his face all screwed up. We were told later that he'd relapsed into the shell-shock he'd suffered during the war. They had to hospitalize him for a while."

Pat never asked a question during the whole retelling, and Billy guessed he'd always wanted to be the centre of attention whenever there was any story-telling going on. John, the ranch hand, never opened his mouth anyway, unless he was asked something, and then he always answered with as few words as possible. The young wrangler, whose name Billy couldn't remember, was fairly brimming over with questions he wanted to ask, had listened in fascination to Billy's story. He started to speak again, but before he could get his question out, Billy put up his hand and said, "Why don't we call it a night."

The crew quickly bedded down for the night in their sleeping bags, except Pat Ryan, who climbed up the little ladder he'd made and attached to the box of the truck, to reach the cot he'd brought along to sleep on. You sly old dog, Billy thought as he crawled into his sleeping bag.

Billy had rolled up his clothes to use as a pillow and as he lay on his back staring up, he felt as though he could reach up and touch the stars. Telling the rig story wasn't as hard as he'd thought it would be. In fact, he found himself feeling that it had somehow been quite cathartic. In minutes the snoring around him began to drown out the crackling and popping of the fire.

The image of the milk cow dangling rattlesnakes from her belly wandered across his mind and brought a small chuckle to his throat, just as he drifted off to sleep.

The next thing he knew it was 5:30 and Pat was already up and about, so Billy decided he might as well get up and give him a hand preparing breakfast. He stirred the fire back to life and then went to the nearby stream to get some water for coffee. He was surprised to see ice forming at the edges of the running water.

After breakfast, John the ranch hand spoke up for once and told everyone where he thought the cattle would most likely be. The crew packed their lunches from Pat in their saddle bags, paired up and headed in different directions. Billy rode with the kid, who admitted to being 15, which Billy thought was an odd pairing, since neither of them really knew what he was doing.

Riding out while it was still dark, Billy became acutely aware as the sun began to rise. At first, from his perch in the saddle, he could see it glinting on the mountain tops, and then he watched it make its way down the mountain-sides until everything was bathed in its bright light. Just before daybreak, a big bull elk ran out in front of them, his head laid back and trumpeting as he ran. Billy thought that probably the old bull hadn't even seen them, as he was more interested in finding his own cows.

"Must be rutting season," Billy remarked to his young friend. "Hunting season opens in another week and I reckon I'll come back and bag that old guy."

The two riders rode in the direction they'd been told, until they came to the boundary fence. Their job was simple: find the cows and their calves and herd them east. Some of the older cows seemed to know from experience what was happening and headed out on their own, while others, after a summer in the mountains, seemed to have turned wild and kept running and hiding in the trees. All day long the two riders scoured every valley and the groves of trees for wayward cattle, constantly coping with the frustration of trying to get the cattle heading in the right direction and having one or two double back and escape into the trees.

For four days the round-up continued and the growing herd was pushed down the main road to the home ranch. If they had missed any cattle, Billy figured, they'd just have to survive the winter as best they could on their own. He thought that maybe that's what John did during the lonely winter days out on the range, round up stray cattle and mend fences.

Billy found herding some two thousand head of cows, calves and bulls down the road easy compared to rounding up the small group he and the kid had had to gathered that had been scattered over twenty square miles. The only difference was the louder and growing cacophony of sound as the herd plodded along the road. Cows bellowed for their calves and the calves bellowed for their mothers. It was quite a sound. The cowboys were all constantly whistling and yelling at the slow-moving herd, and in the rear, Pat never stopped blowing the truck horn. Any oncoming car had to wait patiently as the herd parted and flowed round and past it.

Back at the main ranch, Billy waiting for his pay was surprised to see Pat waddle towards him on his bowed legs with the money. Pat made a show of looking around and then took Billy by the elbow and in a conspiritorial tone of voice, said, "I was talking to the boss and I think I might have convinced her to hire you on permanently. The pay is $50 a month, which is not all that great, but you get free room and board and who knowns, maybe in a few years time you will get your own bunk house and maybe even become ranch foreman someday, What do you think of that? Pat asked and his eyes grew wide as he gave Billy the great news.

Billy hesitated, wondering how he would give Pat his answer without offending him. "I don't know, Pat. I appreciate the offer, but

I've been thinking while riding, that I'm going to go back to the oil patch. I like working around machinery. I sure appreciate the offer though, and with those words, Billy got into his car and drove away.

Back in Nanton though, Billy quickly grew restless again. All his good friends moved on, and there weren't any local girls he fancied dating.

So at supper on the farm one night a few days later, Billy told his parents he was going back to Leduc to work the oil rigs again. He'd forgotten about the old bull elk. He'd be leaving in the morning.

Chapter 3

The first oil rig Billy stopped at when he got back to Leduc was General Petroleum Rig 4. The Tool Push and the Driller were both sitting in the doghouse when Billy walked in and asked about a job.

The Tool Push was a man Billy guessed to be somewhere in his 30s, who for some reason was wearing a tie that showed itself incongruously from under his coveralls.

"So, you got any experience?" demanded the Tool Push without displaying too much interest or introducing himself or asking Billy his name.

"Yep, got some," said Billy equally as briskly. "I worked over at Tex-Can Drilling coupla months ago."

"That Al Schultz's rig you worked on?" asked the Tool Push.

Billy just nodded.

Now the Tool Push took more interest.

"What's your name?" he asked.

"So you're the kid that retrieved the bodies from the blowout!" said the two men in unison when Billy told them his name.

Billy just nodded, but the Tool Push immediately thrust out his hand.

"I'm Art Hansen and I'm sure glad to meet you. This here is Joe McGraw. You ever worked a derrick?"

"Just one shift," Billy replied, "but I know I can handle the job. I'm not scared of heights."

"We're going to finish this hole and then the rig'll be moved to Swan Hills for the winter. You still interested?"

"Yep, I do," said Billy. "I'd look forward to the experience of working in camp job all winter."

Hansen held out his hand again and said: "You're hired. Be here tomorrow morning for the 8 o'clock shift."

When he left, Billy drove back to Ma William's boarding house. When Ma opened the door and saw who was standing there, she threw her arms around him and gave him a bear hug, something she was pretty good at doing, having built up the strength and bulk for it over the years. When she finally loosened her grip, Billy got his breath back to ask if he could have his old bed back.

Ma let out a loud chortle. "Anything for my Billy," she said without hesitation.

The next morning, the Tool Push was waiting for Billy. "I'll show you the ropes and tell you the rules. We have a two-strike ball game here. You get one warning, and the second strike you're fired. Smoking around the rig, showing up drunk, arriving late, not wearing your hard hat, riding the elevators up to the monkey board, or anything else that's just plain stupid and puts the crew at risk, and you're down the road right now. Capishe?"

Billy didn't know for sure exactly what "capishe" meant, but he thought he had a pretty good idea, so he just nodded again to as not to show his ignorance.

"I run this rig by the book, and there won't be any deaths or fuck-ups while I run this show," Hansen said. "Now let's climb up to that monkey board and I'll show you how I want things done."

Billy had only taken about three steps up the steel ladder, when Hansen yelled, "Hold it right there! Never grab the rungs when you're climbing. One of the rungs could give away and you'd go ass-over-teakettles and probably break your stupid neck. Always hold the rails on each side, so that you always have something to hold on to if anything goes wrong, a rung breaks under your foot, or whatever."

Billy climbed the next 90 feet with Hansen right behind him. Once out on the monkey board, Hansen told him in detail how to inspect the safety belt and set its length so Billy could reach out just the right distance to unlatch the elevators.

Hansen also told him that a derrick man had to be able to trust the belt, because it was the only thing supporting him as he pulled the pipes towards him while stacking them into the fingers.

"This here belt is the only thing between you and falling ten stories to your death," Hansen reiterated for emphasis.

Finally back down on the rig floor, Hansen told Billy how to mix mud in the mud tanks, so that it would have the right viscosity to carry all of the shale from the drilling to the surface. Billy listened intently to try to make sure he heard and understood all the instructions, and asked the occasional appropriate question to show he was not only interested but also paying attention.

"Okay," said Hansen when he'd reached the end of his lesson. "Now you go and meet the rest of the crew, and if you run into any problems, you just ask McGraw the driller. I'd rather you ask a dumb question and work safely than just barge right on ahead and make some kinda dumb and dangerous mistake.

Billy went over and introduced himself to the rest of the crew, a little amazed to find he was the youngest of them all. To his relief though, no-one seemed to harbor or show any resentment that he'd been promoted over them to derrick man. When he got a chance to talk to McGraw, he mused aloud that Hansen seemed a pretty thorough guy. "Yeah, he should be," said McGraw. "He used to be a major during the war. In fact, he still likes to be called Major rather than Art."

Billy took his responsibilities seriously and absorbed all that he could about every aspect of the oil-rig. In town, even among the tight-knit rigger fraternity, he could sense the deference that people somehow gave him, and when he looked in the shaving mirror one morning, it dawned on him that it was a man he saw looking back at him, not the scared kid he'd been ten months ago. And the nice difference he also noted was that now he could walk into the beer parlor for a drink without being challenged on his age.

And slowly, being back in Leduc, Billy found his thoughts turning time and again to Candace Crawford. Time was quickly passing, and he knew he'd soon leaving Leduc for the North.

Finally, he decided to screw up his courage and go over her house to see what was happening with her.

Candace's mother opened the door when he knocked.

"I don't know if you remember me?" Billy blurted out nervously.

Before he could hardly finish his sentence, Mrs. Crawford warmly said, "Of course I do, Billy. You came here to take Candace to the theatre."

The warm welcome restored some of Bill's confidence.

"So how is Candace and where is she now?" he choked out.

"Oh, she's fine," said Mrs. Crawford. "She's off attending the U of A and is hoping to become a music teacher someday."

"Well, do you think you could give me her address and phone number, so maybe I can send her a note or give her a call?" Billy managed to say.

Mrs. Crawford smiled sweetly.

"I think she's pretty busy with her studies right now and perhaps now's not a good time for you to call her," she said.

Billy returned to his car knowing he'd been rebuffed. Same old shit! He thought to himself: the town people like our money but they really do hate us roughnecks.

Chapter 4

Laying the rig down and moving it to Swan Hills was a new experience for Billy, and so was camp life. The camp consisted of a half-dozen rundown trailers that each provided sleeping quarters for four men, and there was a kitchen trailer, recreation trailer, wash-room unit, and another couple of dilapidated extra trailers for various other assorted purposes.

Winter struck hard with a vengeance that year, and by mid-November the thermometer regularly plunged to 20 or 30 below.

All the oil stoves in the different trailers seemed to leak, so there was a pervasive smell of fuel oil which stuck to everyone and their clothing all the time. Taking a shower didn't seem to help much, as the water was trucked in from the nearest slough and stunk like a muskrat. Billy decided he didn't dare drink the water or even the coffee because it tasted so bad. Instead he and everyone else drank fruit juices.

The cook turned out to be a miserable old alcoholic but no-one dared challenge any of his meals, for fear of not getting served. It had happened in the past. Amid the reek of oil, most of the food had a fuel-oil taste to it as well. Most of the time off from working was spent playing poker, reading or sleeping. There was little other entertainment to be had. Billy found he could hold his own in the poker games, but he swore one of the players was winning far too often for it all to be on the up-and-up. No-one could prove the man was cheating, but he was raking in more money playing poker than he was from working.

To relieve the boredom of the seemingly-interminable periods when he wasn't working, Bill started volunteering to do extra shifts.

He felt he might as well be making additional money as reading a book. He also became very adept at improvising repairs to odd and ends and different items, working from the toolbox and using surplus pipe and other bits and pieces he can across. He also taught himself how to weld and fit pipe, and pretty soon he was the go-to guy when an emergency came up.

Christmas was a bleak business up in the frozen camp. Not a single decoration was to be found anywhere in the camp, but Billy had started writing Christmas cards to all his family and friends when the thought struck him that he should write one to Candace. He just sent it to Candace Crawford, Leduc, Alberta, and hoped it would find its way to her there.

It was at this time that McGraw the Driller announced he'd had enough and was quitting and going home to his wife and family. The Major approached Billy and said, "Well, kid, you think you're ready to become a Driller?"

Billy was dumbstruck: it had never occurred to him that as a 19-year-old kid, he'd be promoted to Driller. He'd now be in total control of a crew of five men all older and with more seniority than he. Billy had always sensed though that Hansen liked him, and the promotion made him choke a little with pride and pleasure.

"I won't let you down," was all he could say.

Spring break-up was fast approaching and everyone was hurrying to finish their last hole so they could move the rig out while the ground was still frozen. Getting back to his trailer during those last days in camp, Billy found a letter addressed to him on his bunk. It was from Candace, and although it said little of any importance, Billy read it over and over again. Candace said she was glad to hear from him, and that she was fine. University would soon be over and she hoped she'd be able to find a summer job, maybe in Jasper.

The contents of the letter were sparse and brief, but that didn't matter to Billy. What did matter as that she'd written and it made Billy's spirits soar?

Chapter 5

The rig crew was eager to see civilization again. Winter was over and the rig was being moved to Ponoka, so everybody was being given five days off, their first break in five months. All the talk was about what they were going to do with all that time off. Most of the single guys planned to rent a hotel in Edmonton and drink all the beer they could possibly tuck away. It was going to be quite a riot, and the Park Hotel seemed to be the hotel of choice, so Billy decided he would book a room there as well.

When he was asked what he was going to do while he was in Edmonton, Billy replied, "I don't rightly know, but first, I'm going to spend a long, long time just soaking in a very, very hot bath. Then I'm going to buy me a new Ford car - you know the one, the one that's being advertised in the magazine I showed you. I sure like the sleek look of that new 1949 model."

When he awoke the first morning in Edmonton, he was suffering from a mild hang-over and sat on the edge of the bed for a while thinking about what he would do for the next three days. Somehow, sitting in the Park Hotel beer parlor just didn't appeal to him. Knowing the university was just a fairly short distance away, he decided to go and hang out there -maybe he might just run into Candace.

Over at the university, he asked a passing student where would be the best place to meet a friend who was studying there. The man pointed down the street and said most of the main education courses were taken at the Coutts building, and that was probably his best bet. Billy decided to stake out the entrance so he could watch the students come and go. He parked the car in a suitable strategic location beside the curb and leaned against it, his eyes half-closed as he enjoyed the warmth of the bright spring sun. Students sauntered back and forth in front of him on the street, paying him no attention. Then all of a sudden, Candace appeared as if out of nowhere, standing right in front of him like some kind of a mirage.

"Billy!" she exclaimed coming to an immediate stop in front of him, her arms clasping her workbooks.

Billy bolted in embarrassment to a kind of attention. He hadn't rehearsed anything to say to her in case he was fortunate enough to see her.

Flustered, he mumbled something about being in the neighborhood and "maybe you might like to have coffee with me?"

"Sure," she replied, "That's where I'm headed right now. Come on, the tuck shop is just down the street."

She confidently and somehow naturally took Billy by the arm, asking him questions on how he was doing, as they walked along.

In the coffee-shop, she quickly spotted the friends she had been planning to meet, and introduced Billy to them as they joined the group at the table. Billy sat quietly by, listening to the students grouse about their professors and their classes but not really trying to join in the alien conversation which drifted around him. Most of his attention was acutely focused on Candace's presence next to him, her arm against his as she took part in the friendly banter.

Then he recognized an approaching man as the one Candace had introduced him to during their one and only date, at the Leduc movie theatre.

Candace's friend stopped nonchalantly at the table.

"So how are all you little pedagogues doing?" he asked a little haughtily.

"Pull up a chair," said Candace blithely ignoring his superior attitude. "You remember Billy?"

Billy said nothing and her friend took no notice of her question, only looking across at Candace and another of her friends. He made a big production about removing his expensive skin-tight leather gloves, pulling at each finger one at a time and finally tossing them casually on the table. Next he removed his long expensive overcoat and carefully folded it over the back of his chair. The last clothing item he removed was a silk scarf.

"Christ!" Billy thought to himself, "I've never owned a scarf in my life...doesn't this guy know it's spring time?"

One of the other students continued his monologue about the philosophy course they all had to take. What did Rousseau, Descartes or Locke have to do with being a school teacher? He whined. And what's all this stuff about "though he may doubt - he cannot doubt he exists"? What's it all supposed to mean? He said.

Some of the others at the table were just nodding their heads in agreement.

"Well," said Candace's obviously-older friend in a patronizing tone, "the philosophers you mentioned had a lot to do with our modern day western thinking. If it hadn't been for them and all the other writers during the age of enlightenment, you'd probably all be teaching witchcraft, or the fine art of cannibalism or something by now.

"When Descartes wrote that if he had doubts about anything, then it should be possible to arrive at truth based on scientific knowledge.

"I'd say," He continued, "that philosophy is a subject matter that all educators should possess."

Billy had no idea what the heck they were taking about, and decided he didn't care. What he did know that "Mr. Big Shot" obviously enjoyed talking down to everyone at the table, including Candace. Billy could care less, he was in Candace's company and her body was squeezed next to his.

Leaving the café with him a little while afterwards, Candace said she'd walk him back to his car as that was the way she happened to be going anyway.

When they got there, Billy hesitated for a moment and then asked if maybe she'd like to take a drive.

"Alright," she said slightly aloofly, "I've never driven in a new 1949 Ford before. Where are we going to go?"

"I dun no," Billy admitted. "You're the expert on this place. You decide."

Candace directed him to turn off on Fort Saskatchewan Drive and Billy was suddenly stunned by the huge and opulent houses lining the road.

"Wow, look at these expensive homes!" he exclaimed.

Billy drove around Edmonton for a couple of hours and was pleased to find that the conversation between the two of them was non-stop, casual, pleasant and light. Candace seemed to know all about university life and the city, but wanted to know all about camp life, and said how proud Billy must be, becoming a Driller at such a young age. Billy in turn wanted to know all about her life at university life. The subject of the blowout never came up.

Finally Billy asked, "Can I take you out for supper?"

"Why not," she replied. "You're the man with the money around here."

Billy didn't know quite what to make of that after the encounter with the other clearly-wealthy man, so he suggested the MacDonald Hotel, reasoning that the best hotel in Edmonton must also have the best restaurant.

When they pulled into the hotel parking lot though, Candace protested she wasn't properly dressed.

"Nonsense," said Billy, with a sudden rush of blood to the head, "When I tell them I'm Billy Cochrane, they're just going to scurry to conduct us to the best table in the place."

Candace giggled at the audacity of that.

"Well, if they throw us out, we'll tell them that we have been thrown out of better places," she said reassuringly.

But they weren't thrown out and during supper, Billy began to wonder if he had perhaps made a bit of a mistake in picking that particular place. He'd never seen such an array of cutlery at his place setting, and he had no idea what it was all there for. He decided the best course of action would be simply to copy whatever Candace did, and that seemed to go quite well.

At the end of the meal, Billy thought he would press his luck.

"Seeing the night's still so young," he ventured a little more boldly, "maybe we should take in a movie?"

"That's very nice, Billy," said Candace, "and it was a very good supper. Thank you for that. But I have to get home and study for an exam I'm taking tomorrow."

For future reference, Billy paid close attention to the directions Candace gave him as he was driving her home.

When they stopped in front of the basement suite she and a room mate rented, Billy quickly got out of the car and rushed round to open her door for her. And of course, he thought, she can hardly refuse me permission to walk her to the door.

When they stopped in front of the closed door, Candace turned to him and thanked him again for the "wonderful afternoon and supper". The words were barely out of her mouth when Billy pulled her gently to him and kissed her. Somewhat to his surprise and very much to his pleasure, Candace immediately returned the kiss with equal vigor.

When their lips finally parted, Billy took her hands in his own two huge and calloused palms, and managed an invitation to another supper and movie the next day

"Yes" was all she said, before she reached up and gave Billy another quick and parting kiss, before turning to the door.

"I'll pick you up at five," said Billy as he turned to go back to the car.

Chapter 6

Back at the hotel, Billy joined the rest of the crew, who by then were all in various but mostly fairly significant states of intoxication. He ordered a beer and started to slowly sip it, only listening with about half an ear to all the male blathering going on around him. His mind and his heart were both racing at about 100 miles an hour as memories of his time with Candace filled his thoughts. The others were too distracted with their own banter and talk to notice and pay him much attention.

The next day seemed to take an eternity to come to an end, and Billy, never known for his clock-watching, kept on looking at his watch as the hands crept round and the hours crawled by.

Afterwards he decided to take a stroll down Whyte Avenue and buy some new clothes. Considering the food was so terrible in camp, he wondered how he'd managed to gain so much weight. All his old clothes barely fit him anymore. Once back in his hotel room with time still to fill, he looked through the paper to see what movies were on and at which theatre. He finally settled on two, one called Twelve O'clock High, starring Gregory Peck, or another called All the King's Men, starring Broderick Crawford, as ones he thought Candace might enjoy. He'd let her choose which.

Five o'clock did finally arrived and Billy eventually found himself knocking on Candace's door. He was glad he'd bought some new clothes, because Candace looked stunning in her stylish clothes.

"My, don't you look gorgeous!" he exclaimed, taking a step or two backwards to admire the entire effect.

H felt a new surge of confidence taking hold now that he was back with her.

In the car he asked her what she felt like eating and after some discussion they agreed on Chinese food. He then asked her if she'd seen either of the movies, naming them and telling her who the main star was in each one.

Candace said she hadn't seen either but added that she'd heard All the King's Men were a good picture. At least, she added a little teasingly, she thought she'd like one with an actor with the name Crawford. "Besides", she continued, "I'm tired of war and war stories. That seems to be about half of everything they put out at the moment." Billy was pleased as they drove off, that Candace moved close to him, not pressing up against him but definitely shifting so she wasn't sitting on the far side of the front seat either.

Supper took a little longer than expected, so they had to rush to get to the 7 o'clock show in time, arriving just as the lights went down. It was a good movie but Billy found that holding hands with Candace throughout was quite a distraction and certainly the best part for him.

Walking out of the theatre together, with her hand through his arm, Billy commented once again that the night was still young and wasn't there something else that they could do? He immediately felt like kicking himself because he'd used that line the night before, but Candace didn't hesitate.

"Why don't we go back to my place and I'll make you a cup of coffee," she said. "My roommate's gone home for the weekend, so we should have some privacy there."

Back at the suite, Billy perched n the rickety old couch and watched Candace as she prepared the coffee. It was going to be interesting to see what kind of a coffee-maker she was.

As she waited for the coffee to boil, she put a Frank Sinatra album on the record player, and then, when the coffee was ready brought it over and sat down beside him. He quickly pulled her unresistingly to him and they began to kiss with the same passion he'd detected the night before. That encouraged him after a few minutes of kissing, to slide his hand up under her pleated skirt. To his amazement, she made no effort to stop him. He was further stunned when she broke away for a moment, stood up, held out her hand, and said, "Let's go into the bedroom."

There they quickly stripped each other and made love all night long. Time after time Billy dozed off, only to awake and start over again. Her young and pliable body delighted him and he found he simply couldn't get enough of her and her kisses and caresses. In the morning the coffee from the night before was still sitting there cold and untouched and the record player was still spinning.

The quality of the light from the window caught Billy's attention, somehow triggering curiosity in him. He went to the window, parted the curtain and peeked out.

"I see we had a visitor last night," he said.

"Who?" said Candace as she came over to put her arms around him and have a look.

The visitor had been a fresh new blanket of sparkling spring snow.

Billy was pleased there was no sense of unease between them over what had happened during the night. By now, he was sure that this was the girl for him. He turned and put his arms around her.

"Let me buy you breakfast," he said gently

"You really are spoiling me," she said with only mock coyness, laughing with her eyes and smile.

Outside, Billy stopped as he was about to unlock his car

"Come with me," he said commandingly.

Taking her by the hand, he led her over to the park across the street. There he told her to put her hands on his hips and walk right behind him through the snow.

"What are you doing?" she demanded curiously.

"Never mind, just do as I ask."

In the fresh snow, Billy stepped out a huge square.

"This is going to be our new home," he announced. "Now let's step out the rooms.

Candace looked at him strangely, not quite sure what to make of what he was saying, but she quickly caught on and began shuffling her feet through the white blanket around her, as she paced out a giant room.

"And this is the ballroom at the end of the house and here is where the grand piano will be," she stated firmly.

Billy paced off a smaller room.

"This'll be my den," he said. "And we'll put in a fireplace and I'll mount the heads of all the African wildlife I shoot on a safari."

Candace went to the far corner of the rectangle and paced out another quite sizable room.

"This'll be the kitchen," she declared.

Billy joined her and made a smaller room just by the kitchen.

"This'll be the maid's quarters," he said with pretend dignity which he thought befitted a large and rich landowner.

Candace was about to step out another room when he suddenly hauled her down to the ground.

"And these will be the two snow angels that will live here," he said.

They both were giddy from laughter as they made the two snow angels side by side, the wings made by their arms touching at the tips.

Standing up, Candace brushed herself off and started to make a snow ball, chasing Billy back to the car.

"This is to wash your face with," she taunted as she launched her missile. It missed by a wide margin.

After breakfast at a nearby restaurant, Billy announced that all good things have an end and that he had to leave for Ponoka.

Candace wrinkled her face, obviously not at all pleased at the announcement.

"Oh," she said flatly."

"The rig's going to be there tomorrow," said Billy. "I'm going to be needed to help set it up. Besides, Ponoka's only an hour's drive from Edmonton. So when I work the graveyard shift, I can be here in the evenings, and when I work the day shift, I can be here in the evenings as well. It's just when I work the afternoon shift that I'm not going to be able to make it."

She looked down, nodded a little glumly and said, "Okay then. But you better stick to your word."

Chapter 7

On his way to Ponoka, Billy tried to work out with himself just exactly what it was that was attracting him so much to Candace. Was it love, lust or just plain ordinary old attraction?

She's not really a true beauty queen, he thought, but she sure is good-looking enough to turn some heads as she walks down a street. She's quite tall for a woman, but that has no bearing on anything at all. She's clearly intelligent and self-assured, like her mother, and she certainly does have a mind of her own. She definitely likes to have her own way and she won't put up with much nonsense from me. But she's sure got me going – I think I'm in love. I just can't wait to see her again.

The first thing Billy did was to find a place to stay in Ponoka at a boarding house, not unlike Ma Williams' boarding house in Leduc. The only thing he insisted on was that he had a private room all to himself. Then he drove out to the rig site, and was surprised to see a large crowd of people gathered to witness the spectacle of the rig-raising. Big trucks were arriving, each carrying a piece of the rig from Swan Hills. He soon located Art Hansen.

"We should be charging admission for this," he jested.

Confident that the move had gone smoothly, Billy gave everyone a wave and headed back to his car. He'd just covered a few steps when Hansen brought him up short.

"You not going to be in charge of raising the derrick?" he called.

Billy started to turn round, but Hansen just gave him a dismissive wave. He suddenly realized Hansen had far more confidence in him than he did in himself. It could be he mused for a moment, that Hansen's job as Tool Push probably had a lot more to do with him being a Major and in charge of men in the army, than his knowledge and actual experience on a drilling rig.

Raising the derrick from a horizontal position to an upright position, Billy knew, was a very tricky maneuver and not to be trusted to just anyone. Still, Billy was confident as he had done it many times last winter and he was proud Hansen had confidence in him. The derrick would be reassembled on the ground, and then it would be connected to the drill cable and pulled into an upright position by the rig's own power.

Billy knew how careful he had to be, applying just the right amount of power, so that at the last moment the derrick would smoothly come to rest nestled against the A-frame.

From there it was just a matter of bolting everything together and assembling all the out-buildings and other infrastructure.

It took only a day to have the rig up and running, and from then on it was just work as usual. For the rest of that April, Billy drove to Edmonton to see Candace just as often as he could, just as he'd said he would. Candace always protested that he was spoiling her with all the dinners, presents and flowers and other little things, and

Billy always answered that it was his pleasure after all that time "in the bush."

She teased him endlessly that if he didn't stop coming so often, she'd fail her courses and her mother would be mad at her, but each time Billy arrived, he could see how happy she was to see him. The sex was constant and endlessly creative. When her roommate was around, they would make love in the backseat of his car, or just about anywhere that afforded them a little privacy.

With each visit, they became more inventive and daring in their lovemaking, the risk of getting only enhancing their excitement.

Candace landed a summer job at the Jasper Park Lodge, and he intended to fully exploit every minute with her that he could before she left. He offered to drive her to Jasper, but she told him that her mother and father would be taking her - probably just to check everything out to protect their own innocent little daughter-child, not knowing what had been going on behind their backs. The two laughed at how ironical of this.

With Candace gone, Billy realized he didn't know quite what to do with the extra time on his hands, and he usually went go for a drink with the rest of the crew after work.

Hansen took him aside one day.

"I don't think it's a good idea for you to be drinking the rest of the lads in the crew," he said gently. "Officers don't drink with enlisted men. How do you expect to be able to drink with a man and then demand that he bust his ass for you? You have to set an example so he knows you're the boss at all times."

Hansen continued that the lives and safety of the rig would be jeopardized if he weren't able to fire a man who was continually fouling up, just because he's a drinking buddy.

Billy knew what he was saying made sense, but he also knew he could play pranks and roughhouse with his crew, and hopefully they'd still respect him. He wasn't about to become a martinet and have his men hate to work under him. Besides, he reckoned, although Ponoka wasn't as hostile to oil workers as Leduc had been, it was still hard to make local friends there. Most of the oil-patch workers found it wasn't worthwhile getting to know the locals or becoming involved in any organized sports or clubs, because they knew they'd be moving to the next town in the near future.

It wasn't too long after that that Hansen pulled Billy aside one day and asked him if he'd like to play a round of golf after work.

Billy gave him a quizzical look.

"Well, did you ever play golf?" Hansen asked.

"Nanton, where I grew up, had a golf course, and as kids some of us roamed round the golf course, but I wouldn't exactly call it golf," he said.

"Well, Ponoka's got a good little course. I'll meet you there at five."

Billy took that as an order and was there promptly at five. The little clubhouse rented him a set of clubs, and he and Hansen set out. "You ever played hockey?" Hansen asked as they walked out.

"Of course," said Billy, as if it was a silly question to ask.

"Then you should have no problem learning to play golf," said Hansen. "I'll give you a few pointers on how to swing the club and you should do fine."

Billy couldn't see how that would work since the two games were supposedly so different, but as the round progressed he made a few good shots and before long he knew he was solidly hooked. And his competitive nature made him want to be as good as Hansen obviously was. The next day he bought a set of clubs at the local hardware store, and after that he and Hansen and whoever else was around played nearly every chance they got that sunny June and July.

Billy phoned Candace every day at a pre-arranged time and they'd go over the day's events. Billy didn't truly care very much what Candace talked about; he just wanted to hear the lilting sound of her voice at the other end of the phone

The Ponoka Stampede was a big event in the community. Changing clothes in the change-shack after the night shift, a new hand who had been hired when the rig moved to Ponoka, asked whether the other guys were going to watch the parade or not.

"What time does it start?" Billy asked.

"10 o'clock," said the youngster.

"That sounds like it might be a novel thing to do," Billy said. The others agreed it seemed like it might be an idea, and they all agreed to meet downtown and watch the parade. When the time came, all five of them gathered on the steps of the Leland Hotel as a good vantage point for watching the parade as it made its way down the main street. There was the usual assortment of floats, bands, horses and clowns. The one participant that amused just about everybody most was a cowboy all dressed up and riding a buffalo.

"Here comes the combines!" announced Billy catching a glimpse of them out of the corner of his eye. Usually, he knew, the combine harvesters are a signal in most rural towns that the parade's about to come to an end.

"Well, if we're going to get a chair in the bar, we'd best move a move on," said one of the older members of the group.

"Trouble is," said the new kid, or Weevil as all new roughnecks were called, "the bartenders are all going to know me and that I'm underage. They're all going to kick me out."

"What we'll do," said the Derrick man, "is we'll go in first and get a table and put an extra chair with its back to the bar. You hang around for a bit outside while we order the beer and then you can slide on in and take the seat so the bartenders can't see your face."

The ruse succeeded for a while, but in the end one of the bartenders, waiting on another table, spotted the youngster and came over to him.

"McAffery, what the fuck are you doing in here?" he demanded gruffly. "How come you're not outside playing marbles with the other kids?"

"Ah, give the kid a break," Joe the Derrick man cut in. "He's just put in a hard shift on General Petroleum Rig 4."

The bartender's eyebrows raised a little and he seemed to be impressed someone so obviously so young was working on an oil rig.

"All right," he conceded roughly. "You just drink up and then get the hell outa here."

It turned out that that the bartender had perhaps only said it for show. Or maybe it was because of all the confusion of a packed bar.

But he never came back to the table again and left McAffery alone for the rest of the day. McAffery and the rest of the crew stayed and drank uninterrupted all afternoon long. Billy chuckled to himself under his breath: he himself was only 19.

After a time though, Billy excused himself.

"I reckon it's time to get some supper and some shuteye. Twelve o'clock will soon be here," he added, hoping the others would follow his lead. Maybe we'll take in the stampede itself tomorrow," he said, standing up to leave.

When Billy arrived at the boarding house, he was told there had been a phone call for him to return. Billy looked at the number and immediately recognized it as Candace's.

Her voice seemed to be very small and near breaking when she came on the line.

"Hi, Billy," was all she said.

"What's wrong?" Billy asked, alarmed.

"I'm in a predicament," she said, sounding on the edge of tears.

"What happened? Did they fire you?"

"No, no...nothing like that." There was a long pause, and then she added worriedly, "Billy, I'm pregnant."

It was Billy's turn to take a deep breath and long pause.

"You sure?" he said finally, trying to keep his voice as level as possible.

"Yes, I'm sure," she replied with what sounded to him like a tiny edge of impatience.

There was another awkward pause before Candace, close to breaking down, whispered, "Billy, what are we going to do?"

"What are we going to do?" Billy repeated, slowly beginning to gather his wits.

"What are we going to do? – I'll tell you what we're going to do," he continued. "We're going to get married! That's *if* you love me. *Do* you love me, Candace?"

He'd never asked her before and she had never said it in as many words. Nor had he.

"You know I do, Billy. Do you love me?"

"You know I do," he said firmly.

"I don't know what my parents are going to say."

"I don't care what they say," he said. "The important thing is that we love each other and we're going to get married. I have a couple days off next weekend and I'll drive over there and bring you home. We'll tell your parents together then - and let the chips can fall where they may."

Twelve o'clock came and went and Billy was becoming more and more alarmed as his crew showed up late for work. So he was relieved when at last he heard the hurried clattering of footsteps running up the steel steps to the rig's dog-house. He put on his best stern face as the steel door was thrown open. He was about to give them all a good strict lecture, when Billy stopped.

"What in hell happened to you guys?" he said, looking into their faces.

The Derrick man spoke up first.

"Young McAffery here was trying to chase a fart through a keg of nails and we thought we would help him," he said, trying to make a joke out of the situation.

Both of McAffery's eyes were already starting to swell shut, and his nose looked like it was probably broken. The other three members of the foursome were all a little cut and bruised and the worse for wear as well.

"Well, it sure as hell doesn't look to me like you've all come straight from the bar," he said. "So what really happened?"

The Derrick man spoke up again.

"We all went to the rodeo dance," he admitted, "and genius here," he said, pointing at McAffery, "decided he was going to hustle some cowboy's girlfriend - not some roper cowboy, not some little bull rider, no, no, no. He had to pick on a bull-dogger's gal, didn't he, and we had to fight a rearguard action just to be able to get him out of the hall still in one piece."

Billy shook his head, knowing full well he'd been through similar scrapes. And here they all were just as he'd been, still drunk from the night escapades. He'd been warned about that.

He turned to his record-keeping.

"Get the hell to work," he snarled as best he could, knowing that further words were useless at that point.

That night he thought back over his own previous experiences to dream up every busy, nasty and dirty work-task he could think of - and a few more besides - for his crew, as punishment for their behavior.

Only towards the end of the shift did he begin to take a little pity on them. He knew the rig's drill bit needed changing, but instead he eased up on the speed he was drilling for the last half hour and so postponed having to trip the pipe out of the hole. He knew that was a risky thing to do, as one or even all the cones might wear out and fall off the bit, and that would mean big trouble for everyone. He'd have a hard time explaining that to Hansen, who already warned him about being compromised by friends.

But all went well and Billy waved a noticeably less than cheery hand to the crew as the end of the shift finally arrived and them all started departing.

"I'll see all your sorry asses here again tonight," he said bitingly. "Although, McAffery, I doubt you'll be able to see me very well at all."

McAffery's eyes were almost completely closed and Billy was surprised he could see out of them at all.

The following week passed in a blur for Billy. Question after question formed in his mind. Self-doubts came and went as he struggled to dispel them. He knew Candace's father would be strongly opposed to the marriage, and he prepared himself to have to stand up to the older man. He reasoned to himself that he'd be 20 next month and that should be plenty mature enough to enter into marriage. Financially, he knew he was already earning much more than the average Albertan.

Edmonton was still dark when Billy drove through it and it wasn't until the tedious drive to Jasper that he again assessed his predicament. What would happen if he just ignored the whole issue? What if the baby wasn't his? Was there any other way out of it all other than marriage? Was there anyone he knew who could give him advice? Question after question would well up in his mind as he drove.

He thought back to a discussion a group of his friends had around the back table in the pool hall a few years back. Corky McClusky was holding court, as he usually did, with the rest of the kids hanging on to every word he said. Corkey played junior hockey for the Regina Pats and was everyone's hero, including Billy. Corkey was forever recounting his sexual escapades in Regina where young girls threw themselves at the hockey players. This time, Corkey was boasting that he won a bet with another Nanton friend as to who could bang Lucy, the "Nanton town pump," as Corkey called her, in the shortest time. Corkey said that it took him only two blocks after getting her into his car while his friend drove to seal the deal. The crowd around Corkey all laughed a knowing laugh as did Billy. Although four years junior to Corkey, Billy laughed along mimicking the older teens.

Someone, Billy couldn't remember who, asked if Corkey wasn't worried about getting some girl knocked-up. Billy remembered Corkey dismissively waiving off the question by saying that girls knew how to take care of themselves. Again all the older guys nodded their heads in agreement.

Frenchy Smith spoke up and said, "not me, I always carry protection" and patted his back pocket. Frenchy got his nickname, "Frenchy", because he carried a French Safe in his wallet. The circular outline of the French Safe showed through both his wallet and the back pocket of his blur jeans.

"Smith, Corkey replied, the only time that French Safe that you always carry around with you will ever get used is when you show it to the kids on your school bus," to a large round of laughter.

"I don't care, French shot back defensively, it's better to be safe than sorry."

The original questioner pressed on asking Corkey what he would do if he ever got a girl pregnant. Corkey got serious for a moment and told the gathering that he had a friend than knew a Pharmacist and he could get a pill that would solve everything.

As Billy continued his drive, he thought back to that long ago conversation and wondered if there was such a pill. It took years for Billy to realize that Corkey was usually full of shit. Corkey used to tell everyone the local Hutterite colony would pay a man to come and knock up their women so they could bring new blood into their ranks. When Billy was older he challenged Corkey as to how he knew this. Billy asked Corkey if he had ever been paid and when pressed, Corkey admitted that he hadn't, but he had a friend who was paid and when Billy pressed on, demanding to know the name of "this friend," Corkey finally admitted that it was actually a friend of his friend that had been paid.

Still, Billy believed that in some mysterious way, woman knew how to keep from getting pregnant. If this were so, he pondered, how did Candace let herself get pregnant?

Billy gripped the steering wheel tighter and told himself to put all those thoughts out of his mind. He then thought of his parents. He should have told them and alerted them as to his intentions. Billy knew that marriage was the only option that his mother would consider. Anytime a couple's name that lived on the edge of town came up in conversation, Billy's mother would always derisively dismiss them as the two who were "shacked-up." Billy knew that the only support he would get from his father would be, "if you are man enough to get yourself into this situation, then you have to be man enough to get yourself out."

Arriving at the Jasper Park Lodge that weekend, he went to the staff quarters, waiting outside for Candace to spot him and come out.

When she did, Billy instinctively knew he was doing the right thing. He held out his hand and stated, "Mrs. Cochrane I presume."

Then he swept her up in his arms, kissed her and soothed, "its okay, every thing's going to be okay."

Candace's faced quickly brightened and they began to chat and make plans as they made their way back to Leduc.

By the time they stopped in front of Candace's parents' house though, their fears and nervousness had returned and they both looked at each other and the close front door in trepidation.

"Well, we're just going to have to face the music at some time," said Billy. "Let's get on with it, shall we." But he followed behind Candace, carrying her luggage, as she opened the door.

Suddenly Candace's mother was there, rushing towards her, sensing instinctively without knowing exactly what, that something was amiss.

"What are you doing here?" she said warily. "We'd planned on coming and getting you next week."

"There's been a change of plans, Mrs. Crawford," Billy said, stepping in. "Is Mr. Crawford home?"

Mrs. Crawford, now fully alarmed, turned and ran up stairs to get her husband. There was a brief pause as a few words could be heard coming indistinctly from above, and then the two came down slowly and apprehensively together.

"So just exactly what's the meaning of all this?" he demanded.

"Let's go on through to the living room, Mom, Dad," said Candace, who by now had regained a little of her composure.

She got them seated and then announced in as many words that she and Billy were going to get married.

Both the Crawfords looked thunderstruck, not knowing what to say. Then Mr. Crawford regained his voice.

"This is preposterous!" he roared. "No daughter of mine is going to run off to join some oil-rig circus, moving from town to town like a bunch of gypsies!"

The veins in his neck and temples bulged as he fought to control his rage.

"Daddy," said Candace as easily as she could, to try to calm him down, "I think you should know - I'm pregnant."

As she said this, Billy put his arm around her waist, wanting to give a support for her and, in some small way, make a statement that she belonged to him now.

Mrs. Crawford made what almost sounded like a whimpering or choking noise as she leaped up to hug her daughter. Both sobbed in each other's arms for a few moments, while Billy stood there silently watching and looking at his future father-in-law for what seemed an eternity.

Mr. Crawford kept clenching his jaw as he tried to think of what next to say and to form the words. Finally the throbbing pulse in his neck and temple began to recede, and he spoke again.

"Well then, I guess that's settled," he ground out angrily. "Maybe we should have a drink before supper."

As the meal progressed, the conversation eased a little and turned more positive, as it sank in more and more with Mr. Crawford that there really was no alternative but marriage for the two parents-to-be.

But Mr. Crawford wasn't through yet.

"I think the marriage should take place as soon as possible to avoid, awkward questions," he said, fighting the boiling fury inside. "A church wedding is out of the question, so I suggest we go to a Justice of the Peace in Edmonton and get it all out of the way as quickly as possible."

You sly son-of-a bitch, Billy thought. You've had to agree to the marriage and now you're making Candace feel as embarrassed and belittled as possible, just out of a sense of revenge for having had your say taken away from you. Some how, some day, some where, I'm going to throw this right back in your face.

"So," Mr. Crawford said, gathering steam again with added venom and turning to Billy, "just exactly how do you plan to spend the rest of your and my daughter's life? - living and working in the oil patch?"

Billy paused for a few seconds to make sure he could speak without losing his temper.

"My thoughts," he replied, "are that I will work there for a couple more years, and by then I'll have saved enough to buy a farm. There's a neighbor of ours in Nanton that I think will be ready to sell in a couple of years. Between his farm and my father's, I should be able to do okay."

He wanted to say that maybe he could get a chicken-shit job at a chicken-shit bank in some chicken-shit town like this, so he could strut about and act like some kind of chicken-shit big shot, but he bit his tongue.

"And I suppose you will be able to afford a piano for my daughter as well?" Mr. Crawford continued sarcastically.

Candace put out her hand on to her father's arm in a gentle and soothing gesture.

"Daddy...please!" she said.

Mr. Crawford had little else to say after that, and the marriage went off without a hitch. Billy got other drillers to cover for him for three days for his honeymoon. His parents drove up from Nanton for the wedding and even a few of his old chums from there showed up. Only a few of Candace's closest friends were invited, and at Mr. Crawford's insistence, she wasn't allowed to wear a formal wedding dress.

Mr. Crawford also made darned sure everyone knew he was the one who picked up the tab for the small reception after the brief civil ceremony.

Chapter 8

Billy was only too happy to have the wedding behind him so he and Candace could get on with their lives. Their first major purchase was a 40-foot-long trailer which turned out to be their home for the next four years. And during that time Candace made it a point never to complain when it came time yet again to secure all their belongings inside the unit, and once more move on to their next destination. They criss-crossed most of Alberta and a lot of Saskatchewan during those years. Billy's seniority as a company employee and his standing with the firm meant that he could usually avoid camp jobs in the winter, but there was still a lot of moving to be done.

Two new additions arrived in those four years. Crawford Cochrane was born the day after New Year's Day, 1950, and Crawford was joined in the family by Jet, a black Labrador puppy, on Crawford's birthday the next year.

The family's small home was always an active place, with friends constantly coming and going, an intensively active little son and boisterous dog. It was constant bedlam. But somehow, amidst it all, the Cochranes' bank account kept on growing. For some reason though, Billy kept postponing any thoughts of buying a farm. Occasionally Candace would prod him gently on the subject and he'd just dismiss her lightly with: "Maybe next year."

Holidays were only honored if there was a delay in moving the rig, or on the odd occasion the rig was laid up for repairs between moves. The young couple sometimes seized those opportunities to travel to Las Vegas or, on one occasion, to Hawaii. On Crawford's second birthday, Billy built him a skating rink in their trailer park and gave him some skates to practice with. The rink was a big hit with all the children in the park, and Crawford in particular was always demanding to be taken skating. Billy marveled how quickly he learned to turn in either direction.

The year 1953 was a momentous one for Billy: Art Hansen suddenly said one day that he was quitting the rigs and he'd bought a Dodge dealership in Calgary to replace them. Billy was a little taken aback at the announcement but not entirely surprised: there always was a constant turn over of personnel on the rigs. But he was genuinely stunned when the Major said he'd been authorized by General Petroleum to offer Billy his job as Tool Pusher.

As Billy stammered and stumbled for words, Hansen just slapped him hard on the back and said: "Congratulations, Billy - you're now one of the youngest Tool Pushes in the Alberta oil patch!"

Billy could only reflect that he was still only 23.

Alone with Candace later that night, the couple went over their options. Billy felt it was high time they bought a proper, permanent home, as Crawford would soon be starting school.

Candace was adverse to the idea but wondered aloud where it should be. And then she added in a completely different voice, "Billy, I think I'm pregnant again."

Candace's prognostication was confirmed shortly afterwards, and the revelation further galvanized the twosome into considering the idea of a less mobile home more deeply. They discussed the possibilities and Billy ruled out Leduc and Nanton, as he didn't want any in-laws interfering in their lives. Candace said in response though that she didn't want to raise any child in either of the two biggest nearby cities, Calgary or Edmonton.

That led to a compromise to something more central so Billy could commute home as often as possible. They finally agreed Red Deer was a nice little city and that's where they'd buy a house.

"I'll be making nearly $2,000 a month," said Billy, "and that should qualify us for a pretty good mortgage. I'd like to see any other 23-year-old - or 'most anyone else for that matter - making more than me at that age. It's probably four times what a policeman makes!"

Candace told him if his head got any bigger he probably would be able to put his hard-hat on.

But the conversation took on a more serious tone as the realization set in that Candace would likely be carrying most of the main task of raising their children.

"Well, the move isn't for ever," Billy reassured her. "I'll maybe change careers in the not too distant future so we can be together more."

He took a long pause and then added apologetically: "I'm sorry; I've just decided I don't want to be a farmer after all. Just think - with the new job I never have to get dirty again! I can just sit in my trailer, giving orders and watching all the rest of them getting all covered in grease. Oh, and the job comes with a free truck to use."

Billy took her in his arms and he could feel the tension in her ebb away as she began to relax and accept his decision.

Chapter 9

Back on the job, Billy just couldn't sit quietly by in the little trailer, which he now kept parked right on the rig site. He was never quite sure he could trust anyone to do the difficult tasks, and was always visiting the rig floor. He made sure he was the one to lay the rig down when moving or raise it up when they arrived at a new site. He was constantly giving directions and instructions and forever "helping out" when he thought help was needed.

One day he received an urgent call that the hole had caved in and the pipe had stuck. Billy rushed over and immediately took over the controls. The pipe wouldn't budge when he tried to lift it though. The large mud pumps were unable to regain the circulation they needed when they hooked up the Kelly. Several times he strained the engines until they nearly stalled, and still the pipe wouldn't budge. He stopped to try to think the situation through for a moment. Abandoning the hole and the entire drill pipe still down in it was unthinkable. The prospect of losing close to $100,000 worth of drill stem and drilling time wasn't an option he even wanted to consider.

All the crew was gathered around him wondering what he was going to do.

Billy continued to stroke his chin, looking up at the crown of the derrick and then down at the four feet of drill stem sticking above the rig floor.

"Okay," he finally said. "I want everyone to go stand out on the road."

After they had gone, he lowered the elevators down the four-foot length of pipe until they touched the floor. He then gunned the motors to the floor, released the clutch and slammed the machinery into gear to send the elevators upward into the pipe joint. Each time he repeated the action, the whole rig shuddered and shook and groaned under the strain.

From the road, the crew looked on in amazement and apprehension, sure that the crown of the rig was going to collapse. The process was like operating a pile driver in reverse.

Little by little though, he felt he was making progress. Each time he reefed hard on the pipe, he gained about a foot, and every time he reefed he'd check to see if the rig was going to collapse. If it did, he reckoned his only chance would be to dive under the A-frame.

On about the 20th attempt, just as the engines were starting to stall, the drill stem broke free, the engines seemed to catch their second wind and the pipe began to lift from the hole.

Seeing all was well, the crew raced back to the rig floor.

"B-b-boy, Billy," said the Driller, who had a slight stutter anyway, "By G-G-God, every time you r-r-reeeeefed on her, the wh-wh-whole rig squatted like a d-d-dog taking a p-piss!"

It wasn't until they had run back into the hole with a new bit that they discovered Billy had stretched the whole drill stem by 15 feet.

After they moved to Red Deer, Billy tried to live up to his promise to Candace that he'd commute from home to work if the rig was within a 100-mile radius. If the rig was outside that, he said he'd do his best to squeeze in a day or two a week for them to be together. He knew he had to delegate more authority to his drillers, but every time there was some kind of a problem or an incident arose, he also knew he couldn't quite trust anyone but himself to sort it out. He liked to pop up unannounced at any time of day or night, just to keep everyone on their toes. He also wanted to be sure that his routine didn't become predictable, especially when petty theft continued as a constant problem, with wrenches and other tools going missing. It seemed that no matter whose land they were on, the farmer seemed to feel the bags of cement were public property for him to take. The theft of cement and diesel fuel never bothered Billy too much, but he took it very personally when his own workers stole tools from the tool room. To try to forestall the thefts of cement, Billy always took it on himself to give a few bags to the land owner as a gesture of good will. And often the farmer's phone was his only means of communication, so he liked to maintain a good relationship with the farmer and his wife and enjoyed talking about agriculture and exchanging local gossip with them.

The family's black Lab pet, Jet, became his inseparable companion, following him everywhere. The only place he wasn't allowed was on the rig floor, so Jet contented himself with curling up in the doghouse and going round begging for leftover sandwiches from the crew. The constant roar from the rig never seemed to bother him.

Bruce, Billy's old friend from Leduc, now worked for him and asked one day how good was Jet as a hunter.

Billy laughed.

"I have three guns in the gun rack I've installed behind the seat in the truck," he said. "When I take out the .22 out to shoot a crow, magpie, a gopher or something, Jet's mildly interested and will run over to the kill as if to get it, but he never retrieves it. It's as if it's beneath his dignity.

"If I take out my 303, he pays no attention at all, because he knows I'm going to be shooting at a coyote. But if I pull out the shotgun, he just goes completely nuts. His teeth chatter and his whole body shakes and shivers. I tell you that dog will break a quarter inch of ice to fetch a duck."

"Not to mention all the golf balls I see you chipping by your trailer," Bruce cut in.

Both Billy and Candace were happy with their lives though. Candace was well aware of their growing bank account but never again mentioned buying a farm. She knew her husband was an oilman and the black liquid ran in his veins; she wasn't about to try to change that in him.

The second child, Judy, was born in 1954 and Billy delighted in playing with his new daughter. Crawford, even at the age of five, was already showing signs of leaning towards being an athlete and interested in sports. He had pictures of National Hockey League stars all over the walls of his room. Candace continued to be even tempered and patient with all her growing brood, quietly and steadily building a circle of her own centering on the church she had joined and attended with the children.

The couple bought an old upright piano for her to play and Billy remarked that it wasn't exactly a grand as he'd promised, but at least it was a piano and her father had thought they'd never own one of those at all.

Chapter 10

Frank McMillan approached the rig Billy was working on with an assured gait.

"Where's Billy Cochrane at?" he asked as he stepped into the dog house.

The Driller pointed at the rig floor where two feet where sticking out from under the steel floor.

"Those are his feet," he said.

"What's he doing?" McMillan asked.

"We installed a new motor and Billy's hooking up the chain drive." he replied.

"How long's he going to be?" McMillan demanded.

"I don't know," said the Driller. "He's been at it for 12 hours now. He doesn't think the rest of us can manage with out him."

McMillan saw Billy wiggling out of the well he'd been lying in, and went over to greet him. The Driller knew no-one except rig personnel were meant to go out on to the rig floor, but McMillan seemed to exude such authority that he didn't try to stop him.

When Billy stood up, he came face to face with McMillan. Billy was about to offer his hand, but he realized his hand was covered with grease. Frank started to speak, but Billy held up his right hand and index finger as an indication to wait for a moment. Billy then turned to his Driller and made a circular motion with his index finger. The Driller knew that Billy wanted him to engage the new engine. Billy listened and watched intently as the engine turned over. Billy then signaled for the motorman to turn on the fuel to the new engine which promptly roared to life. Satisfied, he turned back to McMillan and beckoned him to the dog house.

"So what brings you out here?" he asked, starting to wipe his hands clear of grease with a rag.

"I came to see you," McMillan said. "You had anything to eat yet?"

"No," said Billy, "and I could eat the ass out of a dead skunk!"

"Then let's drive to town and I'll buy you breakfast."

As they walked to Billy's truck, Billy looked around. He couldn't see Macmillan's.

"Where's your vehicle?" he asked

Frank pointed over to an adjacent cow pasture.

"Right there. I flew in. I hope I didn't scare the farmer's cows too much."

Billy stopped, staring at Macmillan's shiny new plane and shaking his head.

"Well I'll be... go to hell!" he said, amazed.

Over a breakfast of steak and eggs, McMillan began to outline his plan. "Cochrane," he began, "I and a lot of other people have been keeping an eye on you for the past few years. You're considered one of the best Tool Pushers in the business. I don't know if you realize it, but you've been making General Petroleum a lot of money. You consistently drill holes faster and with fewer breakdowns that any other Tool Push around."

"I'm enjoying your flattery," Billy interrupted, "but how in the hell do you know all this?"

McMillan gave a dismissive wave of his hand.

"I make it my business to know these things and I have my ways of finding out," he said.

So what's your point?" Billy said.

"My point is this," McMillan continued, setting down his knife and fork and slowly wiping his mouth. "How would you like to own your own drilling rig?"

It was Billy's turn to sit back in his chair as the weight of what McMillan was talking about slowly began to sink in. He chose his words carefully.

"What exactly do you have in mind?" he said deliberately.

"I believe you're smart enough and hard-working enough to own your own rig and maybe even a fleet of rigs," said McMillan, "and I just happen to know where there is one for sale."

Billy stared at McMillan incredulously and let out a loud sarcastic laugh.

"I'll have to check my checking account first," he said.

McMillan ignored his outburst.

"There's an estate sale of three IDACO rigs coming up this Friday in Shelby Montana. I'll arrange for a loan from the Royal Bank of Canada to buy a rig along with a line of operating credit and personally guarantee it.

"So what's the catch?" Billy asked warily.

"There's no catch. You will drill Arctic Petroleum's wells when and where we want. In fact, we have at least a year's work ahead of us. I'm not asking for any discounts. We'll pay the going rate. I'm sure your new banker'll be glad to hear you're going to have steady cash flow for a year."

"That's it!" said Billy astounded.

"That and one other thing," McMillan continued. "After a five- year period of grace, you'll pay me five per cent interest on your earnings a year. I think that's only reasonable. Any real estate agent would want a five-per-cent commission. Even your church expects ten per cent of your earnings. I suggest we fly right away and inspect the rigs, and if you think they're okay, we'll fly to Calgary tomorrow and see my bank manager."

Sure, why not, Billy thought to himself - why not fly down and take a look, the plane ride should be quite an experience just by itself. He estimated Shelby was maybe an hour away by plane.

Before they could take off, they had to chase a herd of curious cows away from the plane. The takeoff was more than a little bumpy, with the small aircraft bouncing over the rough cow pasture at Macmillan's hands. But once in the air, the scenery of the Alberta foothills and mountain range unfolded beneath them with breath-taking beauty. Big Chief mountain was more majestic from the air than it was from the ground.

Billy's mind was racing too fast to take it all in though. McMillan expected him to make a career altering decision in just two days.

They easily found the small dirt landing strip in Shelby, and quickly found and paid a local to drive them to where the rigs were neatly laid out.

Billy quickly went to work inspecting the three rigs. He knew where all the wear points would be and looked for all the tell-tale signs of neglect and shoddy maintenance. As he went about the inspections, his excitement grew. He began to see himself as a drilling contractor. Owning his own drilling rig had never crossed his mind before, but here he was, looking at buying a rig. As he mentally added up all the pieces a rig needed to be operational, and compared that with what he was examining, he became more and more excited. I'm like Jet going on a duck hunt, he thought. There didn't seem to be anything scavenged from the rigs. As far as he could tell, they were ready to go.

After poking and prodding and looking about for a couple of hours, he went back to McMillan, who was discussing how best to pan for gold with some people who were now gathered around him.

Frank cheerily looked up." All through?" he asked. Billy nodded.

"Can anybody drive us back to my plane?" McMillan asked, looking around.

The man who had driven them in volunteered to take them again, so they climbed aboard, but neither of them said anything on the way, as they didn't want him to know about their intentions.

Back at the plane though, Frank said, "So waddya think?"

"Geez, I don't know," said Billy. "That number six rig looked the best to me, but I'm not sure I'm the risk-taker you are, Frank."

McMillan shot him a quizzical look.

"Don't tell *me* a man who entered a rig spewing out oil and drill stem three separate times, single handedly, to pull out three pals he already knew were dead, isn't a risk taker!" he exclaimed.

"What if I fuck up or there's no more oil to look for and I go broke and you have a guarantee on my note?" Billy said.

"Let me tell you something, Billy Boy: we haven't yet even begun to scratch the surface in this province looking for oil. And if you go broke, you're going to be in good company, because we're all going to be broke right there along with you!"

"Well, I sure do appreciate your confidence in me, Frank." Billy said. "Let me sleep on it, and if I'm in, we'll fly to Calgary tomorrow and see your banker. How much money do you reckon the rig will go for?"

"I'm thinking around $180,000 should be a good deal," said Frank. "Plus, we need to get another $50,000 line of credit to get you going. That should do it."

That night Billy phoned Candace and dropped the bombshell on her. He held his breath as he waited for her reaction.

Candace coolly replied that the decision was entirely up to him.

Then she thought about it for a long moment and suggested that if he was going to go ahead with the deal, she'd want the title of their Red Deer home put in her name.

"That way, even if we go broke, we should be able to keep the house," she said.

Armed with Candace's cautious approval, Billy began making a list of all the things he'd have to deal with and all the questions he'd have to answer to get the rigs up and running. Questions such as, How do I assemble crews? How will all the paper work get handled? Where will I establish my head office? What will I name the company? A million questions leaped out at him, and he started making a list of all the pros and cons he could see ahead, writing them out on a sheet of paper to try to make sure he didn't miss any. He'd spent enough time in General Petroleum's head office to have a general understanding as to how a head office worked. In fact, he had always wondered what all the people did there to earn a living. Still, he was confident he could run a drilling company with about half the people GP had working for them.

Billy stayed up all night wrestling with his decision. One thing he was sure of, he knew how to run a drilling rig. The rest he could learn or hire people to do it for him. He'd long accustomed himself to getting up at five A.M., and on this morning, after a brief snooze, he awoke with the resolve to go ahead with the deal. If the bank would have confidence enough in him to lend him the money and McMillan had enough confidence to back him, then he must have something going for him.

Billy filed his usual morning report back to GP and then waited for McMillan to land his plane in the adjoining field. Finally the aviator swooped out of the sky exactly on time, and landed his little plane. Billy climbed aboard almost before the little light aircraft had come to a stop.

"I knew you'd do it," McMillan said.

Billy laughed.

"These are all the clothes I have with me," he said. "My good clothes are all back in Red Deer. I'm not sure I'll make much of an impression on a banker wearing these old blue jeans, a white shirt and cowboy boots!"

"Don't worry about him. He's an okay guy, not your usual old stuffed shirt," McMillan yelled over the roar of the engines, as the machine bounced over the ground again and the two men started their takeoff.

The Royal Bank building looked to Billy like a stone-walled medieval fortress when they got there, and he couldn't help but be a little intimidated as he followed Frank through the doors. A secretary ushered them directly into the manager's office, saying Mr. Love was expecting them.

The bank manager stood to shake their hands.

"So this is your protégée that you've been talking about," he said, looking Billy over with a critical eye. Billy realized the manager and McMillan had obviously been talking about him.

"Mr. Love, meet William J. Cochrane, of Cochrane Drilling, one of the top up-and-comers in the Alberta oil patch."

This slightly flustered and embarrassed Billy, but now he knew what he was going to call his drilling company.

He stretched out his massive calloused hand to greet the bank manager.

"Pleased to meet you," he managed.

Mr. Love looked down at Billy's hands.

"I can see your hands are no strangers to hard work," he said.

"No, sir," Billy replied politely again.

McMillan quickly got down to business and came right to the point, explaining exactly what they wanted to do and how much money they would need.

From time to time, the bank manager interrupted to ask Billy a pointed and intelligent question. Billy quickly realized he knew exactly what the oil patch was all about.

When McMillan finally finished his proposal, Mr. Love sat quietly rocking back and forth in his swivel chair, in obvious deep thought, still looking in Billy's direction.

After what seemed an eternity to Billy, he looked him squarely in the eye and said, "You're pretty young to own a drilling company, you know."

Billy returned the banker's gaze.

"And you're pretty young to be a bank manager."

He immediately regretted his brashness, thinking that perhaps he'd blown the deal.

There was a brief pause and then the manager let out a guffaw.

"Touché!" he said, standing up. "Perhaps you'd be kind enough to wait in the reception area for a minute while I chat to Mr. McMillan here?"

Outside, Billy could hear their voices through the door, but he couldn't make out what they were saying. The minutes dragged by, seeming like an eternity.

Finally, after what might have been fifteen minutes, the manager poked his head around the corner of the door and asked Billy to rejoin them.

"Mr. Cochrane," he said, sitting back down, "you have a deal. I've given Mr. McMillan the authority on your behalf to buy the oil rig you want. If your purchase is successful, I'll need you to form a legal corporation and come back to me to complete all the paperwork that's required. I'm sure Mr. McMillan will be able to explain some of the technicalities on your return flight."

Billy hardly could find the words to reply.

"Wow!" he said after they had re boarded the plane. "Who'd have ever thought a farm kid from Nanton would ever be able to borrow that kind of money."

McMillan looked Billy full in the eyes.

"Don't kid yourself," he said coldly. "That guy wouldn't give you five cents to see Christ do handsprings. He was either going to lend you the money or lose Arctic Oil's business. It's my neck on the block, and you'd better perform."

There was a new tone in Macmillan's voice as he said this and Billy knew he was serious.

Friday morning found McMillan back in the cow pasture with his plane. Once again they were off to Shelby, this time for the auction sale.

The auctioneer stood on the pipe ramp in front of Rig No. 1. The rigs were numbered 1, 2 and 6. Billy wondered if there ever were rigs 3, 4 and 5 before turning his attention back to the auctioneer, who explained that once the bidding had been completed, the buyer could have any pick of the three rigs that were on sale.

After a long opening song and dance routine about how well the late owner had looked after his rigs before his untimely passing, he started his auctioneer's selling chant, rattling off the words in a high staccato sing-song pitch.

"Who'll open the bid at $250,000?" he challenged.

McMillan had told Billy to keep quiet and he'd be in charge of all the bidding, so Billy positioned himself where he could watch Macmillan's every move and the auctioneer at the same time.

$250,000! Billy became instantly alarmed, shooting a long sideways glance at McMillan, who seemed totally unperturbed and didn't move a muscle, keeping his eyes away from Billy. Billy knew this was far more than they'd agreed to pay, and if the bidding were to start there, they'd immediately be out of the running. So he breathed a sigh of relief when no-one else spoke up either.

The auctioneer paused for a second and started to harangue the crowd about what a fine piece of machinery it was and how cheap they were being.

"All right," he finally challenged, "who will give me $200,000?"

Again there were no takers.

The auctioneer leaned forward.

"Did ya'll come here to steal some of the best iron in the USA?" he yelled.

Still no hands went up, and Billy began to think that maybe he might have a chance after all.

Finally, with a great show of contempt, the auctioneer called: "All right then, let's get the bidding started at $150,000."

Billy shot another furtive glance at McMillan, but his eyes remained expressionless. A hand went up farther across the crowd, and the auctioneer excitedly pounced on it as something to build on.

"$150, 000," he said. "Do I hear $200,000?" Billy's spirits dropped again, as he knew that too was more than they had agreed on.

The auctioneer kept going back and forth between the accepted $150,000 and the requested $200,000, but nobody said anything and nobody was apparently prepared to move to the higher figure. He stopped for a breath or a moment, and removed his cowboy hat to wipe an imaginary bead of the sweat from his brow.

Taking advantage of the short pause, McMillan spoke up.

"$155,000."

The bid instantly brought the red-faced auctioneer back to life.

"Do I hear $160,000?" he asked, pointing towards the previous bidder.

After a short pause with all eyes on him, the bidder finally nodded. But before the auctioneer could begin to restart his calling, McMillan instantly bid it up to $165,000 in the same firm tone of voice.

Billy shot him another brief glimpse. Macmillan's eyes were now cold and glaring like some predatory animal.

The other bidder seemed unnerved by the quickness of Macmillan's bid, obviously alarmed he might lose control of the competition, and get caught in a bidding war he didn't want.

The auctioneer spun back to the original bidder.

"Do I hear $170,000?" he demanded.

The man seemed to become more flustered than ever, with everyone staring at him in anticipation of his response. He looked like a deer caught in a car's headlights.

Then he slowly shook his head. The auctioneer turned his attention back to the rest of the crowd and started calling for a bid of $170,000 then. But despite pleading and wheedling, no-one made a move.

The auctioneer called for any final bids, made a dramatic dismissive gesture and yelled, "Sold!"

Billy jumped up in the air with excitement. He was suddenly an owner of a drilling rig.

The auctioneer turned to McMillan and asked him which rig he was choosing.

"All three of them," McMillan said calmly.

A stunned hush came over everyone as they realized the auction was now over. No-one was more stunned than Billy. They'd never discussed buying all three rigs.

The auctioneer was equally taken aback, as he knew that often the prices went up after the first sale. But he managed to regain his composure and asked who the buyer was.

In his firm, steady voice McMillan replied: "Cochrane Drilling, Calgary... Alberta... Canada."

People immediately began to gather around the two of them.

One asked if McMillan would be interested in selling one of the rigs for an immediate profit, but McMillan just pointed to Billy.

"You'll have to ask Mr. Cochrane," he said and strode away to pay for the rigs.

The man immediately turned his attention to Billy.

"You want to sell Number six for a $10,000 profit?" he said.

Sensing a swelling feeling of pride and confidence in him, Bill shook his head.

Another person stepped up and asked if he'd be prepared to part with a thousand feet of drill stem.

"No way!" he spat dismissively.

Finally, a smaller group of people who had been waiting stepped forward, sensing he was free.The oldest one introduced himself as one of the former Tool Push on the rigs and said the rest of the group had worked on them as well. Maybe he might have jobs for them.

Billy immediately saw this might be a solution to one of his most pressing concerns. He asked some pointed questions and found them to be legitimate by what they said.

Most of all, he said, he wanted to know if the rigs were indeed all in good working order. To his relief, the Tool Push reassured him that as far as he knew, all were in pretty decent shape when they were laid down. Then he added that on last rig he was working on, No. 6, he was sure he could hear a slight knock on one of the engines. Other than that, he said, he was sure they were ready to go.

Billy asked what kind of wages they'd been paid and was comforted to learn their pay had been very similar to that being paid in Canada. McMillan had told him on their flight down that Arctic Petroleum held a large block of leases in the Camrose area and wanted to get drilling as soon as possible. All the seismic tests looked good, he said, and if the field proved successful, there'd be a lot of work ahead for the new company.

Billy wrote down all the men's names and phone numbers and told them were all hired - and that if they had about 20 more friends, they'd be hired as well.

"I'm not sure what the deal is with Americans wanting to work in Canada, but take a look into it and be in Camrose as soon as I can arrange to have the rigs trucked north," he said, secretly sure that they'd all just drive up and go to work. He doubted that anyone would ask any questions.

On their flight home, Billy turned to McMillan.

"You knew you were going to buy all of those rigs back there all along, didn't you?" he said.

"You've heard the story of the young bull and the old bull?" said McMillan, adding without pause when Billy didn't reply: "Well, the young bull said, Let's run down the hill and fuck a couple of those pretty young cows. To which the old bull replied, No, let's walk down and fuck them all."

These were the last words McMillan spoke for the rest of the trip back to Pincher Creek. Billy thought he'd offer some much-needed advice on how to run the new business - or at least be curious about what Billy's immediate plans were - but he never said another word.

And the only thing McMillan said when Billy was getting out of the plane was: "Be sure to see your new banker tomorrow and get everything signed up."

When Billy phoned Candace, he suddenly found he was too numb to be excited. He just matter-of-factly told her they now owned three drilling rigs and were a half million dollars in debt.

Then he went on to reassure her he expected no problems running the drilling rigs, adding though that he'd need a lot of help on the business administration end. Did she think she could handle it?

"I'm sure we can muddle through," she said, with Billy noting the "we" included him as part of the muddle they were going to have to make their way through.

This was all Billy needed to hear. He was now certain Candace was on-side with everything.

"We are going to have to move to Calgary," he said. "So we can be close to all the oil companies and their head offices there."

"Meet me at GP's office tomorrow at 2 P.M.," he said. "That way I can return their truck and tell them I'm leaving. And if we have time, we can look for some land to rent for the new company headquarters -and also go and see Art Hansen and lease four new Power Wagon trucks."

Time didn't permit for any land shopping the next day, but they did stop into Art Hansen's Dodge dealership on the Calgary Trail.

Art immediately spied Billy the instant he walked through the door, walking out of his office to greet him.

"I see you're still walking like an army major," Billy said teasingly. "I suppose you run your dealership like you ran your rig - the army way."

Billy didn't really like Hansen all that much, but he truly respected him. When Billy was promoted to Tool Push, he had copied Hansen's management style. Hansen hadn't been much fun to work for, but he ran his rig by the book, and Billy vowed to copy his style whenever he ever the chance.

"What brings you and your lovely wife to Calgary?" Hansen inquired as he shook their hands.

Billy chose his words carefully. He wanted to make an impact on his old Tool Push.

"I've had a slight change in careers," he said.

"Really?" said Hansen. "What are you doing now?"

"I've just bought three drilling rigs." Billy dead-panned.

Hansen looked at him with a cool appraisal, caught off-guard and looking to see if he was joking.

"I can believe that," he said after a moment.

Billy excitedly told him his story, concluding by saying, "I want to lease four Dodge Power wagons right now, and hopefully, in five years' time, I'll be back in here leasing 20 trucks a year. I want the trucks to be painted gold with black trim, and I want you to paint an oil rig on each of their doors, with the words Cochrane Drilling stenciled underneath.

"I also want each truck fitted with a winch, and an aluminum tool box installed in the truck box. Also install a head rack on each one as well."

"Well, it seems like you know what you want," said Hansen. "Is there anything else?"

"No, I'll install my gun rack myself. Just have them ready to go as soon as possible."

The couple was filling out the paperwork, when Hansen spoke up again.

"You know something, Billy; this doesn't surprise me a bit. You're going to be a big success someday."

Billy spent the rest of that night contacting trucking firms to move his rigs and calling up nearly everyone he knew whom he had ever worked with that had been any good, asking them to come and work for him.

One of his first calls was to Bruce, who had survived the blowout with him. He asked him to become a Tool Push on one of the rigs.

The rest of the hiring could be done on site as the sight of an oil rig derrick stood out like a huge Help Wanted ad for anyone driving by.

Chapter 11

The big rig-moving trucks rumbled onto the Arctic lease site precisely on time. Billy and his new crew were there, waiting anxiously for them, and everyone immediately went to work setting up.

As usual Billy insisted on handling the controls when it came time to raise the newly assembled derrick. In two days the rig was drilling, and the other two rigs also showed up at their new locations in quick order. In quick succession Billy supervised the new rigs' start ups. Sleep was a rare commodity for him during the first two weeks.

And as time went by Billy considered himself lucky no major problem presented itself. All the rigs were operating within a 20-mile radius of Camrose and Billy visited each one at least once a day, grumbling to anyone who would listen that running a drilling rig was no problem; the tough job was dealing with all the messages always waiting for him when he got back to his hotel room.

After two weeks, Dave, his geologist friend from the first rig Billy had worked in Leduc, showed up. Dave pulled his small trailer on to the lease and went to ask Billy where to park it, obviously quite amazed at what he'd seen.

"Do you mean to tell me you're Cochrane Drilling?" he said incredulously.

"Why - does that surprise you?" Billy said smugly with a big grin.

"Well, I'll be a son-of-a-bitch!" was all Dave could say. "Arctic told me to report here and said a Cochrane Drilling was the drilling contractor, but I never dreamed it'd be you who was the Cochrane in Cochrane Drilling."

"Funny how the world works," said Billy. He then told Dave the story of how it had all happened.

Dave could only shake his head in disbelief.

"You've got balls as big as watermelons," he said in wonder and admiration.

Billy laughed.

"Time will tell if I'm a genius or an idiot," he said.

A week later, the first well was nearing Total Depth and everyone was tense with excitement. During the final 200 feet, Dave, as the newly-hired geologist, hardly left the rig. He spent all his time peering through his microscope looking at the shale samples that were constantly being brought to him.

On his return to his hotel room at the end of that, Billy sorted through all his messages and stopped at the one saying it was urgent he contact his banker in Calgary.

He called the number on the slip and Mr. Love himself answered the phone.

"What's up?" Billy demanded

"What's up!" repeated the banker. "What's up is that you're out of money and you're overdrawn $5,000, that's what."

Billy couldn't believe his ears.

"I thought we agreed I could have a $50,000 operating line of credit?" he said finally.

It was the banker's turn to sound incredulous.

"Don't you realize you've spent the $50,000?" he said, his voice taking on a threatening tone. "We're not prepared to honor any more checks and I want that over-draft covered immediately."

Billy pleaded he had nearly finished the first well and Arctic would be sending him a check for $100,000 check in the near future. But the banker was untouched and cut him off.

"You well knew the terms when you signed the contract," he ended stonily.

Billy took a long few moments to recover from his shock before calling Candace to give her the bad news. But he hadn't recovered enough to prevent his tirade when she came on the phone.

"How did you manage to spend $50,000 in one month?" he screamed. "We're are about to go bankrupt after only one month of operation."

Candace broke into tears.

"I had to write the checks as everything was ordered COD because the company has no established credit," she wept.

"So why wasn't I told that the line of credit was overspent?" Billy hurled back.

Candace started to recover.

"Billy," she said with an increasingly strong edge to her voice, "I'm the one that arranged for the sale of our house in Red Deer. I found a place in Calgary to rent. I packed up all our belongings and moved with our two children to Calgary all by myself. I've had to find a school for Crawford. I set up an office in the spare bedroom and I'm the one who tried to set up some kind of book keeping system. And I'm a music teacher, not an accountant. Besides, I think I am pregnant again."

Billy gave no indication of having heard the last sentence.

"Do you think I'm up here in Camrose just twiddling my thumbs!" he fired back, using the momentary pause at the end of the line to cool down a little,

"I guess we should have close to $10,000 in the saving account. Take it out and put it into our company account." he demanded.

"But that's the money that we've been putting aside to buy a farm or some other rainy-day emergency, Billy," Candace objected.

"Just do it!" Billy exploded back, slamming down the phone.

When he got back to the rig, he found Dave waiting anxiously for him. The geologist wasted no time in telling him they had found oil and that he wanted the zone they were in to be cored.

"I'll go back to town and call a coring company," Billy said. "It's going to take a day to drill the core samples and then we'll call a logging company to bring the well into production."

Then Billy felt confident enough in Dave to tell him the banker story and that as far as he was concerned, he had completed the well so he was going to drive to Calgary and demand payment from McMillan.

Dave was silent for a few minutes, and then he took a deep breath and said, "You know, it wouldn't surprise me if McMillan set you up to go broke. Then he could go to the bank and buy your rigs for pennies on the dollar."

"You think he'd do that?" Billy responded in horror, not sure whether to belief the idea or simply dismisses it out of hand.

"I don't know - he's a tough customer," said Dave.

Billy told his Tool Push to do nothing until he goes back. He had to go to Calgary.

Back in Calgary, Billy stormed into Macmillan's Arctic Oil office and, before McMillan could say anything, demanded the $100,000 owing to him for completing drilling the well.

"The geologist wants to core the pay zone, and then the well will have to be brought into production," he said, adding that he wasn't responsible for either of those things, and he wasn't going to do another thing until he was paid.

"What's more," he went on, "from here on there's going to be an extra daily charge for as long as the rig was needed."

He was to further add that if he wasn't paid immediately, he'd pull the whole rig off the hole and abandon it.

Before he could utter this last threat though, McMillan leaned back in his swivel chair with a wry grin and said, "Billy, you sure are some worked up!"

McMillan pulled himself upright and called his secretary.

"Have the comptroller come in and bring the checkbook with him," he said.

Billy slumped into a chair feeling more than a little ridiculous. During the drives to and from the site, he'd worked himself into a rage and he was now beginning to feel pretty foolish about his over-reaction.

"So you say we have stuck oil," said McMillan. "That's excellent news."

Billy regained his composure and apologized.

"Frank," he said, "I miscalculated my costs when drilling this well. In future I want to be paid in three stages. First payment after we drill and run the casing; second payment after I'm two-thirds done; and the final payment upon completion"

Again McMillan smiled wryly.

"That's how all the rest of the drilling companies want to be paid," he admitted.

Billy was about to apologize again, when the comptroller entered Macmillan's lavish office with the companies checkbook.

In a deliberate and exaggerated show of disdain over the amount, McMillan signed the $100,000 check with a flourish, announcing: "Payment in full for well number 38."

He then said that he would order the coring company and logging company out to the drill-site.

Billy immediately rushed to the bank with the check and demanded to see Mr. Love immediately.

Shown into the manager's office and wanting to see his reaction, Billy produced the check with a similar flourish to the one he'd seen in Macmillan's office.

"This ought to help out my bottom line a little," he said sarcastically, continuing condescendingly, "Do you want me to deposit it, or do you want to do it?"

With a final show of importance, he added: "Perhaps you can deposit it - I haven't got time to stand in line."

He then quickly excused himself saying he had other business to do, pausing in the door on his way out.

"There'll be two more checks just like this one that will be deposited next week," he said, having roughly worked out that barring any problems, he should make around $15,000 on each completed well.

The black cloud that had been hanging over his head for the last month was beginning to lift and he was in a very different mood when he arrived at his new home.

"Candace! Your drilling man is home," he yelled. "Let's get naked!"

Over his first home-cooked meal in a month, hastily rustled up to counter his raging hunger, the couple talked about what had to be done to run the company. Both agreed the company needed an office and at least one or maybe even two experienced book keepers. Billy also promised he wouldn't continue at the pace he had been working and would be home "much more" in the future.

He also made a quick call to his American Tool Push and told him that a coring and logging firm were on their way.

"I'll be back as soon as I can," he said, reassured that the American knew as much about drilling rigs as he did.

"There!" he said turned back to Candace, "that's how I plan to run this company in the future: hire good people and delegate some authority to them. I don't have to live on the rig; I can manage most of the problems from our office in Calgary. Soon as everything is under control, I'll be home every night for supper. Then I can watch Crawford play hockey, take Judy to her ballet lessons, and whatever what's-his-name-is help it do its thing.

He laughed as he reached over to rub Candace's tummy.

"In the morning, we're going to look for a new front office and yard space for Cochrane Drilling."

Candace didn't remind him that he had never even reacted to hearing about her being pregnant again.

Chapter 12

By the end of that October, Cochrane Drilling had completed seven wells for Arctic Petroleum, three of which turned out to be good producing wells.

Bill had already signed a contract with another oil company to move two rigs up north for the winter drilling season and he'd have to spend some down time waiting for the muskeg to freeze over, so he planned to use the time to do some needed repairs and repaint the rigs. The derricks would be painted gold and all the out-buildings and substructure would be painted black. This would keep most of the crews busy and the rest could take a holiday if they wanted.

Bill sat in the dog house of his one remaining rig that was still drilling. The Tool Push had gone to town to get some supplies and he was absent-mindedly gazing out the small window at the crew going about their business. He could smell the smell of the slough that lingered on Jet's coat from that day's early-morning duck hunt. Jet was stretched out on the bench, happily licking him in quiet contentment.

Hearing footsteps coming up the steel stairs, Billy turned on his high stool to look at the door as it opened.

Standing in front of him was a medium-built man wearing a tweed suit and a bow tie. His hair was plastered down with some kind of lotion, and it was neatly parted in the middle. His eyes looked slightly owlish in his wire rimmed glasses. He looked as though he'd just stepped out of the 1920s. All he needed to complete the wardrobe, Billy thought vaguely, was a straw boater hat and spats on his shoes.

"How can I help you?" he said, resisting the temptation to laugh.

"I've been told I might be able to find Mr. Cochrane here."

"You're looking at him."

"You m-m- mean to tell me you're M-M-Mr. Cochrane?" the man stuttered. "You own this drilling rig?"

"I don't see anyone else here," Billy chided gently, looking over his shoulder, "unless you are looking at my dog."

The man took a breath and apologized.

"I'm sorry," he said, "I'd expected someone much older."

"Come back in three months, I should be an old man by then," Billy kidded.

"My name is Thor Olsen," the man replied, sticking out his hand.

Billy shook it, wondering what-in-hell this guy could want.

"My name is Bill Cochrane," he said. He didn't like to be called Billy any more. He preferred to be called just straight Bill, especially in a business setting, or in more formal settings, William, but he knew close old friends would always call him Billy, come what may.

"What can I do for you?" he asked once again.

Thor quickly explained that he owned a half section of land five miles away, and he also owned the mineral rights to it. Bill listened as Olsen concluded his story by asking if he would drill an oil well for him.

Bill let out a low whistle and asked Thor if he knew anything about the oil industry in general.

Thor tried to look indignant.

"I guess I know enough," he said shortly. "How much would it cost to drill a well and how soon can you get started?"

Billy's first instinct was to tell the strangely-dressed man to get lost, as he was clear in way over his head, but he was somewhat intrigued with the obvious eccentric.

He looked him up and for a few moments and then explained that the wells he'd been drilling to date in the Camrose area averaged between 2,500 to 3,000 feet.

"If I were to drill a well like that for you, it'd cost $100, 000," he advised, thinking that figure should cool the man's ardor a little.

"Mmm… $100,000... and what does that all include?" Olsen said, seeming undaunted by the huge sum.

"I'll want a $10,000 deposit up-front before I'll even move my rig," Bill said. "And I'll want $30,000 after the surface casing has been set and the blow-out preventer welded on it - that should be at around 900 feet. Then I'll want an additional $30,000 when we're two-thirds completed and the final payment of $30,000 upon completion. If you can raise that kind of money, I can squeeze in one more well before we head up north."

"Mr. Cochrane," Olsen continued, "I own my land free and clear. It is one of the best halves in the area, and I know it's worth at least $30,000. I will sign over title to you to get you started, and I can guarantee you I'll have the rest of the money on time as you've outlined."

Bill was more than a little taken back. He'd thought the man was merely on a fishing expedition and couldn't possibly be serious about investing what was clearly everything he had on such a gamble.

"Wait a minute," he said. "Hold on here...do you mean to tell me you're prepared to gamble everything you have on the long shot there might actually be oil on your farm? What makes you think there's any oil under there? What if we drill a duster! Have you completed seismograph work? Is oil bubbling out of the ground? What makes you so sure you're going to find oil?"

Olsen looked at him.

"I know there is oil there," he said assuredly. "There is oil under my farm...I know it."

"Well, you are a big boy," Bill warned. "If you lose your ass and your farm in this, don't come crying to me. If you really are serious, I'll draw up a contract and we can start next week.

Olsen reached out his hand to shake on the deal.

"I'm deadly serious," he said with finality.

"Alright then," Bill said, shrugging. "Who's your lawyer? We'll meet there tomorrow with my contract and he can fill in all the rest of the information I'm going to need."

After the contract was signed the following day, Bill suggested they drive out to the Olsen farm, as a cat machine would have to be brought in to make a rough road, clear and level the lease and dig a sump hole.

Olsen showed Bill where he wanted the well drilled and Bill outlined what cat work would have to be performed.

Finally Billy stopped and said, "I have to ask you, why you think this is the right spot to drill?"

"Because I witched it," was the surprising reply.

"You what!" Billy exclaimed.

"I'll show you." Olsen said. He went to his car and returned with a coat hanger. He unraveled the twisted ends of wire and holding one end in his hand, began walking in different directions. Over the exact spot, he had said he wanted to drill on, the coat hanger suddenly pointed straight down at the ground and then, as he walked farther away, the points of the rod began to slowly rise up again.

Billy watched in utter amazement.

"I've heard of people that witch for water wells," he said shaking his heading, "but I've never heard of anyone witching for oil wells. Personally I call bullshit!"

"Witching for oil has an entirely different feel than witching for water," Olsen replied evenly. "I was looking to drill a water well, and I couldn't figure out why my witching rod was acting so strangely. And then it came to me that I was standing over a pool of oil. I went to all the wells that you've found oil on, and I witched them, and they acted exactly the same. I came home and checked it out again and got the same results here."

By the time he left, Billy was having serious second thoughts about the contract he'd just signed, fearing that the whole venture was almost certain to have a thoroughly messy ending. On arriving back in Camrose, he decided to do a little checking up on his new business venture.

The first stop was the Alice Hotel bar, which he knew was a popular drinking spot for the local farmers. Four older farmers were sitting around a table in the corner, engrossed in conversation.

Billy walked up to them and asked if they'd mind if he joined them. They waved to an empty chair and invited him to sit down. Billy waved to the waitress to bring a beer for all his new friends and listened in quietly to their conversation for a while. It ranged over a wide variety of farm matters. Finally after a few minutes, he asked if any of them knew a Thor Olsen. All of them indicated in some manner or another that sure, they knew him.

One of the farmers looked at him and asked, "So, what's Thor been up to now? He's always got some kind of hair-brained scheme up his sleeve." Everyone laughed in sympathy.

"You remember the time he wanted everyone to invest in setting up a bottled-water plant on his farm?" one of the others said.

Turning to Billy, he explained that there was a spring on Olsen's farm that Thor claimed had to have the purest water in Alberta, and he wanted to bottle the water and sell it.

"Ever hear of anything so crazy?" he said. "To think anyone would pay money for bottled water!"

They all had a good chuckle laugh over that.

"I wonder how much money he cost all his investors on that deal?" wondered a third farmer.

The last one to speak up had a strong Norwegian accent.

"I recall dat Thor's father Ollie emigrated to Camrose before de turn of de century and built up one of de finest homesteads in Central Alberta," he said. "He built up a herd of registered Angus cattle and produced de best crops. He worked himself to death and den gave it all to his no-good son. Now dat Thor doesn't have a stick of machinery or a single cow!"

The Scandinavian explained that instead of raising his Angus cows, the son had been hell bent on importing some white cows from France, and when none of his imported cattle passed the quarantine inspection, he lost all his money.

"Dat boy will one day lose de whole farm," the farmer predicted.

Alarm bells were ringing in Billy's head as he listened to the farmers tell a series of Thor Olsen stories. But there's nothing I can do about it now, he said to himself, the contract's all signed and the deal is done.

Billy stopped at the rig in the morning and told his Tool Push he was going to Calgary for a few days, but as soon as the well was finished, to move the rig to Thor Olsen's farm, five miles south.

"Olsen will direct you to the exact drilling site," he said.

Chapter 13

Billy and Candace rented a small shop in South East Calgary. There was a 2,000-square-foot shop on the main level and offices on the second floor.

Billy felt he had learned a valuable lesson, and he vowed that he and only he would sign all of the checks issued by Cochrane Drilling. There was only one phone in the office and either he or their newly-hired bookkeeper answered it. Whether going into the office to work or not, Billy always rose at 5 A.M. and was behind his desk by 6 A.M. He demanded that his three Tool Pushes send their daily reports to him by 7 A.M. each day. By 9 A.M. there was a steady procession of salespeople at his door, promoting one product or another in what seemed like a never-ending stream. When it wasn't salespeople knocking on his door, it was people looking for work.

The one-acre fenced yard quickly began to fill with pieces of equipment, new and used. Billy tried to set his afternoons aside for delivering or arranging supplies to his rigs. On rare occasions when he had time, he'd repair items in the shop. The various items and bit and pieces included a General Motors diesel engine he had every intention of rebuilding, but he never seemed to find the time to work on it.

Toots Linder, his American Tool Push, whom Billy had assigned to drill the well on Olsen's property, soon began to complain that

Olsen was becoming a pain-in-the-ass, as he was always under-foot, usually giving tours to people.

"One of these days, that farmer," as Toots always referred to Olsen, "is going to get himself killed."

"Just be sure to tell me when you finish running the surface casing, and I'll come right up," Billy responded.

"That should be some time tomorrow morning," Toots told him.

Billy was at the rig site by 9 A.M, just as the cement truck was pulling away. All the roughnecks were busy mixing cement to cement off the surface casing. Billy talked with Toots for a while and then said, "I guess it's about time to pay a visit to Mr. Olsen."

He drove over to Olsen's farmyard and knocked on the door of the house. When no-one answered, he opened it and walked in. Thor was sitting in an over-stuffed living-room chair, wearing an old housecoat, his hair was disheveled and at least a three days' growth of beard was his on his chin. His wire-rim glasses were sitting on an adjacent coffee table. His eyes were staring into space and were sunken and red-rimmed. Billy could hardly believe it was the same dapper man who had introduced himself so strangely just three weeks before.

Billy was stunned at the change in his appearance and was casting about trying to see how he could best broach the topic of asking for money.

Finally, Olsen began to focus on him, and Billy took this as a cue to make an opening.

"I suppose you know why I am here?" he said as straight forwarded as he could.

Thor nodded weakly.

"We've finished running the surface casing," said Billy, "and if you remember our agreement, you were to pay a $10,000 deposit and then a further $30,000 upon our running the surface casing."

Thor nodded again, so weakly that the movement was barely perceptible.

"Well, I'm here to collect the $30, 000," Billy finished.

There was a long pause before Olsen formed the words, hardly reaching a whispered, "I don't have it."

"You don't have it!" Billy choked out. "What happened to all those investors you were suppose to have?"

Olsen could only manage a feeble palms-up gesture.

Billy stood before him, clenching his fists and riveted to the spot.

"Look," he said with a piercing glare, his eyes boring into Olsen's, "you know the deal...I'm not going to hang around while you feel sorry for yourself. Time is money and I've got holes to be drilling. I'm going to go straight to the rig and order them to cement this hole off and get the rig ready to be moved.

"As far as I am concerned, you're sitting on my land...you pathetic son-of-a-bitch. And remember, I didn't want your land, I just expected to be paid."

Turning to leave the room, Bill spied a double-barreled shotgun leaning against the wall not too far from Olsen's chair. The sight of the gun and the man's obvious mental distress made Billy pause.

Softening a little for a moment, he turned back to the man slumped in the chair.

"Look," he said, "you can use this house until you pull yourself together."

Billy picked up the shotgun.

"And just in case you somehow might screw up the courage to blow your head off, I'm taking this with me."

Back at the rig, Toots was used to Billy inspecting the rig with military precision and making sure it was maintained spotlessly clean, but he was quite unprepared when Billy came storming on to the rig and ordered everyone to drop what they were doing and get ready to move the rig.

"Cochrane Drilling isn't in the business of playing games or giving out charity," he told Toots.

Back in Calgary later, Billy received a call from Frank McMillan.

"You wearing a tie today?" McMillan greeted him.

"You kidding?" he said. "It's tough to run a welder wearing a suit and tie. Why? What's up?"

"I think it's time to introduce you to some of the players in this game," said McMillan mysteriously. "Meet me at the Petroleum Club for lunch, but you'll have to wear a sports coat and a tie to get in."

Suitably dressed, Billy arrived at the Petroleum Club exactly at noon.

A waiter showed him to Frank's table where Frank was having a glass of wine. A bottle rested chilling in an ice bucket. Frank poured him a glass and said, "I hope you drink wine."

"I've never drunk much wine," said Billy. "I'm pretty well a beer and rye whiskey guy."

"Let's meet some very important people in this business before they tuck into their meals," said McMillan. "Come with me."

Parading from table to table with Billy in tow, Frank called out the names of the individuals as he slapped them on the back and shook their hands. Usually he'd indulge in some drawn-out kind of greeting, asking how their wives were, inquiring after their children and other members of the family, before finally getting round to introducing Billy, who was standing self-consciously behind him and wishing he could fade into the walls.

Eventually Frank would turn to Billy and say, "Gentlemen, I want to introduce you to William Cochrane, of Cochrane Drilling, a true up-and-comer." Billy would dutifully shake hands, and several of the people asked him for his business card.

Stopping at one table, McMillan said, "Mr. Cochrane, I'd like to introduce you to the next Premier of Alberta - or maybe even the next Prime Minister of Canada... Mr. Peter Lougheed."

Lougheed politely stood up and said, "Mr. Cochrane, it's my pleasure."

The last table they stopped at, McMillan jocularly said, "Mr. Cochrane, meet the Titans of the Arctic, Jack Gallager and Bill Richards."

The two men traded insults briefly with McMillan and then laughingly extended their hands to Billy.

Back at their own table, Billy asked McMillan if he knew everyone in Calgary. McMillan shot him a laconic look and dryly replied, "No, only the players in the oil patch. Remember this, Billy, in the *real* world; you make more money from your shoulders up, than you do from your shoulders down. Who you know is as important as what you know in this business."

Billy had almost finished his medium-rare steak when he finally spoke again.

"I can't believe that I've just met some of the people I've met today."

Leaving the club, McMillan told Billy to wait a second while he went over to the reception desk.

Returning he handed Billy a sheath of papers and said, "This is the Petroleum Club membership application. I'll nominate you for membership. They hold a lot of nice functions which I think you and your lovely wife might well enjoy."

Billy started to protest, but McMillan waved him, saying, "You should also join the Ranchman's Club as well."

Billy started to protest again when McMillan cut him off a second time. "You like to golf, don't you?" he asked.

"Yeah, but..." Billy assayed weakly

McMillan never gave him time to finish the sentence.

"Then I suggest you take out a membership with the Calgary Golf and Country Club. You curl, by the way?"

Billy stopped dead in his tracks.

"Just hold on a minute," he protested, "there's hardly enough time in the day for me to wipe my ass, let alone do all of the other things you think I should be doing."

"It's not about you doing any of these things, it's about the perception that you do all these things," said Frank. "Listen, my young friend, if you want to have the last rig standing upright in Alberta, you'd better start rubbing shoulders with the people that make the decisions in the oil patch. "Besides, you're making money and all these memberships are write-offs against the company, right?"

Billy had never even thought about write-offs before. Nor had he even hired an accountant as yet, but instinctively he knew that everything McMillan said was probably true and made a lot of sense.

Chapter 14

Billy's promise to Candace about spending more time at home somehow never seemed to materialize. If he wasn't away at one of his rigs, he often worked late and seldom made it home before 9 P.M. Candace took the tack of excusing herself from going to the office and telling Billy that if he couldn't make it home in time to help her with the children, then she'd simply have to spend all of her time raising the kids.

The first winter of the new business flew by, and drilling contracts started piling up on Billy's desk for the upcoming year. Billy reckoned he could use at least three more drilling rigs, so he went back to see Mr. Love at the Royal Bank again, hoping he'd forget abut the way Billy had behaved back at the end of completing the first of his own drill jobs and would lend him the money to buy three more rigs.

Mr. Love looked at him more than a little incredulously and reminded him that Cochrane Drilling hadn't even completed its first year of operation as yet.

At the very least, he told Billy, he'd need a financial statement from his first year of operation.

Billy pleaded as best he could that surely the bank manager should be able to see for himself from the company bank account that it had a healthy balance which was continuing to grow, and he argued that he already had enough work stacked up to justify three more rigs.

Mr. Love shook his head.

"I'm sorry," he said, "but its bank policy."

Billy left in another huff and thought about trying his luck with another bank, but then realized that probably every bank would have the same policies. Trying to cool down, he had to laugh at himself, thinking: "Who do I think I am? Here I am, a 26-year-old farm kid asking for a million and a half dollars!"

The first year of operation quickly drew an end and he found himself going over the annual financial statement with his newly-hired accountant. To Billy it still sounded like accountant was talking another language, using terms like differed earnings, shareholder loans, capital depreciation, and many other technical accountant terms.

Billy felt he had to cut in.

"I'm not sure what all these things mean, but am I correct in saying it looks to me like Cochrane Drilling made close to one half of a million dollars in its first year of operation?" he said.

Again the accountant started to speak and said that yes technically that was true, but that he needed to know and recognize ....Billy tuned him out; he felt he knew all he needed to know.

Billy virtually ran to the bank from the accountant's office. There he again confronted the beleaguered Mr. Love again, pushing the financial statement in front of him and staring intently as the manager began poring over the document, his lips pursed.

Mr. Love said nothing as he went from the balance sheet to the profit and loss sheet. He kept shifting his weight from side to side in his big swivel chair, continually pushing his glasses back up his sloping nose while he made notes. From time to time, he'd tilt his head downward and look over the top of his glasses when he had a question to ask. Then he'd look back down with his chin almost touching his chest, returning to reading the statements.

During the whole process he made small noises that sounded to Billy like tiny grunts. At one point he glanced over his glasses and commented, "I see you own a half section of land in Camrose. Was this your family farm?"

Billy didn't want to get into the whole story, so he merely replied, "Something like that."

Finally Mr. Love pushed himself back in his chair, looked over at Billy and said, "Very impressive."

He cleared his throat with a small Ahem, and said, "Now what was it again you wanted to see me about?"

Billy thought to himself, you phony self important asshole, you know damn' well what I'm here for, but he choked off the words.

"We were taking about you lending me money to buy three new drilling rigs."

"Ahhh, yes," Mr. Love said as if the memory was only now just slowly coming back to him, "what was that amount again that you were looking for?"

"One and a half million," Billy shot back without a second's hesitation. Billy could sense envy seeping out of the banker. Not only had he as a 26-year-old earned such a large sum of money, but Billy was a little surprised at his own audacity in asking for such a large loan to boot.

Billy continued by telling the banker he reckoned he could save on taxes by buying more equipment. He hoped the banker wouldn't press this point as Billy knew he couldn't really explain it.

"You know there is a very real and large danger from expanding too fast," the banker intoned. "Remember Turner Valley... everyone thought that was going to be a huge oil boom, and most of the people involved lost the shirts off their backs. I think this whole Leduc thing will turn out to be just another Turner Valley."

Billy looked at the banker in some disbelief, wondering where he could possibly have been for the past seven years, apart perhaps from the other side of Mars. Didn't the man know what was going on in the Alberta oil patch, or was he just looking for an excuse to refuse Billy's loan application?

Speaking deliberately so as to keep his voice as even as possible, Billy told him, "I drilled thirty six wells for various oil companies all over central and northern Alberta. Fifteen of the wells I drilled turned out to be producers. I'd say this is a little more than a Turner Valley."

"Perhaps you don't have a very good memory of the Great Depression," the banker replied, as he again tilted his head down and peered at Billy over his half rim glasses.

"Look!" Billy said, letting his voice raise an agitated octave or two, "I've paid for the first three rigs I bought in one year, and I'm confident I can pay for three new rigs in three years."

"Yes, but you had Mr. Macmillan's guarantee," Mr. Love pointed out.

"I don't need anyone's guarantee," Billy reassured him. "I've got enough assets. I want to order one rig a month for the next three months. That way, I'll have new crews trained and be ready for the winter season."

"And where do you intend to buy these rigs?"

"Houston, Texas." came Billy's reply without a second's hesitation.

There was another long pause, with Mr. Love twirling his pencil between his two thumbs and forefingers.

"Thanks so much for coming in, he said, "I'll have an answer for you in three days."

Chapter 15

Billy drove home from his meeting with the bank manager to eat a rare lunch with Candace. He showed her the financial statements and then swept her up in his arms.

"Honey," he said, "it's time to build our dream home. I'm going to take the afternoon off and we'll phone a Realtor and go shopping."

Candace couldn't help but be caught up in his excitement.

"So where should we build?" she said.

"Well, to build the mansion I promised you when we got married, it'll take at least five acres. Judy is already showing interest in horses, so maybe we will need a stable as well." He winked at his daughter as he gave Candace a playful shove. "I also insist we have a good view of the Rockies."

Candace also had own list of demands. It couldn't be too far out of the city and it had to be near a school. There had to be good roads, as she was the one that was always driving the kids, she said as she returned the gesture, with a pointed push.

They phoned a Realtor and gave him a list of their wants, and he said he'd come right over as he already had a place in mind he thought would be perfect for them.

Picking them up, the Realtor asked them what they had intended spending. Billy was prepared for that as he knew the Realtor was trying to sum up their wealth and match it to their ages.

"Whatever it takes," was Billy's sly reply. Walking to the man's car, he pointed to his truck with the company sign displayed on the door.

"See that sign on the door that says Cochran Drilling?" he said. "Well, I'm the Cochrane in Cochrane Drilling.

This was evidently enough to impress the Realtor.

"I'm going to show you some properties in Mount Royal that you can use as comparisons," he said. "Maybe the two of you might even be interested in one of them. They're on our way, as the acreage I want to show you is just on down 17 Street."

Billy and Candace nodded their agreement.

The two homes in Mount Royal turned out to be magnificent and stately. Huge hedges and manicured lawns made them appear even more majestic and impressive. Seeing that both the Cochranes were impressed, the Realtor gave them the listing prices and Billy noted he also gave them a sideways glance to see their reaction. This must be a real estate sales trick to gage if the prospective clients would flinch, he thought, another test to see if they had money. So he made sure not to show any kind of reaction at all, keeping his face and eyes expressionless.

"You want to see inside?" the Realtor asked.

"No," Candace said firmly, "we have something else in mind."

"I doubt," Billy joined in, "our neighbors would appreciate my diesel truck waking everyone up at 5:30 in the morning."

Not long afterwards the Realtor pulled up to one of his Acreage For Sale signs, announcing proudly but rather unnecessarily, "This is it."

The three of them walked the perimeter of the five-acre parcel as the Realtor babbled on that some day Calgary would grow out this far and he had no comparable piece of property this close to Calgary, or at least any with nearly as good a mountain view as this one, and that he thought it was an excellent property.

Billy cut him off.

"So what are they asking for this?" he asked, coming straight to the point.

The realtor's voice dropped to a well-practiced conspiratorial note.

"I hear there are divorce problems and I think we can get it with an offer of, say, $10, 000," he said.

"$10,000!" Billy exclaimed. "We just sold our house in Red Deer a year ago for that amount."

"Well, you know, this is Calgary," the Realtor wheedled.

Billy asked the Realtor to wait in his car out of earshot for a bit, as he and his wife wanted to talk, and the couple strolled on their own.

The Realtor went and waited by the car, watching them from a distance as they walked and talked in a measured way. Suddenly they stopped and both were waving their arms and pointing excitedly in all directions. The discussion went on and on. After what was perhaps a half hour - it certainly seemed that way to the Realtor – the duo returned to the car.

Candace had no sooner sat down than she exclaimed breathlessly: "We'll take it!"

The Realtor turned to look Billy, who was sitting behind him, for his reaction. Billy just shrugged and said, "She's the boss on the housing project!"

Leaving the property, the Realtor pointed out the nearby Burt's General Store.

"You can always use that as your landmark to find your property," he said.

Arriving back home, the twosome continued with their plans. Candace kept on asking how much they could really afford. Billy replied affably that he had no idea, and suggested instead that they hire an architect to help them, and see what he thought it would cost.

"You'll be in charge of building the house and I'll be in charge of building a new storage and office site," he reminded her. "Just keep me up to date!"

It took only two days before the bank manager phoned Billy.

"I've got good news for you," he said. "The bank has approved your loan application. You can go ahead and order three new rigs."

Chapter 16

Sorting through his mail a day or two later, Billy was irritated to be interrupted by a knock on his door. Looking up, he saw a man about his age walk in and stick out his hand to him. This person obviously isn't here to apply for a rough necking job, Billy thought to himself.

The man introduced himself as Skid Blake.

"And you must be Mr. Cochrane," he finished.

"Just call me Bill," Billy corrected him, sizing him up as a business prospect of some type.

Without being invited, Blake moved a chair close to Billy's desk and sat down, leaning forward to rest his arms on top of the desk.

That's a bit impertinent, Billy thought. No-one's ever done that to me before.

"Jesus Christ, Bill," Blake said, taking the initiative in the conversation, "you've got paws on you like a polar bear! You know something... I read recently that a man's dink is usually three times the size of his thumb." He turned his head on an angle and laughed. Not an ordinary laugh, Billy noted, but instead he just sucked air in and out rapidly over his clenched teeth. He flashed a huge gap-toothed grin and his eyes lit up when he made his sucking-noise laugh.

Somehow though, took an instant liking to the man.

"I hope I don't have to take my dink out to prove your theory," he rebutted.

"Christ, no, you're probably hung like a donkey and you'd leave me with a life-long inferiority complex," the man replied.

"So what can I do for you?" Billy asked, deciding it was time to get down to business.

"You can drill an oil well for me...that's what you can do."

Billy had heard that one before but this man didn't look like a farmer.

"You have an oil company I presume," he said.

"Yeah, several of them. You see, I'm a stock broker and promoter by trade, and I usually get involved with the stocks I sell."

Seeing the puzzlement on Billy's face, Skid laughed again.

"What I do is form a company, take it public so it can be traded on the stock exchange, find some land that has some promise, draw-up a beautiful prospectus, hype the hell out of it - and then sell my shares to some suckers in the US or Ontario," he said. "Ever since you guys discovered oil in Leduc, I've been making money hand over fist."

He turned his head sideways again and gave another of his unusual laughs.

Billy joined in with a chuckle of his own.

"Ever hit oil?" he said.

"Hell no! Most of the time we don't even drill the wells!"

Billy folded his arms and chuckled again, staring hard in the man's eyes.

"So why'd you come to me?" he said.

"Well," Blake admitted, "we need to keep our credibility up, and we plan to make our next well a showcase one."

Billy gave his head a slight shake.

"I drill wells for money, not pretend money," he said. "You want to wildcat for a well, then I guess that's your business, but I live in the real world."

"That's exactly my point, I've come here to find out how much it will cost to drill a well and how soon you can drill it."

"Where's your property?" Billy demanded.

"I bought some mineral rights from a farmer near Crossfield."

"Crossfield," Billy murmured almost under his breath, rubbing his chin as he considered the prospect. "I'd guess the pay zone - *if* there is a pay zone around there - would be around five thousand feet. I don't know as I've never drilled around there, and you're probably looking at around, say at least $100,000. But I won't be able to get to it for three months.

"Perfect!" Skid replied. "That'll give me lots of time to get the good news out about the exciting new oil play at Crossfield. I should have a couple hundred thousand dollars in Giant Oil and Gas's account by then."

He let out yet another of his infectious laughs.

"I'll write you a deposit check right now and you get ready to drill in three months. Got any thing to drink to celebrate this new partnership of ours?"

Billy was so completely taken aback by the brazen request that he just responded, "Sure, why not."

He quickly managed to produce two glasses that were anything but clean.

"I guess they'll have to do," he said, "and all I have is whiskey and water."

Skid pushed his chair back and put his feet on Billy's desk.

"Fine with me," he said

Wide-eyed at Skid's effrontery, Billy managed to blurt, "I realize it's not much of a desk, but it is *my* desk!"

Skid promptly took his feet down and pulled the chair back up to the desk.

"That's another thing I wanted to ask you - you sure don't have much of an office for a successful drilling company CEO."

"So what makes you think I'm successful?" Billy asked, deciding to go along with Skid's bald-faced in-your-face approach.

Skid took a large swallow from his glass.

"You'd have to be pretty incompetent not to be making money with a drilling rig these days," he said. "So how did you come to own drilling rigs?"

Billy told him the story about Frank McMillan and the Montana auction.

Skid whistled.

"Frank McMillan!" Skid shouted, coming halfway out of the chair. "Frank McMillan, eh! Frank got his start in the oil business the same way I did, as a stockbroker. He's got to be the luckiest son-of-a-bitch in the world! Some people fall into a barrel of tits and come up sucking their thumb, but Frank always lands right on his feet. He's luckier than a silly with a bag full of pricks. Mind you, he's also a cut-throat manager and doesn't take any shit from anybody, no matter who they are."

"So how'd you become a stockbroker," Billy asked, instantly regretting the question as he felt he should instead be dismissing the man and getting back to his paperwork.

But he was also intrigued by Skid's peculiar behavior and his stupid but catching laugh. He poured the two of them another shot of whiskey and sat back to listen to Skid's response.

"Oh... both my parents are doctors and they wanted me to go into medicine as well," said Skid. "But I can't stand sick people. So I went into studying commerce instead. I rarely attended classes though, and spent most of my time playing poker at my frat house.

"How did you pass your courses if you never attended classes?" Billy asked with a mixture of disbelief, wonderment and curiosity.

"Everyone called me the phantom. I usually found someone who took good notes and pay them for them, and then I'd just show up for the exams. Never did get my degree though. I found all those pretty co-eds far more interesting than any course the university had to offer. I love the action out here in the real world. University is over-rated if you ask me. You married?"

"Yup, three kids."

"Yeah, me too, three kids and three marriages, and this third marriage aren't looking too hot either."

"Didn't you ever hear that verse in the old cowboy song about, 'Can't afford to split my half one more time'?" Billy said kidding.

"Guess not," Skid replied wryly.

Billy was so taken by Skids self-depreciating humor that he opened up and the conversation slid over into how he and his wife were planning to build their new home and new storage yard and office.

Skid seemed genuinely impressed and asked all kinds of pointed questions, finally ending off: "I think I'm in the presence of a mogul!"

He tossed off the last of his drink and invited Billy to join him for another at Hy's Steak House.

"All the lads should be there and all the beautiful secretaries should be arriving soon as well," he said.

"Who are all the lads?" Billy demanded.

"If you don't know that, you must surely come. There'll be a lot of people that you should get to know...and I don't just mean the secretaries."

"Don't you go to the Petroleum Club?" Billy asked.

"Nahhh...I'm a member there, but it's too stuffy for me - and besides, they don't allow women in there. If you want to meet the oil crowd that wear suits, go to the Petroleum Club; if you want to eat a good meal and meet the real hands-on oil crowd, go to Hy's; and if you want to get laid, go to the 400 Club! Come on, lets go," he said, standing up to leave.

Seeing Billy look apprehensively at the pile of paper on his desk, he added, "Come on, all that can wait until tomorrow!"

"Easy for you to say...you probably get to work by six am to catch the opening of the Toronto Stock Exchange and are finished by two," Billy said. I have to get to work by six and usually don't get out of here until nine at night."

When Billy walked into Hy's, Skid was there waving frantically to him to come and join him. He was sitting at a table with five other men and immediately began a round of introductions. Billy paused when he was introduced to Alvin Nahajowich. Alvin held out a hand as big as Billy's and said in a big booming voice, "So you're *the* Bill

Cochrane, of Cochrane Drilling! You don't know me, but I'm Alvin - of Alvin's Trucking.

Skid piped in, "I bet you five bucks that you can't spell his last name."

Billy ignored him and continued on with his conversation with Alvin.

"Well, well," he said. "I've hired you to move my rigs on many occasions, but we never have met - pleased to meet you."

Billy returned Alvin's iron grip with an even harder grasp of his own. Alvin took this as a challenge and the two men began squeezing as hard as they could. Billy took some pride in Alvin finally giving in and releasing his hand first.

Next he greeted Ned Hamilton, who had been the geologist on several holes that Billy had drilled.

Everyone at the table was involved with the oil patch in one way or another, and Billy soon became thoroughly engrossed in the conversation as it swirled around the latest news and bits of gossip. He also noted that there seemed to be a steady stream of girls who would swing by their table for a time and chat with Skid. Skid obviously enjoyed their attention and he'd usually make some sexual innuendo or comment to them. None of them were the least put off by his flirtations, and most had a fast comeback line that they'd obviously practiced and was equally sassy. Skid would point to Billy and introduce him as "the new kid on the block".

A waiter came by to ask if anyone was interested in the steak special.

Skid instantly took control.

"Yes, and bring us a couple of bottles of your good red wine," he said.

The waiter brought the wine and began writing down their orders. Stopping at Alvin, he said, "Yeah, I know - knock off its horns and wipe its ass."

Billy thought vaguely that he should perhaps phone home, but he was home for supper so seldom now that he no longer even bothered to call. Taking the afternoon off was a rare treat, he thought, and I might as well enjoy it.

Skid's way of paying the tab at the end of the meal was also a new experience for Billy. Skid grabbed a cowboy hat off one of the men's head and told everyone to get their credit cards out. This was obvious a well-accepted ritual around him, as no-one protested and everyone threw their cards into the hat without any more prompting. Skid held the hat up in the air and asked the waiter to reach in.

"Pick a card, any card," he told him.

The waiter gave the card to Skid and Skid looked at it.

"And the unlucky loser is - Cochrane Drilling!" he announced.

Billy was a little chagrined, as he wondered whether he wasn't perhaps being set up, but Skid passed the hat round and everyone retrieved their credit cards.

"You're getting off lightly, Cochrane, the bills only for $235. I've seen it as high as $500. If the bill is over $500, we draw two cards."

"I can't believe my good luck," Billy replied sarcastically, but he took the good ribbing in stride and paid the bill.

As they were about to leave the restaurant afterwards, Skid thanked Billy for the meal, winked and said, "I think I'll have just one more drink." He steered his way back in and over to where two pretty girls were sitting.

"Want to join in?" he invited.

"Naah… I've got a busy day tomorrow," Billy said.

He picked up Toots, his top Tool Push, and flew to Houston the next day to look at the three new rigs he was ordering. He wanted all the latest features on them that he'd either heard of or read about. Eventually satisfied with what he saw, he completed the purchase. The manufacturer guaranteed the delivery of the first rig in a month, with the other two to follow at one-month intervals. Billy felt that Toots was the one employee he could truly trust and completely rely on, and he told him over beers that he doubted he'd be able to keep up to six rigs running what with all the daily problems, so he planned on making Toots a Field Superintendent to help out on the management end.

The discussion over the duties of a Field Sup took several hours and required many beers. The one thing he knew about Toots that most impressed him was that he was as meticulous about order and cleanliness as Billy. The two men made a list on who should be promoted to man the expanded drill fleet and how they would recruit new men.

"Sometimes I feel like a juggler with too many balls in the air." Billy admitted.

"Yeah I know," Toots replied, "and riding a unicycle at the same time!"

Billy felt like a kid starting to open presents at Christmas time when the first rig arrived from Houston. He immediately shipped it to Grande Prairie where he had a contract to drill six wells. Billy followed the rig north as he had no intention of allowing anyone else but him raise the new derrick for the first time. And once again, the rig ran smoothly and Billy was happy with his purchase.

Back killing time in Grande Prairie, Billy's thoughts turned to Johnny Laboucan, his friend who had been killed in the Leduc blowout he'd been involved in. Billy felt he owed it to Johnny and try to find his mother, so he could explain Johnny's death and see if the money and the few belongings Johnny had had, had reached her. Billy had no idea just how he might find the little cabin that Johnny had described to him during their many conversations. And no-one knew anyone named Laboucan in the area.

Finally, Billy went to the post office, and a clerk there confirmed that yes, indeed, they did have a Mrs. Laboucan on their general delivery list. She gave Billy a general idea on how to find the little cabin, and he set off to find it. When he did so, it was just as Johnny had described it, located about 15 miles west of Grande Prairie. Billy knocked on the door and a frail Metis woman opened it a small crack.

"Mrs. Laboucan?"

"Yes?" she said hesitantly.

Billy quickly introduced himself and explained the purpose of his visit. Mrs. Laboucan's face remained expressionless as if she was used to receiving bad news, and he began to wonder about the wisdom of coming and perhaps opening old wounds. After all, it had been eight years since the accident now.

She never invited Billy in but stood listening to his story as he stood on the dirt pathway leading in front of the cabin. Her only reaction was to nod when Billy asked a question of his own.

Finally he ran out of questions and didn't know what else to say. There didn't seem to be anyone else in the cabin and Billy thought that maybe all the younger brothers and sisters Johnny had told him about had left home. So he turned to leave, and then suddenly stopped, reaching for his wallet and pulling out a $100 bill.

He handed it to the Métis woman, but again her face failed to register expression of any kind. Billy mumbled a goodbye, got back in his vehicle and drove back to town, wondering what kind of a life the wizened woman must be living.

Chapter 17

Back in Calgary, Billy was startled when a short time later Skid walked into his office without knocking. It was obviously not a habit he had formed. He pulled up a chair and asked how Billy was coming along with their plans to drill Skid's well.

"I should ask you how the fund-raisin's going," Billy responded.

Skid let out his sucked-through-clenched-teeth chuckle.

"You know what Barnum and Bailey say...there's a new sucker born every day," he said. "Actually, I feel real good about this well and I'm going to hang on to my shares. Usually we just 'run the box' on a wildcat well, but I've got a feeling we're going to hit oil and strike it rich this time."

"What do you mean 'run the box? `" Billy asked.

Skid looked at him and realized he knew nothing at all about how the stock market and brokerage firms worked.

"It works like this," he explained, putting his elbows back on Billy's desk and tilting his head to one side in the strange way he had. "I get about four other brokers involved and we sell my stock to each other creating an illusion of a lot of action on my stock. Soon, real investors start taking an interest and coming on board, and the share price starts climbing. Then, with a few rumors strategically placed in the local papers - which I write because most newspaper people are just plain too lazy to investigate or even write the stories themselves, especially if you give them a bottle of whiskey - pretty soon you've got some *real* investors buying in.

"When I think it's time to bail, I sell my stock. Then I change the name of the company and start over."

Skid's eyes sparkled as he let out another of his laughs. He could see Billy was catching on to his scheme.

"What I most enjoy doing though, is buying and selling lease lands that have mineral rights," he said. "That's why I always hang around the oil crowd. A lot of the conversation is just bullshit, but you never know when there's going to be some real little jewel of information that leaks out."

"So what are you going to write this time?" Billy asked.

"Oh I don't know, let's see, how about, Leduc-sized Oil Formation Thought to Lie Beneath Crossfield's Rolling Farm Land," he said, visualizing the headline. "Then I'll wait a couple of weeks and write another column: Giant Oil Poised to Drill a Discovery Well into the Crossfield Oil Play. Then, just as we start drilling, I'll issue a press release saying something like, Large Crowd on Hand as Giant Oils Spuds in its First Test Well in the Exciting Crossfield Oil Play. By this time I'll have taken in several partners, and raised Giant's initial offering price per share from five cents to hopefully twenty cents."

"Just so long as I get paid I'll be happy for both of us." Billy said a little ruefully, laughing along with Skid at his outrageous story.

Skid turned serious for a moment though.

"The Petroleum Club's having a Halloween party this Saturday," he said. "What do you say my wife and I swing by your place and pick up you and that wife of yours, and the four of us go to it?"

Billy thought for a minute, realizing that he and Candace rarely went anywhere even with another couple.

"That sounds like fun," he said. "I'll ask Candace and give you a call."

Not unexpectedly the idea was an instant hit with Candace, and she gave Billy a hug.

"We never go anywhere anymore," she admonished him. "You work all the time and I spend all my time raising the kids. This is the first time you've been home for supper in a month. After supper, I want you to take a look at some plans the architect has drawn up for the new house.

She chattered happily on as she prepared supper.

Looking at the plans afterwards, they both decided excitedly that they needed to make revisions. He told her he hoped she'd told the architect they'd budgeted a total of $100,000 for their home, and that included his fee.

"I want you to tell him that building should start June 1," he said, adding an explanation that by then he'd have completed his winter drilling season and, to be on the safe side, they ought to have ample cash in the bank.

Chapter 18

Billy phoned Skid three days before Christmas and told him he might have a Christmas present for him.

"So what's up?" said Skid.

"We've got some oil showing up at your well in Crossfield!" said Billy.

"Great news!" Skid exclaimed. "Let's take a run out there this afternoon. I'll be at your office at one." Then he hung up.

True to his word, Skid walked into the office exactly on time.

"Come on! Get a move on, let's go!" he said.

Billy was becoming quite accustomed to Skid's impetuosity and had made sure to be ready to leave.

"I think we should take my truck in case we get stuck in a snow bank in the car," he said.

"You always leave your truck running?" he said.

"Only when it's 20 below zero," Billy said.

Jet materialized from some warm resting spot someplace and when Billy told him he'd have to stay home, the big Labrador obediently returned to his resting spot.

"Even your dog obeys your orders," Skid remarked in some awe.

Billy ignored the comment and cautioned him not to get his hopes up too high about the well.

"Often they'll just give you a sniff and that's all it is," he said. "It's not worth bringing into production."

Skid had been to the site many times though, and he was happy they were in a four-wheel-drive truck pushing through some freshly drifted snow.

"What's the next step?" he asked as the rig came into view.

"The next step is to wait for Haliburton to come and run a drill stem test," Billy said. "Haliburton has tools they attach to the drill stem that will give you the pressure and potential flow, things like that."

Entering the dog house, Billy asked the Driller where Bruce the Tool Push was.

"He had to run into Calgary for some things," the Driller said.

Billy nodded.

"So what's the crew doing outside?" he said.

"Oh, they're putting together a flare line to the sump," the Driller explained.

Billy asked a few more questions and then excused himself.

"I'll be right back," he said.

A half hour went by with Skid asking the Driller all sorts of questions and the Driller becoming increasingly anxious with Billy's absence. Finally he went and opened the door and looked out, before closing it again quickly.

"Jesus Christ, I can't believe this!" he said, throwing on his coat and bolting out at high speed. Skid followed and stopped at the railing to look at what was causing such an alarm.

Billy was carrying a length of four-inch pipe over one shoulder and a 48-inch pipe wrench in his other hand.

Skid pulled his collar up over his ears and went down to investigate.

By now the Driller was flapping his arms around like a wounded duck, trying to insert himself into the centre of the activity. Billy had pulled on a pair of coveralls and was wearing his hard hat with the liner pulled down over his ears. Manning the pipe wrench and giving orders, he soon had the line constructed.

Back in the dog house, the Driller was profusely protesting that Billy needn't have done that, but the company boss just shrugged and said it looked to him like the crew didn't know what they were doing and had needed a hand.

"Those boys will be some surprised when they find out who the new hand was out there," the Driller mused as he began to relax a bit.

"Just be sure no-one lights a cigarette around here," Billy said.

Skid stood up and suggested they return to Calgary, but Billy said he wanted to wait a few minutes, as the four o'clock crew would be arriving any minute. When they arrived, both the incoming and outgoing crews all crowded into the dog house sorting out their lunch pails. One of the young roughnecks was complaining loudly that he thought his toes were frozen.

Billy took the incoming crew's Driller by the arm and told him the Haliburtan truck should be there soon, and what he should be doing to get ready for them.

"Bruce'll probably be back soon in any event," he said. "If he's not, Haliburtan will tell you what they want done. Just one other thing - don't let her freeze up."

Billy stripped off his coveralls and returned them to the storage box in his truck. Looking into the box, Skid saw there was quite a collection of items.

"You must have about half of everything you own in there!" he said.

"Pretty much," Billy replied, "the only difference is now that I don't carry my golf clubs any more - and I do carry a case of Crown Royal whiskey in their place."

"A case of Crown Royal!" said Skid, instantly warming to the idea. "You drink that much whiskey?"

"Nahhh, but you never know when you'll need to smooth some farmer or oil big-wig," he said. "There're a lot of doors to be opened in this business."

On the way back to Calgary, Skid suddenly said, "Take it on an experts advise, they serve up excellent hot rums at Hy's!"

"Alright," said Billy, "hot rums it is."

Many of the people they found drinking in the establishment were becoming familiar to Billy. He and Skid joined Alvin, Ned Hamilton and a couple of others Billy didn't know. One was Al Crane, who owned a large seismic company, and the other was Boyd Halburt, who ran a large construction company.

An earnest discussion ensued about who had the most important job in the oil industry. Crane suggested if he didn't do the seismic work, no-one would be working because nobody would be able to find oil.

Halburt scoffed that if it wasn't for his 50 caterpillars; there wouldn't be the thousands of miles of cut lines that "you doodle buggers" need to get around.

Everyone made a case for themselves and eventually the discussion turned to what is the best vehicle to own.

Billy took serious interest in the conversation, as he wanted input on this issue. Vehicle breakdown in the frozen northern terrain was a constant problem for anybody in the area and especially for everyone at the table. Everyone had an opinion on broken axles, broken springs, weak transmissions, faulty gear boxes on the front wheel drive etc.

And when comparing bang for the buck, everyone had an opinion o that too. Billy ended up no wiser as the conversation wound down, but over the years he had noticed the truck makes that were being driven were constantly changing.'

When asked what he thought, Billy just shrugged.

"I dive Power Wagons I lease from Art Hansen," he said.

Skid suddenly threw up his hands and interrupted.

"I almost forgot - I need two more curlers for the Oilman's Bonspiel," he said. "Cochrane, you must have curled before. You're in!"

"Now hold on a minute," Billy replied. "I haven't got time for a three- day drunk right now."

"You gotta come," Skid insisted. "Everybody who's anybody in the oil patch will be there - not to mention loads of good-looking babes."

He winked broadly.

"Here's the deal," he continued. "I'll pick everyone up in my car a week from this Friday. And I'll make all the reservations."

Billy shook his head slowly, wondering what on earth he'd got himself into now.

The combination of Hy's huge steak and several drinks put Billy in a more and more mellow mood, and when Skid suggested they wander over to the Petroleum Club to play some poker, Billy readily agreed.

"Have you played?" he asked Billy.

"It'd be pretty hard to spend a winter in the bush and not know how to play poker," Billy said.

"It's Wednesday, so all the boys should be at choir practice," Skid responded.

At the club, the two men took seats at the table where the game of choice seemed to be Texas Hold'em. Billy played conservatively, hoping to get to know his opponents better. Skid, on the other hand, seemed to plunge right in and play with reckless abandon.

The one player Billy decided he needs to be wary of was one of the senior partners in one of Calgary's most prominent oil and gas law firms.

The man had a bushy salt-and-pepper mustache. He had removed his suit jacket and appeared to be all business while he was playing. If Skid won a hand on a bluff, he'd invariably show his two hole cards and look at his opponent with his head tilted and give his unique clenched-teeth chuckle. He and the lawyer seemed to be doing most of the winning.

Around one in the morning, Billy was ready to leave.

"You coming to get your car or you want to take a cab home and come and get the car in the morning?" he said.

Skid said to wait for a couple more hands and he'd leave with him.

The very next hand the lawyer, whose turn it was to deal, flopped an ace, jack and seven of spades. Skid led off the betting with a $100 bet and everyone else folded, except the lawyer.

The next card dealt was another seven. Skid said all the cash he had was $40, but if he had $40, 0000 he'd bet that too.

The lawyer removed his glasses and held them to the light, seeming to examine them for dirt. He then deliberately shone them on his tie. Everyone was watching closely, waiting to see if he was going to make the call. Billy knew that everyone - including himself - was speculating what each man had for a hand.

After an extraordinary long delay from fiddling around with his glasses, the lawyer finally spoke, looking defiantly around the table.

"I believe," he said, "this is a no-limit game, so the gentleman's entitled to bet any amount he cares to - just so long as he can cover his bet. I call his $40 bet."

He then dealt the last card, a meaningless two of hearts. Everyone knew the card could hardly affect the two players' hands.

"Your bet," the lawyer said, fixing Billy with a cold stare.

Skid spread his elbows on the table and with his head tilted as always, looked the lawyer in the face.

"I bet $40,000." Only this time there was no chuckle as he spoke.

It was the lawyer's turn to react.

If I were to lose, you know I'd have a certified check for you at my office tomorrow at ten o'clock in the morning. Now, if I were to win, how exactly do you plan to pay me?"

The table was deadly silent.

"If I lose, which I doubt I'll do," Skid said, "I have 450,000 shares of Giant Oil stock that traded at 10 cents a share to day."

"I see, you have $45,000 worth of blue sky against my certified check," said the lawyer. "If I were to try and sell all those shares tomorrow, it'd drive their price down into the ground, to zero. I'm very aware of some of your oil stories, my friend."

Skid bristled visibly at this remark and stabbed a finger at Billy.

"So tell them, Billy, how much do you reckon those shares are worth from the prospect we've seen today?"

Billy was taken back by being put on a spot in the centre of the discussion.

"I can't really say," he mumbled, "the well is showing signs of being a producer, but then..." He just shrugged his shoulders.

Skid turned to the lawyer.

"That well is going to be a gusher, and the shares are going to be worth a dollar each in a couple of week's time," he stated flatly.

Again the lawyer seemed to deliberate for a long time.

Finally he said: "That's a very large bet. I accept."

Skid immediately triumphantly slammed down his pocket aces.

"Beat this!" he challenged.

By now everyone was leaning forward to see what the lawyer laid down for a hand. Slowly he turned over a seven and the cold hard fact suddenly started to hit everyone that he might have four sevens.

In what seemed to be an eternity, the lawyer turned up the last seven.

Skid sat stunned, starring at the cards. People began to stand up to leave, not a word was spoken by anyone. It was as though they had witnessed a murder.

The lawyer broke the thick, hanging silence.

"Mr. Blake, I expect to see you in my office at ten A.M. tomorrow with the transfer document in hand and completed.

Then in a low voice he added, "Please don't make me have to chase you."

Billy didn't speak a word on the drive back to his office to get Skid's car. He had no idea what to say.

Finally Skid spoke. "Merry fucking Christmas." Not another word was exchanged until they reached Billy's office and Skid started getting out of the truck.

"You know something, Billy," Skid said. "Alberta is just like a Holstein milk cow: just when you get a full pail of milk, she'll step her foot right into it."

Then out of the blue, he said: "What do you say we take our wives out to the Petroleum Club's New Year bash this year?" He said it quietly and gently as if the evening's events were already forgotten.

Billy nodded in wonderment. How could his friend just dismiss such a gigantic loss so easily?

****

The next day Billy was busy finalizing plans for the company Christmas party. He'd delegated most things to his secretary, but he was busy writing checks for bonuses and he had to calculate how long everyone had been working for him and how each one was to be rewarded. It had been another banner year for Cochrane Drilling, and Billy didn't want to go cheap. He booked rooms for all the Tool Pushes who could make it and for their wives at the Paliser Hotel. All the catering would be done by the hotel, so he had only to finalize the awards ceremony itself.

His secretary interrupted his thoughts and told him there was a land man to see him.

Billy was perplexed that a land man would want to see him and why he would be working so close to Christmas.

"Show him in," he said.

A young man Billy's age walked in and introduced himself. After a few Christmas pleasantries, he came to the point.

"We note that you own a half section of land five miles south of Camrose."

Billy nodded.

"So?" he said.

"We're prepared to make you a lucrative offer for your mineral rights and drilling rights on that property."

"Are you now?" said Billy, "and just who are 'we'?"

"I'd rather not divulge that right now," the young man stonewalled.

"Well, in that case, I'd rather not have any dealings with you," Billy replied, "and if you don't mind, I have work to do."

"But," the young man stammered, "but you haven't heard what we're preparing to offer you."

Again Billy mimicked his tone. "And I'm not prepared to listen."

The man virtually slunk out of Billy's office, leaving Billy wondering what that had all been about.

He really hadn't thought about his Camrose farm for a couple of years now. He made a note to make some calls early in the New Year and find out what was going on up there.

The Christmas party turned out to be a great success, and Billy thought everyone seemed truly surprised and delighted with their bonus checks. Many of the men there seemed to be very uncomfortable in a tie, he noted with some amusement, but he knew at the back of his mind Candace had grown away and more distant from much of the oil crowd. She seemed to enjoy herself throughout the party though.

"We've come a long way from our 32-foot trailer," he reminded her.

"Yes she concurred, but we had grate times in it."

Billy closed the party by noting Christmas time was for kids and it was about time for all of them to be getting home to their families. Next year we will hold our party a week earlier, he promised.

The Petroleum New Year party proved to be a glittering affair and "everyone who's who from the Alberta oil patch" was there. Billy was beginning to recognize all the important movers and shakers and Candace turned out looking stunning in an expensive black dress and diamond necklace that Billy had given her for Christmas. She seemed, he observed, a lot more comfortable with this crowd than she had been with all the assorted oil workers present at their own Christmas party. He could tell she was impressed when he introduced her to someone she'd read about or when he pointed out some of the local celebrities at the event.

Billy too recognized that he too was overcoming his own insecurity and was beginning to feel at ease as he made casual conversation with many of the big players in the Alberta oil patch.

Mr. Brinkerhoff made a point to say hello to him and Candace and that pleased him.

Skid's wife Carol positively gushed her excitement at being among such powerful and august company. Skid, sucking on a big cigar, remarked to her that maybe everyone else was saying the same thing about them.

As the evening progressed, Billy felt some one take his arm. When he looked around, he saw it was Frank McMillan.

"Billy boy, happy new year," Frank purred. "I've been meaning to talk to you."

Billy said nothing and let Frank continue.

"It has come to my attention that you own some land in Camrose that still has mineral rights," he said.

"Ah," Billy replied, "so you're the 'we' your land man was talking about when he visited me. Slow of me - I should've guessed that."

"Yes," said Macmillan, "that was unfortunate: I should have come and talked to you myself. In any event, our seismic testing indicates your land might have some potential. I suggest we sit down now and work out some kind of a deal that will be beneficial for both of us."

"I'll think about it, Frank, but - and please pardon the pun - frankly I've already got a hole one-third drilled on the property.

McMillan made a small gesture to wave that aside.

"One has to be careful," he continued, undeterred. "Those oil pockets around Camrose are small and one can easily miss them just by being out 200 yards. I wouldn't want you wasting your time and money drilling dry holes."

"I'll think about it," Billy said again and turned to go back to his table.

When he got there, Skid leaned over and asked, "What did that vulture want?"

Billy didn't respond right away, as he was pondering Frank's initiative.

"McMillan wants to make me a proposal on some land I own in Camrose," he told Skid.

"If McMillan wants to do a deal with you," Skid said, "then I recommend you do it yourself."

Back home that night, Billy and Candace engaged in an unusual bout of intimacy. When they'd finished, he remarked that that was the first time they'd sex in at least a month.

"I know, Candace replied, "you're gone all the time and I'm usually frazzled raising our kids. Things will improve, I promise."

Skid showed up as promised with his big new Chrysler New Yorker to take his team of curlers to the Bonspiel. The other was in the car when Billy climbed in, and the first bottle of whiskey was opened before they reached the outskirts of Calgary. Curling stories began to fly as the big car raced down the Calgary-Edmonton highway.

Skid told them he'd be the skip as he had skipped a team that almost won the Alberta schoolboys' provincials. Everyone knew that "almost" in Skid's vocabulary could mean almost anything but they didn't dispute his taking command.

Hamilton remarked it was a good thing they were curling now, because 20 years before they would have all had to own their own rocks and the rocks would have had to be loaded into the car as well. He continued on at length with a story about how, when he was a kid, an old farmer he knew was so proud of his rocks that whenever anyone fired a fast takeout at them, he'd run over, scoop up the one about to be knocked out and exclaim "That's good!"

Skid pulled his car into a no-parking zone in front of the Hotel MacDonald and suggested they all go in and register. Billy pointed out that they were in a no-parking area, but Skid dismissed him by saying they'd be back "out in a few minutes".

One of the Hotel ballrooms was set up as the Bonspiel headquarters. A Dixie Land band was playing in one corner and booths were set up all through the ballroom. Everyone was already in some state of inebriation and people Billy knew were shouting at him to have a drink. The evening quickly disappeared into a haze, and when Billy next looked at his watch, it showed just after two in the morning.

Hamilton held out another drink that some hospitality booth had just poured and Billy waved it away saying he was done for the night.

"We've got to be at breakfast by seven and on the ice at eight," he reminded his team-mates. "Tell Skid to bring my suitcase up to the room when he comes. I'm going to bed."

Hamilton and Gould woke Billy up at 6:30 the next morning. Letting his two friends into the room, they all noticed at once that Skid wasn't in his bed and it had never been slept in.

Gould said he saw Skid heading out of the ballroom around one that morning, and with one of the hostesses under his arm.

"That figures," Billy grunted.

Skid's absence left them in a difficult position. All of their suitcases were in his car and all they had to wear were the suits they'd had on when they arrived. They finally decided to take the shuttle bus to the rink, enjoy a hearty hospitality breakfast and hope for the best that Skid would show up.

At the curling rink it was if the party had never stopped. After Billy had consumed about three vodka-and-oranges, Skid breezed in as if nothing had happened. The team immediately demanded where their curling clothes were, as they had to be on the ice in ten minutes.

Skid grabbed vodka, and with his patented laugh, replied that he had no idea at all where the car was. It had either been stolen or towed away, he said.

"No matter," he continued, ""We'll simply curl in our suits."

"What about our brooms?" Hamilton demanded.

Skid shrugged his shoulders.

"Sweeping is seriously over-rated," he intoned blithely. "I'll hang my necktie out of the fly of my pants and you aim at that."

Going out on to the ice, Billy noted that all their opponents were uniformly dressed with fancy sweaters, with their names on the back of them. Each was taking a turn at sliding out of the hack and doing elaborate stretching exercises.

Skid pulled a bottle of whiskey out of his jacket pocket and set it down on the walkway. He held out his hand and introduced himself cheerfully to each of the opposition in turn. At that point, Billy gave up, decided "what-the-hell," and they all might as well have some fun and play along.

Fortunately, the opposition all took it as a great gag and went along with it, laughingly shaking hands with the team.

Well, Billy thought, the game should be over in about three ends and then we can all go and have a look for Skid's car. No-one swept any rocks as they didn't have any brooms, and when one of their teammates finished throwing, he'd take a slug from Skid's whiskey bottle and sit down.

Skid was matching all three of his team-mates drink for drink, but rather than being knocked out in just three ends, he somehow managed to make one incredible shot after another. It was almost as if he was playing by instinct and the opposition quickly quit smiling and started watching sullenly as Skid succeeded in making shot after shot, finally needing to execute a double take-out with his final stone to win the game.

All seven people were jammed in the back of the rings when Skid's final stone was delivered. When he made the shot, Billy looked around and saw that nearly everyone in the rink was watching them, all clapping and laughing.

One old timer slapped them all on the back as they were leaving the ice, and proclaimed that they'd added yet another piece of folklore to the Oilman's Bonspiel.

Celebrating at the bar, Skid went over to the draw board. When he returned, he noted dryly noted that their next game "should be a pushover". Hamilton took the lure.

"Who are we playing?" he asked as casually as he could.

"Some nobody named Matt Baldwin," said Skid, heading out to retrieve his car from the police compound.

Baldwin cleaned them off the ice in three ends, and they all made a long drive back to Calgary in silence, except for Hamilton. He noted that if they were to come back next year, they'd all have to train a lot harder.

"D'you mean curling or drinking?" said Skid.

The first thing Billy did when he got back to work was look up his old friend Dave the Geologist, whom he had got to know on his first job as a roughneck.

Billy knew that Dave was familiar with the Camrose geological field and he wanted his opinion on his Camrose land. Billy quickly located him and, after the usual opening pleasantries, asked Dave what he wanted to know. Dave tried to protest and said he was bound by professional etiquette, so he couldn't divulge any information. He wasn't about to divulge seismic information that was paid for by some other company. Billy wasn't sure what he could ask his friend, since he knew well the predicament he was putting him in. So after a few moments' silence mulling over the puzzle, Billy asked him if he thought he was being foolhardy to drill a well on his own land.

"Just say yes or no, and that's the very last question I'll ask," Billy promised.

There was another long pause. Billy then answered his own question by saying, "I'll take your silence as a no.

Moments later Billy called Toots and told him to move Rig No. 4 to Camrose after it had completed its present hole.

Just as he hung up, there was a knock on the door and Ethel his secretary poked her head round it.

"There's someone waiting to see you, who says he's an old friend from Nanton," she said.

"Show him in," Billy gestured.

Walt Cornish came in and greeted Billy warmly, then settled into a chair in front of the desk, taking off his cowboy hat off and sitting it on his knee.

Walt was five years older than Billy and his parents owned a mid-sized ranch at Nanton. Billy asked about many of his old friends, explaining that he always seemed to be in too much of a hurry going through Nanton, either on his way somewhere or on his way back home.

Walt brought Billy up-to-date on who had died and some of the local gossip.

"Everybody talks about you; you're a local hero," he said, his voice rising slightly with evident excitement.

Finally, Billy asked Walt how his chuck wagon racing was doing.

"That's what I've come to see you about," Walt said. He picked his cowboy hat up and agitatedly fingered the brim around in a circle.

"The sport has changed so much lately," he said a little sadly. "In the old days you harnessed up four of your fastest quarter horses, and away you'd go. Now, everyone's claiming thoroughbreds from the race-tracks and converting them into chuck wagon ponies. Some work out pretty well and others don't adapt. Pretty soon you have a helluva investment in horses.

"So... what I've come here to talk to you about is sponsoring my outfit. I'll put your drilling companies name on my tarp and pay you ten percent of my winnings. I know it's not much, but look at the exposure you'll get at every stampede, especially the Calgary stampede."

Billy gave a wry smile as if he had heard this pitch many times.

"How much are you looking for, Walt?"

"Would $3,000 be too much to ask?"

Billy let out a long sigh.

"You know, I have four season tickets for both the hockey and football teams, and I rarely get a chance to go...I have four tickets to the Calgary Philharmonic orchestra and I never go...I have a membership at the Calgary Golf an Country Club, and I seldom get a chance to play... and everyday there are requests from everything from Girl Guides to who knows what for a donation of money.

"Then there are requests to take out advertising in every magazine that has ever been written."

Walt, his head bowed, mumbled, "I know...I know." He got up to leave. "Thank you for your time," he said as he turned towards the door.

"Hold on there," said Billy. "Where are you going? You're forgetting your check."

Hardly had Walt made his joyful exit with his check firmly tucked into his wallet, than Billy called Skid.

"Skid, are you still the CEO of Giant Oil?" he inquired, already knowing the answer.

Skid laughed his usual sucking laugh.

"As far as I know."

"Well," said Billy, "I have some very bad news. Your well at Crossfield has turned out to be a dud. The drill stem test shows the pay zone isn't economically viable, and I recommend you abandon it."

Skid gave a rueful laugh.

"I don't suppose our lawyer friend will be too happy when he hears this," he said.

"Well, look at it this way," Billy offered. "Neither of you are out of pocket any money, and you're famous as the man who lost his oil company in a poker game."

Leaving for lunch shortly afterwards, Billy stopped at Ethel's desk and told her he was thinking of making her responsible for handling all requests for donations.

"I can't seem to say No," he added bemusedly. "I'll be back by two. If there's an emergency, you can reach me at Hy's."

At Hy's, Billy scanned the room for Skid, looking forward to hearing Skid's latest escapades and his endlessly endearing and charmingly self-deprecating sense of humor. Seeing him not, he spotted several of the usual and settled down to have lunch with them. Opposite him was a man he hadn't met. Billy extended his hand.

"I don't believe we've met," he said. "The name's Bill Cochrane, Cochrane Drilling."

The stranger held out his own pudgy little hand and gave Billy a very limp handshake.

"My name's Woodward Conridge III, CONFLEXO Oil," he said in a heavy American drawl and with what Billy thought was a slight smirk, as if to imply: "Who the hell is Cochrane Drilling?"

Billy decided to ignore the snub and the man along with it.

Ordering his steak, he turned his attention to Alvin.

"You keeping busy, Alvin?" he asked.

Alvin ignored his question, answering it instead with a question of his own.

"You know who CONFLEXO is, don't you?"

"Yeah, I know who CONFLEXO is," he said.

Woodward still had a sardonic and self-satisfied grin on his face, looking like the cat that ate the canary. Billy took further stock of the man and his soft little hands. He had obviously never spent any time in "the field" and he wore an expensive suit that was far more suited to the Petroleum Club than Hy's. To Billy, everything about Woodward looked soft and flabby. Even his belly protruded beneath his belt.

But Billy's curiosity was piqued and he decided to find out more about the man. Just because my first reaction was negative, he thought, I'd better stay on the good side of him. Maybe CONFLEXO was going to drill some wells?

"I detect an American accent, but I can't really place it," Billy said, hoping to coax Woodward into a serious discussion. He also knew from experience that most Americans can't resist telling people what state they're from.

"I'm from Oklahoma. Tulsa, Oklahoma."

Their food arrived ending any further discussion for the moment.

Billy noted during the meal though, that if anyone made a joke, Conridge would always add a put-down line, turning it back on the teller and making it appear as though the joke-teller was the likely perpetrator.

This had always irritated Billy, as he knew people like that hated ever to be the butt of any joke themselves.

"Sorry, folks, but I got to run," he said. "Whose turn is it to pay today? Time to pass the hat."

Woodward spoke up with his high, feminine-sounding voice.

"No need for that, CONFLEXO's paying today."

Billy left thinking that he'd have liked to stay for a couple more drinks, but he also knew from experience that if he didn't leave then, there was always the great likelihood of his never leaving and all of them ending up in the 400 Club at around four in the morning. Not only did he have some pressing work to do, he wanted to get home, as he'd promised Candace to join her to over the housing magazines an architect had left them. They'd have to make a decision soon if they wanted to get started – and there were so many options to explore – such as style and size of house.

Billy was leaning towards a huge house with a frontier-cabin look but Candace was adamant that she wanted a modern look. Billy tried to persist, telling her that the architect recommended to him was Gordon Atkins. Atkins, he was told, was well-known for specializing in designing homes featuring massive wood beams, floor to ceiling windows, angled skylights, cathedral like ceilings, and an all around feeling of spaciousness.

"Tell him when you talk to him, if I'm not there, to design the biggest damn' cabin ever built," he said, "and we want a mountain view from every important room in the house."

Chapter 19

The phone rang at 2 A.M. and Billy groggily answered it. "Boss," said a voice at the other end, "sorry to bother you at this hour, but your well in Camrose is showing some life. We've got strong oil showings in the mud tanks and the tailings coming over the shaker smell strongly of oil."

"Be right there!" said Billy's springing instantly to life.

Candace didn't move: she'd taken to wearing ear plugs to ward off all the late night calls that came to their home.

Billy reached for the suitcase he kept packed and ready for emergencies like this. He was out the door in a matter of moments, and drove the 180 miles to Camrose in three hours, a high speed considering the road conditions.

Arriving at the rig, he quickly changed into his coveralls and steel toed boots and immediately took charge. After looking at the tell-tale oil signs, he made two phone calls in quick succession, to his old friend Dave the Geologist.

Apologizing for the early hour of the call, he came quickly to the point, asking him to come to the rig and provide everyone some expert advice.

The second call was to Halliburton, ordering a drill-stem test. The crew started preparing for Halliburton and Billy took all the precautions he could to be ready for a blowout just in case.

After two days of drill stem tests and taking core samples, he was waiting nervously for the results. Finally Dave came over.

"Sorry, Billy, I've go some bad news," he said. He hadn't even finished the final words of the sentence when Billy exploded.

"Fuck!" he said, and threw his hard hat against the doghouse wall.

Alarmed, Dave threw his hands up.

just kidding!" he said. "You got a great looking well!"

He went on to say that the zone had the potential for 300 barrels per day but, given government regulations and common sense, Billy could realistically expect a producing well of between 75 and 100 barrels of production per day.

Billy did a little dance, and then turned to Dave with an alarmed look on his face.

"You know something - I know fuck all about running an oil company," he said. "All this time I've been drilling this well, I never gave any thought to what I'd do if I struck oil! You mentioned government regulation. What the hell are they and what do they mean?"

Dave scratched his head and said, "Well, for starters, there's a code called Good Petroleum Practice. One can only extract so much oil at a time, so as to not bugger up the formation and also not to rob your neighbor of his oil. And..."

Again before he could finish his thoughts, Billy cut him off.

"How about moving to Calgary and running the oil production division for me?" he said. "I'll pay you what you want, and you'll be in full control. We'll grow this company together."

Sensing some alarm and hesitancy on Dave's part, Billy pressed on.

"I'll pay you $40,000 a year - plus bonuses - and you won't have to spend the rest of your life in some God-forbidden place staring through your microscope in some little shack on an oil rig lease."

Billy could sense he was starting waver.

"I'll even pay your moving cost to Calgary," he said.

Dave still hesitated.

"I don't know, Billy, I'll have to think about it. I'll talk to the wife and get back to you."

Billy stayed on in Camrose for a couple more days and supervised the installation of the "Christmas Tree" valve on his well. Then, before leaving, he stopped into the farm house to see if Thor Olsen still was living there.

When Olsen answered his door, Billy sheepishly held out the man's shotgun and said, "I thought I'd better return this."

Olsen had apparently been working at his kitchen table, surrounded by a pile of paper. Billy hadn't been sure how he'd be received since he was sure Olsen would think he'd duped him out of his farm and mineral rights.

Olsen waved Billy to sit down.

"You want a cup of coffee?" he asked.

"Sure," Billy said as a friendly gesture. "I guess you've heard I struck oil."

"Yes...yes, that was no surprise to me," Olsen replied.

"You're not bitter?" Billy said; a little surprised.

"That's life," Olsen said dismissively. "But look here, I'm drawing up plans to patent my new carburetor that's going to revolutionize transportation. If I can get the Big Three car companies to buy in, I'll make millions. I've already been offered $10,000 by a big oil company to buy me out. $10,000 is peanuts to what I'm going to make.

"Seeing you're here though, would you consider lending me $10,000 to cover the costs of registering the patent and starting up a publicly traded company? I promise you your investment will pay handsome dividends."

Billy stood up.

"Sorry, Thor, I won't do that. But what I will do is to give you free use of your old farm. You can live here and rent the land out for a little income. Just don't run a cultivator over my pump jacks."

Billy returned to Calgary afterwards feeling like he'd eased his conscience somewhat, and drove directly to the new home construction site.

Candace and the architect were standing on the acreage looking at a roll of plans.

"Change in plans," Billy interrupted. "Expand the floor area to 10,000 feet and also add the wine room we were talking about."

Both Candace and the architect looked at him with some consternation.

"Honey," said Billy, "we've struck oil and there's a lot more where it's coming from."

Candace gave him a huge hug and the architect shook his hand.

Billy's next stop was at the construction site of his new office and storage yard. He approached the building contractor and said again, "Change in plans. I want 10 additional office spaces added.

"Hang on o second," the contractor said, "that's going to cost you..." and as he paused to figure out the new square footage.

Billy waved it off.

"I don't give a damn what it costs," he said. "Just get it done!"

When he finally returned to his office, he stopped at the front desk and Ethel presented him with a thick stack of phone messages.

Then she hissed, "That man is in your office again."

Billy knew instantly whom she meant, and wasn't surprised to find Skid sitting there enjoying a glass of Billy's whiskey with his feet propped up on his desk again.

"Just heard the good news," he said. "That old battle-axe of a secretary of yours said she reckoned you'd be back soon, so I availed myself to your hospitality. I just about had to barge her out of the way to get in here."

"Just imagine that," said Billy feigning sarcasm, "a secretary doing her job!"

Skid leaned on Billy's desk, cocked his head to one side, and said, "So tell me about it."

"No big deal," said Billy, "just a hundred barrels a day producer. Mind you, I plan to drill three more sister wells on my property, and with a little luck I should be able to get 400 barrels a day of production."

"Four hundred barrels a day!" Skid thundered. "At two bucks a barrel, that's eight hundred bucks a day!"

"My, but you are good at math," said Billy.

"You got to let me take you public," said Skid. "I'll have you farting through silk for the rest of your life."

"Why would I want to do that?" Billy said playfully. "Then I'd probably end up losing control of my companies. I don't need some public watchdog looking over my shoulder and having to issue financial statements every quarter or whatever,"

"I can make you a ton of money, my friend," Skid wheedled.

Billy took a sip of his whiskey.

"We'll see," he said, going on to recount the bringing of the well into production and what a thrill it had been. Then he told about visiting Olsen and jokingly told Skid he should help Thor with his new company.

"Yeah, right, I've heard that kind of story a thousand times," said Skid. "What I do have is a new gold mining venture in the North West Territories. It should be good for a good pay day."

"I've been meaning to ask you something," Billy said, changing the subject. "Who the hell is Woodward Conridge the Third?"

"Oh! So you met Mr. Conridge."

"Yeah, at Hy's a week or so ago."

Skid obviously enjoyed the question and mulled it all over before saying that he'd need another drink to tell the story.

"Woodward Conridge the Third," he said after being suitably supplied and speaking as dramatically as he could as he intoned each of the man's names for emphasis, "is purported to have married into the famous E.W. Marson family, the Tulsa oil tycoon, and rumor has it that CONFLEXO Oil, Marson's oil company, sent him up to Calgary just to get rid of him.

"I personally don't buy that, because when you get talking to him, he does know what he's talking about. I truly believe he came up here to size up the oil potential for CONFLEXO.

"He come off as a faggot to me," Billy mused.

"He's not a faggot, but he is a pervert," said Skid.

"What do you mean by that?"

Skid assumed his favorite posture, leaning over with his arms on Billy's desk. Billy knew this was a sure signal a conspiratorial story was about to unfold.

Skid let out a signature chortle.

"You know Karen that always hangs out at Hy's and the 400 Club?"

Billy slowly shook his head trying to place her.

"Sure you do, she's the one with the short dark hair, no tits and an ass on her like a twelve-year-old boy!"

Billy smiled at the description and replied that he thought maybe he knew the female Skid was talking about.

Skid was warming up to his story and let out a few more blast of air through his clenched teeth.

"Well, I was fucking her one time and she told me a story about Woodward. Apparently he owns a big house in Mount Royal that his wife never comes to because she hates Calgary.

"So on this occasion he lures Karen to his house with the promise of cocaine. They get into snorting some of the white stuff, and he suggests they play a game of hide-and-seek.

"Karen figures, what the hell and agrees. So she tells me she has to strip naked and he gives her a cat-o-nine-tales whip and tells her she has to find him and whip his ass. Woodward hides in one of the upstairs bedroom closets until Karen eventually finds him

– which didn't take too long. She told me she goes from bedroom to bedroom bare-buck naked and yelling out, ready or not here, I come! She was cracking the whip all over the furniture as she went.

"When she finally located Mr. Woodward Conridge the Third," said Skid savoring the name all over again in a slightly more deferential tone, "he runs out of the closet shrieking like a stuck pig, with her chasing him and whacking his ass with her whip!"

Both Billy and Skid were almost doubled over laughing, as Skid told his story. Catching his breath and rubbing the tears of laughter out of his eyes, Skid continued: "Wait! There's more!

"So there's Woodward wearing a pair of women's pantyhose and running around his pool table with a hard on that is about three inches long! And Karen's chasing him whipping his butt."

Billy was now on one knee laughing.

"That's too much!" was all he could say.

Skid quickly made Billy promise to not repeat the story to anyone, as Conridge might come in handy some day. But the following day as he went into Hy's for lunch, he couldn't help wonder if the butt of the story might be there.

"Hey, Cochrane, you're just the man I want to see!" Ned Hamilton called out.

Everyone else at the table was reaching out to shake his hand and congratulate him on the success of his well.

"Not many secrets in this town," he muttered.

As Billy sat down and the hubbub settled down, Hamilton told him why he had wanted to see him.

"A one-day opening has just come up at our hospitality lot for Stampede week," he said.

"What the hell are you talking about, Hamilton?" Billy demanded, perplexed.

Hamilton explained that a group of service companies rented a parking lot at Sixth Avenue and Fourth Street during Stampede week. They hired a catering company and band for the week, and the company - or in some cases, maybe even a couple of companies - would got together and host a pancake breakfast.

"The idea is to send out invitations to everyone you do business with as a PR promotion," said Hamilton. "The catering companies handle most of the manpower and provide the grill, plates and glasses, and all the other shit, and you go around and press the flesh or, if you want, cook a flapjack or two."

"I see," said Billy, "so what will this cost me?"

"Around $1,000, plus your booze costs."

Billy mulled this over as he ate his lunch. He could see there would be some good PR to be had - *and* he could write the whole venture off against the company for tax purposes. Finally, he thought, this might be fun, and it could be his contribution to the annual event.

He also told himself that if Hamilton was asking, then he was sure Hamilton and his seismograph company would be taking a spot as well. Hamilton was a very successful geologist and he'd moved on to build up a very successful seismographic company.

If Hamilton thought it was all worth his time, Billy mused, and then it was probably a pretty good deal. Finishing his lunch he got up to leave.

"So, what's the hurry?" Hamilton demanded. "I've just ordered a couple of more bottles of wine."

Billy explained he'd just got back and had to catch up on some paperwork.

"Count me in for one day though," he said. "What day is that?"

Hamilton took out his notebook from his front pocket.

"July 10th," he said.

Billy made a quick mental note and left before they could talk him into drinking more of the wine. He found he was learning the hard way that if you didn't leave by two, you'd probably end up spending the afternoon downtown.

Back at work, he told Ethel to make up 300 tickets for the pancake breakfast and send them out to all the oil and service companies that were on their directory.

"When you finish that, get ready to move," he said, "We're moving in to our new offices and shop next Monday, finished or not!"

Billy took great pride and pleasure in his new office. He personally designed the sign on the front entrance to the building, stating in large gold letters, COCHRANE DRILLING CO. Under that it had COCHRANE OIL AND GAS.

He also personally designed the inside of his own office, complete with separate bathroom and large closet, where he kept a complete change of clothing. A sliding wall panel opened to a complete bar, and expensive leather furniture decorated the large room. The centre-piece was his large mahogany desk. The walls were adorned with various animal heads he'd shot and had mounted.

But much to his chagrin, he now had nine full time office staff, seven working in the office and two out in the yard - along with, on any given time, another 200-300 employees in the field.

Chapter 20

Billy's morning routines were predictable. At 6:30 the morning reports began trickling in. He needed this information to pass on to the oil companies he was drilling for and for his own information, so he could know what was going on out in the field.

Usually Toots was present for these calls and listened in on the speaker phone, or often he would take the calls himself. At nine o'clock he'd meet with Dave and go over the latest developments on the oil-and-gas front. These meetings were becoming increasingly tense as Dave constantly whined and complained about everything, and Billy found it more and more irritating. And the past year had actually seen Cochrane Oil and Gas lose money. Dave knew Billy was disappointed in the year's results, and he took to defensively pointing out that it was expensive to buy oil leases from the provincial government - and also how expensive it was to have all the land seismographed.

Billy knew all this, but what bothered him most was the number of dry holes they drilled. He didn't say anything to Dave about it, but it was obvious he felt Dave was slipping and doing a poor job interpreting the seismograph results. During one of their previous meetings, Billy commented that they might just as well wildcat their drilling, as all the seismograph testing didn't seem to help. The comment dug deep into Dave and Billy thought for a second he was going to bawl, but he pulled himself together and the meeting ended not happily but without tears. The comment rankled though, and it was lying under the surface at the end of their meeting as Billy asked Dave to help out next Wednesday at their hospitality booth, by cooking pancakes.

By the look on Dave's face, Billy thought he'd just asked Dave to jump in and shovel out a mud tank. Dave hesitated and lamented, "I hope this doesn't reflect on the oil and gas's side bottom line."

"I'm sure we can figure something out," Billy muttered almost to himself as Dave went out the door. "He's just blown $500,000 on dry holes, and he's worried about the price of vodka and pancake batter!"

Later on, Billy watched as Candace pulled on some new jeans and then she asked asked how she looked in her blue jeans and blue cowboy hat.

"Fine," he fibbed.

"I think I look fat in blue jeans," she said.

Billy said nothing and it occurred to him that he'd never ever seen his wife in blue jeans - and yes, she did look fat in their snug fit. Since their third child was born, she'd steadily gained weight, trying – and succeeding - to disguise it by her choice of clothing. She even wore a bulky nightgown when she went to bed.

The caterers had everything ready to go when Billy and Candace arrived downtown. Billy rounded up some help to unload the twenty cases of vodka he'd brought in his truck. By 8:30 a lineup was forming to get in. Billy made two signs: one read Orange juice, and the other said Kickapoo Joy juice. He taped them on the five-gallon cream cans, then he set Dave to mixing up the vodka and orange juice while he, Candace and Toots starting cooking sausages and pancakes. When they opened the gate, the crowd surged in.

Billy didn't recognize a single face and reasoned the tickets he'd sent out were probably handed down to junior staff in the companies. He looked over and saw Dave carefully measuring out the juice mix and the vodka. Billy went over.

"You'll never keep up at this rate," he said, grabbing four bottles of vodka and pouring them all simultaneously into the cream can, then contemptuously splashing in four gallons of orange juice.

Watching this, Dave whined he couldn't pour all the drinks by himself.

"You don't pour!" Billy ordered. "Let them use the ladle and pour their own drinks." He plunked a ladle into the vodka pail.

At nine, the western band began playing and soon the party was in full swing. Billy was enjoying himself and regularly took a break from serving pancakes to do an impromptu doh-say-doh and little dance left and right with Candace.

Halfway through the morning, Dave excitedly tapped Billy on the shoulder.

"There are people passing tickets through the fence to people on the street!" he said. "They've got to be stopped!"

Billy shrugged." Who cares!" he said.

Dave persisted though, indignantly asking Billy how come he didn't care who was eating their food and drinking their vodka.

Billy gave Dave a withering look.

"For God's sake, man!" he spat. "This is the Calgary Stampede! People are here to have fun!"

"Quite a party you got going here, Billy!" Skid said, dropping by.

One drunken young lady was dancing on top one of one of the tables, and Skid suggested slyly that maybe he'd better help her down before she hurt herself.

"I think," said Billy, "she'd be a lot safer on the table than being 'helped down' by you."

During the morning, several top oil people took the opportunity to stop by and thank Billy for the invitations.

Billy laughingly mock-apologized, saying he was sorry he was responsible for so little work getting done today at many a downtown office.

By 11 all the vodka had been either drunk or spilled, and Billy said it was time to wind everything down.

On the way home he suggested to Candace that they take the kids to the midway that afternoon.

"I might as well take the afternoon off, as there'd be little happening at the office," he said. "Nothing gets done during Stampede week."

Candace agreed enthusiastically; there were so few opportunities do things as a family. She dressed Judy up in a smart little red-and-white dress and the five of them all set out to the Stampede grounds.

Things started out badly at their very first stop, a merry-go-round with wooden horses with saddles for the passengers to ride. As they waited their turn to get on, Billy could see Judy had her eyes on a big white stallion that was being ridden by another little girl. When the ride stopped, Judy tried to rush forward to get on her chosen horse, but another girl beat her to it. Judy stood by the horse and sulked as the carousel started up. Billy noticed Candace didn't spot this as she accompanied five-year-old Johnathon to a horse and stood protectively by him during the ride. Judy eventually climbed on another smaller horse near her mother, but she was clearly disappointed that she hadn't got the horse she wanted, pouting throughout the ride. Billy glanced down at Crawford at his side, who showed haughtily that at the great age of 12, it was far beneath *his* dignity to ride on a stupid merry-go-round.

Billy felt a barb of irritation. From where he stood, as a five-year-old boy Johnathon should have been able to ride by himself on something as tame as a carousel. But he also knew how protective Candace was of him, so he bit his tongue, not wanting to make an issue of it under the circumstances.

Their next stop was at a food stand, where Judy took no time to spill orange pop down the front of her dress. Candace wiped it up as quickly and as best she could, but her actions and comforting words did little to stem the tears and howls to which Judy had now descended.

And from then on, nothing they did for the rest of the afternoon could make Judy happy.

By the time they passed the strong-man exhibit, the tears weren't flowing any more, but Billy knew the afternoon was close to being a wipe out. So to try to help the youngster along with his pouting sister's behavior, he asked Crawford if he'd like to try and ring the bell.

"I will, if you will," Crawford said, looking up eagerly at his he-man father.

The proprietor showed them how easy it really was, taking a practiced and easy swing with the large mallet. Not surprisingly, he rang the bell with a resounding clank. Crawford took the mallet from him and gave it a hefty swing, and was clearly dismayed and disappointed when the ball only went up half the pole. He stepped back and handed the mallet to his dad.

"All right, everyone stand back," said Billy, taking aim for a mighty blow. He crashed the mallet down on target, but the ball didn't travel much farther up the scale than it had with Crawford.

Everyone standing around was having a good laugh at that when Judy spoke up and demanded she be given a turn too. Billy paid the man his money, then stepped back a little to give her room and watch as she tried to lift the mallet. Finally, with much effort, she managed to lift it enough to let it fall and make contact with the striking platform. The ball only moved very slightly, making the other four Cochranes laugh even harder. Judy's dignity was hurt still further and she turned away, sulking even more.

Still Billy and Candace continued going out of their way to try to cheer Judy up. They coaxed her on to different rides; they asked her if she wanted to see any of the exhibits they passed; they even bought her some cotton candy. Nothing helped, and she continued her dark mood, her bottom lip protruding and her head bent forward, her shoulders hunched.

Finally, as the afternoon heat closed in on them, Candace suggested that maybe they'd better get Johnathon home as he was clearly getting tired.

"Tell you what," said Billy brightly, "why don't you take Judy and Johnathon home, and Crawford and I'll stay for the evening rodeo and chuck wagon races. What do you think of that, Crawford?

Crawford looked up at his dad, his beaming smile answering the question. Both he and Billy were relieved to be free of Judy's constant whining, and the two of them relaxed as they watched the rodeo.

When the chuck wagons entered the track, Billy pointed out the Cochrane Drilling tarpaulin on one of them and explained to his son how and why that was.

The Cochrane wagon eventually ran in the last heat, and to Billy and Crawford's delight, it won. The way Joe Carbury gravelly intoned the words the Cochrane Drilling rig as it raced to first place gave Billy a great thrill and swell of pride, and he decided his $3,000 investment hadn't been a bad deal after all.

It especially gave him pleasure to see Crawford jumping up and down with excitement and cheering the chuck wagon on towards the finishing line.

Leaving the grandstands, Billy asked Crawford if he'd like to go to the barns and meet the drivers and outriders. Crawford received the suggestion with enthusiasm.

In one of the barns Billy soon found Walt Cornish chatting with some of the cowboys and introduced him to his son.

Walt called over the riders and participants standing around.

"Boys, I'd like all of you to meet Mr. Billy Cochrane, Cochrane Drilling, and his son Crawford."

One by one, they all came over to shake Billy's hand and also Crawford's. One of the outriders asked Billy if he had any roughneck jobs open for him, and Billy told him to drop by his office in the morning to fill out an application.

Walt handed Billy a beer.

"I guess you're a little young yet," he said, looking down at Crawford.

Crawford sat next to Billy on a hay bale as Billy sipped on his beer and noted with satisfaction the notice Crawford was taking of the deference everyone was showing them. He didn't want his son to grow up cocky or spoiled, but he sure did want him to grow up confident. He hoped that one day Crawford would work for Cochrane Drilling, and he felt he should mix with "real" people just as soon as possible.

Just then Warren Cooper, the rodeo announcer walked by. Both Walt and Billy called to him in unison, as Cooper was another Nanton native. Cooper sat down and rolled his customary Bull Durham cigarette. And always, when he lit his cigarette, there was invariably a hot ash that fell on his tie. Billy doubted Cooper owned a single shirt or tie that didn't have holes burned in them.

"So, Coop," Billy inquired, "has anyone claimed that wallet yet?"

"What wallet?" Cooper grunted.

"You know the one," said Billy. "Every year you announce that Helen Hunt has found a wallet, and if you have lost yours, you can go to Hell-en Hunt for it."

Everyone laughed at how Billy had turned Coop's corny old traditional joke around on him, and Coop harrumphed good-naturedly at their laughter.

Chapter 21

A few days later, Ethel poked her head into Billy's office. "There's a Mr. Woodward Conridge the Third out here wanting to see you," she announced.

Billy immediately put down what he was doing.

"Show him in," he said.

What in hell does Conridge want to see me for? he wondered.

The rotund man seemed to glide into the office, which impressed Billy with just how agile such a fat man could be.

He extended his powerful right hand to shake the man's pudgy little one.

"So what brings you here to our little low-rent district?" he inquired curiously.

Instead of sitting down, Conridge looked around the office, scanning the animal heads and other items Billy had mounted on the walls.

He wandered over to the large sheep head.

"Very impressive," he said. "Nice Rocky Mountain Bighorn. By the look of that one-and-a-quarter curl, I'd hazard a guess this one could be registered in the Boone and Crockett registry."

Billy was even more impressed that someone like Conridge should have such a knowledge or interest in that particular field. Like all hunters, he was proud of his trophy.

Getting up from his desk, he joined Conridge in front of the head.

"Shot that one in Waterton Park," he said. "I hired Andy Russell as a guide. Have you maybe heard of him?"

Conridge's blank stare answered his question, so he explained briefly that Russell was a famous out doors man, naturalist and guide.

"Anyway," he continued, "after a two-day ride we spotted this ram up on the opposite mountain. He must've been about 600 yard away but I was able to drop him from there - then damn' near killed myself climbing up to the ledge he was on! The most work I've ever done in one day - having fun, dragging that critter out.

"But I don't suppose you came here to listen to one of my hunting stories," he added, returning to his desk.

Conridge dropped in a chair in front of the desk, leaning forward and instantly becoming all business.

"If my information is right," he said, "I believe you have 12 producing oil and gas wells right now."

Billy was taken aback. Conridge's knowledge of his business was spot on.

"Something like that," he conceded, without giving the exact number away.

Conridge's eyes seemed to disappear behind all the baby fat in his cheeks. He began making a pitch for Billy to sell out to CONFLEXO, pouring out a jumble of facts and figures at high speed.

Billy tried to concentrate on what he was saying, but his mind kept wandering off to the story Skid had told him about Conridge's perverted little sexual bout with Karen from Hy's. He kept having to force himself to pay attention to what the oil businessman was saying and keeps from breaking into a broad grin right in front of him. The image of Conridge being chased by Karen with her whip was too ridiculous, especially with the man in question now sitting before him, and he had a hard time not bursting out laughing

"So, how much money are we talking about?" he asked to help keep his expression serious.

"Well, we'd have to do a proper assessment," said Conridge, "but I'm pretty confident we'd provide you with more money than *you*'d ever be able to spend."

He emphasized the *you* condescendingly.

Billy ignored the emphasis, developing something of a new respect for the man. At least Conridge seemed to know his business.

But there was no point in drawing the meeting out.

"At the moment Cochrane Oil and Gas is not for sale," he said firmly. "But I'll keep this in mind,"

After Conridge had taken his leave, Billy turned his attention back to the upcoming house-warming party he'd had promised Candace, promising to provide her with a list of oil people he wanted invited. Candace was excited that her parents would also be staying with them for a couple of days at the time of the party.

Billy wondered a little ruefully and apprehensively how he should greet his father-in-law. The two of them hadn't ever been exactly close after their first encounter, even though Billy didn't hold a grudge against the old man for his unpleasantly-worded objections to his daughter marrying the oil man. He recognized the older man had only been looking out for Candace's best interests and the older man was pleased the couple had given their son the family name to keep it going.

Still, Billy rarely accompanied her when she went home to visit her parents, and this would be the first time the Crawfords had ever stayed over with the Cochranes.

Should make for an interesting little time, he mused. He'd never even invited his own parents, as he knew they wouldn't come.

Billy had promised Candace to be on his best behavior and at least be home for supper when the Crawfords arrived, so, true to his word, he was home when the car drew up and Candace excitedly showed her parents around their mansion - with Billy tagging along. Mr. Crawford took it all in silence.

"Quite a place you have here," he said finally.

Billy wasn't quite sure how he meant that and thought of a couple of cutting answers he could give, but decided to leave the hatchet well buried.

"Nothing's too good for your daughter," he said, shaking his head.

Candace had saved pointing out the grand piano in the huge living room for last, and Billy could no longer help himself.

"We thought we'd move out of our trailer first, before we bought that," he said lightly.

Everyone had a little chuckle at the jest and the ice was broken.

In the meantime, Billy was thinking of the party. He knew it was going to be the talk of Calgary for days afterward and that it was being widely anticipated by all those invited.

When the day arrived, he'd arranged that as the guests arrived, they were met by a butler, who took away and stored their coats. Waiters and waitresses scurried about, pouring drinks from behind a couple of tables, others moving around offering trays filled with appetizers. Billy felt more than a little awkward and even out of place in his newly-purchased tuxedo, even though it was his own home. He knew he'd never been comfortable with making small talk. So in the end he was only too happy to see the last of his guests leave, and he slumped into a large chair, savoring a drink.

Skid, of course, didn't really regard himself as guest but a part of the family, so he'd stayed behind and he plunked himself down in a chair next to his host.

"Well!" he said. "That was some party! Jesus Christ, Billy, this home is bigger than the Lougheed Mansion!"

"That's because oil wasn't discovered when the Lougheeds first came here," said Billy.

Two weeks later, Billy was in the office when he received a frantic call from Candace. She was almost incoherent.

"You must come home right away!" she practically screamed into the receiver. "Judy's in trouble."

"What kind of trouble?" said Billy, instantly alarmed?

"She stole something from Burt's Store, and he insists both her parents must be present to bring her to his store - or he says he's going to go to the police."

"Go to the police!" said Billy. "What in hell did she steal? Jesus Christ, Candace, you're making this sound like our seven-year-old daughter committed some kind of an armed hold-up or something. Can't you handle this by yourself?"

"No, I can't!" Candace stormed back. "And don't you take that tone and attitude with me! He's the one who said you'd have to be there too!"

She sounded on the edge of tears, whether from fury, anxiety or frustration Billy couldn't tell which.

"Okay," he said, a little more soothingly. "I'll be there right away."

When he got there, Candace was still crying, but a little more calmly. Judy just looked sullen.

Entering Burt's Store, Billy introduced himself and Candace. Judy didn't need introducing. As soon as he saw her, Mr. Burt went into a tirade, pointing his finger accusingly and threateningly at Billy.

"This," he ranted, "is how criminals get started! And it's usually the result of poor parenting!"

Billy could feel himself redden and get angry too.

"All right!" he finally cut in. "Just exactly what *did* my daughter steal and how much was it?"

This provoked even greater outrage in Mr. Burt.

"That's not the point!" he raged, continuing to point his finger towards the couple. "That's typical! This is exactly what I mean - you rich people, you think you can just buy your way out of everything!"

Billy felt like breaking the man's finger off and inserting it into a tender part of the man's body. Candace could sense his growing fury heating up beside her, and moved in to try to calm the situation down a little before it turned physical, apologizing and promising desperately that they'd take all his good advice to heart.

Burt seemed to calm down a little, slightly mollified by the mother's earnest appeal. Judy, Candace promised, hadn't heard the last of this from her parents.

"Okay, then," said Mr. Burt, regaining control of himself. "I guess I can take you at your word, and I won't call the police – this time! But you owe me ten cents for that chocolate bar she took."

Arriving home with Candace and Judy, Billy was still choking back his outrage, but he realized he had to get back to the office.

"I'll deal with you, young lady, when I get home tonight," he told Judy menacingly. She stomped off into the house from the truck, knowing full well nothing more would likely be said from either of her parents. It never had been before, despite all her temper tantrums and shenanigans.

Chapter 22

Dining at Hy's the next day, Billy dawdled with Skid after lunch, enjoying the wine.

"That was a pretty impressive performance you did, promoting that gold mine in northern B.C." he told Skid.

Skid poured them both another glass of wine.

"Well, a guy has to make a living the best he can," he said with fake modesty and a twinkle in his eye. "So, how's everything going in the fast lane?"

"I honestly don't know," Billy answered morosely. "I buy a new rig every year, and all it means is just one more headache. What I know how to do best is to dig holes in the ground with people I know. Now I'm spending most of my time with lawyers and accountants and other assorted jackasses and pains-in-the-butt.

"Did you catch that guy on the Ed Sullivan show the other night, which spins plates on sticks? Every time he got a new plate spinning, one of the others would begin to wobble and he'd have to keep rushing around speeding them up to keep them from crashing to the ground, while at the same time he was adding new ones. That's how I feel! I think that's me up there! I've got too many fucking spinning plates on the go.

"I'm drinking too much, and I haven't had a decent piece of tail in months. Candace takes about four different kinds of pills every day - for who knows what - and all she can talk about is how Judy disrespects her. Seems to me she spends all her spare time going to her philharmonic functions. Now she's joined some kind of a weird church. I don't get to see Crawford play hockey or ball, and I worry about my daughter."

Before Skid could say anything, he continued: "My youngest son never goes outside and instead just hangs around his mother playing the piano. Next thing I know, he'll probably turn out to be a homosexual!

"So, is this really what making money's all about? I'm heading up to Edson tomorrow - we're drilling on our property up there, and they're having all kinds of trouble with a tricky formation we're in.

"So I'm just going to load up my old dog and hang out in the dog house up there for a couple of days, where no-one can bother me."

When he arrived in Edson, he found the shale formation the rig was in was continuing to shatter, and the drill was continually going off line on the hole. No-one - including Billy for once - had any real answers, so they kept trying different bits and experimenting with different drilling techniques.

On the second night, Billy was sitting by himself in the hotel bar, when one of the young roughnecks from the rig stopped in to buy some beer from the takeout.

He came over and introduced himself to Billy.

"I remember your face," said Billy.

"I'm getting married soon and my friends are holding a stag for me tonight," said the roughneck. "Why don't you come on and join?"

It only took Billy a minute to think about it.

"Why not?" he said. "It's been a while since I've been at a stag."

Billy walked into the farmhouse later with a couple bottles of Crown Royal whiskey, and soon found himself in a stook game with a bunch of young strangers. All the young players seemed to be distracted for some reason and kept on taking turns going to the window and looking out.

Finally, around midnight, the one at the window called: "They're here!"

There was a knock at the door and in reply to the joint invitation to come in, in walked two Edmonton hookers. In the blink of an eye, the atmosphere became electric. Most of the players at the card game in the kitchen left to go the living room where the two women were setting up for their strip act. For Billy, between playing cards and amusingly watching the two girls disappear all night long into bedrooms, the night flew by. The sun was shining through the windows before he knew it.

Billy stood up.

"Well, thank you for your hospitality," he said to his hosts. "I guess I better be getting home."

It was three o'clock that afternoon before Billy pulled up in his driveway. There were cars parked everywhere. What in hell's going on? he wondered.

There was nowhere for him to park, so he drove his truck up on to his lawn.

Entering the house, he was met by a total stranger who asked him snootily if he should be there.

Billy, still a little drunk and hung-over, rubbed the two-day-old growth of whiskers on his chin, looked around at all the vehicles.

"I'm wondering the same thing myself," he said with a slight slur, a little bemused.

As he went in, another of the guests guessed who he was and hurried over.

"You Mr. Cochrane?" he inquired in a whisper.

Billy looked at this new face in puzzlement.

"Yes..." he said wearily.

"I'm sorry, sir," the man said in a whisper. "Please take this seat here." He gestured to the one he'd just vacated.

No-one else in the room even noticed or paid any attention to Billy's arrival. They were all concentrating on a stringed quartet playing round the piano.

Billy scanned the room and didn't recognize a single person until he spotted Candace also sitting near the piano. To try to keep from falling asleep he tried to focus on the music, but his eyes kept shutting.

Finally he could fight it no more, and, his chin on his chest, he sank into a deep sleep in the large chair.

He only awoke when Candace shook him. Opening his eyes, he found everyone had left. He'd slept through the whole thing.

"Really, Billy!" Candace said, mildly rebuking him. "If you have to snore, you must do it in tune with the music! Now, don't forget, next Thursday we're hosting a dinner for the hospital board. Number one, I want you here; and, number two, I want you to stick around and help entertain the guests for me, and not slink off to bed at the first opportunity."

"Why don't you just send a check to the hospital board and save yourself and everyone else all the fuss and trouble?" Billy said, already bored with the whole idea.

"Because I'm a member of the board," she reminded him, "and we're trying to increase an awareness of the need for a new wing at our hospital."

"Well, all right then," said Billy a little grumpily. "I'll be sure to be here. But you make sure you sit me beside someone who's at least a little interesting."

"The last dinner we had," she recalled, "you seemed to be taken by Captain Elfort."

"Yeah - because he was a captain in world war one, with some interesting stories to tell," said Billy. "It's those people you invite that sidle up to me with their hands clasped behind their backs and use such words like extraordinary, splendid or delightful, that tees me off." He imitated some of their toffee-nosed accents in saying the words. "That's when I excuse myself and head off to bed. *They* don't have to get up at five o'clock in the morning! Where do you meet these people anyway? And whoever talks like that anyhow?"

"Now you listen to me, Billy C!" Candace admonished, "I don't run off to bed when your oil buddies sit around and get drunk and say words like shit or fuck!"

Billy was speechless. In all his married life he'd never heard her use words like that before.

After a moment though, he broke into a grin.

"All right, all right," he said, holding his hands up in surrender.

"You've got a deal."

Chapter 23

All the regulars at Hy's were all abuzz about the new oil and gas play in Fort St. John, British Columbia, when Billy walked in a few days later. Rumors were flying back and forth about who the players were and how big a field it was. As usual, the people that knew the most were keeping quiet and said the least.

When asked, Billy shrugged and said *he* didn't have any rigs in the area. The conversation drifted away to the world-championship boxing match being held that evening between Muhammad Ali and Floyd Patterson.

"What day *is* this?" asked someone who the worse for wear was clearly already.

"November 22," said Conridge, "and the year is 1965 - in case you've forgotten that too!"

Skid asked if the bout was being televised, and Ned Hamilton chimed in.

"There's nothing like watching a heavyweight championship fight live," he proclaimed. Everyone turned around and started demanding how he would know - where had he ever watched a live championship fight. In all the joking and teasing, no-one noticed Conridge slip away.

He came back to the table shortly afterwards and sat down grinning, looking in more ways than one like the very fat Cheshire cat in Alice in Wonderland. The debate was still raging about the individual merits of each fighter and who was going to win, when Conridge interjected.

"Would any of you gentlemen like to go to the fight tonight?" he said loudly, so as to be heard above the raised voices.

It was if a gun had gone off. Everyone at the table stopped in mid-sentence. Conridge suddenly had everyone's full attention.

"I just made a few calls," he said offhandedly. "My plane leaves at 2 P.M. precisely. I made a call to an old friend at the Sands Hotel and he just happens to have three rooms he comped, and six tickets to the fight. So who's in?"

Skid practically jumped on the table.

"Me and Billy," he volunteered quickly.

Billy shot him a look of astonishment, but he knew he wouldn't be able to resist going. Almost as instantly, four other hands went up around the table.

"Great!" Conridge said. "See you all at the CONFLEXO hangar at two - and don't be late."

Billy looked at his watch.

"That only gives us an hour to get ready," he said. "Better get going and he led the stampede out of the restaurant.

As he hurried by her to his office, Ethel stood up, reached out and attempted to hand him a bunch of messages. He ignored the offered paper, went in and quickly dug out a clean suit to change into, throwing just a clean shirt, underwear and shaving kit into his ever-ready suitcase. Then he charged into the shower, as Ethel shouted to him through the bathroom door, trying to give him instructions about which of the messages were the most important and needed to be answered.

He quickly toweled himself off, wrapped the towel round himself and emerged, to brush past a startled Ethel again.

"Later," he said. "I don't have time for that now."

"What should I tell all these people?" Ethel queried her voicing rising slightly in panic at the aspect, as she followed him to the door, still waving the wad of messages.

"Tell 'em I was called away on an emergency," Billy retorted, his voice tracking off as he turned and ran to his truck.

The 12-seat CONFLEXO jet was already on the runway with its engine idling in preparation for takeoff when Billy drove up. He was so excited, just like the rest of the group, that he hardly even noticed the very buxom female flight attendant.

Sitting down next to Skid, he asked, "Tell your wife you're going?"

"Naaah," said Skid. "Why catch shit twice?"

As soon as the plane had take off and leveled out at cruising altitude, Conridge's flight attendant began serving drinks. Everything anyone ordered, she made a double.

"You see that?" Skid asked, keeping an eye on her in wonder, "she's drinking shot for shot with the rest of us!"

Conridge, who had been sitting up front in the co-pilot's seat, stood up.

"Gentlemen, may I introduce Wanda, she's available for any of your needs on this trip. Enjoy!"

Suddenly it hit Billy what Conridge was talking about. It didn't escape Skid's attention either. Halfway through the flight, he disappeared to the back of the plane. His fairly brief vanishing act didn't escape Conridge's attention. When Skid made his way back to his seat, Conridge announced: "Gentlemen, meet the newest member of the Mile-High Club!"

Skid just grinned.

Nearing Las Vegas, Billy noticed Wanda was becoming quite drunk and could barely pour the drinks. He'd never looked back during the flight to see who else had made the trip to the back of the plane, but he couldn't help but seen Wanda lurch by and try to plunk herself down on Conridge's lap who was sitting in the co-pilot's seat. Slipping off his knees, she fell against the instrument panel, tripping some switches and causing the pilot to lose control. The plane started to nose-dive towards the earth. Conridge cursed and quickly pulled her away from the controls. The pilot immediately reached over to reset the switches. In moments, he'd regained control, bringing the plane out of the nose-dive.

The incident had taken only a matter of seconds, but Billy noticed there wasn't much conversation during the last half-hour of the flight after that. Thinking back later, he decided it was the only time he'd ever seen Conridge without that silly smirk of his on his face.

A limousine was waiting for them at the airport as they landed, and it quickly whisked them away to the Sands Hotel. Everyone was milling around while Conridge handled the check-ins. Billy couldn't hear what was being said most of the time, but he could make out Conridge's rich Oklahoma accent announcing "Woodward Conridge the Third and CONFLEXO" to the receptionist

Conridge managed to finish the check-ins in short order, turning triumphantly to the group.

"Gentlemen," he said rather like a ring announcer, "here are your tickets to the fight - and it gets better!" He paused for dramatic effect.

"Here also are tickets to Sinatra's late show to night. Everyone's on their own from here on in."

In the room with Billy, Skid did an impromptu dance, slapping him on the back.

"First we take the Sands, then we bring this town to its knees!" he declared. "Did you get a look at those cocktail waitresses?"

Billy shook his head at him.

"Wasn't that gal on the plane enough for you?" he said in some awe.

"You kidding?" said Skid. "I'm just like that old black hunting dog of yours - bring out your shotgun and he starts to shake, shiver and his teeth rattle. I'm the same way around women."

When he got to the arena where the fight was to take place, Billy couldn't believe the excitement. There was a feeling of static electricity that buzzed in the air before, during and even after the fight.

On the way out afterwards, he ruefully noted that the $5 minimum bet he'd spotted at the blackjack tables on the way in had all of a sudden mysteriously moved up to $50.

For him though, Frank Sinatra's show turned out to be almost as exciting as the fight. During every lull in the performance, Skid would run out and place a bet at a nearby table, then quickly return to catch the next song.

After the performance, Skid told him he was going to play craps and break the house.

"I guess I'll be somewhere in the room playing blackjack," Billy replied.

In less than an hour, Skid was back, tugging at Billy's sleeve.

"Can you loan me a couple of thou?" he said, adding more than a little unnecessarily, "I'm having a bit of a bad spell."

Billy started to try lecturing him about his gambling losses, but Skid blocked him before he could hardly get the first few words of protest out.

"You're the gambler here, Billy boy! You lose $100,000 on a dry hole - and you lecture me about losing a few lousy thousand dollars?"

Billy laughed at the irony and went to the cashier to get some money for him. Then he settled back into his blackjack game and watching the promenade of men and women dressed to-the-nines parading around the casino. He recognized a few celebrities and realized everyone that was there was there not just to see but to be seen. He'd never witnessed so much jewelry, especially on some of the black women.

Sipping on a drink, he was startled a little while later, when a well dressed man tapped him on his shoulder.

"Are you Mr. Cochrane?" the big man asked politely as he turned to face him.

Billy cautiously admitted he was.

"May I speak to you a moment?" the man said, stepping back and beckoning him away from the table. Billy instinctively looked nervously at the stack of chips in front of him on the table, but the stranger quickly assured him the dealer would look after them for him.

Away from the table, the man quickly identified himself as a security employee with the hotel.

"Did you accompany a Mr. Woodward Conridge to Las Vegas?" he said.

Billy nodded, starting to become alarmed with the big man's stern countenance.

"What's this all about?" he demanded.

"Mr. Conridge has had an accident," the man said. "Would you mind gathering up your chips and coming with me." It sounded more like an order than a request, so Billy quickly stuffed his chips into his pockets.

Turning back to the man, he said, "I want my friend to come also."

He went over to the craps table Skid was at, tapped him on the shoulder and whispered into his ear, "Come with me."

Skid was about to protest, but looking at Billy, he sensed something serious was wrong. He grabbed up his chips and left the table, trailing after Billy and the big hotel employee.

The man opened the door to a deluxe suite. There, sitting naked on the bed, was Conridge. He was covered in blood and Billy could see bits of red stuff everywhere. Conridge was blubbering incoherently as another hotel security man stood impassively off to the side.

"Holy hell!" said Skid, the first to find his voice. "What the hell happened to you? You just get robbed?"

Woodward nodded dumbly, and Skid turned to the security man.

"We need to get the police in here," he said.

"I don't think," the security man replied evenly, "that either you, or Mr. Holloway, or the Sands Hotel want to see the police involved in this."

Billy went up to Conridge to try to comfort and calm him and it was then that he noticed for the first time that Conridge still had a spiked dog collar around his neck. A whip lay on the floor on the other side of the bed, with flecks of red on it, and Billy also spotted a couple of syringes laying on the nearby night table. All over Conridge's corpulent body there were bright-red striped and angry-looking marks, some of them still oozing blood.

Billy looked sharply at Skid to see whether he'd seen the same things and the two of them stood there transfixed for a moment, not knowing what to do or say.

The silence was broken by one of the two security men.

"We should be able to identify whoever was responsible for this by the video tape," he said. "The hotel will deal with this little matter discreetly, without any fuss."

"Well, please have the hotel to send up a doctor right away," Billy said.

"That's already in hand," said the bigger of the security men, the one who had collected Skid and him from the gaming tables.

Billy turned to Skid again.

"As far as we're concerned," he said on behalf of the two of them, "this was a mugging that went a little too far, and it's all going to stay in Vegas. What happens 'in Vegas stays in Vegas?

Chapter 24

The going away party a few days later for Joan, one of the office assistants, started harmlessly enough.

Billy decided to stay on at the office at the end of the regular work day and join in the little celebration the rest of the staff had organized. He wanted to get a better look at Joan's replacement, a younger woman called Judy. The only thing he knew about the new girl, which he could confirm himself, was she was a knockout to look at - which was decidedly odd, he thought, because Ethel had usually only hired competent people who tended to be on the plain side.

And of course the name had stuck with him, because it was the same as his daughter's. He also knew that during the changeover over-lap training period before Joan left, Judy had taken to personally delivering the handful of messages to his office each day, rather than Ethel. And it seemed to him that she always lingered a bit. That intrigued him.

By nine o'clock on the night of the party, everyone was in fine spirits, and to be very relaxed from all the alcohol. Quite a number were dancing to music from the radio. Billy got up from his chair and went into his office to go into the bathroom and relieve himself. He didn't notice Judy slide into the office behind him, quietly pushing the door closed behind her. He was startled to see her there when he heard the door click. Judy was leaning back against it in a provocative pose.

Without a word, Billy took two quick steps towards her and swept her into his arms, kissing her on the mouth and neck. Judy almost immediately slid down his zipper, reached in, pulled out his rapidly-hardening cock and began playing with it.

Staring into his eyes, she slowly went on her knees and started licking the now-stiff member. After a few moments, she broke off her gaze, taking him fully in her mouth and sliding his now-throbbing rod deep down her throat. In all their married years, Candace had never done that, and Billy couldn't believe the sensation he had, as he ejaculated into Judy's receptive mouth.

It was all over with in just a few minutes and they quietly rejoined the party, apparently with no-one having noticed their absence together.

Annual Christmas parties were becoming more and more elaborate as time went on, Billy noticed as he worked on bonus checks for the company party. The bonus checks had kept on going up each year as well. He decided to move the company party to the Calgary Inn from the venerable old Paliser Hotel. But the format remained the same: following an excellent dinner Billy summarized the year's activities and ended the speech by pointing at the big Christmas tree in the corner.

"There are your Christmas presents, under the tree!" he said.

He always enjoyed the mad scramble, with everyone trying each employee's envelope and people calling out each other's name to hand them the one with their name on it. It always looked more like an Easter egg hunt than Christmas.

The one change that Billy made for this year's party was that he booked a room at the hotel for Judy and him. He knew Candace would either tire or become bored with the oil crowd before too long and would want to go home early. She always did, and Billy made some excuse to stay.

Over the next few weeks, Billy's thoughts became quite fixated on Judy, and plotted every conceivable excuse to spend time with her. He paid for a high-end apartment for her and claimed it as a business expense needed by Cochrane Drilling guests. He let his hair grow long to keep up with the current fashion for younger people; and he bought a new Corvette and left it for Judy to drive as long as she didn't drive it to work - or up some tree someplace.

Looking into the mirror each morning, Billy cursed himself ruefully for his unfaithfulness of the night before, and he regularly vowed to break off the relationship. But his resolve only lasted until Judy showed up for work in the morning in her short mini skirt. And when she brought in new messages, she took to standing in his en-suite door, where she knew no-one else would be able to see her. She'd pout provocatively at him and lift up that teasing little skirt, pulling her panties to one side and rubbing herself in front of him. As she did so, she'd roll her tongue over her lips, knowing she was driving him crazy with lust as he sat at his desk, the boss of all he surveyed.

It was a bright February day almost two months after the Christmas party and his hours of passion with Judy, when Bruce called Billy to break some bad news. The night shift had just twisted the drill bit off.

"How in hell did that happen?" Billy exploded into the phone.

Before Bruce could answer, he screamed, "Never mind! I'll be right there."

The drive to Rocky Mountain House gave Billy time to think about where he was going with Judy and how the relationship had developed in the last several weeks. He knew he was in an almost impossible situation, yet he had to have her. Many times she was late for work or even missed out entirely, and by now he felt certain she was screwing other men. But then again, he rationalized, *he* to was a married man.

Pulling up to the rig after the phone call, Billy's blood began to boil again. The crew was standing around waiting for the service company to arrive with the 'fishing' tools.

"Okay," he demanded, "what happened?"

Bruce had held the Driller and roughneck back from going home, as he knew Billy would want some answers to some direct questions.

"I had to take a quick crap and left the Roughneck here to squeak the brake," said the Driller. "I *told* him to keep the weight gauge at 20,000 pounds…" His voice trailed off.

"I didn't know I'd put that much weight on the bit," the Roughneck said dispiritedly. "The brake slipped out of my hand."

Billy ignored the boy's lamentation and turned back to the Driller.

"Take a crap, my ass!" he said. "You went for a smoke and you left a quarter-of-a-million-dollar drill rig in the hands of some

18-year-old weevil! Pack your stuff and get the hell of this property! I don't want to see your face again!

"As for you," he said, turning back to the kid, "you're fired as well."

The two men started to slink off the floor.

"It wasn't the kid's fault," Bruce tried to intercede quietly.

"You know the problem with you, Bruce?" Billy said. "You're just too damn' soft. You're losing it too! You set up that guy to Driller and because of you we're going to lose money on this hole. Pack your stuff and go home to your wife in Leduc."

"You're firing me, Billy?" said Bruce, astounded. "You're firing the first person you met on your first job as a roughneck 17 years ago?"

"You heard me, Bruce!" Billy ground out. "I'll take over and get that god-damned bit out of the whole."

Arriving back home after the job was done, Billy was met at the door by Candace. He could see she was upset about something and he decided to take the bull by the horns.

"What's the hell's the matter with you?" he snarled.

"It's Judy," she said fighting back the tears. "The principal phoned and said she's been skipping school."

"Great!" said Billy. "So now we have to go to the school and have some god-damned school teacher point his finger at me and tell us we're bad parents! Where is she? Where's Judy? I'm going to have a talk to her."

Judy came down from her bedroom with a sullen look on her face.

"Come with me, young lady," Billy said, leading her by the arm and practically dragging her to the stable he'd built for her behind the house. "Look at this! You're not even looking after this expensive horse we bought you! There's horse shit everywhere and you promised if we bought you a horse, you'd look after it properly and clean up behind it. Its coat hasn't been combed for a week! We put you in Girl Guides. And you quit! We put you in ballet lessons, and you decided you didn't like that, so you quit! We put you in figure-skating because you wanted to skate like Crawford, and you quit! You just had to have a horse, so we put you in riding classes and bought you all the expensive clothes that go with it - and just you look at this! Now your mother tells me you've been skipping school! If that's the way it's going to be, I'm going to sell this horse - you're not even spending the time you're out of school looking after it. If that's the way it's going to be, I'm going to sell it!"

Judy's expression never changed as her father ranted on.

Finally, her arms folded across her chest, she looked him hard in the eye with angry glare.

"Fine!" she spat out. "I don't care! You never come to see me do anything anyway!"

She spun on her heel and stomped out of the stable back to the house, ran up the stairs to her room and slammed the door.

Billy was left to vent his anger by grabbing a shovel and cleaning up the stable.

Cooling off slowly, he realized with some regret that there was more than a nugget of truth in what she'd said.

His mind was elsewhere though as he meticulously set about scheming towards an Easter-break getaway skiing at Banff with his secretary. It was unlikely, he mused, that Candace would even bother to ask him just where he'd been for two days during a long weekend, but as a backup he came up with elaborate ruse just in case. Then he booked an expensive suite at a lodge and started looking forward to a little romantic time away with his lover.

Billy had only skied a couple of times in his life, and he knew from asking her, that Judy had never skied in her life. No matter though, he decided to himself, this promises to be a nice exciting, romantic and hopefully passionate little adventure for the two of them.

When they got there, Judy enrolled for a half-day learner's course, and Billy set about tackling the nearest easy slope. Each time he finished a run, he looked over to see how Judy was making out. It seemed like she was spending most of her time holding on to the instructor's arm, supposedly struggling to stand up.

Eventually, exhausted by the time the early afternoon arrived, the two of them retreated to the lounge near the ski-lift.

While they were waiting for their drinks to come, Judy suddenly got up and went over to a tall, muscular young man leaning against one of the barroom's support beams. Billy sipped on his drink alone and watched out of the corner of his eye as Judy openly fawned over the man, who was deeply tanned and had a pair of sunglasses perched on his head of shoulder-length, rather dirty-blond hair.

Billy noticed he looked like a very keen and athletic skier but seemed to be totally disinterested in Judy, nonchalantly taking an occasional sip at his beer. Billy couldn't help but see Judy continually touched him as she chattered away.

Eventually she returned to the table.

"Who's that?" Billy heard himself asking.

"That's Hans, my instructor," she replied, perhaps a little too offhandedly.

"I figured he'd probably have some kind of Swiss name," Billy said sarcastically.

The couple had the most expensive meal at the most expensive restaurant that evening, but Billy noticed she continued to seem distracted. He wanted to return to the room, drink some wine, light some candles, soak in the hot tub and then take her to bed, but Judy talked him into going out instead, to a popular nightclub and dance-place.

Entering the room, his worst fears were quickly confirmed. Loud rock music blared out from the speakers and garish lights played ceaselessly over the dance floor. Judy was quite bubbling with excitement though, and made a few dance steps as she and Billy made their way over to a booth. Billy slouched wearily into it. In almost no time, before Billy spotted him, Judy asked him if he minded if she went over to talk to her instructor, who he saw was laughing with a group of like-dressed skiers.

Billy felt he'd been trapped, but he didn't know what to say. He didn't want to appear anxious or threatened or that he'd had his pride wounded, so he airily waved her away.

"No problem," he shrugged.

During the evening though, he silently endured Judy's entreaties to dance with her. And every time he refused, she'd respond by asking him if he then minded her dancing with someone else. The evening spun out into eternity with Billy drinking morosely in the booth and watching her shamelessly dance in an openly-flirtatious way with the resorts young ski instructors.

Several times he caught one of the young men looking at him as they talked, and he knew they were talking about him. He didn't dare get up and go back to hotel, leaving Judy alone, but he couldn't figure out a way to get her out of there without causing a scene. The more he drank the more miserable he became.

The night at the dance-place came mercifully to an end - at closing time - and the two finally made their way back to their room together. He made a feeble attempt at initiating sex. For the first time since he'd known her, Judy said she was tired, turned her back to him, and went to sleep.

Little was said on their drive back to Calgary the next day, and Billy unenthusiastically returned her kiss when he dropped her off. Driving away, he heard Jerry Lee Lewis came on the radio singing "Middle Aged Crazy." An angry and bitter tear came to his eye as the lyrics washed over him.

"Don't look for the grey in his hair, 'cause he ain't got any;
He got a young thing beside him that melts in his hand;
He's middle aged crazy trying to prove he still can.

He's got a woman he's loved for a long time at home,
Ah, but the thrill is all gone when they cut down the lights'
They've got a business that they spent a while coming by.
Been a long uphill climb, but now the profits are high.
But today he's forty years old going on twenty
And he hears of sordid affairs and he ain't had any.
And the young thing beside him you know she understands
That he's middle-aged crazy, trying to prove he still can.

Chapter 25

Billy's mood hadn't improved by the time he went to work on the Monday. Of his thirteen oil rigs, only six were actively drilling. Dave didn't show up at the office for their usual 9 o'clock meeting, and Billy went to Ethel wondering where he was.

When Ethel told him Dave had booked out to attend a convention, Billy exploded.

"Conventions, board meeting, committee meetings, staff meetings, every god-damned committee in the oil patch, he's on it!" he said. "I wonder if it's ever occurred to him his job is to find oil for Cochrane Oil and Gas!"

His mood darkened farther when Ethel told him Judy hadn't showed up for work that morning either. She went on to say that she thought Judy should be fired. Her work was shoddy and she came to work late far too often, she said.

"Let me look after it," Billy said, trying to smooth her ruffled feathers.

Two days later, Dave returned to work and reported to Billy's office for their usual morning meeting. Billy started by asking how the convention was, but before Dave could get three words out his mouth, he cut him off.

"I think it's about time you started worrying more about Cochrane Oil than some Geologist's convention," he said, with more than a touch of bitterness.

Dave was taken back by the outburst.

"Are you saying I'm not doing a good job here?" he replied.

"I'm just saying that your success rate at finding producing wells is far below industry standards," Billy accused.

Dave was shocked into silence for a moment, finally coming up with a rather lame: "I've got excellent credentials as a geologist."

Billy looked him angrily in the eye.

"That may be so," he said, 'but I think a farmer in Camrose with an unraveled coat hanger can do just as good a job as you."

Dave stood up with a look of disbelief on his face. He knew the incident Billy was referring to. And it could only mean one thing.

"You firing me?" he demanded.

Billy jerked his head towards the door.

"Don't let the door hit you on the ass on your way out," he said.

Shortly afterwards, Judy came in with a handful of messages, and Billy took the opportunity to tell her Ethel wasn't at all happy with her work performance.

"So why *are* you so late so often?" he said. "It's a real habit with you."

Judy quickly listed off several excuses and as she was talking, stepped into Billy's bathroom doorway, to pull up her skirt and expose herself.

Billy looked down at his desk and shook his head.

"All right, all right, I'll be over to your apartment at 10 this Friday," he said, knowing he was beaten.

The appointed time came and went with Billy waiting alone in the apartment, hoping against hope that she'd show up, but fearing the worst. Finally he left and moved his truck to an inconspicuous spot on the road outside where he could watch the entrance, retrieving a bottle of whiskey from a paper bag on the floor behind his seat. He began to drink while he waited, keeping an eye on the building entrance and parking lot.

Finally, at 2 o'clock in the morning, the company Corvette he let her drive pulled into the parking lot. He watched as a young man emerged from the driver's side, with Judy following. Billy watched the two of them enter the building arm-in-arm and waited until the apartment light came on. Then he decided to wait a little longer, reckoning the man wasn't going anywhere any more that night. Rocking back and forth in his seat, he softly banged his forehead against the steering wheel in frustration, anger and disappointment.

On the following Monday morning, Judy cheerfully bounced into his office with his usual stack of messages. He looked up at her, fixing her with a baleful look.

"So, what happened to you last Friday?" he asked as though he didn't know.

"Yeah, sorry," said Judy. "My grandma got taken sick and I had to leave town to go and take care of her. I tried to phone you, but I couldn't find you."

Billy decided that wasn't the right time or place to confront her, cursing himself for a fool when she left the room, sickened by his stupidity and weakness.

Dragging his mind back to his work, he was interrupted by a knock on the door. Ethel was standing there with a worried look on her face.

"What is it?" Billy asked anxiously.

"There's a gentleman out here that demands to see you."

"Show him in," Billy said, wondering why Ethel had looked so concerned.

A mousy little man strode in.

"Are you Mr. Cochrane?" he said, without introducing himself.

"Yes."

The man reaching into an inside pocket, produced a business-sized envelope, and tossed it lightly on the desk.

"You have officially been served," he said formally, turning and leaving, with the large envelope lying in front of Billy.

Billy opened it, right away recognizing the contents.

"Hmmm," he mused as he read. Frank McMillan was suing him for $1 million.

I wonder where he came up with that figure and what took him so long? thought Billy. This ought to keep my lawyers busy for a good while.

Two days later Billy received a call from the bank. Officials there wanted to meet with him immediately. Shortly afterwards, three senior officials filed into his office. Billy didn't know any of them: they didn't include the old manager, who had recently retired. Besides, Billy recalled, he hardly ever went to his bank any more.

He asked them politely if they'd care for some coffee, and pleasantries were exchanged while it was brought in and served.

Finally one of the bankers, speaking with a strong English accent, came to the point.

"Mr. Cochrane," he said, "we note that your account with us is seriously overdrawn."

"Oh, I wouldn't use the word seriously," Billy said. "I know I'm nowhere near my limit."

The Englishman didn't respond. Instead, one of the others asked a little condescendingly but in a more conciliatory tone, "Are you perhaps having business problems?"

"No more than anyone else," Billy replied turning to him. "It's quiet everywhere. It'll pick up again this winter."

"We note," the Englishman put in, "that your cash flow is seriously down."

"No more than to be expected," Billy replied evenly, aware he was starting to become annoyed at the tone in the Englishman's voice.

"Then would you please explain to us why you have purchased 13 drilling rigs - when, as you have just said, you knew there'd be times when there'd be no work for them?"

Billy did his best to explain the situation, but the Englishman kept coming at him with his irritating questions and his irritating accent. He closed by asking Billy how he could have got into such a predicament.

Billy looked from banker to banker.

"An old rancher once told me that when things got tough in the cattle business, hold on to the cow's tail and she'll pull you through," he said.

The Englishman snorted.

"What's that got to do with anything?" he said.

Billy leaned back and put his cowboy-booted feet up on his desk.

"If you're so god-damned smart," he challenged, "how did you folks come to lend a farm kid from Nanton with a Grade-10 education all that money? Did you happen to notice those drilling rigs in my yard? Well, they're going to be the cow that's going to pull me out of the mire - and the 350 people I write checks for every month! They're going to pull us through this tight spot we're *all* in. And besides, three of the holes Cochrane Oil and Gas drilled on my leases last winter in the Virginia Hills oil play are solid producers and I expect good success again this winter.

"As soon as we can solve the logistics of getting the oil to Edmonton I predict I'm going to have an additional 30,000 barrels of increased production a day."

The head banker, becoming alarmed at the growing confrontation, spoke up to try to smooth things over.

"I'll come to the point," he said. "It's come to our attention that you are being sued for $10,000,000."

"Ahhhh," said Billy, not bothering to correct the number, "so that's what this is all about! Good news sure travels fast in this town! Let me guess: Frank McMillan put the squeeze on you. Well, if McMillan thinks he can panic me into selling my oil and gas portfolio, he and you better have another thought coming. What makes you think I owe McMillan a single red cent? My lawyers tell me that even if McMillan can prove his case – which he can't – it'll take years for the case to come to trial. I don't know where McMillan even came up with the figure from. I think he must have calculated the gross number of dollars I've ever earned in my entire life, multiplied it by five, and thrown a dart at a board to see what other kind of other multiplier he could come up with.

"I don't take this all that seriously and you shouldn't either. I may owe him some money, but how much will finally come out sometime way into the future.

"But I guess you don't care about that, seeing how he's such a big client of yours!"

His speech was greeted by a stunned silence.

The head banker stood up.

"Mr. Cochrane," he said, "the Royal Bank is calling in your loan - effective immediately. Good day!"

Billy was left seething as the bankers started to troop out of his office.

"The Royal Bank will come crawling on its knees to get my business back - and I'll tell them, when they fire you three piss-ants, I might consider it!" he yelled after them.

Billy knew he could leave that and most of his other problems safely to be dealt with by his lawyers and accountants; but he knew it was only he who must deal with Judy.

There was only one place left where he felt he could take refuge, sort out his problems and restore his confidence, and that was on one of his rigs. He phoned Candace and told her he'd be gone for a couple of days and would be back on Sunday.

"Perhaps you could have a roast ready for me when I get back," he suggested.

He got in his truck and started heading for Caroline, where he had landed a contract to drill seven wells.

Chapter 26

Taking Jet along in the truck, Billy hoped he'd also be able to find time to wander in the bush and hunt some grouse along with supervising spuding in a new well. There was nothing that gave him more satisfaction than raising the derrick on a new well-site – apart perhaps from his duck-hunting with Jet. He likened setting up a rig to raising a sleeping giant and always joked with those around him that the rig was getting an erection.

It was tromping through the bush alone with his dog though that gave him time to think. It allowed him to decide that he'd solve the problems he had control over - and the rest would have to sort them selves out. They'd just have to play out on their own.

It was a magnificent Alberta fall day, and Billy loved the fall colors and smells in the air in that area at that time of year. After his time out in the countryside with Jet, he returned to Calgary with his spirits much improved.

Entering the house, he was surprised by the greeting he got, which instantly dismissed any thoughts of a roast beef dinner. On the contrary, he realized with a start, the atmosphere seemed positively funereal. He found Candace silently crying in the corner of one of the big chairs in the living room.

"Hey, what's the matter?" he said, rushing over in alarm.

Candace took her face from her handkerchief.

"It's Judy," she said weakly.

"Why? What's happened?" Billy asked, feeling his alarm growing.

"She hasn't been home for two days."

"What?" said Billy? "What makes you think there's a problem? She's done this before."

"She said she was going to stay at her friend Amanda's place," said Candace. "But I phoned to check on her and Amanda said she never showed up there. She's been hanging out with a different, older crowd lately, and I don't like them. They all look so weird. I'm worried she's maybe taking drugs, and I'm worried she's going to run away to Haight–Ashbury, or some place like that, that you see on TV."

"Why didn't you tell me about this sooner?" Billy asked, trying to stem the flood of tears and fears pouring out of his wife.

It didn't help. Candace returned to her weeping, and Billy knew that was all the answer she was going to give him.

He knelt down beside her and took her gently in his arms to comfort her.

"I'm going to find her," he assured her. "Where do you think she is?"

Candace could only shake her head to show she had no idea, and continued with her weeping.

Crawford was out, so Billy went to Johnathon's room and asked his younger son if he knew where his sister was. Johnathon, aware of his mother's noisy tears, only shrugged his shoulders, held up his hands and shook his head.

"Well, where does this Amanda live?" Billy pressed.

Johnathon began to explain.

Billy interrupted him.

"Come on," he said taking his son by the arm. "You're going to show me."

Johnathon directed him to a house a short distance away, and he went to the door. Amanda's mother answered his harsh raps, and, when she saw Billy standing there asking for Amanda, she became defensive.

"What's this all about?" she said.

Billy quickly introduced himself as Judy's father and explained that Judy was missing and her daughter might be able to tell him where she was.

The woman finally relented and called Amanda to the door. The young girl was both sullen and uncooperative. As Billy asked each of his questions, she twisted back and forth with her arms crossed, refusing to look him in the eye and keeping her gaze fixed on the ground.

"I dunno," was all she said to each question

Before long, Billy was pleading with her, saying that if she didn't tell him, his wife was going to have a nervous breakdown. This moved Amanda's mother to action, and she began to participate in the interrogation. After a few moments, Amanda wilted under the pressure.

"You might try this apartment building in Bowness," she said adding a rough description and the area.

Billy dropped Johnathon back at the house, telling him he must tell his mother he'd gone to look for Judy. Then he screeched out of the driveway before Candace could emerge from the house.

Cruising around the general area Amanda had given him, Billy spotted a dilapidated two-story walk-up apartment building that fitted her description.

Pulling into the side of the road, he watched the building for a while, noting the comings and goings of different hippie-looking people. Before long, he decided he needed to take a gamble and follow one of the men into the building. From a safe distance, he slyly noted the apartment number the man went into. Waiting for a moment, he knocked on the door, practically forcing his way in past the bleary-eyed and scruffy-looking young man who opened it.

Inside, he found himself in a room with several young people lounging around on cushions and a chesterfield. Most were smoking marijuana.

"I have reason to believe that my daughter might be here," he announced firmly in a loud voice. The words were just barely left his mouth when he caught a glimpse of movement out of the corner of his eye.

Turning, he was too late to ward off the force of the beer bottle as it smashed against his skull.

On the edge of unconsciousness, he felt himself dragged out and thrown down the flight of stairs. He lay sprawled for several minutes, trying to drag his brain back to consciousness. He felt like he was watching the end of a movie reel as abstract images flickered in his mind. Lapsing in and out of consciousness, he was vaguely aware of the leering, laughing faces looking down at him from the top of the stairs. Finally he summoned enough strength to stand up and teeter back to the car. Reaching for his handkerchief, he managed to staunch the flow of blood down the side of his face. Slowly the pain in his head began to be displaced by rage, but he also saw he had to work out his options and not do anything rash. He ruled out calling the police as he didn't want any complications which could further involve his daughter. He considered calling some of his friends to come and storm the place. They'd certainly have made short order of the place and its occupants.

Finally he reached a conclusion.

"Fuck it," he said to himself. "I can deal with this bunch of punks by myself.

He opened the car trunk planning to arm himself with a tire iron, but when he looked in, he immediately spotted a hockey stick autographed by Gordie Howe.

He'd bought it at some charity auction and forgotten about it. Taking it out, he swiftly broke it over his knee, creating a three-foot long weapon. He grunted quietly to himself with satisfaction.

Then he slipped into the building, hiding in a small alcove so that he could creep in behind the next person showing up at the apartment to buy drugs.

It wasn't a foolproof plan, he recognized, but it should work, especially if it was a woman. His luck held and he quickly moved up behind a woman as she entered the apartment block, moving silently up the stairs behind her. Staying out of sight from anyone inside, he loitered a few steps behind, knowing that the punks inside would now be very cautious who they opened the door for.

Whoever was inside obviously recognized the woman, because he quickly undid the chain and opened the door for her. Billy instantly rushed the door, knocking the woman down in the process as he threw his weight against the half-opened door. In the second before he threw it open, in the gap he recognized the man who had opened it as the nasty-looking one who had cold-cocked him with the beer bottle. Before he could move to defend himself or block Billy, Billy cracked his head open with the hockey-stick.

Stepping over the mans prone body, he stepped into the living room to an audience of startled young men. Four men were sitting around a table playing cards; the rest were sitting and lying around in a zombie-like state, listening to the music that continued to spill deafeningly from the radio.

One of the men at the table started to stand up to challenge Billy and got whacked with the jagged end of the broken hockey stick for his trouble. The punk sat back down against very suddenly, and the rest seemed to cower back as Billy threatened each in turn with the stick.

At that moment, another hippie-looking punk came out of the hallway buttoning up his fly.

"Hey, dudes, who's next?" he asked without looking up from fumbling with his buttons.

Then looking up, he came face to face with Billy. Billy gave him a hard blow to the side of his face, sending him reeling to the floor at the feet of his friends.

Billy strode down the hallway and threw open the first door he came to, peering into the semi-darkness.

"Judy?" he called into the gloom, unable to make out even the vaguest shape in the space beyond.

A small familiar voice came back. "Daddy?"

"Come on, sweetheart, we're going home," he said.

He reached in, fumbled for a switch, found one, and quickly pulled a sheet from the bed. Wrapping it round her and with her under one arm and him brandishing the hockey stick with the other, the two of them made their way out of the apartment.

Back at the house, he drove round the back and he and Judy went in through the back door. He told her quietly to go to her room and get cleaned up.

"This is going to be our secret," he whispered to her, knowing though that he was going to have to give Candace some kind of an explanation.

When he went into the living room, Candace didn't even seem to notice he'd come in. She still had her face buried in her hands, still in tears, and she didn't look up. He knelt down with his face in her lap and felt her hands reach out to the top of his head.

Before he could say anything, Candace spoke first.

"I'm sorry," she said. "I'm so sorry; I've been such a total failure, a failure as a mother and a wife."

"Shsss," he soothed, "Don't say such a thing."

"It's true," she insisted, still weeping. "If I'd paid more attention to you, you'd never have taken that blond secretary floozies of yours as a mistress, and Judy wouldn't have got herself mixed up in a drug crowd."

Billy was startled. Candace obviously knew everything. Without saying anything, he took her hands in his, put his head on her shoulder and cried along with her for a long time. It was the first time he'd cried for longer than he could remember. His shoulders shook with sobs as all the emotions of the recent months started to pour out of him.

Finally he raised his head and looked into her blue eyes.

"I'll fix it," he said. "I promise. I'll fix everything. It'll be okay - you'll see."